PLANET MISSION

PART ONE

DAVID CLAIBORNE

Dear Maggie and Herman,
I hope you enjoy reading.

Your friend,

7.21.2021

P.S. wish I was working
on Star Wars too.

CROWN
UPSIDE
DOWN

Copyright © 2021 by David Claiborne

First edition July 2021

Cover and interior design by KUHN Design Group
Cover illustration by Chris Petrocchi
Edited by Amy Partain

ISBN 978-1-7369971-0-9 (hardcover)
ISBN 978-1-7369971-1-6 (paperback)
ISBN 978-1-7369971-2-3 (eBook)
ISBN 978-1-7369971-3-0 (Kindle)

Published by Crown Upside Down LLC
18695 Pony Express Drive #2091
Parker, CO 80134

CONTENTS

THANKS

I would like to thank my beta readers: Ethan, Louise, Terry, Dori, and Rico.

Thanks also to Brittany and Shawn, without whom this project might not have been possible.

Thanks to my illustrator, Chris; to my designer, Steve; and to my editor, Amy.

Thanks also to all those who offered words of encouragement, large or small, and who showed interest in this project.

FOR MY WIFE, MICHELE.

PROLOGUE

Good evening, everyone. I'm Mia Morales with the Administration Broadcast Service. We have a special segment for you, an exclusive, with someone who has something very important to say. Joining me is Molly McDaithi, daughter of Ioachim and Anne McDaithi, proprietors of the infamous Good Samaritan Central Park Clinic. Good evening, Molly. Did I say your name right?"

"Good evening, Mia. Yes, it's Mac-Day-Hee, you said it right. Thank you for having me, and for giving me the opportunity to address the controversy in the proper way."

"It's my pleasure. I understand that you have a prepared statement?"

"I do."

"Is it also correct that you had the aid of the Administration in preparing this statement?"

"That's correct, Mia."

"How wonderful, Molly. How fortunate we all are to hear this, and with the blessing of the Administration behind it, please go ahead with your statement."

"Thank you, Mia," Molly said, and began to read:

> *My fellow citizens, worker positions, civil servant positions, esteemed colleagues, veteran positions—thank you for your*

service—entertainers, and administrators. I am humbled and honored to have the opportunity to come before you today through the generosity of the ABS and with the cooperation of our great Administration. I am the daughter of Anne and Ioaichim McDaithi, proprietors of the controversial Good Samaritan Central Park clinic, which I am sure you know of from news reports over the past several months. I am here in the name of our great Administration to renounce the actions of my parents and the intolerance they spread in the city of New York. I am also here to apologize for their insensitivity to anyone who may have been offended by them, and by the presence of a faith-based organization in the city. The presence of a religious group in such a historic landmark as Central Park sends a dangerous message that their teachings and beliefs are acceptable and puts disadvantaged people at risk. It is a shame that some still cling to the argument that we should partner with…with bigots in order to fight the problems facing New York.

"*On behalf of the community I represent, and the Administration, whose aid in preparing this statement I am eternally grateful for, I renounce Good Samaritan as an organization. I renounce the Central Park Clinic, which this organization with the aid of my parents, has set up. I demand that they leave the city immediately or risk further reputational harm with members of the disadvantaged community, New Yorkers, the Administration, and the wider public. Thank you for your time.*"

"Wow," Mia said. "That was incredible. And so brave. So brave."

"Thank you, Mia," Molly said.

"I want you to know how proud I am to be able to host you here. And I want to stress for you and our viewers just how important what it is you have done. How are you feeling?"

Molly gave a nervous laugh. She began to tear up a little and bit her lip.

"It's alright, Molly. I am here for you. The entire Administration is behind you," Mia said.

"It's hard. It really is," Molly said.

"I can only imagine," Mia replied.

"I feel relief, but sad at the same time. I know coming here and making this statement today was the right thing to do," Molly said. "The right thing for the community and for my family."

"I could not agree more," Mia said. "I also understand that this is not the end of your service to the Administration?"

"You're right. I'm not finished yet," Molly said.

"You are going to be joining one of the Administration's sponsored missions?" Mia asked.

"That's correct. The mission departs in a little less than two weeks. I leave for training right after the interview. The Administration asked me to join the mission, and I am honored that they asked me," Molly said.

"And how long will you be in training?" Mia asked.

"About a week," Molly said.

"A week? Is that long enough?" Mia asked.

"I sure hope so. Missionaries normally undergo rigorous testing and training. It can take months, not to mention the years of vetting and preparation to ensure all missionaries are in good standing with the Administration. I have to do it all in a week," Molly said.

"You've more than proven you are deserving of good standing status. Someone like you is sure to succeed," Mia said.

"Thank you for your vote of confidence," Molly said.

"And where is the mission headed?" Mia asked.

"To the colony on the fourth moon of Polus," Molly said.

"Incredible. Simply incredible. Molly, your bravery and commitment are an inspiration to us all. I want you to know that I'm not just saying that. You inspire me. I hope that someday I can show as deep a commitment to the Administration and our community as you are showing here today."

"Thank you again, Mia. I have no doubt you have already shown that and much more. I only hope I can be worthy of the faith that you and the leaders of the Administration are putting in me."

"Thank you for joining us, Molly. I'm sure our viewers are excited to see how this mission unfolds. I know I am. I'm Mia Morales," Mia placed heavy emphasis on the second syllable of her last name and rolled the *R*. "This has been an exclusive from your very own Administration Broadcast Service. For the glory of the Administration."

"…For the glory of the Administration," Molly echoed.

CHAPTER ONE

NOT A CELEBRITY

Welcome aboard to our celebrity!" A woman hovered in front of the open airlock a few inches above the floor, hands on her hips, she struck a confident pose. "I'm Doctor Bebe, but you can call me Jazzy."

"I'm Molly. Molly McDaithi," Molly said, extending her hand, fingers straight out and tense expecting to shake Doctor Bebe's hand. "Thank you, but I'm not a celebrity. I was just on the news a few times. It's nice to meet you."

The doctor took Molly's hand loosely with her fingertips, wrist arched upward and hand relaxed downward toward the ship's deck. "Likewise, Molly. I'm the mission doctor. I'm in charge of the health of the crew and missionaries on our journey out, and once we reach Polus IV, I'll be setting up a clinic for the colonists. Isn't that exciting? I'm excited," Jazzy said.

"That is exciting. That should be great for them," Molly said without a trace of excitement in her voice.

The pair wore the same standard-issue uniform, all blue-grey including the shoes except for a white undershirt with its official regulation logos, designed to provide unity to all members of a mission. Yet, Doctor Bebe had arranged her uniform in a way that made it her own while still conforming to regulations. She wore her long white lab coat, the mark of her profession as was her right, over the rest of her uniform. Her hair was tied up beneath her mission cap, also standard issue for the mission.

Molly pulled herself forward by a handrail and floated aboard the Arca. Her duffel bag trailed behind her and struck her when she stopped, causing her to lurch. She rubbed the back of her head where the bag hit her, feeling insufficient next to Doctor Bebe.

"That was brave of you though, going on TV and denouncing your parents to support the Administration. I don't think I could have done it. I don't think any of us could have," Jazzy said, smiling. "That's why we think of you as a celebrity."

It seemed that the doctor was doing her best to make Molly feel welcome, but Molly got the impression it was strained. She grabbed a metal handhold to prevent her forward momentum from pushing her into her new shipmate. But her duffel bag continued to move and bumped into her back again. It knocked her cap askance over her forehead and hid her green eyes for a moment until she readjusted. "Oof. I'm not used to zero-G yet," she said.

"Don't worry, just follow your training," the doctor said. "We should have gravity again once we're under way. You did have zero-G maneuvering training, didn't you?"

Molly nodded her head. "I did, but I got the accelerated version. It was only a couple hours in a simulator."

"I'm sure it will be just as good as the weeks of training we all received. MFASA overdoes everything. Can I tell you that I am just so glad that the Administration assigned you to us, even if it was at the last minute? It is such an honor to have someone like you on the mission. It's going to be so good to have another woman too. Can you imagine being the only woman a mission? A person could go insane. I was told that you'll need to see me personally. In a professional capacity, I mean," Jazzy said.

"That's right, I have a script here." Molly pulled her phone from the pocket of her jumpsuit, and with a flick of her fingers sent the prescription to Jazzy, who pulled out her phone and reviewed the order, clicking her tongue.

"Oh. That must be so difficult. I am here to support you in any way you need," Jazzy said, as she touched Molly's elbow and lowered her voice. "You know this is truly nothing to be ashamed of. With the proper medication, therapies, and coping strategies you will almost certainly recover. Perhaps fully."

Molly lowered her head and looked around. No one else was on the deck, thankfully.

"Oh, don't worry, *Molly*," Jazzy said, leaning in and emphasizing her name, "I am bound by professional regulations and ethics to keep the nature of our doctor-patient relationship strictly confidential. I assure you that all your information will be held in the highest standards of confidence. By me specifically."

"Thank you, Doctor Bebe."

"Please. We're going to be working together for at least a couple of years. Won't it be great? I know we're going to be friends. But you'd better call me Jazzy. Everyone else does."

"Yes, I think it will be great, Jazzy."

"Jazzy, is she aboard?" scratched a voice over the intercom. Jazzy held her phone up and responded, "Yes, she's here. She just arrived. I've got her."

"All hands, prepare for departure," the voice said.

"Director, only the captain may use the ship's intercom, except in case of emergencies," a different voice said. "We will depart at our scheduled time in approximately twenty minutes. Please stow your gear and take your seats for departure and initial acceleration."

"That was Director Waters," Jazzy said.

"Which one?" Molly asked.

"The first one. The one in charge of the mission. We're still working some of the procedures out with the captain. You'll meet him before we get under way."

"The captain or the director?"

"Don't be silly, Molly. The director, of course," Jazzy said. "Though I'm sure you'll meet the captain personally in due time. There aren't that many people aboard the ship. The Administration chartered passage just for us. We'll have plenty of time to get to know each other on our way to Polus IV. Let me take you to your quarters. They're just a couple of decks below this one. We're still in zero-G while we're docked at Luna Terra," Jazzy said.

"The sooner we have gravity the better for me," Molly said.

"Quarters and bunks are generally aft, and the common areas forward," Jazzy said, explaining the ship's layout to the new arrival. She pushed off the wall and turned deftly, propelling herself toward a ladder. She grasped it and pushed herself down through the deck in a single motion. "Follow me, Molly," she said as her head disappeared below the floor.

Molly started to follow, but her duffel bag got stuck on the edge of the deck and she lost sight of Jazzy.

"Are you coming, Molly?" Jazzy called.

"Yes, just give me a minute," Molly said. She pushed and twisted the straps, but the bag was stuck. At last, she gave a great shove with her feet that both freed her bag and pushed her downward simultaneously, but she regretted the effort at once as her grip slipped and she almost spun off into the corridor. Molly caught the ladder and jerked both elbows around one of the rungs, hanging on. Her duffel bag carried on. "Oof!" she said as the bag's strap tugged on her shoulder.

"Just take your time," Jazzy said.

Molly looked around. Four grey doors lined either side of the corridor. They were quarters according to a small panel next to the door. Molly looked down the ladder to where Jazzy was, still one deck lower.

"My room is all the way down there?" Molly asked.

"You were last to be assigned to the ship, so you got the quarters at the back," Jazzy said. "The others were taken already."

"Alright," Molly called back as she contemplated her next move. "I better just take them one at a time," she said to herself.

"Just take them one at a time," Jazzy said.

"Thanks," Molly said. She had to concentrate too hard to be exasperated by Jazzy's handholding.

Molly went through one more deck plate and pulled herself to a stop next to Jazzy, who floated above the deck, looking as if she could fly. "What's back there?" Molly asked, looking further down the ladder as she grasped the rungs with both elbows again. In spite of, or perhaps because of, her efforts to maintain stability, her feet began to float awkwardly behind her.

"Use your core, your stomach and back muscles, to control your extremities," Jazzy said. "It doesn't take much. That's better. The deck below this is mission cargo, and below that is engineering. The deck you came aboard on houses the receiving airlock, and above that are the common areas, crew quarters, and cockpit. This is an old ship, but it's nice. The Administration commissions only the best for its missionaries. You'll hardly feel the engines vibrating, even this far back."

"That's good. Is one of these my room then?" Molly asked.

"Take your pick. They're all unoccupied," Jazzy said.

The deck had four doors like the one above it. Molly reached for the closest one and saw the panel. "Twelve. At least this will bring me some luck," she said.

"Don't be silly, Molly. You know there's no such thing as luck," Jazzy said.

The door slid open as Molly touched it. "Are you sure this one is available? Someone's name is on the panel."

Jazzy maneuvered forward and peered at the label. "There's no one on this mission by that name. It's probably from a previous passenger. The crew must not have changed the name plates yet." Jazzy tapped the name plate with her finger, and with a couple of swiping motions located the proper menu. "*M-O-L-L-Y* is it?" she said as she replaced the name. "Don't worry. It's just us missionaries and the director, the captain, the flight surgeon, and a couple of crew. Their quarters are all forward."

"There are two doctors on the ship?"

Jazzy shook her head. "There are, but he's only trained to provide care during the journey. Even then he's there primarily for the crew and captain. I'm the mission doctor. Does this one look like it will work?"

Molly nodded and turned her attention to the cabin. She assumed they were nearly identical, and at that moment did not care so much how it looked. Most of all she wanted to stow her things and find stability.

"Once you stow your duffel—and you know you need to really stow it, as in secure it. You received that training?"

"Yes. I'll make sure it's strapped down. Even the accelerated training was good for that."

"Good. After you stow your duffel, come join us in the observation lounge three decks up. Once we're all strapped in for the initial acceleration, we should be able to depart."

"We don't stay in our rooms?"

"Regulations state it's safest if we're all buckled to seats for departure. Plus, after we get under way, Director Waters and I will want to brief everyone on the mission and begin our training."

"So soon? It will take weeks to get there."

"We don't want to waste a moment. There's a lot at stake on these missions, for us and the Administration, but especially for the director. Success could mean big things for any of us—better standing, better positions in the Administration, better housing, improved licensing, but especially for him. Did you know the president-elect was a mission director? Director Waters and I have set personal goals of achieving all our mission objectives, including the optional ones, something no other mission team has done before. We are going to be the best prepared team the Administration has ever sent. Come join us as soon as you can, okay?"

Jazzy pulled up on the ladder with her fingertips and floated up through the deck. Molly pulled herself into her quarters. The door shut automatically behind her.

The cabin was relatively small, but not the smallest she had seen. The floor was aligned to her left which made sense since once they got underway that direction would be "down." It was yet one more thing to disorient her, but she reminder herself that in zero-G it did not matter and tried to shrug off the feeling as she reoriented her feet. Molly found a narrow locker, but what it lacked in girth it made up in height since it ran floor to ceiling. Molly stowed her bag and strapped it down as she had been taught.

Turning around she saw a large screen on the opposite wall. Screens like this were ubiquitous. The Administration gave them freely to anyone who wanted one to encourage their use. They were versatile, and could serve as a television, a workstation, an entertainment center, or communication platform. Each one was linked to the Administration's LiFi network. Many people put them in their private homes. Her parents had not, however. The screen was dark, but eventually it would display news and announcements with the occasional regulatory update, both for their mission and those intended for the general population.

Each screen had a built-in camera. For that reason, she had never liked them, particularly in private rooms. They were for video calls, but she never trusted them. She had difficulty trusting any technology for that matter. She had only acquired her first phone during mission training. Perhaps her distrust of technology was a quirk she had acquired from her parents. Above the screen was a small shelf with a bar containing some clothes hangers. Molly started to take off her mission jacket to hang in front of the screen but thought better of it as she felt a slight chill in the air.

It was time to join the others. She managed to maneuver herself out of the room and up the ladder through the two decks above hers. At last, she pulled herself through the next bulkhead into a much wider room. This deck was open from wall-to-wall, wider and taller than any other corridor she had been in yet, but the room only contained two rows of chairs. Molly stopped where she was, unsure of how to make the transition to the seats absent a handhold, and unsure of whether it would be unseemly to crawl hand over foot along the floor to get there.

"Here's our celebrity," said a man who pushed off one of the chairs and floated toward her. He caught himself gently on the bulkhead when he reached her, absorbing the momentum of his movement with his elbows. He wore the same jump suit, cap, and jacket as everyone else, but his jacket was embroidered with his title: 'Mission Director.'

He extended his hand to Molly. She hesitated, not because she felt unfriendly, but she was uncertain of whether she should let go of the ladder to do so. The others in the room turned to see the new arrival. Jazzy pushed herself out of her chair and floated back.

"She's not a celebrity, Director Waters. She said so herself. Isn't that right, Molly?"

"That's right," Molly said.

"Let me introduce you to Director Waters," Jazzy said.

"It's nice to meet you," Waters said, smiling and pumping Molly's hand firmly and vigorously. Molly wished he would not pull so hard and gripped the ladder harder with her other hand. Waters saw that she was uncomfortable.

"You didn't get the full zero-G training, did you?" he said.

"No, only the accelerated version," Molly said.

"Don't worry. We'll have gravity again once we get under way. The training only really matters at stations. Everywhere else we're going will have gravity," he said with something of a smile in his eyes. His manner put Molly at ease. "Let me help you to your seat," he said extending both of his hands to her.

"Please allow me, Director Waters," Jazzy said, and moved between them.

"Thanks, Jazzy," Waters said, and pushing off he floated back to his seat. "I'm sure we'll get to know each other much better, Molly. Welcome to the mission team."

Jazzy took Molly's hand and pushed off the bulkhead. She towed Molly along for a few meters to the row of chairs farthest back. Molly reached out and grabbed the seat with both hands. Jazzy guided her into the seat. "Think you can buckle yourself in?" Jazzy asked.

Molly nodded. "Yes, thank you," she said politely. Jazzy flashed Molly a smile, then spun back around and floated to the front row of seats where she hovered next to Waters. Molly buckled herself in. It was a five-point harness that ran across her shoulders and fastened on either side of her waist, and then again over the chest. This was the kind of harness she liked.

"We're lucky we don't have to wear helmets for departure," said the man in the seat next to hers. "Otherwise, our heads would be latched to the headrest and we wouldn't be able see."

"What would there be to see?" Molly asked. "This doesn't seem like much of an observation lounge."

Her question answered itself as the walls faded to transparent and revealed space outside, visible through deck-to-deck windows that curved with the sides of the ship right up to a beam that ran stem to stern behind their heads. It was as if they were seated on a platform floating in space itself. Through the port side windows they could see Luna Station. Earth was visible in the distance off the starboard side, nothing more than a blue marble with swirls of white clouds. Everything else was endless blackness punctuated occasionally by a few points of light.

"Oh, dear God," Molly said, gripping the armrests of her chair.

"Be careful," whispered the man sitting next to her. "That kind of language could be offensive. Especially coming from a missionary."

"Of course. My mistake. I apologize," Molly said.

"I'm Joon-baek Kim," the man said and extended his hand, "mission botanist."

Molly pried her hand from the armrest, shook his hand once, and quickly returned it. "Molly McDaithi. Exobiologist."

"I think you're a bit more than that. Everyone here knew who you were before you boarded the ship. What was it like being on the news?" he asked.

"It really wasn't that special," Molly said. "I don't know why people keep bringing it up."

"For a lot of people, it would be a great honor to be on one of the Administration's news programs. First time in space?" he asked.

"Yes," Molly said.

"Mine too. Isn't it great?" he said.

"It is. Truly great," Molly said. She looked down at the floor in front of her to avoid looking out the windows.

"Have you seen the greenhouse yet?" Joon-baek asked. Molly shook her head. "You're lucky. Your quarters must be right above it. The rest of us all got assigned rooms on the same deck. Waters said he wanted to keep us together to help build mission cohesion. But if I had gotten to choose, I would have picked a room back there by yours. It's fantastic. The greenhouse. It helps recycle the ship's air and water. The captain has a collection of tiny trees he promised to show me too. I can't wait until we get under way so I can see it."

Molly calculated carefully how rude it would be if she did not look up to respond when a pair of figures walked down the very wall of the room, mechanically clanking with each step. They stood facing the group, awkwardly facing directly down, perpendicular to the floor.

"They have magnetic boots," Joon-baek said, answering the question written on Molly's face.

"Why don't we all have those?" she asked.

Joon-baek shrugged. "Probably outside of the budget. There are weight considerations too, you know. You really only need them in zero-G, and even then, they're mostly a luxury if you know how to maneuver."

"They seem worth it to me," she said. She noticed another man sitting in the row of chairs in front of them. "Who's that?" she asked, but one of the men with magnetic boots began to speak before Joon-baek could respond.

"Hello, everyone. I see our last passenger has arrived. I'm Captain Jackson, formerly of the U.S. Navy." He addressed Molly directly as the only one to whom he had not been introduced.

"Thank you for your service," intoned everyone in the cabin in unison.

"Thank you. This is Doctor Stephens. He is the flight surgeon. He'll take care of you should anything happen on the journey out. This is my ship, the Arca," he said with a gesture. "We'll be getting under way soon, but before we depart, by regulation, I need to go over the safety briefing."

"Captain, I think I should address the mission team. It's part of my role as director." Waters said.

"That won't be necessary, Waters," the captain said curtly.

"It would really be appropriate, Captain," said Jazzy. "He is the director."

"Regulations proscribe that I deliver the safety briefing, Doctor Bebe. It will only take a minute. Then the rest of the trip is yours."

"They don't seem to like each other," Molly said in an aside to Joon-baek. "They can't have known each other that long." Joon-baek just shrugged.

"This ship is bound for Polus Station in orbit of the fourth moon of Polus," the captain continued. "If that is not your destination, get off now." He paused with a big smile, waiting for his passengers to react. Joon-baek chuckled. Jazzy turned around and shot him a look.

"The journey will take several weeks. The first half will be the acceleration phase, followed by a deceleration phase. The ship will have gravity again as soon as we're under way, except for a few brief minutes while we transition to deceleration mid-trip."

"Thank God," Molly said a little too loud. It was her turn to get a look from Jazzy.

"Remember to be careful about your language," Joon-baek said.

"Below each seat, and stowed in each of your quarters, you will find an emergency vac suit in the event of a hull breach." Doctor Stephens unfurled a suit in front of them all. It floated listlessly, limbs flailing in all sorts of impossible directions. "You put them on just like your jump suit, zip them up, then pull the hood over your head and zip that down too." Doctor Stephens demonstrated putting on the suit as Captain Jackson spoke. "Once it's on, pull the orange tab on the front of the suit to start the flow of oxygen. The suits self-seal once the tab has been pulled." Doctor Stephens pretended to tug the tab, then folded the suit back up.

"The ship is equipped with battery-powered emergency lighting in the event of a power failure. In the event the ship is a total loss, you are to evacuate to the Captain's Yacht, my quarters in other words, aft of the cockpit," Captain Jackson jerked his thumb up and behind him, "which also acts as an emergency lifeboat."

"Can so many things go wrong?" Molly said to Joon-baek.

"They can't. They won't. This is just a speech they have to give," Joon-baek said.

Captain Jackson continued, "That is the only time passengers are permitted on the upper decks, which are strictly reserved for crew and ship operations. Please understand that we are here to serve you on your voyage out to Polus Station, but those are private quarters. We are all going to be very close for several weeks. Everyone will be better served if we respect each other's personal space. We'll stay out of your quarters, and you stay out of ours. If there are no questions, then I think we're ready to go."

The captain and Doctor Stephens clunked down the aisle between the seats and checked everyone's harness to make sure it was secure. Their movements seemed strange, they pulled themselves forward with their feet as they walked. Finishing the harness check, they walked up the bulkhead to the upper deck. Molly had to look away, as seeing them walk up a wall brought back her feeling of disorientation. A few moments later they heard the captain's voice over the intercom.

"We'll be departing in a minute. Once we start accelerating you will feel a strong push toward the back of your seat like a car making a hard turn. This is normal, then once we activate the dampers you won't notice a thing. At that time, you will be free to move about and conduct your business."

"This is going to be fun," Joon-baek said.

"Oh?" Molly said, wanting to say something to be polite, but not sure just what. She was too focused on "accelerating" and avoiding looking at the windows to think of much else.

"It will feel just like Earth once they activate the dampers," Joon-baek said.

"I can't wait," Molly said.

The sound of thrusters off-gassing resonated through the ship, followed by a barely perceptible movement. They could see the ship separating from Luna Station through the windows.

"This doesn't feel much like acceleration," Molly said and relaxed a little.

"We're just maneuvering away from the station," Joon-baek said. "The real fun comes after we pass the moon."

"I thought this was your first time in space," Molly said.

"It is, but I read a lot. It was also part of our training," Joon-baek said.

"I don't think I got that part," Molly said.

Luna Station grew smaller and smaller as they pulled away. Strangely, it seemed to shrink in the distance like a camera zooming out, almost as if they had never been close to the station at all. The ship's thrusters fired again and the Arca began to rotate on its axis while the station receded in the distance. Though she could barely feel the changes, the sensation of turning while moving sideways was odd. Then the Arca's thrusters fired to arrest their movement away from the station and change their trajectory forward past the moon in sort of a sliding arc. They could feel the ship begin to move faster.

"This isn't so bad," Molly said, relaxing even more. Then there was a roaring sound they felt more than heard as it vibrated through the entire ship. As if a rubber band suddenly snapped, they rocketed forward, released on their journey. Molly was pressed back in her seat.

Joon-baek gave out a whoop and smiled next to her. "Here we go!" he said.

They accelerated for several minutes then seemed to slow, but Molly assumed she was just becoming accustomed to their momentum.

"The dampers are now active," Captain Jackson's voice said over the intercom. "You should have gravity now. It will feel slightly heavier than Earth, though in no time at all you won't notice the difference. You are free to move about the cabin and conduct yourselves as you see fit, with respect to the ship's rules. The Arca will be where you live for the next several weeks, so make yourselves at home. Welcome aboard."

The others unfastened their harnesses and stood. Molly undid her harness, and although she knew she should be able to stand she was surprised to find that she could.

"Alright, everyone," Jazzy said. "Let's break for fifteen minutes while we rearrange the observation lounge for training."

By unlatching their bases, the chairs slid easily over the floor. They moved them toward the walls. Jazzy tapped her foot on the floor just in front of the chairs, which caused a pair of long tables to rise out of the floor. She tapped the windows which turned opaque in response. She flicked a presentation from her phone which projected on the opaque walls. She then flicked the presentation toward the other missionaries where it projected above the tables.

"Don't you think I should do the set up?" a man Molly had not met yet asked in an aside with Waters. "I am the mission's media specialist after all."

"Do you want to tell her to stop?" Waters said. That seemed to put an end to the discussion.

"That's Beau Lee," Joon-baek looked back over his shoulder and said to Molly. "He's an audiovisual specialist from the Administration."

"Everyone, take your seats. It would probably be best if we all sat on the same side. You can sit there, Molly," Jazzy said. "Director Waters, do you want to begin?"

Waters walked to the head of the table where he rotated the projection to face him. He leaned forward and rested his palms on the table.

"Welcome to space, everyone. And welcome to the MFASA mission to Polus IV. I also want to extend a special welcome to Molly McDaithi, whose presence with us as a fellow missionary is the result of a special arrangement with the Administration. Welcome, Molly. You have not been with us to this point, but know that you are fully one of us, a full member of my team. I want to begin with the principle at the heart of our mission. This is the same principal at the heart of our society, and at the heart of all that we do. This is also the principal which you, as missionaries, must keep in mind constantly throughout your service: For the glory of the Administration."

"For the glory of the Administration," they intoned together.

CHAPTER TWO

THE DAILY BRIEFING

The Arca's loudspeakers clicked and popped, though Beau barely registered the noise in his early morning sleep, having long become accustomed to the ship's various noises at this point in the journey. Then the sound of a gong and bass drum clashing caused him to sit straight up, now very awake. The captain's wakeup call for that morning, a selection from a composer whom Beau assumed was long dead, featured percussion and a strong brass section. Beau reached for his phone and watched as an app identified the song: "Fanfare for the Common Man" it told him.

Beau heard Director Waters emerge from his quarters outside. Waters passed hastily through the hall and ascended the deck for his ritual morning discussion with the captain about his wakeup calls. The captain's fun did not matter to Beau. He had become accustomed to waking up to music.

In fact, he had been having an uncomfortable dream and was grateful for being awakened. Though he did not particularly want to remember the dream, he could not help but try. Space, vast, unchanging, and empty seen through the transparent metal of the portal in his quarters was good for contemplation. He let his mind wander until the music entered his thoughts again. Beau arose, changed his shirt, put on his uniform, and made his way to the observation lounge.

He smiled as Waters climbed down the ladder from the cockpit. The captain had ejected him yet again. Stern rejoinders followed Waters as he descended the ladder. Beau moved to the wall and tapped the observation glass. It turned opaque with his touch. He scrolled down the touchscreen, looking for the Daily Briefing.

"Thank you, Beau. I've got it," Waters said, who pressed his thumb to the screen, biometrically authorizing use of the mission's LiFi allowance. The Daily Briefing began to buffer.

Other missionaries began to fill the lounge over the next several minutes, some with their phones ready to take notes or sync with the LiFi to watch the briefing themselves.

"Let's get started," Waters began.

He looked around the faces in the room. "Has anyone heard from Molly yet this morning?" he asked.

Beau looked around himself. Given the size of the team, it was easy to see that Molly had not emerged yet. It did not seem so important to Beau that she be there. Molly was an exobiologist, and so long as they remained in space, she did not have much to do except review previous research. Given how little was known about the fauna on Polus IV, she had probably already read and re-read everything available multiple times by this point in their voyage. Even so, it was apparent that her participation mattered to Waters.

"I'll go find her," Beau said.

He climbed down the ladder past the airlock, through the deck with his quarters to the deck below where Molly's quarters were.

He reached her door and could hear a muffled voice. He raised his hand to knock but the door suddenly slid open and Molly stood before him.

"Good morning, Beau," she said. She was congenial. She did not seem surprised to see him.

Beau glanced into her room briefly and saw what he thought looked like a genuine paper book on her desk, but Molly took a step forward and forced Beau back into the hall, and the door quickly closed behind her.

"All ready, Beau?" she asked.

"It's time for the daily briefing. Do you have a real book?" he asked, motioning at the closed door.

"Ha, oh that. I like to read and doodle sometimes. I don't have a whole lot to do, you know. It's also a classic way of documenting new wildlife. Drawing, I mean."

Beau was a little perplexed, but equally curious. Regulations strictly controlled what they were permitted to bring aboard, both for concerns of weight allowance and for concerns of mission suitability. No materials that could compromise the integrity of their mission were permitted.

"How did you get permission?" he asked.

"I didn't. I found the book in one of the drawers in my quarters. I think the previous passenger must have left it there. The pencils I brought though. I just had to give up some other stuff. It's all about weight. A pair of socks and an extra shirt is more than enough for some pencils and a few sheets of real paper."

"But why not just use your phone or a mission tablet? Wouldn't that be easier?" Beau asked.

Regulations strongly preferred that the missionaries carry out recreation on their phones. Electrons and data storage weighed nothing for starters. Well, not nothing, but it was negligible. It also permitted the Mission Director to perform appropriate monitoring of the team to ensure they remained capable so he could alert the Administration of any unorthodox deviations.

"Probably. I prefer the old way of doing it. And I'm not used to having a phone. Sketching is more fun anyway. There's something about paper and pencils that isn't the same on a phone. It feels more human too. Shall we?" she said, redirecting his attention.

"Yep. Everyone else should be ready to begin."

Ready they were. The Daily Briefing had finished buffering, and as they climbed up the ladder into the observation lounge, Waters began to stream the day's lesson.

The studio and the official Mundial Federated Air and Space Administration readers came into view. Beau recognized one as

DeClare White, a female staffer from the MFASA's media division at headquarters where Beau worked back on Earth.

"Good morning, missionaries. As always, the Earth is indebted to you for your commitment to the important work we do. I am DeClare White."

"And I am Nonce Washington," said a man sitting beside her behind a news desk.

"And this is your Daily Briefing," they said together.

Beau cringed a little. They were called readers, and it was an apt term. DeClare and Nonce ably read the script, but that was the best that could be said of their delivery. Beau wondered why the Administration would not simply hire paid entertainers for these positions; it certainly had enough money, and many would fall over themselves at the opportunity to advance their standing. Or the Administration could simply give the information to the director for him to pass on. These briefings were always so wooden and uncomfortable they were almost comical. The staff apparently loved doing them, however. It was quite the honor to be selected as a reader, and he understood: the information they were presenting had been carefully crafted and edited, and it was essential that they read exactly what was in front of them.

"Today's news includes three new words that have been granted cautionary status on the official registry of offensive terminology," DeClare continued.

"Wow. Three new words. That is quite incredible, DeClare."

"Yes, it is, Nonce. As you know, the Department of Inclusivity and Diversity works to ensure that our society remains both inclusive and diverse, and part of that is ensuring that we all are aware of words that may offend those around us, especially our missionaries. That way we can speak carefully and appropriately at all times."

"That is an important job. I am so glad that we are able to communicate this important message to all of our missionaries," Nonce responded.

"I am too, Nonce. That is why we present this briefing on a daily basis," DeClare continued. "Today's words are *surplice* and *amice*."

Beau had a notion those words were not pronounced that way, but it did not matter.

"Be careful saying words like that, DeClare."

"I will, Nonce. We're both excited to caution our missionaries with the third word of the day: *thurible.*"

"Wow, just hearing a word like that sends chills up my spine."

Beau was certain Nonce was decidedly unchilled.

"It makes me glad we are informing people about these offensive words."

"Me too, Nonce. More information, including a full list of cautionary words and the Administration's official style guide for speech, may be found at..." Beau's attention wandered as DeClare read out an entire internet address, letter by letter, slashes and dots included.

"Let's not forget that the official registry includes references to Western religions in general by association, as well as curses, swearing, and any speech that could be construed as offensive or hostile by a listener, or someone who may become a listener. Our viewers can use this as a guideline if they ever have a question or have not had a chance to review the latest additions to the registry. And now it is time for the Daily Lesson."

"Thank you, Nonce. Our missionaries may be working with people of religious affiliation and may witness expressions of belief in *god.* So it's important they are prepared to be the recipients of offensive speech and use the coping strategies from their training to address the situation."

"Oh! Be careful, DeClare. I think that *god* is one of the cautionary words on the official registry."

"You are right, Nonce. But we have received special permission from the DID to use that and other words today in our briefing so that we can communicate this very important message."

"I am glad we were given permission, because you had me worried for a moment there, DeClare."

"I was a little worried too, Nonce."

"Ha ha ha," they both laughed in unison. Or rather, they read the sound of laughter in unison.

"What other news do we have to present today, DeClare?"

"Today is an especially important day, Nonce. This morning we received official confirmation that the Department of Human Services has successfully taken custody of several children from a collective of religious sectarians in New York state," DeClare read. "The Department was complying with a court order that the children be remanded into custody. This followed a court decision last year finding that the Administration does indeed possess the authority to grant itself guardianship in circumstances that the Secretary of Human Services deems to be harmful or deleterious to children."

Nonce continued reading where DeClare left off, "Following the court order, several of the parents from the opposition group agreed to send their children to Administration schools, where they will receive a proper, approved course of education. However, several other parents issued a public statement stating that they would continue to educate their children themselves, triggering the Department of Human Services' action. The children of the parents who refused to comply with the court order were taken into protective custody."

"This represents an important step in giving these children a proper education, Nonce. It is also important that everyone respect the decisions of the court. This step by the Department of Human Services represents an important action to preserve the integrity of our secular society," DeClare read.

"It certainly does, DeClare. We applaud our fellow government agency for its good work," Nonce read.

Molly stood up suddenly. Every head in the lounge turned to face her.

"Excuse me," she said. "I don't feel well. I think I shouldn't have skipped breakfast this morning."

"Of course, Molly," Waters said. "Please take as long as you need."

Molly hurried from the lounge and down the ladder.

"This concludes our Daily Briefing," continued the broadcast.

"Thank you. For the glory of the Administration." Nonce and DeClare said in unison.

Waters paused the playback and minimized the screen, once more revealing the starfield through the observation window behind him. "You all know the nature of these presentations. I'm afraid the Administration tends to oversimplify and generalize things to ensure that the message can be understood by the broadest possible audience."

"The Administration mandates that its programming and documentation be written at no more than a sixth-grade education level precisely for that reason," Beau chimed in.

"As far as I know, that's correct," Waters confirmed. "I don't think we need to review the briefing any further. However, it is important that you all understand completely so that you can interact appropriately with the colonists once we arrive on Polus IV. For that reason, I will be asking each one of you to cover some of these concepts for us. I have asked Jazzy to get us started. Are you ready? Will you need to use the screen?"

Jazzy nodded her head and stood up. "I only need a couple of slides for my presentation. Glory to the Administration," she said, and began her presentation.

Glory to the Administration, Waters thought to himself. *What are the implications?* He stared out the observation window, lost in thought while Jazzy spoke, unaware that the entire mission team was watching him and awaiting his direction.

"Director Waters?" Jazzy said. "I'm finished."

"Oh. Thank you very much, Jazzy," Waters said and brought himself back to the present. "For the remainder of the day, everyone should review their individual mission parameters and training in preparation for our arrival at Polus Station. The captain informs me that Polus itself should be visible as early as tomorrow."

CHAPTER THREE

WHAT THE STAKES ARE

Waters sat at the desk in his quarters after dismissing the rest of the missionaries. Jazzy was in the room with him, as she often was, which made it crowded. Although as director his personal space was the largest on the ship next to the captain, it was still somewhat confined. In addition to the pieces found in each room, his quarters had an extra table for private conferences and meetings as the need arose.

Jazzy sat at the conference table. She appeared to be streaming a program over the LiFi as was her habit in the morning. She had her feet up on the chair with her knees leaning to one side against the arm rests. She wore a slight smile on her face, intent on something on her phone. She was probably using his LiFi allowance. As director, he was afforded a generous amount of bandwidth, but it was still limited. He preferred to work alone. But considering the consequences of explaining that to her, he preferred to tolerate her presence. Even if he had asked her to give him some privacy, she probably would not have taken him seriously anyway.

Their mission team was a small one and had no need of a lead, but Jazzy had deputized herself as second in command anyway. Waters did not protest. He enjoyed the benefits of their relationship and having a woman in a leadership role looked good for the mission. She often spoke up regardless of whether she was officially in a position to do so.

Informally formalizing her authority simply recognized the state of things as they were. She often advised him of her opinion. As the mission's physician, she had a close relationship with the rest of the missionaries. This made her presence advantageous due to the insight she could offer on the team's state of mind. This was a kind of accountability he liked to hold over the mission team. The information she offered allowed him to exercise his authority better.

Waters returned to his phone and sorted through their mission objectives: convince the colonists to adopt a secular form of governance and accept a seat in the Colonial House. This would bring them back under Earth's authority and was the Administration's primary goal, which made it his as well. The Colonial House was a body that advised the Administration and President on interstellar and intersystem topics, typically by passing various non-binding resolutions. The goal was both high stakes and low stakes: high, in the sense that if the colonists refused to join the Colonial House, Earth might remediate them through supplemental education or even resettle them; low, in that the Administration could select a representative either way. That was the better outcome for the Administration in a sense, since it could select a representative with strong loyalty to Earth.

Each missionary had two purposes on the mission. The first was to study the fourth moon of Polus. The second was to improve the colonists' education on a wide variety of subjects, including proper governance, education, healthcare. These were all good things unto themselves, and things in which he believed. He felt for the colonists, and strongly desired to improve their lives and the colony itself through what the Administration offered. He knew the rest of the missionaries felt the same way. His role was to liaise with the leaders of the colony on governance; Jazzy's role, as the mission physician, was healthcare.

They had two biologists on their team. One was a botanist, an exobotanist specifically, whose objective was to study the flora of the moon, especially the Polus fruit, a plant with purported medicinal properties. However, Jazzy did not give much weight to reports that a plant could be such a universal source of healing.

"Tall tales told by worker positions. Not dissimilar from fish stories men have told for millennia. It is a nostrum, nothing more," she had said. Her feeling was that, at least, the healing properties couldn't be ascertained without industrial processing to extract the organic compounds responsible, followed by laboratory study, clinical trials, and the development of a manufacturing process and formalized distribution system. To her, it was at best folk medicine, and at worst, a primitive ritual. She was the expert, which meant it was primitive folk medicine to Waters too.

The second was an exobiologist who would catalogue and study the moon's life. She had become something of a minor celebrity on Earth, a status that had lasted for a few news cycles. Long enough for her to become a recognizable face even after interest faded. That interest was likely to revive upon the completion of their mission, which would work to their benefit. Even so, as a late comer, she had not had the opportunity to bond with the team during training. Her relationship with the other missionaries suffered for that and other reasons.

MFASA had mandated her presence on the team. Waters only accepted her after MFASA Director, now President-elect, Stanisdottir had explained the situation, and still Waters had only reluctantly agreed. Her presence was part of a corrective action against persons of note on Earth, themselves also minor celebrities. Those persons were her parents: doctors who had been made to testify before an Administration hearing about the unorthodox opposition beliefs their organization professed. They had been subjected to remediation, as was appropriate.

Thinking about the news coverage made him uncomfortable. He was surprised the Administration had not suppressed its content more. Her parents had been inappropriately expressive about their faith during the hearing. The word alone made him and others uncomfortable. It was somewhat unsettling that her parents and their organization would be so open about what should have been a private matter, nothing more, especially in a public setting. Waters shook off the thoughts and moved on.

Their team also had a media specialist for the purpose of document-ing the mission, but also to produce news reels suitable for viewing on Earth to help maintain support for the Administration and MFASA's projects. That person was Beau Lee. Waters had fought hardest to keep him with the mission. MFASA's stance was that anyone could point a phone and record footage, and media specialists and their equipment were too expensive for space. Waters countered that while that was true, it took training and skill to capture footage in a competent and aesthet-ically pleasing way, including editing the footage to tell the true story of their mission, and tell it well. Stanisdottir countered that they could simply transmit the footage to Earth and have someone do the same thing, but finally conceded when Waters pointed out that LiFi was often spotty or even unavailable in the colonies and deep space. That meant regular transmissions would not be possible, especially consider-ing that large volumes of footage required a lot of bandwidth. She did not necessarily think that was sufficient to justify an additional mis-sionary on its own, but it had been sufficient as a negotiating point for bringing Molly along, thus Beau got to remain with the team. Beau never knew that his position with the mission was in jeopardy, and Waters preferred to keep it that way. Waters knew the value of special-ists and was glad to have him.

Waters for his part was an attorney by training, a JD. He only prac-ticed law for a brief time before accepting a civil servant position with MFASA. He really enjoyed this work and particularly their mission: advocating for a better, more equitable society through government solutions. Not only that, but a directorship was also a well-known step-pingstone to status with the Administration, to MFASA Director, or even the presidency eventually.

He glanced at Jazzy and saw she had finished her program and appeared to be doing actual work. In addition to educating the col-onists on the benefits of modern medicine, part of her charge was to demonstrate the benefits of free and public healthcare. If the colonists accepted a role in the Colonial House, access to Administration-spon-sored healthcare would be theirs. He simply could not understand that they lacked something as fundamental a human right as healthcare—healthcare! That had been one of the many topics on which the missionary team had been trained to help them understand and therefore work better with the colonists. That the colonists still paid for many services that had long ago been deemed public goods was difficult to understand. As far as he knew, the colonists also had nothing resembling Earth's college and university system, which perhaps was part of the problem.

Waters returned to the table of contents and surveyed the other topics briefly.

"Have you seen the story that came through this morning?" Jazzy asked, interrupting his train of thought.

"Which one?"

"This mission director. The one from the mission to Vega."

"No. What happened?"

"Their mission was apparently unsuccessful."

"That's not so much of a story in itself," Waters said. "Colonists can be pretty intractable. The Administration will simply appoint a representative for them and provide remediation for anyone who needs it."

"That's a given, but that's not what I mean," Jazzy said, as she flicked the story over to Waters's phone. "Listen to this: *Director Jenner of the Vega mission, pictured here, was stripped of her position and licensures by the Administration and faces the possibility of transfer to opposition member status. MFASA, the government agency that oversees all extraterrestrial activity, including spaceflight and missions, reports that the mission failed to meet one of its objectives.*"

"That's new," Waters said. "It's not unusual for a mission to not meet multiple objectives, so not meeting one shouldn't be surprising. MFASA's mission objectives are usually unreasonable; everyone knows that. It's part of the point. That's one way to justify assuming colonial oversight. Do they say which objective caused all this?"

"It doesn't say," Jazzy said. "We're going to meet all our objectives, right? Including the optional ones?"

"Of course, we are. That's why we've been training our missionaries daily."

"We'd better. This is important for us," Jazzy said. "Success here could mean a position for me with the Department of Health. Maybe even a mission of my own. For you—"

"I know very well what it could mean for me. Believe me. I understand what the stakes are. This is new though."

"We have to succeed," Jazzy said.

"We will succeed," Waters said emphatically.

CHAPTER FOUR

A WEEKLY MEETING

A relatively large general use recreation room, which both the crew and passengers shared, sat forward of the Arca's observation lounge. It had a flat smooth metallic floor and walls. Three times a day the crew organized the room as a cafeteria, setting up chairs that were otherwise stowed against the bulkheads. The rest of the day the floor was clear, and the room open for general use.

Regulations dictated that each missionary stay physically healthy, which included at least twenty minutes of cardiovascular exercise six days a week, permitting one day for recovery. The regulation was a holdover from when most ships did not generate artificial gravity but had survived. Exercise helped stave off bone density loss and muscular atrophy common to zero gravity environments. The routine also ensured that all crew and missionaries had at least one thing to do nearly every day to relieve stress and boredom. It was no longer medically necessary since nearly all ships had gravity of some kind. The Administration was slow to change, however, so the regulation remained. As such, the recreation room became a de facto exercise room much of the day.

Waters, who was getting ready for his workout, saw Beau walking out of the rec room and tossed him a towel. Beau snatched the towel out of the air and batted at the sweat on his face.

"It's humid in here today," he said. "I don't usually sweat this much during work outs."

"You're just out of shape," Waters retorted.

Beau chuckled. "How many pullups do you plan to do today, *Director* Waters?"

"All of them. How many did you do?" Waters asked.

"Twenty-one," Beau said.

"I'll probably do more like thirty then," Waters said

Beau twirled his towel around, twisting it into a fine whip.

"Besides, with your form, I don't think a single pullup was done today," Waters said, angling his hips forward to dodge Beau's towel snap.

"Beau, wait just a moment," Waters said as Beau fled for the door.

Beau heard the change in Waters's tone and turned to face him. He could tell Waters needed something, although he wrapped the towel around his hand, just in case he needed a defense.

Waters was glad that Beau stayed. Though Waters was on good terms with all the missionaries, his title caused the others to be reserved around him. 'Director' meant a certain deference no matter his relationship with the missionaries. Waters was certain that even Jazzy often answered according to regulation around him. The regulations had value in that they maintained a level of expectation for behavior, thought, and speech. The regulations did not, however, broker much independence. Time spent individually was an opportunity for expression.

Waters noted one of Beau's drones slumped near the door. "You know, part of the purpose of recording the mission is for documentation purposes," he remarked.

"Yeah, that's why I'm here," Beau replied.

"I don't mean documentation in the sense of a documentary," Waters said. "I'm talking about behavioral documentation. In case anyone should engage in any deviant or unorthodox behavior. They told you that during your training, right? That part of your job, the job of anyone recording the mission, is to be alert for potentially concerning behavior?"

Beau thought back to his training. He was certain he had been told as much. A human resources specialist on loan to MFASA from the DID had spent a day briefing the missionaries, including separate breakout sessions for education on the responsibilities of their individual roles. Beau had only pretended to pay attention, though he did not want to admit that to Waters. The MFASA selection process was so vigorous that it would be unheard of for a missionary to deviate from the regulations, so he did not think it would come up. "That was part of our training. I don't expect I'll need to report anyone from our team, though," he said.

"It's everyone's responsibility to report deviant behavior or unorthodox thinking, of course. The point is that you're the one whose documentation can support any concerns," Waters said.

"It's a big responsibility," Beau said. "I don't think we'll need it though. I mean, you've seen the team. We've been together for weeks now, even accounting for Molly being gone for training. If anything was going to come up, it probably would have by now."

"It's important," Waters said. "Anyone can be on their best behavior for a few weeks. Even several months. I want to ask you to do something, as a favor."

"What?"

"Would you pay special attention to Molly?"

"Why her?"

"She's important to the Administration and to the mission. She represents everything our mission stands for."

"You mean because she renounced her parents' religion?"

"And supported the Administration, yes. And accepted the benefits of a unified society under our Administration's vision. She put aside her family for these values. That's what we're going to be asking the colonists to do."

"She's living proof that it's possible," Beau said.

"Exactly. She is," Waters said. "She's more than just another denouncer; she's a symbol. For the Administration, for MFASA, for our mission. So, would you keep an eye on her for me?"

"Sure. Why though? She's been fine so far."

"We need to be sure she's genuine. Let me know if you see anything that's not one-hundred percent on mission standards."

"You mean make sure her public denunciation was genuine."

"Yes that, but also make sure she has what she needs and that she is a part of the mission. I haven't told the others, and they don't really need to know, but her performance is one of our supplemental mission objectives," Waters said.

"And you and Jazzy want to meet all the objectives," Beau said.

"That, yes, but I have a feeling this is more than just a supplemental objective for MFASA."

Back in his quarters after his workout and freshly showered, Waters brought up the system interface in his quarters. He was still toweling off his hair, though he was dressed once more in his official MFASA jumper, complete with Director patch. The user interface scrolled across the portal in his room, partially obscuring the stars outside, though little points of light broke through occasionally behind the menus and windows. He pressed his thumb to the screen, inhaled deeply, held his breath for a few moments, then slowly exhaled and opened a channel to Earth. It was time for his weekly one-on-one with his boss.

The face of a woman appeared on the screen. "Mundial Federated Air and Space Administration. This is Freja, how many I help you?" said a woman.

She was Freja Stanisdottir, director of MFASA, the government agency for which Waters and the entire mission ostensibly worked, although he was the only official employee of the agency. The remainder of the team were the result of a public selection process. Even Beau was just a contracted specialist. He had worked his way to his position after more than fifteen years with MFASA, having begun as a first-line representative. His promotion to Mission Director had been under Stanisdottir's predecessor and, as she had informed him, more than once, had not been a unanimous selection. Even so, he was proud to be directing his own mission and had committed himself to doing what was necessary to see its success. Stanisdottir, by contrast, was a cabinet secretary appointed by the President. Though the average tenure of someone in her position was no more than a few years, proven once again by her incumbency to the presidency, his integrity still obligated him to do his best for her.

"Good morning, Freja."

"Good morning, Waters," she replied, using his surname. Her formality took him somewhat aback. "Is it time for our weekly appointment?"

"It is. And since today is Friday, may I wish you a happy 'your' day." Waters chuckled, trying to lighten the mood a bit. Director Stanisdottir's expression did not change. "You see," he continued, "'Friday' was named for the old goddess Freya—Freya's day—which eventually got shortened to Friday." Either she did not get the joke, which was unlikely, she did not think it was that funny, which was probable, or she was not in the mood, which was most likely.

"I'm glad you only said so in private," she continued. "I remind you, Waters, that references to religion of any kind, even dead and forgotten ones, are grounds for a grievance on the basis of offense. It is imperative that we guard our language carefully to maintain a positive working relationship with all of our employees."

She was not in the mood. "I understand, Director," Waters replied. "Of course, you are right. It's only because I am comfortable that you know me well enough to understand that I make no assumption or reference to thinking of any kind that religion is appropriate workplace discussion. Still, I hope that your Friday is going well?" he said.

"That's alright," she said, ignoring his polite inquiry. "We're all learning, and we'll get there eventually. Very well. Where shall we begin? Let me check my notes." She swiped her hand to move various items around her screen as she searched. "That's right. We had one of your staff for whom we needed a regularly scheduled update, and one I needed to follow-up on. Who shall we start with?" she asked.

"It does not matter. I am ready to discuss them all," Waters replied.

"Alright then, let's start with the easy and move to the difficult. Tell me about Beau Lee?"

"Beau remains a perfectly competent member of the team. He attends briefings appropriately, consistently uses standardized language, and he attends to his duties as required. He has participated in all training sessions. In preparation for our arrival, he is collecting footage and running regular diagnostics on the video equipment to make sure it functions correctly and that he can document the mission as per his position," Waters reported.

Stanisdottir showed no response. "What is your assessment of our ability to reach our target goal?" she asked.

Waters considered for a moment. "We, together with Beau, continue to work as hard as we can to ensure that we get as close to one hundred percent positive response to the mission documentary as we can." He paused. "I feel the need to register my concerns with a target goal of one hundred percent, though. It is not reasonable to expect one hundred percent audience satisfaction and saturation. MFASA's target—"

"The Administration set its targets using a thorough and scientific analysis process. I'm surprised that you would question them," Stanisdottir interrupted.

For the Administration, 'scientific' meant not so much a process as a predetermined conclusion that must be supported. "Of course. The Administration's methods are sound," he said. "Even so, I continue to register my concern that MFASA is being set up for failure. These targets—"

"The Administration controls our funding, as you know. These targets were set after input from testimony of licensed members before Congress."

"Of course, we would like to achieve complete saturation and satisfaction; that's everyone's goal. It's just not possible. There will always be people who dissent or refuse to participate. And the testimony you're referencing was mostly just the wishful thinking of activist groups and their attorneys taking advantage of representatives who have only the slightest education on the matter, and even that may be generous."

"I hear what you are saying. But this is our budgeted goal, and if we are to maintain our current level of funding, this is the target we must meet—you—must meet. Now then, tell me about McDaithi."

Molly.

Molly was a welcome member of the team. She was also, in his opinion, the least skilled member of the team. Unlike the rest of them, she did not yet have a doctorate. She had been in the middle of her studies when she joined the mission. Her family background was problematic, and she was the least deserving of the honor of participating in an official Mission to one of the colonies. She was still a missionary, however, and a member of his team. Furthermore, he was determined they would all succeed. Her success meant his success.

"Molly continues to perform as expected, given her skillset and duties, which, of course, given her purpose on this mission, is difficult to evaluate. During flight she is limited to reviewing data provided by Polus Station to make sure she can successfully identify as much wildlife as possible once we are on the surface, which she has mastered, not to mention her preparatory training and education."

"What about the agreement?" Stanisdottir asked. "Has she been compliant with the conditions of her participation?"

"She has. We have received no indication nor report that she has engaged in any offensive behavior thus far. Her denunciation appears to have been genuine."

"Has the screen revealed any deviant behavior?" she asked.

"We continue to have difficulty monitoring her, and all missionaries for that matter, using the screens in their quarters. The ship is an older model, and my understanding is that the screens were installed during a refit. The only space in the quarters was below a clothing rack. Most of the screens are obscured, including Molly's. We can only monitor them effectively if they choose to watch something on their screens, which isn't often given that most people use their phones."

"I'm sure you can come up with a solution, Waters. She is an important asset for the Administration. I am counting on you to manage her participation in the mission successfully. Have you tried monitoring her LiFi traffic for data?"

"Of course. She rarely uses her phone though. I understand how important she is to the Administration," Waters said.

"And what about your crew?"

"I am confident that they are all very much aware of the appropriate orthodox protocols and behavior, and that, given their extensive training, each and every one of them would immediately report any heterodox actions directly to me. As for—"

Waters stopped. He was about to express the difficulties he had with the Arca's captain, and to a lesser extent, the flight surgeon. The Arca was a contracted vessel, and Jackson the owner. He did not fall under MFASA's authority. Jackson needed only to comply with the stipulations of his contract, which were that he successfully transport the mission from Earth to Polus Station. By law, a government contract could not dictate the manner or methods; only the specific goal a contractor must meet. He thought better of lodging a protest with the director. She would only insist it was his responsibility to ensure the captain was kept under control, and that he keep any heterodox material from the mission and its team.

"Yes, Waters?" Stanisdottir said.

"I was going to say, as for Molly's inclusion in this mission, I would once again like to register my dissatisfaction. She is the only member of the team I was not permitted to participate in selecting. I am not a warden or disciplinarian, and neither is any other missionary. This mission is too important to risk with the potential of aberrant and heretical thinking compromising its integrity. Neither do I appreciate being used as the Administration's implement of coercion, especially without being consulted first, and especially without my consent."

"So noted, Waters, as I have done so before. Do I need to repeat the purpose of her presence on this mission?" she asked.

Waters considered asking her to do so just to have the satisfaction of wasting a bit of her time but decided against it. "No, of course I understand. It is simply not the choice I would have made."

"That is fine, and you are free to express your views with me, so long as you only do so with me. I trust that you are maintaining confidentiality in this matter?"

"Of course, I am. Confidentiality is one of our most important values."

"I expected nothing less. You only need to complete the mission with her as part of the team. She was given a position consistent with her known capabilities in part to make your stewardship easier."

"I understand," Waters said.

"Very good. Well, I have another meeting to attend to in a couple of minutes. Is there anything else we need to discuss at this time?"

"There was one more thing, Director. Do you remember a few weeks ago, there was a group of children remanded into Administration custody in New York state?"

"Vaguely. What about it?"

"Was Molly's family among them?"

"I do not know for certain, Waters, but I don't believe so. That would be the purview of the Department of Human Services."

"I only ask because if it were the case, the Administration would have violated its agreement with her, and she would be under no obligation to comply with the mission."

"I'll check if it's that important to you. Alright then. We have a scheduled call again next week at the same time."

"I have it on my calendar."

"Good. I'll talk to you then. Have a good weekend."

One day was practically identical to the next during spaceflight, so the concept of a weekend was meaningless, but he replied, "You too," anyway, and ended the call.

"You handled that very well, *Director Waters*," Jazzy said coyly, as she emerged from the corner of his cabin where she had been watching from a spot the camera could not see her. She wrapped her arms around his shoulders and gave him a peck on the cheek.

"Thank you, Jazzy. You know I value your support," Waters said.

"The call's done. You can let go of the official tone now, you know," she said.

Waters winced a bit. She was right. It was hard to stop speaking officially when one did so often.

"Don't worry about Molly. She obviously came aboard in a low mental state. All the signs were there: reduced affect, psychomotor slowing. She arrived with a diagnosis of depression. It can only be worsening given the degree of boredom and isolation she is subject to. I have been administering a placebo in place of her prescribed med, so she is sure to remain in that state and more easily controlled," Jazzy said.

Waters had reservations about treating a member of his team that way, even if mental health management, along with calculated nutritional suppression, was compliant with the Administration's guidelines for containment of potential deviance. Jazzy was right, though: keeping her bored and listless was the easiest way to ensure she did not cause any problems and did not compromise the mission given her lack of training. After all, if she could betray her family, even if for a good cause, who was to say she would not betray the mission?

"We should check to see what she's up to," Jazzy said. "Bring up the screen in her room."

"I was telling Stanisdottir the truth during the call. It's not going to show anything," Waters said.

"Let's just check. I may have an idea."

Waters stepped over to the screen in his own quarters, activated his override, and swiped to Molly's room. The screen had patches of light peeking through, but the only thing they had a clear view of were shirt sleeves and pant legs.

"It's as I said."

"Doesn't she ever watch TV?" Jazzy said.

"She doesn't, and she's the only one. No wonder she's so bored," Waters said.

"It could also be part of her constellation of symptoms, but that would be unusual. Depressed people find it all too easy to fill their time with mindless tasks like television," Jazzy said. "Maybe we can get the crew to do a special pre-arrival cleaning of each of the quarters. As a gift. Or we could implement the pre-arrival quarters check protocol."

"How would you justify that?" Waters asked.

"The usual health and safety reasons should work fine," Jazzy said.

"I'll think about it. We're due to arrive at Polus Station soon, though. I'm not sure what we can learn at this point in the trip. Or what we could do about it. You should get back to your cabin before—" Waters began, but Jazzy was already dressing.

She hugged and kissed him again, then gave Waters a tender look of superiority. She tapped the door which began to slide open, but she arrested the motion with her hand to check that no one was on the deck outside, and then silently slid into the hallway. The door shut itself behind her.

Beau looked down the ladder from the observation lounge above and watched Jazzy cross the hallway to her own room before turning away, feeling the confusion of both shame and envy.

CHAPTER FIVE

CHASING APRICOTS

At the sound of a gong crash followed by two pulsing drum beats, Beau awoke and sat up straight in bed. This time he did not need to check his phone to know the captain's wakeup call selection; there were only so many songs like that. Even at just one a day he had heard each several times now. Outside his quarters Beau heard Waters's footsteps land with thuds and clangs as he rushed up the ladder to confront the captain about this daily ritual for the umpteenth time. "He's done this every day for weeks now. You'd think he'd be used to it," Beau said to himself. But no, Waters and the captain had danced to songs of the captain's choosing in this way each morning since their departure.

Beau lay back to contemplate falling back asleep when he noticed a distinct blue glow coming through the portal. He sat up and looked outside. Where for weeks there had been nothing but blackness pointillated by stars, now a massive blue gas giant swirling with storms and currents dominated space: Polus.

They were arriving. Or, as the captain had warned them, they would arrive within a few days of sighting the planet. The planet's massive size belied the actual distance the ship still had to travel before reaching the station and their final destination. This was where their work really began. This was why they had trained. This was why they endured weeks of travel: the opportunity to set foot on an alien moon, and to

bring modernity to a people who had left such things behind generations ago.

Outside on the deck he heard Waters say, "He locked me out of the
cockpit. Can you believe it? He locked the Mission Director out," followed by a door opening that Beau assumed meant Waters had entered
his quarters. He must have been talking to Jazzy. While MFASA regulation strongly discouraged romantic relationships between missionaries, Beau had heard the regulation was only loosely adhered to, and
it would seem his mission was to be no exception. They tried to be dis-
creet, but there was truly no hiding it. The regulation did not make
sense anyway. Forbidding romantic relationships seemed inconsis-
tent with the Administration's official stance on human sexuality. Still,
MFASA reasoned that unity excluded exclusivity, and for that reason
they excluded romance. Beau could think of other reasons too, among
them jealousy. Or perhaps it was simply that Waters had a companion and he did not.

Beau sighed and kicked his feet over the side of the bunk, making
up his mind to get up. He rinsed off in the shower, dried, and stepped
back into the narrow confines of his quarters, grabbing the jumpsuit
that hung in front of the screen in his room. As he replaced the hanger
he noted a drone camera sitting on the shelf above the screen and felt
a bit guilty. For the first couple weeks he had documented everything
with enthusiasm. Then everything settled into a routine and there really
was not much more to capture. The footage started to look the same, as
did the edits he transmitted back to MFASA. Preparing weekly news
reel submissions for a situation where nothing changed was not just
challenging, it was maddening. He brought it up with Waters, who in
turn informed him the Administration had not budged on its metrics,
not for him or any mission objective.

He reached for the drone camera, hesitated, then decided to take
it down and made his way toward the door. It opened in time to see
Jazzy's back disappear into her own quarters, as he had predicted. He
decided he had time before the daily briefing and began to wander.

He climbed down the ladder into the second deck of empty quarters, which was empty except for Molly's room, then kept going. The starboard side of the deck below was full of crates and equipment for the mission, all securely stowed for flight. The port side bulkheads had been removed to make way for the captain's greenhouse. They called it the greenhouse, but it was more like a botanical garden in miniature. It was full of small, fast-growing plants, most of them edible, and other larger species of various sizes and colors underneath blue and magenta LEDs. Barely a square centimeter was not covered in foliage of some kind, including the ceiling which bore creeping vines, grapes, wisteria, and other plants of which Beau did not know the name. The plants helped clean the air and recycle the water aboard ship. They also made for more interesting ways of staving off Ricket's disease besides daily vitamins. The captain had a collection of bonsai trees interspersed among the other plants. This deck smelled of earth and wet soil. It tended to make Beau a little homesick, so he did not like to spend time there. Joon-baek was in the greenhouse already, working on something with a pair of scissors in his hands.

"Up already, Joon-baek?" Beau asked.

Joon-baek turned away from his work and gave a cordial smile. "Good morning, Beau! The captain asked if I wanted to help in the greenhouse. It's time for partial outer canopy defoliation on a couple of his fruit-bearing trees. I wanted to get started before our briefing today to make sure I get it done before we arrive at Polus Station."

"I think I'd rather get some extra sleep," Beau said.

Joon-baek went back to work. "I don't think I could sleep for thinking about this."

Beau could think of a lot of things he could sleep through, including tree trimming, but that was why he was the media specialist and Joon-baek was the botanist. He continued to the deck below which housed engineering. It was generally darker there save for a few red LED lights. It smelled a bit of ozone, like static electricity. There were no bulkheads here; pipes and conduit lined the walls. The floor was a metal grate, which covered more pipes and conduit. Coming around a central bank of two large cylinders whose purpose he did not understand he was surprised to see Molly sitting on the grated floor with her back to one of the machines.

"I'm sorry, I didn't realize someone was down here," Beau said.

Molly didn't respond. She faced straight ahead, a dull look in her eyes. She was relaxed but not calm. It was more the absence of expression he saw there.

He could not tell if she had heard him or not, so he cleared his throat. "Joon-baek's awake already too. I know it's exciting getting close to the station, but I didn't expect everyone to be up so early."

Molly stared ahead, apparently lost in some morass of thinking consistent of many things and nothing at all judging by the look on her face. Whatever it was must have been too important to acknowledge him.

"I'll just leave you alone then," Beau said.

Molly raised a listless hand and tossed what looked like a bit of crusted bread against the pipes on the opposite wall. It made a tiny ping. As it bounced off a cleaning robot zipped silently out of a slot to intercept the crumb just before it fell through the grate. A pair of brush tipped extensions emerged and sucked up the crumb into a tiny metal door before the bot retraced its path to the slot.

"Even he has something to do," Molly said, her face unchanging.

Beau felt uncomfortable. "I'm sorry?"

"I don't," Molly said.

"What do you mean? Aren't you the team's biologist?" Beau said.

"There's no reason for me to be here," she said.

"I don't think I understand you," Beau said.

"It's alright, isn't it? It's only betrayal if you cause harm. It's alright if what you did was for good, even if people don't know it," Molly said.

Beau took a step back. He knew Molly was not always in good spirits. That had something to do with why she spent time with Jazzy each week, but he had never seen her like this. He motioned over his shoulder with his thumb. "I should go get Jazzy."

Molly finally moved. Turning her head away from him, she wiped her eyes with the back of her wrist. "No, don't get her. I'm fine. Here."

She handed him half a piece of crusted bread. "This is about the most entertaining thing to do on this ship." Beau hesitated, then walked forward and took the crust.

"What should I do with this."

"Watch."

Molly broke off three pieces and tossed them one after the other in different directions. The cleaning bot was on the crumbs before they hit the ground.

"I haven't been able to beat it yet," she said.

Beau admitted it was amusing but handed the bread back to Molly. "I think I'll pass. I don't want to be accused of making a mess. Are you sure you don't want me to get Jazzy?"

"That's alright. I might talk with Doctor Stephens later," she said. She rose, it seemed with great difficulty and even a bit of stiffness and hesitation like she was uncomfortable, and said, "We should probably go get breakfast before today's briefing."

Beau and Molly climbed the ladder to the common room. Waters was already seated at a table with Jazzy and Joon-baek who filled three of the table's four chairs.

"There you two are. I hope you're keeping everything appropriate," Waters said when he saw Beau climb onto the deck with Molly behind him.

He meant it as a joke, and Molly managed a small smile. Beau did not think it was something he ought to be joking about. "Of course. What you're implying would be against regulation," Beau said with a significant look.

Waters waved the comment off with a twinkle in his eye. "Just remember, Beau: regulation for thee but not for me. Come on, sit with us."

"The captain saved some apricots for our arrival. They're from one of his trees. You can cut them up into your cereal," Joon-baek said.

Beau looked at the three occupied seats. With only one seat open and being a little concerned about how he had encountered Molly that morning, he decided to eat with her. "It doesn't look like there's room for all of us. I'll get a different table with Molly."

Waters looked shocked and concerned. "That was insensitive of me. Let's pull up another chair."

The fifth chair at a table for four, which was already on the small side, made breakfast extra crowded. They bumped elbows as they ate. Molly chased an apricot around her bowl of loopy fruits, but Beau noticed that she made little progress. He was going to say something when the captain climbed down to the deck from the cockpit and cleared his throat.

"Everyone, I'm excited to announce that thanks to some solar wind that was on our side, we are going to arrive at Polus Station a few days early. Tonight, in fact." There was a general stir in the room as commentary and excitement arose from missionaries and crew alike.

"So much for my idea," Jazzy said to Waters.

Captain Jackson continued, "We'll prepare for arrival at eighteen-thirty, and no, it won't be anything like our departure acceleration," he said to Molly, "though we will be without gravity temporarily until we dock. Make sure to sweep your quarters twice. Anything you leave aboard is mine until you get back to Earth."

The room filled with excitement. For the crew it meant the opportunity for leave; for the missionaries, it meant finally starting their mission in earnest.

"This is too exciting," Waters said. "Let's forgo today's briefing and training so everyone can get ready for our arrival."

"We should be able to get everything in. The briefing is important," Jazzy objected.

"You're right, but our arrival is important too," Waters said, over-riding Jazzy.

"I bet he pays for that later," Beau said to himself.

"Everyone take the rest of the day to get ready. Welcome to Polus!"

CHAPTER SIX

POLUS STATION

The arrival at Polus Station was uneventful. They were without gravity for just a few minutes, which they spent strapped to their seats in the observation lounge. Once the Arca docked, the station's rotation provided artificial gravity.

Departing the Arca was bittersweet for Beau and Joon-baek. It had been their home for weeks, even months. It was welcome for Waters and Jazzy. They could hardly contain themselves at the prospect of being in control of their own situation once more. Molly seemed indifferent until they climbed out of the airlock. She looked up and immediately returned her eyes to the floor.

"Are you alright?" Joon-baek asked.

"Not again," Molly said and kept her eyes pinned to her feet.

Polus station consisted of three rotating helixes, each with a diameter of several kilometers, connected by several pylons to a central core that spanned the length of the station. The transparent ceiling of each helix made virtually the entire station visible, Polus, the moon below, and space beyond from nearly any vantage point. Each helix rotated independently. The effect was like being in the loop of a roller-coaster which itself was rotating within two other loops.

The missionaries stumbled where they stood as something passed beneath their feet not unlike a small earthquake. Molly grabbed Beau's arm involuntarily.

"What was that?" Jazzy asked.

"It's probably a gravity shift," Joon-baek said. "Every once in a while, the worker positions transfer power in the core to do maintenance. That can cause a temporary fluctuation in the helix's rotational velocity like the one we just felt. Most people become accustomed to the movement within a few days. Some never do and suffer a feeling akin to perpetual sea sickness."

"Perpetual sea sickness, huh?" Molly said.

"We all were tested for suitability to the environmental demands during our training, both from a physical and psychological standpoint," Jazzy said. "It's unfortunate that the Administration would put someone who did not receive the same screening in an environment like this."

Molly shrugged in reply, resigned to her situation.

Despite their initial disorientation, the clear metal ceiling let in light from Polus' star and permitted the people working and traveling through the station a spectacular view. They could see people moving and walking about in other helixes, some of them upside-down from their point of view.

Molly looked up again, seeking to acclimate herself as Joon-baek had said. "Oh, help," she said and clutched Beau's arm tighter.

"Try keeping your eyes on Polus," Joon-baek said and took Molly's free arm. "It will appear to stay fixed relative to our position. That should help with the disorientation."

A woman carrying a large tablet with perfectly straight hair, white slacks, and a white blouse met them. "Hello, everyone. Allow me to be the first to welcome you to Polus Station!" she said. "My name is Tegan, and I'll be your designated civil servant position. If you'll please show me your phones…"

The team pulled out their phones. Tegan tapped her tablet in the direction of each. "I have just given you access to the rooms where you'll be staying. If you'll please follow me."

Several worker positions arrived and began to unload the Arca.

"Will they bring our bags to our rooms?" Jazzy asked.

"Of course…," Tegan checked her tablet, "*Doctor* Bebe."

"You can call me Jazzy."

Living quarters were stacked two and three high along the sides of each helix. Docking airlocks punctuated the apartments periodically.

"Each helix has three docking airlocks, so the station can accommodate up to nine ships at a time," Joon-baek said.

"That is correct…," Tegan checked her tablet. "Would you say your name for me, please?" Tegan asked.

"Joon-baek Kim," he said.

"…June Bug Kim," Tegan repeated.

Something distracted Joon-baek from correcting her pronunciation, and he suddenly turned from the group and pressed his hands against the station's transparent hull. "Ohhh!" he exclaimed and craned his neck to get a better look. "Is that a P-4W patrol ship?"

"Yes. The P-4 is part of the equipment assigned to the officer positions on the station," answered Tegan. Others from the group moved closer to the window to see what had Joon-baek so excited.

"It has wings," Beau said to no one in particular. "It looks like an airplane."

"What you cannot see from this angle is the cabin," Tegan said. "It is quite large, and capable of carrying several passengers; or accused persons, as may suit the needs of the officer positions."

"Do you think we'll get to see inside?" Joon-baek asked. "I hear it's state-of-the-art. It has a titanium alloy-reinforced airframe and hull, so it's supposed to be nearly indestructible, and it's one of the only ships capable of both atmospheric flight and spaceflight. They're very expensive."

"How did you learn so much about our station? Have you been here before?" Tegan asked.

"No. I just like to read," he said. "The P-4W is also armed with a computer-vectored turret-mounted thirty-millimeter railgun."

"Why would you need a gun in space?" Beau asked.

"It's just a precautionary armament for our officer positions—" Tegan checked her tablet, "Missionary Beau Lee. They've never used it. Except for target practice. Though I believe the official reason for purposes of regulatory compliance was clearing celestial bodies that might threaten the station. That made for difficult paperwork since the system has no asteroid belt. But never in an enforcement situation. I see you are a botanist, Missionary Joon-baek Kim," Tegan said as she tapped her tablet. "Perhaps you could have a career as a civil servant position providing tours if your other position does not work out. Would you please continue? I would be interested to hear what else you know about the station."

"Let's see," Joon-baek said to himself. "The south terminus on the central core is where the space elevator will eventually anchor, allowing delivery of supplies and permitting transportation up and down the cable. Until its completion, however, the station and moon below rely on regular drops and shuttles for the exchange of goods and people."

"So, how will we get down to the moon then?" Jazzy asked.

"You will be taking a dropship to the surface," Tegan said.

"I was hoping we'd be done with ships for a while," Molly said.

"Oh, it's an enjoyable ride, I can assure you," Tegan said.

Molly responded with a noncommittal noise.

Tegan stopped after a few minutes and motioned to the façade. "Your rooms are in this bank of housing." She referred to several tiny balconies that extended over the walkway where they stood. "During your brief stay, please do not hesitate to reach out to me; I am at your service according to the description of my position." Then Tegan turned and departed.

"This may be your last opportunity to use the LiFi for a while," Waters said. "So if you still have time on your bandwidth allowance you may want to use it before we land on Polus IV. Colonies are notorious for having poor signal reception."

Joon-baek gave an involuntary shiver.

"What is it?" Molly asked.

"I was just thinking of calling my mom."

"You don't want to talk to your parents?"

"It's not that I don't want to talk to them. Well, I do and I don't. I want to talk to them, but my mom always asks questions. She always wants to know if I'm successful. I'm a missionary botanist for the Administration! But it's not enough. She keeps bugging me about grandchildren too. I don't even know any girls. Excuse me, women. I did not mean to be offensive."

"Don't we count?" Molly said.

"We're missionaries, so according to regulation, no, you don't count," Beau said.

Molly pulled on their arms teasingly with the barest hint of a smirk on her face and said, "Maybe the regulation is more of a guideline."

"No public displays of affection, please," Jazzy said and looked back at the three with a mocking smile. Joon-baek hastily pulled his arm away and blushed as he suppressed a smile himself. Beau pulled his arm away a bit embarrassed.

Waters planted his feet in the speech giving position they had all seen him take before. They turned toward him and put on their best listening faces as he began. "Take the rest of the day to explore. We leave tomorrow. Seeing Polus IV below us makes me eager to get started with our mission, and I'm willing to bet you all feel the same way…where did Molly go?" Waters interrupted himself with the question.

Molly was indeed not to be seen.

"How could we lose her? She was just here. There are only five of us." Jazzy said.

"Maybe she just went to her room already," Joon-baek offered.

Waters cast a significant look at Beau, who returned a plaintive look of his own. He was eager for some free time.

As if he had read Beau's mind, Waters said, "You can explore the station while you look for her."

"I'll check her room," Joon-baek said.

"Being alone may not be good for her," Jazzy said.

"Why?" Beau said.

"It would be inappropriate of me to disclose the reason; it's confidential," Jazzy said.

Joon-baek hopped down the steps. "There's no answer at her door."

"That doesn't mean she's not inside and just wants to be left alone," Beau said, sympathizing with her presumed attitude a little.

"Beau?" Waters said in a tone that asked for his help but also suggested that if he declined that he was willing to use his authority.

"Alright," Beau said with resignation.

"Thanks."

Thus, Beau began his search. He would rather have joined the others. They would probably walk together, but this was his job for now. "So much for getting the afternoon off," he said to himself with a bit of resentment. Not so much towards Waters: he was doing his job as Mission Director. Molly did not have an excuse. He picked a direction and began to walk.

Trees, plants, and even grass-covered medians lined the inner beltway of each helix. A combination of natural light from the transparent metal ceiling and supplemental artificial lights lit the helix. As the day wore on, Beau noticed that the artificial lights grew dimmer, simulating Earth's twenty-four-hour cycle.

A noticeable rumble surprised Beau. "Was that thunder?" he said to himself.

A fine mist covered him as he looked up. He fled to shelter under a balcony as artificial rain fell around him. The plants turned a healthy green under the moisture and his nostrils filled with the smell of wet dirt again. He pushed down his nostalgia. The rainwater spilled gently over the walkways, cleansed them and washed gently into grates, headed some place where it would be processed and recycled.

The station's residents apparently took little notice and continued their business. Some drove under the cover of small electric carts, others produced umbrellas, and others simply ignored the rain. It stopped within a few minutes, and Beau resumed his journey.

Beau was impressed by how ordered the helix was. Without the regularly numbered airlocks he might have gotten lost. He was both surprised at how little time it actually took to traverse the helix and dismayed by how long it was. The helical design meant that although the station had a diameter of only a few kilometers, each helix was several kilometers long. He was tired by the time he finished walking the length of one, and irritated by the time he finished the second. He sat down on a bench, removed his shoes, and rubbed his toes beneath his socks. His feet and legs ached. He was tempted to ask one of the worker positions zipping around on carts for a ride, but his pride, and an unwillingness to admit to a worker position that he needed help, kept him walking.

He was about to start on the third helix when his irritation got the better of him and he said to no one in particular, "This is a waste of my time. We could have missed each other at any number of intersections. She's probably back already."

Although reluctant to report back to Waters that he had not found Molly, he decided he had done more than enough. He boarded an elevator to the central core to transfer back to the helix where they stayed. The elevator door opened, and he pushed himself into the central core's zero-G environment when he spotted a woman with dark hair wearing a matching MFASA jumper, anchored firmly to the metal deck by a pair of gravity boots.

"Molly?" he asked.

She turned and smiled, "Hi, Beau." She stood next to a young man. "This is Sullivan Jakeson. He's an engineer on the station. He's been explaining to me how the core works."

Beau nodded. The young man did not make eye contact and said "Bye" awkwardly before floating off deftly down the corridor.

Beau felt a flush of anger. "Where have you been? I've been looking for you all day. Waters sent me to find you."

"He did? Sorry, I guess," she said sheepishly. "I thought he had dismissed us."

She appeared to be genuinely sorry, and Beau's anger faded, but he resolved to remain at least a little annoyed.

Molly read the change in his features and explained, "I couldn't stand feeling the hard floor below me and looking out at everything at once in space. I felt like I was constantly going to float away. So, I came here."

"I thought you hated zero-G?" Beau said.

"Captain Jackson gave me these," she said and tapped her boot's heel with her toe. The boot clanked as it attached itself back to the deck. "There aren't many windows down here, and they're small."

"So you've just been down here all day?"

Molly could see the absurdity of preferring to spend her free time in a metal tube with little light and few people, and she shuffled a bit, embarrassed. "I wanted to be alone too. It's not that I don't like you all. I just wanted to be by myself with my thoughts for a while. We've been so close together for so long I didn't think anyone would mind."

"It's been hours. Forget it. Are you ready to go back?" Beau asked.

"Sure. Beau?"

"What is it?"

"Thanks for coming to get me."

CHAPTER SEVEN

HOW YOU FALL FROM SPACE

They met at platform nine the next day at precisely thirteen-thirty for their departure to Polus IV per Tegan's instructions. The platform was nothing more than a space in the ring with an airlock and a large "nine" painted on the doorway. The missionaries felt irritable. They had been instructed not to eat beforehand to limit discomfort during the drop. Since their departure was in the mid-afternoon, none of them had eaten breakfast or lunch. Dropships could theoretically depart at any time, but it was most efficient to time the drop for when Polus Station aligned with the space port below.

The airlock doors opened and to their surprise, Captain Jackson stepped out to greet them. "Good afternoon. You lucky people get to have me as your pilot at least one more time. If everyone's here, come aboard. We'll launch in about twenty minutes."

"Molly's not here yet," Beau said.

"Well someone better go find her then," the captain said. "If we don't make our drop window, we have to wait another hour-and-a-half for the station to come back around, and you all are looking peckish. I don't need a bunch of hungry missionaries spoiling my fun."

Waters gave Beau another look when they heard a woman say, "I'm here." Molly came running up to the group, her duffel over her shoulder. Beau noted that she was wearing her gravity boots again.

"Everything alright?" Beau asked.

"I'm fine," Molly replied.

Captain Jackson was already in his flight suit, but the rest of them needed to get dressed before they could depart. "Here, put these on," he said. He tossed a helmet to each of them as they boarded the ship. Stuffed inside each helmet was a flight suit.

"Why do we have to wear these?" Jazzy asked, "We're just going to take them off again in a few minutes. We're all in good enough shape for the trip. We passed MFASA standards."

"They're to keep your insides from becoming outsides," the captain said. "Make it quick: we don't want to miss our window."

They made it quick as they could, then found their seats.

The interior of the drop ship was austere in comparison to Polus Station. The passenger compartment consisted of metal walls covering a metal frame. So little attention had been given to creature comforts that the interior had not been finished. The seats looked like they had been taken out of a museum. There were no windows save for the cockpit, which was visible through a narrow doorway.

Worker positions delivered their equipment and secured their gear and cargo using straps, nets, and a system of channels and locks built directly into the floor.

"This is archaic!" Joon-baek said.

"Yeah, it's—" Molly began.

"It's incredible!" Joon-baek finished.

She was about to say "concerning," but she did not want to dampen Joon-baek's enthusiasm. Molly took some comfort in seeing that she was not alone. Jazzy did not look happy with their accommodations either. She was having a spirited discussion with Waters near the front row of seats, but Molly could not hear what she was saying from where she, Beau, and Joon-baek helped the worker positions stow the equipment.

They finished and fastened themselves in. As they sat in their seats, one by one their helmets snapped back into place, locking their vision forward and immobilizing their heads.

"Is this normal?" Molly asked.

"Perfectly normal," Captain Jackson said. He walked up and down the rows of seats pulling on their harnesses and shaking their helmets to make sure they were secure. He finished and made his way to the cockpit.

"Don't you have to give us another safety talk, Captain?" Jazzy asked with just the barest touch of sarcasm permissible for decorum.

Captain Jackson turned and looked at her with a special gleam in his eye. "Oh, I think this will be much more fun if you experience it without any preconceptions."

"All systems clear checks, tower. Docking clamp control has been transferred to you. Ready to drop," they heard the captain say as he fastened his own harness.

"Roger, dropship. Computer-controlled launch system engaged. Prepare for docking clamp release in approximately one minute."

It was the longest minute of their lives. Molly was strapped in so tight she could barely move. She certainly could not turn her head. She felt like part of the ship. Her heart pounded inside her chest and they had not even moved.

"Standby for departure. Three–two–one."

There was a hydraulic whoosh and mechanical clang as the docking clamps opened. Instantly the drop ship shot away from Polus Station at incredible speed arcing toward the moon below as the ship cast off. The force of their acceleration pressed Molly into her seat.

She was just starting to adjust to the acceleration when the radio crackled, "Altitude 128 kilometers. Aft steering jets cut off. Engine cut off."

"What do you mean engine cut off?!" she said aloud. She heard Jazzy's voice in front of her and thought she must be making a similar protest, but could not hear her.

The cabin lit up with the glow of fire outside the ship, visible and bright through the windows of the cockpit. As the ship plunged into the atmosphere the friction of their descent pushed the dropship through the air so hard that it ignited. A deafening roar filled Molly's ears as they entered the atmosphere.

"Initiating eighty-degree bank."

The dropship banked so far to port that it was almost perpendicular to the surface below. The force pressed Molly against the side of her restraints. The ship banked to starboard, then back to port, then starboard again. Each turn threatened to throw them from their seats. Two massive explosions like thunderclaps sounded right outside the ship. Several passengers gasped audibly, though Molly could not tell who. They were losing speed, but Molly found herself glad she could not move. The back-and-forth motion would have battered her were she not practically bolted to the chair.

"S-turn series complete. Beginning descent. Manual control restored," the radio said.

"Thank you," the captain replied.

"What have we been doing besides descending?" Molly wondered aloud.

At last, the drop ship stopped turning. The roaring decreased, but they still plunged nose-down to the moon below. Molly gripped the armrests and clenched her teeth. Her toes tingled.

"It can't be as steep as it looks," she said to herself.

"We're descending at an angle of nineteen degrees," Captain Jackson yelled back into the cabin. "That's about seven times steeper than most flights land on Earth. Perfectly standard procedure. Think of it like going down a water slide."

"It's steeper," Molly said with increasing dread.

They could see the spaceport approaching through the cockpit windows. The dropship did not seem to be slowing. Molly could hardly believe what was happening to them. "Why aren't we slowing down?" she said aloud, although she doubted that anyone heard her.

The captain raised the nose at last. The descent slowed perceptibly, but not enough for comfort. She could hear more hydraulics at work and said, "Probably the landing gear," as the dropship surfed onto the landing strip. Molly heard two loud screeches to her left and right, then a third screech as the front tires contacted tarmac. Molly's body accelerated once more, this time forwards as the dropship braked suddenly. "That's the parachutes deploying," the captain called out.

"They use *parachutes* to slow down?" Molly said. It was all too primitive.

Joon-baek gave a whoop and started clapping.

The dropship rolled forward into the space port, coming to a stop at last, and the engines powered down. There was an audible sigh of relief from inside the cabin. Many of the missionaries tried to remove their harnesses. The ship had stopped moving, and they were eager to get as far away as they could. Captain Jackson came aft and assisted with the restraints. Molly fell forward out of her seat when the captain unfastened her harness. He helped her onto her feet and gave the back of her helmet a friendly smack. Molly wobbled forward and found Jazzy. They leaned against each other, bonded in mutual misery.

"And that is how you fall from space," Captain Jackson proclaimed.

"Why weren't the engines on?"

"No need. The dropship glides into the spaceport. It's very efficient."

"Gah!"

Captain Jackson was chipper and alert, energized by the drop. The missionaries were not. "Drops aren't for everyone, but I love them," he said with a genuine grin just as he came to help Waters.

"I can see why the regulations state not to eat anything before a drop," Waters said.

"It's not a regulation. I just got tired of cleaning out helmets, so I have the station tell you not to eat anything," Captain Jackson replied. "I tell them it's a MFASA policy or some nonsense. No one ever bothers to look it up. I always eat a big breakfast the day of a drop."

"Captain…" Waters began, but he suddenly felt too ill to argue.

Captain Jackson did not need him to speak to understand what he was thinking after weeks of travelling together. "You'll see me no more soon enough, Waters. After you get off this ship, you may never see me again. That probably goes for the rest of you too. It's been my pleasure to be your captain. This is what I was made for."

CHAPTER EIGHT

DATELINE: ALPHA CENTAURI

Captain Jackson opened the hatch and a blast of fresh air filled the cabin, so fresh it almost hurt to breathe, as if the wind had been knocked out of them. The air felt thin like the top of a high mountain, and they needed to breathe deeply to get enough oxygen. Their bodies screamed for air, yet the air itself felt so alive they could hardly stand it. After weeks of breathing the recycled and reprocessed air in the confines of air-tight vessels, they had become accustomed to stale, lifeless air tinged by ozone and aerosolized metal ions. Even the air on the space station, which had been downright garden-like compared to the Arca, was a pale comparison to the moon's atmosphere.

The light was bright too. The vibrance coming through the hatchway was like they had been living underground for weeks. They blinked and winced, gasping, and shielding their eyes while breathing deeper than they had in some time.

"I'd say it would help to leave your helmets on, but those belong to the ship and I need them back," Captain Jackson said. He did not seem to be affected by the strange air of the moon, nor its light. "I'll need your suits too." The team set about removing their equipment. "Just hang them on the wall over there," the captain added.

A self-driving stairway pulled up to the hatch, and they got their first view of the spaceport. The main building sat on a vast flat plain, raised above the concrete tarmac. The terminal itself was all windows interrupted by metal beams every few meters, though they could not see inside as the finish on the windows reflected the light with a wine-dark sheen. With the exception of an automated flatbed moving toward the dropship to collect their equipment, there was very little activity to be seen, and there were no worker positions in sight. In the distance, beyond the terminal, they saw massive structures like pyramids with an enormous column rising from its apex.

"The space elevator. Still under construction," Joon-baek gasped, both from a combination of awe and the difficulty he had breathing.

Two enormous anchors stood imposingly large above the terminal at the elevator's base, nothing more than enormous weights to counterbalance the mass of the cable system itself. More than two-thirds of their bulk was beneath the surface where they were secured to bedrock. Cable already reached hundreds of meters into the sky supported by a massive scaffolding like the skeleton of a skyscraper, though it was not nearly as thick as it would eventually be. The scaffolding supported the cable until worker positions attached it to the terminus at Polus Station in orbit beyond the upper atmosphere. Once connected, the station's rotational momentum would pull the cable into space and relieve some of the stress on the anchors. At that point, worker positions would remove the scaffolding and thicken the cable to operating size.

The area around the budding space elevator contained several long industrial buildings. "Those are probably the materials manufacturing facilities," Joon-baek said, his breathing improving slightly, as he followed everyone's gaze around the space port.

The terminal was surprisingly small with a half-dozen gates and only one of the jetways extended, presumably theirs. To their dismay, the jetway was also quite far from the dropship, meaning they would have to go down the stairway, cross the tarmac, and up another stairway to reach the jetway to the terminal.

"Why did we land so far away?" Waters asked.

It was a rhetorical question asked out of exasperation more than anything, but the captain responded anyway. "This is where the ships normally land by regulation. We could land closer, but we aren't allowed to. Too much risk of accident, or something like that. The spaceport doesn't have the equipment to pull the dropship closer to the jetway yet, so we take the stairs."

The team descended the stairs one by one, gripping the rails to steady themselves. Jazzy grasped one of Waters's hands on one side and Molly's on the other, holding them up at shoulder height for balance. Beau looked back at the spectacle. He was certain that holding their hands that high made them less stable, but Jazzy looked pale, and he thought anyone offering advice also risked a verbal savaging. Just the same, he imagined himself in Waters's place. The rest of them didn't look much better, but they all made it into the jetway. Despite being back on solid ground and not having eaten for several hours, Jazzy went from pale to green, and looked as if she might really be sick.

"I thought public displays of affection were forbidden," Molly said, referring to Jazzy's monkey grip on their hands, as she tried to lift Jazzy's spirits.

Jazzy could not manage a reply.

They emerged from the jetway wheezing from the minimal effort, but inside their breathing improved. The spaceport was clearly still a construction site. Most of the paneling and glass were in place, but there was no trim. Conduit and metal frames showed through the ceiling and floor. A few non-native potted plants showed that someone had attempted to add some aesthetic ambience. There was little furniture, and that which was present was either in crates or still wrapped in protective plastic.

"This reminds me of my grandmother's house," Joon-baek said.

Most members of the mission team were still disoriented and stressed from the drop, but there was little time for rest and recovery. A chipper voice, inappropriate in its contrast with their physical state, greeted them. "Right this way, please! Gather here, everyone!"

the team heard as they shuffled out of the jetway, some still wobbling as they walked.

The instruction came from a petite woman in a starched white button-down blouse with a short white necktie, a white knee-length skirt, white stockings, and white shoes. The ensemble emphasized her blonde hair, which was closer to platinum on its own without the emphasis of her white civil servant uniform. "That ensemble makes her look like porcelain," Beau commented.

"Don't be rude," Molly said, though Beau had a point. Her eyes, which were a brown, almost mahogany color, were the only thing about her that was not white.

"Thank you! Please gather around here. My name is Alice. I am a civil servant position here on Polus."

"Don't you mean Polus IV?" Waters said in more of a statement than a question.

"That's an excellent question! May I ask your name?" Alice replied.

"Director Waters. Alex Waters."

"He's the Mission Director," Jazzy contributed.

"That's essential to know," Alice replied. "You and I will need to have a specific briefing later."

"I should probably attend as well," Jazzy said, apparently feeling better.

"Of course," Waters agreed, "that would only be appropriate."

"Very well," Alice said, "two for tea and me." Beau and Waters looked at each other sideways. "Allow me to continue. My position description includes duties as a concierge."

"How does someone get selected to be concierge at a place like this? That must be very competitive," Beau asked.

"Indeed, you are not wrong. It is a competitive process with rigorous selection requirements," Alice replied, followed by a period of silence she chose not to fill with further explanation. Beau noted that she had not really answered the question.

"Let this be your first introduction: You are correct, Mission Director Waters. Polus refers to the gas giant you see behind me," Alice said, gesturing palm up to the enormous, impossible-to-miss planet. Everything about her movements and speech was precise and balanced. Yet her contrived demeanor was full of grace and poise. She had clearly performed the same speech many times before, yet she betrayed no displeasure. "We are on the fourth moon, properly known as Polus IV. Colloquially, however, we refer to it simply as 'Polus.' While incorrect, it is also not strictly incorrect, as you will reflect that it only makes sense to name the habitable body in the system, rather than that which it orbits."

The team looked as if they were not at all sure that made sense, but they were also in no condition to argue, though the motion sickness of the drop had begun to fade.

"You have just 'dropped' into the future Polus *IV* Spaceport. Also combined construction site and manufacturing facility for the future Polus *IV* Space Elevator," she said, emphasizing "IV" slightly each time. Alice paused unnecessarily to allow this information to sink in.

"I'm not sure whether she's mocking or acknowledging my question," Waters said quietly.

"If there are no additional questions at this time, then you will please accompany me. This way," she said, turning on the balls of her feet, leaving them no opportunity to ask regardless.

"What about our equipment?" Joon-baek protested. He showed no ill effects from the drop. He was not looking at Alice but was staring at the plain through the windows. Joon-baek was anxious to get to work. The flora consisted of mostly short grasses, and small, scattered patches of brush as far as the eye could see, which was probably no more than a few kilometers in any direction. Low clouds sat on the horizon, and they obscured the terrain around them.

"Your things will be brought to your bunk for you, which has already been pre-assigned according to your position," Alice replied. "I'm surprised you were not briefed on this prior to your arrival."

Waters blushed a bit. "Mocking, she was definitely mocking," he said to himself as he followed the concierge.

"This way please," she said, definitively ending the possibility of further questions.

Alice led them into an adjacent room, which was a small, circular, darkened amphitheater illuminated only by diffuse lighting around the edge of a domed ceiling. A table at the center held a new projector, but there were no seats installed consistent with the state of the rest of the terminal. The contrast between the pristine and complete new display and the haphazard surroundings was jarring. It was reminiscent of a planetarium. They expected an orientation film. They were not disappointed. A veteran position stood near the door, but Alice did not introduce him, so they filed past him into the hall.

"Please feel free to be seated," Alice offered.

They looked around, confused. There were no seats to be had. Alice herself seemed to meld into the walls as a film began and they gathered around the table, which lit up on queue. A rectangular screen materialized on the surface of the table, and a film began to play.

"It's in an older style," Beau said, leaning towards Jazzy. "No longer strictly regulation, but still in use."

Jazzy nodded politely in reply.

The light on the table focused a bit sharpening the image.

"Dateline: Alpha Centauri. Disaster!

"Have you ever wondered why all positions at a space elevator construction facility must have a clean, shaved face? Look how handsome! Have you ever wondered why mustaches are so popular at space ports? Looking good, buddy! Well wonder no more! It all began on Alpha Centauri b.

Before we travel light years to our destination, let's talk about the manufacturing process. Don't worry, I assure you this will be important later. The core of each MFASA space elevator is a cord of high-tensile cables, each made of millions of tiny strands of carbon nanotubes. Each space elevator has its own manufacturing facility for producing essential components. It is more efficient, and effective, for each space elevator to have its own manufacturing facility rather than transporting millions of tons of material through space. (See regulations for more details.) A byproduct of the manufacturing process is a fine particulate carbon dust. But wait just a minute: the dust itself is harmless. Unless you breathe it. Hundreds of years ago on Earth, many workers died from a disease called new-mow-cone-eye-oh-sis after inhaling similar dust during mining operations. For this reason, each manufacturing facility has a negative pressure ventilation system that captures the dust, protecting the worker positions inside from harm. Just like you. Together, we ended the 'black lung!' That was, until...

Disaster! Colonial terrorists unreasonably motivated by remediation of several Alpha Centauri b colonists to Earth for Supplemental Education engaged in an act of terror. These terrorists, who had no resources to permit any resistance thanks to the efforts of your Administration, resorted to launching a simple piece of garbage at the unfinished space elevator. The debris collided with the cable at thousands of kilometers an hour knocking loose the scaffolding and causing the cable and assembly to plummet several kilometers onto the manufacturing facility below. The fall released that normally harmless carbon particulate in a cloud that covered the new space port. Hundreds of worker positions just like you became sick. Some died. The space port itself was severely damaged and construction set back several years. It was only through the efforts of MFASA that the worker positions were able to recover and lead normal lives.

"No thanks to you, terrorists! To ensure nothing like this ever happens again, your Administration instituted several important regulations designed to keep you safe. Colonists must now pass strict background checks before travel; each manufacturing facility and space port is equipped with enough respirators to serve every position; and all positions must remain clean and shaven (except for that mustache, you handsome devil!). These regulations, along with the capture and prosecution of the notorious terrorists and the resettlement and remediation

of the colonists responsible, help keep you and your fellow worker and civil servant positions safe.

"So, remember, worker positions. Remember, civil servant positions: the only safe facial hair is the venerable mustache. Shave daily, and always wear your respirator!"

The film closed with an outdated version of MFASA's logo.

"Really," Molly said, who seemed more concerned over the film than it deserved.

"It's just an educational film. I'm sure that could never happen here," Beau said.

"I'm sure it never will," Molly shot back, a defiant look on her face. Beau had the impression he was not understanding something, but let it go.

"Are there any questions about the film? No? Good." Alice said, seeming to materialize out of nowhere at all. "You will each now be issued your own personal respirator in accordance with the regulations described in the film. The respirators are also equipped with a condenser to help you breathe when outdoors. Wear them at all times, shave daily, and be safe, civil servant positions! Remember to don your mask before helping others don their own."

A worker position pushed a crate into the amphitheater. Alice began handing out masks to the missionaries. Waters stepped forward to help.

"Where's your mask, Alice?" Waters asked. He was determined that every member of the mission would follow this regulation. None of them wore facial hair, so that was handled. The success of the mission could not be compromised, so they needed to get masks as soon as they could.

"Why, it's right here, Mission Director Waters," Alice said, indicating one of the respirators from the crate.

The missionaries finished donning their respirators.

"Do we really have to wear these?" Jazzy said.

Behind them, a muffled roaring and an increase in the room's illumination announced the departure of a shuttle rocketing back to orbit. Their dropship stayed behind.

"That shuttle is departing to return to Polus Station, carrying worker positions who have taken leave, and materials to supply the station. Regulations dictate that at least one dropship remain on the surface to facilitate evacuations if necessary. Your dropship will remain behind to fulfill this role until another arrives. Has everyone finished putting on their respirators? Good," Alice said. "To answer your question..."

"Jazzy."

"...Missionary Jazzy. Yes, you really have to wear them. I will now introduce you to your assigned veteran position. Please greet Lieutenant Thomas Atkins. Thank you for your service, Lieutenant."

"Thank you for your service," the missionaries echoed.

Lieutenant Tommy Atkins stepped away from the doorway towards them. He was a bit taller than average, but stocky. He wore his hair in a typical military cut, and his uniform with the sleeves tight rolled. His face was shorn of any hair, and he had no mustache. He was also not wearing a respirator.

"Lieutenant, where's your respirator?" Waters asked.

"It's right here, sir," the lieutenant said, pointing to his belt from which there indeed hung a respirator. "Regulations exempt veteran positions from the requirement to wear a respirator unless the immediate situation requires it. You can review section 005 D2a for more information."

"How do you breathe outside?" Jazzy asked.

"I've had time to acclimate, and no longer need the supplemental oxygen your respirators provide." This did not seem to be the first time he had answered a similar question. Waters and Jazzy were satisfied.

"It is the lieutenant's time to speak," Alice reminded them with a significant glance.

"This concierge..." Waters said to himself, annoyed.

"Missionaries, I am Lieutenant Tommy Atkins of the United States Marine Corp," the lieutenant continued.

"An anachronism," Beau said quietly to Jazzy. "The Marine Corp is part of the Mundial Defense Force and hasn't been specific to the

United States for decades. At least he's a real first lieutenant judging by the silver bar on his collar. That means he's not fresh out of training."

Jazzy nodded politely.

"You may call me Tommy," the lieutenant continued, looking each missionary in the eye as he spoke. "And to answer your question, it is in accordance with our fine tradition that we continue to call ourselves United States Marines."

Beau tried to pretend it was not him to whom the lieutenant was responding.

"It will be my pleasure to serve as your veteran position. My mission is to guard and protect you, maintain your safety, including protection from local fauna as needed, and to guide you where it is possible for me to do so. This is the scope of my mission, and it is limited to this. Although I am attached to your mission, my position remains under the purview of the Corp, not MFASA, and it is to the Corp that I will report. I will be armed where none of you will be. I look forward to working with you," he concluded.

"Thank you for your service," they all said once more.

"That means you will have a gun, lieutenant?" Beau clarified.

"That is correct. I will be armed with a rifle. It will be my responsibility to keep and maintain it. You don't need to worry about it," Tommy replied.

"Are the animals dangerous?" Jazzy asked.

"No, ma'am; the animals are not dangerous."

"Almost all of the animals on Polus IV are herbivores, or eat plankton and krill, or fish," Molly said.

"Thank you, Molly—" Jazzy began.

"—And thank you," Alice interjected. "Are there any more questions for the lieutenant? No? Then let me welcome you to Polus!" she said, stepping forward to activate a pair of automatic doors, which opened to their first proper view of Polus.

CHAPTER NINE

A PANORAMA
OF NOTHINGNESS

A sweeping panorama of nothingness welcomed them to Polus. Other than the construction project, which was very much in process, the impression of Polus Beau gathered from the terminal had been correct: a vast plain covered with only scattered grasses, scrub brush, and vines. Mostly low, sharp, pitted rocks covered the surface, as if thousands of tiny bubbles had burst and left their impressions behind. Vines or creepers with what looked like seed pods grew abundantly. The plain had the brownish-grey appearance of dead grass in winter. There were no trees except for short, stunted examples in pots throughout the terminal, placed intentionally to help make new arrivals more comfortable.

Tommy put on his cover as they stepped outside.

"This is it?" Beau said.

"It's still not quite spring here," Joon-baek said. "That's why everything is brown."

"It's not what I expected," Jazzy said.

"It's perfect," Molly said.

Beau wondered what she could be seeing that they did not.

"Joon-baek's right, everyone. It's still winter. Everything would be brown on Earth too. We're mostly here for the colonists anyway, not for the moon," Waters said.

They met their first inhabitants: worker positions who were assigned to construction. Some passed them on the terminal sidewalk, some rode on machinery, some drove heavy equipment. None wore respirators.

"All of your phones have been updated with my contact information should you need anything," Alice said, but her tone suggested she did not expect them to need anything. "Please do not hesitate to contact me. For the glory of the Administration."

With that farewell, she stepped back into the terminal, the automatic doors closing behind her. She removed her respirator as soon as she was inside.

Waters stopped a passing worker. "Why aren't you wearing a respirator?" he asked.

"Hah!" exclaimed the worker and continued on his way. His face was covered in stubble. He did not seem to have shaved that week.

"Those men have not shaved!" Waters said with a touch of alarm, pointing at a passing flatbed loaded with long beams. Several different positions rode in the back. Many had credible beards.

Tommy pulled his cover a little lower over his face. "I should take you to where you'll be staying," he said.

Tommy led them to a complex a few hundred meters away, earning a number of stares, comments, and gestures from worker positions they passed. They kept their heads down. It was already difficult to breathe on Polus, and despite the supplemental oxygen they were receiving, the masks seemed to make it more difficult still.

At the complex, several rows of temporary trailers had been laid out in a neat grid with enough room between for a vehicle to pass to serve as housing for the worker and civil servant positions on site. A combination of foot and vehicle traffic had beaten down most of the vegetation. The remaining gravel and crushed rock served as roads and paths. Grass and vines were abundant around the edges of the trailers where traffic had not taken its toll. The trailers were universally painted the same color: straight-from-the-factory-beige with beige trim.

"Brown, just like the rest of this place. We're not staying in barracks, are we?" Jazzy asked.

"No, you are not," Tommy said. "These are portable trailers, manufactured right here on Polus. Inside you will find no bunks. Each trailer is fully equipped. You will have to share, but you won't have to bunk up. These are like houses. They're not bad, and much nicer than barracks. Believe me."

"Where do they get the wood?" Joon-baek asked. "I didn't see any trees."

"No wood. These are one-hundred percent synthetic. Most of the material is mined right here," Tommy answered. "There is a forest about one-hundred and fifty miles west of here. You could get wood from there if you wanted, but it would be more hassle than it's worth."

"How far is that?" Waters asked.

Tommy looked surprised at the question. "What do you mean?" he said.

"I mean, how far is a hundred and fifty miles? I'm surprised the military still uses the outdated and imperial measurements."

"It's nautical miles, which we still use," Tommy said. "They're based on the circumference of the planet and work just as well as metric units since they're based on a fixed standard. And it's about two-hundred and seventy-five kilometers, give or take, to answer your question."

"Even so, I'd appreciate if you would use the metric system when you're around us," Waters said.

"I don't think so," Tommy said. Ignoring the shocked look on Waters's face at his curt reply, he continued, "You can take those things off now. No one here wears them. And you look ridiculous. Besides, you'll never acclimate." Tommy had just about enough of the respirators.

They removed them reluctantly, rubbing and scratching at their heads where the masks had left little lines forming an oval like a picture frame around each face.

Waters protested a little, but still removed his respirator. "Why have this regulation at all then?"

"You saw the movie," Tommy said. "It's impossible to work in these things for more than a few minutes though. Most people think Alpha Centauri b was a freak accident too. Virtually no one believes a group of colonists, most of who just got rounded up, would even be capable of pulling something like that off."

"You mean resettled," Waters said.

"Sure, resettled," Tommy said. "Wear the mask if you want, but you'll be the only one. Worst of all, you'll miss out on all this fresh air."

He was right. The air had a pleasant and crisp feeling to it like a fall morning. They still breathed heavily, though not because of the content of the atmosphere. It was virtually identical to Earth in that regard. They had become winded just walking to the trailers, like they were hiking at altitude.

"It does feel good to breathe," Joon-baek said. "Much better than the air on the station."

"Once you're here long enough, you'll like it even more. It makes you feel like you're growing, the way you feel after a good workout. Tired, but fulfilled," Tommy said.

"So, if each trailer has two bedrooms, does that mean we'll have roommates?" Jazzy asked.

"Correct," Tommy answered, pulling out his phone. "You'll be staying two to a trailer: Waters and Lee. Bebe with Mc – Mc-Die-thee?"

"Mac-Day-hee," Molly said.

"McDaithi. And Juhn Bike Kim with me," he finished.

"Joon-baek. You said Kim right."

"June Bug it is," Tommy said.

Joon-baek let the mistake pass. It was not the first time someone had mispronounced his name, and he knew the lieutenant meant nothing by it. "You're staying with us?" Joon-baek asked. "Not that we mind, it's just, well, I guess you are part of the mission now."

"That's right. I'll be staying with you, eating with you, traveling with you. You'll have to get used to me. Especially you," Tommy said, directing the last remark at Joon-baek.

"How do you know you're not staying with me?" Joon-baek replied.

Tommy laughed and smacked Joon-baek on the shoulder.

"Why can't we pick who we stay with?" Jazzy asked.

"I don't see why you can't," Tommy said. "These assignments came directly from MFASA before you arrived."

Alice drove up in a train of carts with a worker position. The first cart carried their personal luggage. The second and third carts carried their equipment.

"Alice," Molly said. "Will you be staying with us too?"

Jazzy shot Molly a look that said, "shut up!"

"Unfortunately, no," she replied. "I have my own trailer elsewhere."

"Do you have to share a trailer too?" Jazzy asked.

"There are several empty trailers here. Civil servant positions are not permitted to share a trailer with worker positions, so no, I live alone."

"Do you mean to tell me there are empty trailers all over the place, but we have to share?" Jazzy said. "We've been cramped up on a spaceship for weeks, just dropped out of the sky, and now we can't stretch our legs out a little?"

"I'm sure we could fill out the requisite paperwork to have you assigned to a different trailer if you would prefer one of your own. We will have to wait until the next ship arrives at Polus Station to permit the wake carrier wave relays to transmit your request over the LiFi, although the signal here is spotty at the best of times, which may increase your wait time. Once you submit your request, MFASA's civil servant positions on Earth have up to sixty days to complete processing, at which time they will transmit the response back again at the next opportunity, bearing in mind the aforementioned considerations."

"Fine. Let's do that then," Jazzy said.

"We're supposed to leave for the colony in a couple days anyway," Waters said. "We can manage until then. I'm sure we can make other arrangements in the meantime."

"Please be careful," Alice said to Joon-baek.

He was already back at the second cart, dropping and pulling their carefully packed equipment to the ground looking for his gear. Alice stepped down from the lead cart and began going over tags, looking for Joon-baek's duffel. Tommy, Beau, and Molly walked over to help, while Waters took Jazzy aside to the far corner of the trailer. They spoke in a low, deceptively quiet and intense voice that Beau recognized from when his mom had scolded him in public as a child. Jazzy was better at the voice than Waters. In spite of not being able to hear anything, it was clear she was not pleased with the arrangements. The others just averted their eyes and stacked bags on the gravel.

"Here's yours, Beau. And here's mine. I'll go get settled," Molly said.

"Just a moment," Waters said, walking back to the group. He and Jazzy had apparently reached an agreement. "Beau, can I talk to you?"

Beau and Waters walked a short distance away. Jazzy collected her bag and walked up the ramp into the nearest trailer.

"Isn't that our trailer?" Beau said.

"Well, yes," Waters said. "Look, Beau. I need you to swap with Jazzy."

"What? Why? I know you and Jazzy have a thing. Everyone does, but that would be a flagrant violation of both regulation and how MFASA has chosen to order the mission," Beau said.

Waters put his hand on Beau's shoulder and pulled him a little farther from the rest of the group. "I need you to keep this quiet, because it's protected health information."

"Should you even be telling me then?"

"It will help you understand the situation. Jazzy is the mission's doctor, right? Well, Jazzy has been treating Molly since we left Earth. Prescribing her meds and everything."

"Treating her? For what?"

"Jazzy says it's acute depression, a grief reaction due to something that happened to her back home."

"Acute? We were in space for weeks?"

"She said that sometimes even an acute episode can last a long time, especially if the person failed to receive resolution. Because they have a professional treating relationship, it wouldn't be appropriate for them to stay together like that. It's unethical. Their treating relationship is already questionable since we've all become friends on the journey out. Besides, Jazzy needs a break from seeing her patient all the time."

"That makes sense," Beau had to concede, though he suspected the real motivation was much less noble. "But what do our mission guidelines say about male and female missionaries staying together? What about the relationship policy?"

Waters looked a bit uncomfortable. "You know as well as I do no one follows those guidelines. Do you have any idea how many couples come out of missions? And no one's telling you to sleep with Molly." Beau blushed a little, surprised at the comment and taken aback. He liked Molly fine as a colleague but had never considered her romantically.

"I was more worried about you," Beau said.

"There are two bedrooms. It will be fine. For both of us," Waters said. "Come on, Beau. I can't ask Joon-baek to swap because of Lieutenant Atkins. It's already clear I don't have any real authority over him even though he's part of the mission now."

Beau was silent for a moment. He felt like a sucker, especially after walking the length of the space station searching for Molly. He relented anyway. "Alright."

"Thanks," Waters said. "I'll owe you one later."

"You're welcome," Beau replied sarcastically.

Waters grinned back at him and went to grab his duffel bag from the cart. "You'll tell Molly, won't you?"

"Me? That's your job!" Beau called back, but Waters was already on his way through the trailer door.

Beau turned around and saw Molly still unloading the carts. At least she was not already unpacking. "Molly. Hey. We need to change the trailer assignments. You're going to share with me instead of Jazzy. There's two bedrooms so it should be okay. Waters said—"

"Great," Molly interrupted.

"What?" Beau said.

"I said that's fine."

"Oh," Beau said, confused but relieved. Molly kept unloading the carts. "I guess I'll start moving things in then. Which bag is yours?"

Molly picked up one of the large duffels and tossed it at Beau. It struck him with more force than it had a right to.

"Sheesh. What did you pack?"

"You know. All things according to regulation. The bricks and rocks are MFASA standard and everything."

Beau wasn't sure how to respond, so he grabbed his bag, which seemed unaccountably lighter, and walked through the trailer door.

CHAPTER TEN

YOU'RE ALRIGHT

Joon-baek sat at a makeshift bench he had built outside the trailer he shared with Tommy. He set it up as soon as their supplies were unloaded. He was pleased to find that the focus of his study, the vine with its fruit-like seed pods, was everywhere. It grew like a weed right around the trailers. He was eager to begin his work before they set out for the colony. The bench was covered in a piece of thin perforated sheet metal he had found in a dumpster, scrap from what had likely been some industrial walkway, a discarded piece of construction waste. The perforation worked well for his purposes, as it allowed excess water and dirt to flow through. The crate which carried his equipment sat overturned with its lid askance next to the workbench. He could not set up his actual workstation until they arrived at their final destination.

A rig of several multi-colored LEDs hung over the bench, carefully selected to match the wavelengths of Polus' light. Below the lights Joonbaek had placed rows of grow pots ready for planting. The prevailing theory was that creating conditions as close as possible to their natural growing environment would allow his botanic collections the greatest chance of survival. That was as good a place to start as any. To that end, he had cleaned and sterilized the surface, and set to work preparing his workstation. He needed a water source, but that necessity had been fulfilled by connecting a line to the trailer's gutters. He thought a rain barrel was best suited to the task, but that was something he had not scavenged yet. There were no open streams or bodies of water for many miles around; all water for the space elevator was pumped from an aquifer below the surface.

He concentrated on labeling and arranging several samples of the vine and its fruit in pots according to their size and collection date. Joon-baek's purpose on the mission was dual. He had successfully passed the tests and interviews to become a missionary and was as qualified to work with the colonists as anyone. His grant, however, was specifically to study the cultivation of Polus fruit. He was determined to be the first to successfully grow the vine domestically.

"There hasn't been one of our guys yet who's been able to make that stuff last more than a few hours," said a passing worker position, though Joon-baek had not asked him.

"That's why I'm here. I hope to find a way to domesticate and transport Polus fruit," Joon-baek replied, visibly and vocally excited, but not really looking him, intent instead on what he was doing. Joon-baek lifted a pot, turned it to look at the date, and then placed it in line.

"Hill," said the worker position, extending his hand. "Construction foreman at the space elevator worksite." Hill was large, but not fat. Like many of the worker positions he wore a beard and mustache, contrary to regulations.

Joon-baek took his hand and shook it briefly before returning to his work. "Joon-baek Kim, missionary botanist. What are you a foreman of, Hill?"

"I work for the Aerosolized Hydrocarbon Fuel and Fittings Local."

"You're in charge of the gas?"

"That's what most people would call it. But the five-dollar name gets us more funding and respect."

"What are fittings?"

"Oh, you know, various parts and accessories associated with gas transportation, exchange and use. Good luck, on your project, Joon-baek." That sounded like a farewell, but Hill remained. "I'll bet you one session of your LiFi bandwidth allowance that none of those plants survive until morning."

"How long have you been here, Hill? Long enough to know your bet is a safe one, I'm sure. No bet; for now," Joon-baek replied, still absorbed with his work.

Hill advanced and placed both of his palms on the workbench, intruding into the workspace. Joon-baek attempted to ignore him and continue working. "Why not? No confidence? Any idiot can grow a plant," taunted Hill, teeth showing under a friendly but challenging grin.

Joon-baek stopped and looked up at Hill, making eye contact for the first time. He looked from one eye to the other. He was not intimidated. He had several older brothers and knew what a ribbing looked and felt like. Joon-baek thought the challenge over for a moment. He avoided using the LiFi anyway: his family always asked questions to which there was no possible answer, and he preferred his work to TV.

"Alright, Mr. Hill. One LiFi session it is, unless even one plant is alive in its pot tomorrow."

"It's a bet," Hill said, and stuck out his hand for Joon-baek to shake. Joon-baek took the hand for the second time that day, unsure of the protocol for bets. Hill shook it vigorously. "Are you a golfer, Joon-baek?" Hill asked, satisfied now that their bet was confirmed.

Joon-baek was in fact a golfer, it being a sport that regulations deemed tolerable since person-to-person contact was not part of the game, and therefore devoid of inherent violence. "I am, but I didn't bring my clubs. They weigh too much."

"Don't worry about that. You can borrow from one of the boys," Hill said.

Joon-baek flinched a little at Hill's use of the offensive term "boys," the proper application of "worker positions" being preferred, but he let it go. He had heard that worker positions tended to be much rougher in their interactions and tolerance for such behavior among other positions had been part of their missionary training.

"We usually meet in the evening after everyone gets off work on the road just west of here. You should see how the golf balls fly here!" Hill continued.

"It sounds like fun," Joon-baek said. "I'll be there as soon as I get everything planted."

"Don't forget your phone. I won't mind if you want to turn over that LiFi balance early." Hill turned and walked off but called back over his shoulder. "I wonder how much I'll be able to barter for a LiFi session on a clear, high-quality government channel."

Low clouds still obscured the horizon for several kilometers as Joon-baek walked along the road out of the space port, such as it was. It was only identifiable as a road due to the vehicle and foot traffic that had made it out this far and worn away the vegetation. He brought Tommy with him. Hill along with a handful of other worker positions were right where they said they would be.

"Joon-baek! I'm glad you could come. I see you brought the lieutenant. Did you bring your phone?" Hill asked, as he walked up.

"Did you bring yours?" Joon-baek retorted.

Hill smiled and motioned them over and showed one of the clubs: a driver. Joon-baek looked them over. It was like nothing he had seen before. He could see they were all using similar, though unique sets of clubs. Both the clubs and golf bags were clearly handmade, though not of poor quality. On the contrary, they seemed exceptional, and of good weight and balance. Joon-baek took a couple of practice swings. Just the right amount of flexibility too.

"Did you make these?" he asked, though he already knew the answer.

"All of us did. We make our own stuff here. Carbon fiber and titanium, both from construction waste," Hill added quickly, wanting to make it clear there was no diversion of Administration property taking place. "After hours, the machinery is available. You should see some of the projects the guys get up to. One of my guys made a scale model of Polus Station with moving habitat rings, working lights and everything," Hill said, just before taking a swing and launching a ball hundreds of meters onto the plain where they lost sight of it. "What did

I tell you? These things really fly! Take a swing," he said to Joon-baek, then he turned and handed Tommy a club too. "Here, lieutenant," he said.

"No bets this time, Hill," Tommy said.

"Still sore, huh?" Hill said. Tommy waved him off as he took a crack at a golf ball. It launched well but sliced to the right.

"I'd like to see that sometime. The model, I mean," Joon-baek said, genuinely interested and curious how worker positions could manage to produce items of such quality. He took a tee, which looked like it had been 3-D printed, and pushed it into the ground. The gravel and rock resisted, but it stood stable. After a couple of practice swings, Joon-baek sent a ball sailing every bit as far as Hill had. The club performed even better than it looked.

"Nice," Hill said.

"Nice," Joon-baek said, indicating to the club. "I haven't hit for a few months, but a few more days of this and it'll come back to me."

"We'll have to bring a range-finder next time to see how far you're hitting them," Hill said.

They hit balls until it was too dark to see. Joon-baek was very tired and surprised that he would become winded by an activity as simple as hitting golf balls. Tommy even improved his slice.

"Come on," Hill said. "You probably don't want to be out after dark. Who knows what kind of bird might sweep down on you?"

As if Hill's words had turned on a switch, the plain suddenly filled up with a soft orange lights.

"Whoa! What is that?" Joon-baek said.

"It's the Polus fruit," Tommy said. "They're bioluminescent. Hill's right. We should get back."

"But it's so great! Don't you want to see it?" Joon-baek said.

"I guess we're just used to it after being here for months," Hill replied. "Come on, you look wiped out. The lights will be there tomorrow."

Hill trotted up to Joon-baek's workbench the next morning with a grin of smug anticipation. He had his phone in hand, ready to collect.

Joon-baek had risen early to begin work and was at the workbench. Hill pulled up short. His grin turned to drop-jawed disbelief. Some of the plants were indeed dead, the smell of their rotting flesh hung in the air. But a half-dozen were clearly still alive. The fruit still glowed in the low light of the early morning.

"How did you—" Hill began as he drew closer, but he quickly saw. Joon-baek had drawn up several vines into pots, though they were still quite rooted to the ground.

"That's not what I meant!" Hill began, the visible parts of his neck flushing with red hives. "You still owe me!"

"I don't think so, Hill. Our bet was that not even one plant would remain alive, *in its pot*. Several are alive. If you don't think this is fair, next time be more specific about the terms," Joon-baek said.

Hill looked skeptical, but then a grin spread across his face. "Alright, Joon-baek. I'm an experienced gambler; I should have known to be specific. A bet's a bet, and a loss is a loss. Here," he said, pulling out his phone.

"I wouldn't have any use for the extra bandwidth. Keep it," Joon-baek said. "In fact, we're leaving in a couple days. I probably won't use mine anyway, so why don't you take part of my allowance?" Joon-baek pointed his phone at Hill's and swiped over several LiFi credits.

"Joon-baek, you're all right," Hill said.

CHAPTER ELEVEN

THE LIFI NEVER WORKS

ater that evening, Beau sat at the table in his trailer's common room reading news stories on his phone. Rumors of the limited LiFi access on the colonial planets, Polus IV included, were proving to be no exaggeration. He had not received any updates on his ABS account yet. The text-only stories he downloaded on Polus Station sufficed for now. He flipped through each story absentmindedly while he ate a sandwich. It was much easier to pick a story to read when it had a thumbnail image to go with the headline; even easier when it included a video. "This must be what old news pages were like," he said to himself.

He had not felt like unpacking yesterday when he threw his duffel on the bed in his room in the front bedroom. He still felt that way and was living out of the bag. He had figured that Molly would want the back room. It was slightly larger and more private, so he had left that to her. She came in and asked which room was hers and had been in there since. She could not possibly have that much to unpack, but he did not want to bother her and was enjoying the time to himself besides.

Other than the bedrooms, the trailer had a small bathroom off the hallway between the rooms, and a kitchenette he could see into if he stooped to peer between the cabinets and bar. The trailer was tacky. The exterior was standard factory brown, and the interior was not much better. Everything was shades of gray. A light gray table, creamy gray laminate flooring, primer gray walls, a cloud-gray couch. It was as if the factory had applied a coat of primer then called a stoppage. Beau knew better, however. Color theory suggested that grays, browns, and beiges were the most calming and least likely to promote conflict. Warm colors had the opposite effect. Virtually nothing MFASA produced had any warmth. The drab, rainy-day color scheme was probably the result of research to ensure the best chance of success for those working in the outer colonies of space.

He finished his sandwich and got up to see what else he could find. The answer was not much. He opened the refrigerator to see the same things he had seen his first and second trips to the kitchen. He hoped in vain he had missed something, or that something might look appetizing this time. Supplies seemed to be limited, a fact he did not appreciate as he was still famished from the previous day. While he stood staring into the humming void of a refrigerator full of not much more than processed cheeses and meat, there was a knock at the door and then without waiting for someone to answer Tommy and Joon-baek walked in laughing. Their hands were full of snacks, and Tommy had several bottles. Beau hoped against hope it was both not water and potable.

"Well, this is boring," Joon-baek said. "You should see our trailer. Tommy decorated it. Much nicer."

"I've been here longer," Tommy explained.

Tommy was no longer in uniform. He wore denim jeans and a T-shirt, which Beau reflected was rather retro of him. The shirt bore a pinup dangling in and around the letter "I" and wearing not much more than a brown fedora and a belt with a whip. On the back it said, "It's Indy in '02." Beau was certain such an image would not pass DID approval.

"I don't care where you've been or how long because you brought food," Beau said, helping them with their snacks. "There's nothing in my refrigerator. Where did you get all this?"

"Like I said, I've been here a while," Tommy said. "You get to know the civil servants a bit, and they'll get you things you wouldn't believe.

It helps to know people who are placed higher in the Administration. They don't even ask for a favor in return. The beer's from the construction guys though. They brew it right here in one of the foundries. They put together a metal vat and use the Polus fruit. They're really ingenious."

"You should see some of the stuff the worker positions have put together," Joon-baek said.

"So, beer may be a stretch. It's more like a cider, but there's nothing else, so it does the job," Tommy said, passing out the bottles.

They popped open the bottles, said cheers to the mission, and took a drink. It was not bad, but Tommy was right: it was different. Perhaps it was the weeks they had gone without or the moon's strange atmosphere or the lack of food, whatever it was, the brew went straight to their heads.

"That's one way to preserve a fruit," Joon-baek said with a satisfied sigh.

"I heard people," Molly said, emerging from her bedroom.

Tommy handed her a bottle with a "cheers." She opened it and took a drink. Tension flowed from her. She grabbed a seat with the rest of them at the table. She had changed into casual clothing, or as casual as was possible for the team. This meant white undershirts with the MFASA logo on the sleeve and a pair of lightweight cotton-blend pants.

"I always thought those pants made better pajamas," Beau said. He looked again and realized she had probably been sleeping since yesterday and regretted the remark.

"Allow me to welcome you to Polus by taking your money. You know how to play poker?" Tommy asked.

"Gambling is against regulation," Beau said.

Joon-baek shuffled uncomfortably a little.

"What is it?" Beau asked. Joon-baek didn't respond.

"So it is, but you didn't answer my question," Tommy continued.

"I know a little," Beau said. He knew very little. He knew it was a game, that it was played with cards, and that other civil servant positions frowned on it as more of a worker position game.

"I don't. What's a poker?" Joon-baek asked.

"None of us have any money anyway," Molly said.

"What? No money?" Tommy said, feigning astonishment. "We'll just have to find something else for you to lose then. The workers mostly trade LiFi, but that's not worth anything where we're going," he said as he went to the cupboards in the kitchenette. He returned to the table with a box of the cheap knockoff generic brand of Loopy Fruits, which the trailer's previous occupants had left behind. Tommy opened it and dumped a pile of the stale, faded pseudo-sugar frosted colored loops on the table.

"Everyone count out twenty to start. Don't eat any of them," Tommy said too late as Joon-baek tossed a handful in his mouth.

"Why not?" he said.

"Never mind," Tommy said.

Joon-baek worked the cereal out of his mouth into a napkin.

Beau thought that poker was a simple enough game of probability after they had played a while. Yet he did not understand why he could not win when he had good cards. At times Tommy would fold when the cards suggested he might win. At other times, Tommy threw loopy fruits into the pot despite a poor hand, eventually scaring the rest of them into folding for that round.

"Let's try something a little different," Tommy said when they had almost finished the beer. He dealt everyone a pair of cards. "Don't look at them," he said. Instead, Tommy took one of the cards and held it face out to the rest of the team and pressed it to his forehead for a couple of seconds until it stuck. "Everyone do this, then you can look at your other card but don't show it to anyone else."

From outside came a rumble that vibrated through the trailer.

Tommy rose and went to the door. "Must be a storm coming," he said, his tone and manner changing instantly.

"What's the big deal?" Beau asked.

"This isn't Earth," Tommy said. "Storms here are no joke. How did this one sneak up on us? We usually get advance warning."

"The LiFi hasn't been working right since we got here," Beau said.

"The LiFi never works," Tommy said with a note of frustration. Tommy went to the door, opened it, and stepped outside onto the landing. Low clouds covered the expanse of sky above them. An eerie green the color of tarnished copper tinged the horizon, and the air carried the smell of ozone and cut grass. Light reflecting from the gas giant above usually prevented the moon from ever becoming fully dark. Now, however, the sky was growing dark as a starless night.

"We have to go now! We need to get to the spaceport. We can shelter in the lower level," Tommy said.

"What is it? What's going on?" Beau asked. He and the others stood, but slowly and reluctantly, not really understanding.

"The storm. We have to take shelter. Have you ever been in a tornado?"

Their faces were blank. They all knew of tornados, had read about them, but they mostly occurred in rural areas, and therefore mostly affected worker positions. The most important cities rarely saw weather events.

"Of course not. Right," Tommy said.

"Isn't the space elevator closer? We can use the service tunnels," Molly said, trying to be helpful but not fully comprehending the situation herself.

"Maybe," Tommy said. "Either one. Let's go."

Tommy went outside and banged on Jazzy and Waters's trailer door but got no answer. He tried to walk in, but the door was locked. The rest of the team joined him outside, but within a few steps they stopped short.

The clouds above the spaceport churned and rotated low and slow. Broad at first, then tightening like they were pouring down a drain. Small tendrils shot down and up from the clouds. A siren wailed from somewhere, barely audible in the whipping wind. Sheets of rain pulled toward them across the plain. Tiny droplets carried on the wind spattered against their faces. Suddenly a tunnel of clouds larger than the spaceport itself descended in a roar, engulfing the building. The pitiful wailing siren broke off completely.

"Shit. Too late. Back inside!" Tommy said.

"That's an offensive word!" Joon-baek said.

Tommy pushed Joon-baek back toward the door. Beau and Molly did not need to be told twice. They ran back inside.

"Help me, Beau!" Tommy called.

He ran to Molly's bedroom and grabbed the mattress from her bed, dragging blankets, pillows, and sheets behind him.

"What about Alex and Jazzy?" Beau called after him.

"Get your mattress and bring it out here," Tommy yelled, trying to be heard over the wind.

Tommy stood Molly's mattress up against the wall of the trailer. Beau struggled with his mattress. It was a straight shot into the hall-way from Molly's room, but Beau's room was off the hall. His mattress became stuck between the doorway and wall. Molly and Joon-baek grabbed the end and pulled, manhandling it out the door. Tommy shouted something, but they could no longer hear him. At last, the mattress passed some unknown threshold of resistance and slid into the hallway. Molly and Joon-baek tumbled backward onto the floor. Tommy grabbed the mattress and put it up against the wall opposite the first.

He was shouting again. Still they could not hear, but did not need to. They all sat down between the mattresses and pulled them down over their heads. The trailer shuddered and rocked. The constant spat-tering of rain stuck in their ears, occasionally punctuated by thuds as pieces of debris hit the trailer. Then the spattering changed to batter-ing, as if a crowd had decided to pelt the trailer with rocks.

Beau's heart pounded. His lungs itched. Tiny stabbing pains pulsed through his body. First his stomach, then behind the top of his sternum, then below his ribs, never staying in one place for more than a second. He wondered if this was what it felt like to die. Time seemed to slow. They experienced everything with an uncanny intensity. Every ebb and flow of the wind outside, every collision of wreckage, every shudder of the trailer. Beau had a moment of clarity in which he remembered his position. He pulled his phone from his pocket and recorded.

After a few minutes, constant heavy rain replaced the wind. They felt relieved, but sat still for several more minutes, wary of moving. At last they pushed the mattresses off and saw that the sky had lightened. Finally, as one they sensed it was okay to move. They all stood up and went to the door.

Outside, destruction was everywhere. The trailer directly across the way was simply gone, leaving nothing but the rectangular footprint of its foundation. Tommy's and Joon-baek's trailer was intact, but part of the roof was missing. The walls of Waters's trailer had completely collapsed inward in a heap.

"Alex!" Beau said, running to Waters's trailer. "Alex! Alex!"

"Oh, Jesus, help," Molly said.

They ran to the trailer and tossed aside what they could, furiously tugging at the ruins. "Alex! Jazzy!" they called. After a few seconds, Waters called back.

"Here we are! We're here!" Waters called out.

"Help us!" It was Jazzy.

"They're over here!" Beau shouted as he climbed over the rubble of what used to be their trailer.

The others climbed up, grabbed hold of the collapsed wall, and counted together—one, two, three—then pushed what was left of the outer wall over into the road. As the wall fell away, Waters and Jazzy popped out like Jack-in-the-boxes with their arms splayed wide and flopping. The sight was so absurd and comical that everyone laughed from relief despite themselves. Beau dragged Waters out of the rubble by his arm pits. Joon-baek and Molly grabbed Jazzy and carried her just a little too far in their enthusiasm.

"I'm out, I'm out!" she said.

"Are you okay? Are you hurt? What do you need?" Molly and Beau alternated asking.

Waters and Jazzy stood up in the road, turning around, patting their legs and arms.

"I think we're okay," Jazzy said.

Small fragments covered them. Their hair was white with dust and was starting to cake in the rain. Their natural skin tones were unrecognizable. Everyone was soaking wet, but they all seemed okay. Then, they heard a groan and snap as the far wall of the trailer collapsed inward.

"The wall that we pushed off must have been holding the other one up," Joon-baek said.

"You two bastards are lucky," Tommy said.

Neither of them argued.

As the excitement and adrenaline ebbed, the rain began to seep into their skin and they realized they were cold. Everyone began to depart. Joon-baek, Beau, Molly, and Tommy went to change. Joon-baek and Tommy's trailer was untouched except for superficial damage to the roof. Other than the interior mess created by their mattress fort, Molly and Beau's trailer was also intact. Jazzy and Waters located their clothing in the debris, only to find it ruined by the storm and collapse of the trailer. There was no point in trying to salvage anything. The storm had left Waters and Jazzy with effectively nothing.

Tommy brought out a few emergency ponchos, large unwieldy plastic things. After changing and donning a poncho themselves, Beau and Molly shared spare T-shirts and pants with Waters and Jazzy.

"Maybe Alice has something for you," Tommy said to the pair of now homeless missionaries. "I'll take you to her." Tommy, Waters, and Jazzy started walking back to the spaceport, which did not seem to have suffered much.

"The spaceport looks fine," Beau said as he kicked a piece of trash out of the road.

"Makes sense," Joon-baek said. "It's almost entirely made of metal and concrete. Even the windows."

"I hope everyone's okay," Molly said.

Joon-baek surveyed his makeshift workbench. The storm had ripped his watering system apart. The potted plants and samples were overturned on the ground, their contents spilled or broken. The plants he had kept attached to the vines, however, appeared fine. Joon-baek set about righting the workbench, scooping up the surviving plants and rearranging his project.

Worker positions began to drive and move around, doing what they could after the storm.

Molly and Beau went into their trailer to put their bedrooms back together. As Beau pulled Molly's mattress back into her room, a thick book bound in red leather dropped out of the sheets. Molly scooped it up and held it to her chest with the cover facing inward, and took it into her room. She came back out and took the mattress from Beau.

"I can do this, Beau. Thank you," Molly said definitively, pulling the mattress away from him and dragging it the rest of the way into her room.

Beau watched her work the mattress back in alone. He wanted to help, but the suddenness of her insistence startled him, and he left her alone. Beau tugged and pulled his mattress back into his room, the effort of maneuvering it around the corner and through the door leaving him out of breath. Once the mattress was back in place, he plopped down on his bed and stared at the wall, on the other side of which was Molly's room and the book she had dropped. On the station, he had seen the same book. She had told him it was just loose paper for sketches, but he was certain she had a Bible. He had never seen one in person, but the style was unmistakable. He recognized it from some of his college classes.

As missionaries sponsored by the Administration, religious materials, while not strictly forbidden, were almost unheard of. Why would she have a Bible? Shouldn't she have realized after all the training and courses required for this mission that there was no reason to believe in God? Or maybe, she held onto those beliefs because she had not received the full training? This was a mission to educate the colonists. Without knowing all the specifics, Beau knew there were reasons Molly was on the mission that were not consistent with the usual qualifications and procedures, but why would MFASA permit someone with potential religious sympathies on a mission? Did they not know? She was a biologist—an exobiologist at that. Did she still take religion seriously? Beau stood and stared, cutting a hole into the wall of Molly's room with his eyes, but said nothing.

"She's still a member of the team. She's still a friend. I'll just have to try and understand better," he said to himself.

Beau was pondering all of this when Molly emerged from her room and poked her head in his doorway. "Did you record any of the storm?" she asked.

Beau snapped out of it. "I did."

He pulled out his phone and they walked over to the common room table. He selected the footage, and pinched and flicked it above his phone, which projected an image above the table they both could see. The video was dark and noisy. Barely anything was recognizable.

"You can't see anything," she said disappointed.

"Yeah. I'll have to watch the rest to see if any of it is usable." Beau was disappointed too. This storm was a significant event. It could easily have been edited to show their heroism and triumph, but it did not look like he had enough clear footage for that kind of documentation.

"It doesn't seem half as bad as it felt at the time," Molly said. "Maybe Alice can get you access to the cameras from the spaceport and trailer complex? There's also the cleanup. That should be good to film. Waters will understand. He'll be able to explain it to the Administration. We had to be concerned about safety more than anything else."

"True," Beau said. "And yeah, filming the cleanup and seeing if any spaceport cameras captured it is a good idea."

She was right. He could probably find good footage from the spaceport, or any number of screens and cameras in the area, and the cleanup itself would make for some good shots. But he was still disappointed he missed the main event.

Their attention was pulled outside by the sound of a cart grinding to a stop then pulling away again. Beau and Molly peeked out, then both went out to see about Jazzy and Waters, whom Alice had just dropped off. Alice had apparently also loaned them the civil servant position's choice attire because Jazzy and Waters were dressed completely in white from head to toe. Waters wore a white button-down long-sleeved shirt and white pants. Jazzy wore a white blouse and white skirt under her temporary poncho.

"She gave us five more just like this," Waters said, seeing the looks and stares from the rest of the missionaries.

"All of them white?" Beau asked.

"All white," Jazzy said.

"What about your mission uniform?" Molly asked.

"Ruined. There's nothing left. I don't think there's anything salvageable either. She assigned us a new trailer too. One of the empty ones a road over."

Beau suddenly felt very tired as the day's events began to catch up to him, and he noticed the others' shoulders slumped a little, and thought they must be tired too. The rain had stopped, and the clouds cleared for the first time since they landed. Polus loomed bright in the sky. It felt very cold all of a sudden. They looked at the damage around them. The scope of it seemed to hit them for the first time.

"Has anyone seen Tommy?" Beau asked.

"He went to get our transport. The sooner we can get out of this place, the better," Jazzy said. "It's been hell so far."

Now there was not much else to do. Waters and Jazzy said good night and walked to their new trailer. Joon-baek turned his attention back to tinkering at his workbench but had thrown on a puffy mission jacket to ward off the chill. He would probably keep working for some time. Beau and Molly went back inside their trailer.

"Goodnight, Beau," Molly said as she headed to her room.

"Goodnight, Molly. Molly?"

Molly paused for a moment in the doorway and looked back over her shoulder at Beau.

"We're still friends?"

"Of course, we're still friends. Goodnight, Beau."

"Goodnight."

CHAPTER TWELVE

THE WORST TRIP
OF YOUR LIFE

Beau emerged from his trailer the next morning to see an enormous six-wheeled vehicle parked outside of Tommy's and Joon-baek's trailer. A crew of worker positions was already cleaning up wreckage caused by the storm. They disassembled and tossed rubble and debris into the back of a covered truck, and a heavy weight descended periodically to compact the debris.

"Worker positions will molecularize the wreckage for recycling and reprinting into new components at the factory," Alice said, appearing seemingly out of nowhere to answer a question no one had asked.

Beau jumped. "Alice! You startled me!"

"I do apologize."

"What about Waters's and Jazzy's stuff?"

"Our understanding was that their clothing and possessions were no longer useable. It too will be recycled for reuse at the factory. I took the liberty of supplying them with new clothing yesterday."

"Yes, we saw." An awkward pause ensued. Alice clutched a tablet to her chest and stared at Beau but said nothing. "So, what are you doing here, Alice?"

Tommy and Joon-baek emerged from their trailer. Molly came out as well.

"Today is your departure day. As your concierge, I am here to make sure that your journey's start is uneventful," Alice said. "Certainly, your Director has shared the schedule with all of you?"

"No, something else kept us busy most of yesterday," Beau said. He was astounded that Alice did not seem more concerned about the storm or the ruination of the trailers. "We're not staying to help with the cleanup here?"

"No. Your Director in consultation with Doctor Bebe has escalated your departure. Allow me to demonstrate the features of your rover," she said, referring to the enormous six-wheeled vehicle parked between the trailers.

"What about the gigantic storm that destroyed this entire place last night?" Beau said, exasperated. "Were there any casualties? Don't you need help?"

"I can assure you that we are fully equipped to handle the cleanup from such an event. As you can see, reconstruction has already started."

"I can see that, but I mean, was anyone hurt? Is everyone okay?"

"There were minor injuries only among some of the worker positions. A few were reportedly and unadvisedly playing golf instead of sheltering in the space elevator's base and suffered minor abrasions."

"That's it?"

"That is it."

"What about the spaceport? What about the elevator? What about the trailers? These got destroyed!"

"The spaceport was designed specifically to withstand such storms. Its metal alloy construction is quite sturdy."

"This all seems too casual, Alice."

"I can assure you, that this is not our first such event. If you have no more questions, please allow me to demonstrate the features of the rover."

"I'll handle it," Tommy said. "I've used them plenty."

"It is part of my position's duties, Lieutenant Atkins," Alice said.

"Don't let me stop you then," Tommy replied, knowing further argument would be futile.

The rover was a monster of a vehicle, the wheels almost as tall as any of the missionaries. The cab was a long, rectangular shape with a bay of windows at the front like a cockpit. The cab sat just above the front tires. They would have to climb to get inside. Alice delicately kicked her foot between the first and second tires and a small stepladder folded down leading up to the door.

Inside it was spacious, but they still had to stoop while inside. Beau sat on one of the bench seats, where there was plenty of room to stretch his legs. Another row of bench seats and two seats in the cockpit area for a driver and passenger filled out the front of the rover's interior. Behind them was a large area for cargo, though they could have fit another row or two of benches if needed. Parts of the roof and sides were transparent. Between the two rows of benches there was a hatch. When Beau reached up and popped it open, another step ladder descended and he stuck his head out. Tommy popped up next to him, the hatch providing room for both. The top of the rover was covered in solar collection panels. Towards the front was an array of navigation and communication equipment; to the rear was a set of folded metal bars. Beau turned around and bumped a tubular set of controls. The bars unfolded into a honeycombed arm.

"We get generic Loopy Fruits to eat, but I bet that controller alone cost thirty-thousand dollars," Tommy said. "They could plug in my nephew's game controller for about fifty bucks and do the same thing. Stick your hand in."

Beau put his hand in the tube and it formed to fit his arm. The folded metal bars at the rear opened into an arm with two fingers and a thumb that mimicked his movements. He wiggled his fingers and the electronic arm opened and closed its claw. He made the "okay" sign, and the arm pinched two clamps together and held the third up delicately. It was not perfect, but it was a good approximation.

"Cool," Beau said.

"No rude gestures, please," Tommy joked.

"That is for loading and unloading equipment," Alice called up from inside the cab. "Please do not recreate with the expensive equipment."

"Oh, we're going to do nothing but play with this," Tommy said, not at all worried about Alice's purse-lipped response.

"Hi, Alex!" Beau used the mechanical arm to wave at Waters and Jazzy as they came around the corner of a trailer. Waters grinned and jogged toward them. Jazzy crossed her arms.

"They need two arms. Then you could back two rovers up and box," Tommy said. Beau obliged him by making a fist and punching motion with the arm. The motion rocked the whole rover.

"Please!" Alice cried.

"Better not get her too worked up. She might get friendly," Tommy said, and popped back into the cab.

Beau reluctantly pulled his arm out of the tube and went back inside. The mechanical arm automatically returned to its rest position along the back of the rover. Waters climbed up the step into the cab.

"This thing is great," he said.

Alice proceeded to walk them through the uses of the switches and buttons on the console of the cockpit. There were only a few of them. She pinched the display screen and flicked up the projection screen and began explaining the various menus, how to activate various systems and customize settings, and Beau's mind began to wander.

"I think I should be the one to drive us as the Director," Beau heard Waters say, breaking out of his introspection.

"Don't worry, Waters. You'll get plenty of chances to drive. We all will. You'll wish you hadn't by the time we're done. This is going to be the worst trip of your life," Tommy said.

"It can't be worse than falling from space," Jazzy said.

Tommy only smiled in reply.

"I am sure your journey will be an uneventful one. I wish you all great success in your mission," Alice said. "For the glory of the Administration!"

"Guess it's time we load everything then," Beau said. He and Tommy looked at each other for a moment before they both sprang for the hatch, eager to operate the arm, only to find that Joon-baek was there already. Rather, he was still there. He had been there since

Beau had vacated the seat and had not left the "Armatron," as he called it, since.

"This thing is great!" Joon-baek said. "It's just like a toy I had when I was a kid!" He had donned a helmet from the enviro suits and played with the arm.

"Beau!" Waters called from outside the rover. "Come help get things set up outside."

"Guess we'd better get everything ready to load then," Beau said, dejected.

Alice disappeared without anyone seeing her go. The missionaries opened the rear hatch and set about loading the rover.

Tommy was not wrong about it being their worst trip ever. The colony was nearly three-hundred kilometers from the spaceport, and to get there they had to cross the plains, a marsh, navigate the forest and foothills of a mountain range, and then cross the mountain range itself to finally reach the settlement.

"This won't be too bad," Waters had said. "Three hundred kilometers isn't that far. It should only take us a few hours to get there. It would be less than a day's trip on Earth."

Waters's estimations were quickly shown to be flawed. Polus had no roads. As flat as the plains looked, every bump and hole, rock, bush, shrub, arroyo, gully, and hill became an obstacle. Even the grass, which not far from the spaceport grew tall enough to obscure the rover's wheels, was an obstacle. It was tough and springy. Were it not for their machinery they would have worn themselves out. The terrain limited the rover to traveling no faster than a few kilometers an hour. The enormous wheels of the rover handled the terrain fine, mostly, but it was built for durability, not for comfort. With only the benches inside to sit on, the missionaries were tossed against their restraints with every bump, each jolt transferred directly into their bodies. After less than an hour, most of them gave up and moved to the floor or used duffel bags as makeshift cushions. Joon-baek was the only one still sitting in a seat. He napped, somehow, leaning forward against his safety belt.

The enviro suit helmet he still wore knocked arrhythmically against the side of the rover whenever they hit a bump.

"How can he sleep like that?" Tommy asked.

There was no way to answer that question.

They spent several days driving over the plains, long enough to become accustomed to the monotony. They only stopped to swap the batteries. Waters and Jazzy, anxious to reach the colony, pushed them onward.

At first, Beau was intent on documenting every moment of their journey. He regretted missing the storm, the mission's biggest event so far. Though Alice promised to send him footage from the spaceport's cameras, it was not the same. He stood in the top hatch and watch the terrain roll by. There was not much to capture, however, and after a while he mostly used it as an excuse to stand. He admitted, though, that there were some lovely sights. Bluffs and canyons in the distance with sides painted deep reds and oranges; colors in the sky, especially the night sky; distant trees and plants with leaves the color of no plant he had ever seen before. Water flowing in great tracts reflecting the sky in glassy relief.

One thing they had not yet seen was any wildlife, much to Molly's disappointment. Not even a bird. Plants, however, were abundant. The Polus vines and its fruit were everywhere. It would have been obnoxious were the fruit not so tasty. It seemed like the farther they traveled from the spaceport, the sweeter it became. It was also very filling. Just a bite was enough to satisfy them for many hours.

"We may die of boredom, but we won't go hungry, at least," Jazzy said.

"How could you be bored?" Joon-baek said, fascinated by each new blade of grass.

Sleeping at night was another puzzle altogether. They really had no choice but to sleep in the rover instead of making camp. Early on, they had discovered that the grass was not only tall, but incredibly dense. It was not just that there was a lot of it packed tightly, although that was true. It was also that the grass resisted being trampled. Trying to push through it was like trying to run through water. There was no flattening it down to pitch a shelter to speak of. So, when none of them wanted to continue driving at night, they stopped. Tommy slept under the stars on the roof, a feat the others could not be persuaded to attempt for fear of rolling off in their sleep. The interior of the rover was not too bad, albeit crowded. A couple people could lie down between the benches if they alternated head to foot. There were also the driver and passenger seats, which reclined and were the most comfortable. Those quickly became the most coveted seats in the rover.

Although they managed, they grew tired of the routine. They snapped at each other over little annoyances, until one morning their spirits lifted when the grass began to break, and they spotted trees in the distance.

CHAPTER THIRTEEN

A POLAR BEAR

t was slow going. There was no path, only a general direction. The sight of the trees that had lifted their spirits proved false hope. They did not seem to be getting any closer.

"The trees on Polus are enormous," Joon-baek explained. "They would be visible from many kilometers away."

The whine of the rover's electric motors filled the cabin with white noise. Although the grass was no longer as dense, the terrain remained rough and they jostled back and forth uncomfortably from time to time. They had been traveling for several days, and the difficult trip sapped their energy. No one had the will to start a conversation. Those who attempted to pass the boredom with naps risked an unceremonious awakening from unwelcome bumps.

Waters grew worried. He was thinking of their schedule and goals. He had significantly underestimated the difficulty and time the journey would take.

Molly, whose turn it was to drive, said nothing but looked uncomfortable. Jazzy sat in the front passenger seat with her knees drawn up and eyes closed, failing to sleep.

Tommy had enough of the inside the rover. "I'll take a turn up top, now," he said.

He passed through the hatch and found Beau holding a strap

attached to the rover's antennae with one hand and struggling with a pair of binoculars with the other. He was seated on the roof, hunched over, and looked miserable. Beau acknowledged Tommy with a grunt as the lieutenant came through the hatch but made no other motion. He was leaning against one of the protective hoops that surrounded the antennae, forming a makeshift stool.

Tommy shrugged, hooked himself to the antennae, and hunkered down next to Beau, holding on for stability.

"Aren't you going to go inside?" Tommy asked. "There's room now with me up top."

Beau shook his head from side to side slowly. "The fresh air feels better," he said. He looked as if the rover's next lurch might rob him of his lunch.

Tommy made a gesture that said "whatever you want." Beau relaxed a bit and allowed the lash and hoop to take the weight of his body a little more. This might have been pleasant under normal circumstances. The rover was crowded and the windows small. The roof had the best view, and everything was new and different. However, the trip had worn them all down, and motion sickness had set in for some. Beau was determined not to ask Jazzy for any medication; he felt a strange combination of excitement and discomfort talking to her under normal circumstances. Besides, he didn't want her to think he was weak.

It was growing late. The gas giant loomed large in the sky above, seeming to mock their progress with its unchanging, unshifting dominance, ever the same no matter their struggles. The setting sun was low enough to shoot its rays under the clouds that had been with them all day. Although, it made everything seem golden, the blinding light slowed their progress further. According to schedule, they had intended to reach the colonists that day. It was clear that would not be happening. Not today. Probably not tomorrow either.

The heads-up display told Molly that the batteries were close to empty. She swept the widget off the screen and onto the tablet on the console. The clouds had prevented the batteries from recharging efficiently, a fact that was contributing to their slow progress. If tomorrow were sunny, they might be able to continue. Now, however, they needed to start thinking about a place to spend the night.

Suddenly the rover broke through the tall grass, lurched down a small embankment, and came to a stop in a bog. Tommy and Beau toppled forward, gripping the straps that held them to the roof. The rover's wheels continued to spin, kicking up water against its sides and sinking the craft past the wheel hubs. Molly dragged the throttle back to suspend the drive. The rover was very much stuck.

"Why didn't you warn us!" Waters's voice cackled over their phones at Tommy and Beau on the roof. He was irritated, but they all were growing less patient the longer their journey took.

It was a stupid question. No one could see anything through the grass, which was taller than the rover even now, and the sunlight pouring under the clouds made it difficult to see. Something like leafy green duckweed floated on the water, completely obscuring the bog below. None of them could have possibly known what lay beneath, and their exhaustion was in danger of getting the better of them. In any case, it was clear they were not in a mere pond.

"Try again," Waters said to Molly. She moved the throttle forward. The wheels spun and kicked up a peat-like plant, painting the sides of the rover. Molly brought the throttle back. It was no use.

"There's solid ground just ahead," Tommy called from the roof. "It looks like it's covered with low grass. If we can get there, things should go smoother."

Waters and Joon-baek leaned forward to peer through the rover's windshield. Even Jazzy stirred. A few meters farther they could see the grass. Beyond that, towering trees signaled the edge of a forest. The same forest they needed to traverse to reach the colony.

Tommy hopped down on one of the tires. Holding onto the enormous treads, he tested his footing. "The weeds feel thick enough to walk on," he said.

Waters looked to Joon-baek. "Given how sturdy the rest of the vegetation has been, he might be right," he answered in reply to the unasked question.

They soon tested the idea. Tommy was first. He stepped off and put his weight on the peat. The plant matter gave way beneath him slowly, but he found that if he kept moving, he could stay on top.

"Here goes," he said. He let go of the tire and sprung out across the top of the bog, comically lifting his knees and feet extra high to stay abreast of sinking. With a few quick steps he made it to solid ground, huffing from the effort.

Waters, not to be outdone, opened the side door, and imitating Tommy stepped out onto the bog. He promptly fell face-first into the muck, soiling the white clothes Alice had given him. The distribution of his body weight kept him from sinking, but Tommy had to walk back to help him and ended up knee-deep in the bog himself. Together they walked to shore where Waters shook him off.

"I can manage myself," he said, becoming even more irritated at being embarrassed.

The others followed cautiously. Eventually all made it to solid ground. "This grass is especially tough," Joon-baek remarked, stepping onto the close-cropped hard ground which crunched and squeaked beneath their feet like cold snow. "It almost looks like it's been cut." Joon-baek bent down to examine the plants. He brushed the grass with his hand, and with a cry he pulled away sharply. His hand was scratched deeply. Blood oozed from where he had touched the ground. "It's sharp!" he cried. Jazzy tended to Joon-baek as best she could, glad to have something to do after days of monotony.

"Everyone, be careful." Waters warned, stating the obvious.

Molly went back to the rover and grabbed a tarp. She spread it over the ground and bent down to observe the grass. "It looks almost as if it's been eaten close to the ground. Like sheep or goats would do back home," she said.

Jazzy drew a breath in suddenly and froze in place, Joon-baek's bandage dangling in her hand. Not more than thirty meters away, an enormous beast emerged from the tree line. It was larger than the rover, which was no small feat. White fur covered its body. It had four large limbs thick like tree trunks, and six tiny wings set on its back just between its shoulders, comically small compared to its bulk. It ambled forward towards the bog with a series of muffled grunts and gave a satisfied shake. Waves of light passed across its fur as it ruffled and shook. With a relaxed sigh it dipped its massive head into the bog, plunging its snout through the peat. It sucked in water with a slurp and raised its head high. Jaws opened to reveal large plates of teeth like baleen. The animal sprayed the water back over the bog through its teeth. Liters and liters came out in a fine mist. Finishing, the beast turned and dipped again.

"A Polus bear," Molly whispered, hunkering down.

"A polar bear?" Beau said.

"It's feeding," she said.

"Quiet!" Waters hissed through his teeth. "There are no polar bears here. It's a Polus bear; one of the native species."

The Polus bear finished spraying the water from its maw and crunched on something lazily for a few seconds, rotating a bit and dipping its snout into the bog once more. With its muzzle immersed, it looked up at last and fixed its dark eyes on the mission team. In an instant it extracted itself from the bog and reared up onto its hind legs. Four front feet pawed the air. It gave a deep sonorous bellow that echoed off the trees. The team covered their ears and recoiled. It was monstrous and terrible at its full height. It lingered there on two legs for a moment, looking at and through them. Flashes of bright light traced striped patterns across its fur. Jazzy let out a cry and bolted. Joon-baek and Beau followed without a word.

"No, don't run!" Molly shouted.

With the sudden movement, the Polus bear dropped onto all fours, its weight sending a shockwave through the ground, and fled to the trees with a speed that belied its size, flashes of orange coursing its fur. It was gone in moments. Jazzy tripped and fell headlong onto the sharp grass. She put out her hands to brace her fall, the sharp grass scratching her palms, forearms, and legs terribly, tearing the clothing Alice had given her. Joon-baek and Beau, unable to stop their momentum, tumbled over Jazzy, receiving the same injuries and worse from the rough grass.

"Stop! It's gone, it's gone!" Molly shouted, running up to them, try-ing to calm them as they scrambled to their feet ready to take flight once more, their wounds already red with blood.

"We need to get out of here!" Beau shouted.

"It's gone!" Molly repeated. "Why did you run? Running from any animal could prompt it to chase you." Waters and Tommy trotted up behind her, looking back over their shoulders cautiously.

"Of course, we know that," Beau countered. It was his turn to be embarrassed. Beau turned away to avoid Waters seeing his exasper-ated expression, but Tommy could not contain himself or did not care to. He grinned. "Wipe that smart grin off your face, soldier——" Beau said.

"I'm a Marine."

"I don't care what you are," Beau said, frustrated, tired, embarrassed, and angry because of it. "I may not be Director, but I report to MFASA just the same. This will certainly go in my documentation, which your superiors are sure to read."

With the Polus bear gone, adrenaline subsided and they calmed. As it did, the three who had fallen noticed their wounds. Jazzy tried to flex her fingers and gasped in pain. The others fared little better. Joon-baek's jacket had survived the tumble and protected his torso, but it was full of tears and rips. Beau's jump suit and Jazzy's white suit were in tatters.

"My hands!" Jazzy cried.

"You should see your face," Tommy quipped.

"Tommy!" Molly said, surprised at how flippantly he treated the whole situation.

Jazzy shot him a look that somehow managed to be both plaintive and murderous. It was the wrong thing to say and he meant something else by it, but he was right. Her face was cut, bleeding, and covered in dirt. Her hair was in uncharacteristic tumbles about her head, little strands like tendrils sought escape in every direction.

"Don't pay the veteran position any attention," Beau said. "Speak-ing of positions, where were you when that thing came out of the trees?"

Tommy just snorted and walked away.

"What good is having a rifle if you're not going to use it?" Beau asked.

"Can you help?" Waters asked anyone in general as he tried his best to tend their wounds.

"I'll do it," Molly said.

"Ha!" Jazzy said with scorn. She was embarrassed too. "You didn't warn us about the Polus bear. What makes you think you're of any use right now?"

Molly reddened but ignored Jazzy's comments and tended to Joon-baek, who had found a rock and sat down. Beau walked with Jazzy back to the rover.

"I'm sorry," Joon-baek said. "I should have known better. We don't know anything about this place, and here I am sticking my hands into strange plants and losing my head."

"It's nothing," Molly responded. "None of us are used to this place. Here, Tommy, Alex, take these and go help the others."

"What am I supposed to do with these?" Waters asked as he received the bandages Molly passed to him.

"You saw what Jazzy did earlier for Joon-baek?" Molly asked.

"Yes, I saw—"

"It's that simple. Clean it and bandage it."

As the sun set and the blue light of Polus once more filtered through the clouds, they worked patching each other up. They decided to spend the night in the rover, wanting no more encounters with bears of any kind, polar or Polus.

"I doubt the bog would make any difference to one of them. They're big enough," Tommy commented.

"Hush," Molly said.

When they got to the rover, they found its doors shut.

"The wounded need room to recover," Beau called from the rover's hatch. "That won't leave space for the rest inside, unfortunately. I will tend to Jazzy tonight at least."

"You expect us to spend the night outside? Who knows what else comes out at night?" Joon-baek said.

"I understand," Beau said, as he disappeared back inside the rover.

Molly, although she was not eager to spend the night outside either, felt obligated to speak up since animals were her expertise and part of her responsibility. "I don't think we have anything to worry about," she said. "The moon's fauna is almost entirely made up of herbivores. I don't think the Polus bear is dangerous, just big."

Joon-baek was not convinced. "What's to say one of the exceptions won't find us? Even if they are herbivores, that monster could have crushed us without a second thought. Healing or not, the rest of us are injured too—"

"I'm fine," Tommy chimed in. He seemed to find the whole situation to be great fun. "And she's right. Polus bears aren't dangerous. Far from it. We probably just scared that one."

"You can be the first to sleep outside then," Joon-baek said.

"Joon-baek, I understand your concerns, but my injuries are very real," Jazzy's voice came over their phones.

Waters spoke up. "It's alright, Jazzy. We can make room."

Their phones went silent as Waters and Jazzy switched to talking directly. Jazzy argued that her position as the mission's physician merited special consideration; Waters responded that her wounds were no worse than everyone else's, and there was plenty of room for them all in the rover. In the end, they compromised: only Joon-baek, Beau, and Jazzy, the three who were injured, could stay inside. Molly, Waters, and Tommy, who were uninjured, had to give up their places in the rover.

"Makes no difference to me," Tommy said.

"I suppose that's the best we're going to get," Waters said, although he was not eager to test the accuracy of Molly's assessment of Polus IV's fauna any more than the other missionaries.

Molly did not bother to offer an opinion. With the decision made there was no use arguing, but they were not looking forward to spending the night outside either. Razor sharp grass aside, which seemed all too capable of shredding their equipment, Joon-baek was right about the Polus bear. Whether it intended to or not, an animal of that size could hurt them. Sprawled out asleep on the grass they made much easier targets for even accidental crushings.

The three clambered up the tires and on top of the rover. With Tommy's help they spread out tarps over the antenna like a tent and prepared to spend the night under the stars.

CHAPTER FOURTEEN

A WONDER

The night turned out to be cold; very cold. The three missionaries who lay under tarps on the roof of the rover huddled close around a small heat lamp, blankets pulled over their shoulders, watching their breath form little clouds. None of them were comfortable. They had tried to sleep for the first hour or two. One-by-one they realized they would not be sleeping that night and sat up. They were too cold and tired to talk, but there was a sort of camaraderie in being miserable together.

Late in the deepest part of the night the clouds cleared. Polus began to cast its pale blue light over the surface of the moon, illuminating everything around them. Molly, Waters, and Tommy saw the light through the gaps in their makeshift shelter and peered outside. There they saw a wonder.

The bioluminescent Polus fruit that had illuminated the gravely plain near the space port was familiar to them, but this was a new world. The needles of the gigantic trees towering high above them were aglow with a green truer than any shade they had seen before. The razor grass that had given them so much trouble formed a luminescent carpet that stretched along the banks of the bog. The bog itself teemed with life and color. Below the water's surface tiny creatures, no more than points of glowing pink light, skittered about, nipping up bits of algae, which itself gave off a dim luminescence. The duckweed that covered the bog was alight with tiny green circles, the edges of each individual leaf shining distinctly. The tall prairie grass behind them was aglow. The whole moon seemed to be a new creation beneath the light of Polus, that giant dominating the sky above.

They forgot the cold for the moment, instead gazing in awe. It was like standing in a painting, like flying through a comet's tail or reaching a rainbow's promised source. Everything that existed cried out for joy at its being, as if in the light of Polus they saw not only the features of the moon, but that life itself in fact *was*.

Then the clouds returned, hiding Polus once more, and the lights faded. Waters's phone cackled and they remember again that they were cold.

"What are you doing up there?" Jazzy's voice cackled.

Their movements must have disturbed the rest of the missionaries. They guessed that those inside the rover were not sleeping much better than those outside, though they must have been warm at least.

"Did you see that?" Waters asked.

"See what? It's night outside. There's nothing to see," Jazzy replied. "Did you decide to practice your dancing steps because you couldn't sleep? You're making a racket. Please, sit down and let us get some rest. We all need it."

They crept back into their makeshift tent and resumed their vigil over the tiny heat lamp, though now its dim heat seemed insufficient, even disappointing. Their thoughts turned to what they had seen, mixing colors green, gold, pink, orange, and yellow in their mind's eye. These visions slowly blended into a cascade of vivid dreams, and they slept where they sat.

The three sleeping on the roof were awakened by the sound of the rover's door opening, followed by the chittering of Jazzy and Beau. The clouds had cleared, and the morning sun shone brightly through gaps in the makeshift tarp. Birdsong and the buzz of insects filled the morning air. One by one those exiled to the roof stretched and breathed deeply, feeling surprisingly refreshed and good-natured in contrast to the missionaries who had the benefit of sleeping inside, who seemed to want nothing to do with each other.

Waters stepped out of the tarp and immediately stood bolt upright. Molly and Tommy followed, and they stood abreast in a line, fixated on the shore. They counted a troop of six Polus bears assembled at the edge of the bog. Three of them bore tiny riders, or at least they looked tiny atop the massive beasts. Three riderless animals stood attentive, fawning affectionately over the tiny figures atop their kin.

After the surprise wore off, they saw that the figures themselves were human. The two groups considered each other for what seemed endless minutes until Jazzy saw their visitors for the first time and gave a cry.

No doubt, these were the colonists. Each one appeared quite proud, even noble. They wore high boots, carved glasses with a single thin slit across the front, and shirts or a hooded covering like a poncho that was decorated with woven patterns. Waters wondered how the colonists could move about safely in this terrain considering how many injuries the missionaries had suffered the previous day in just a few minutes outside the rover.

Each colonist carried a long staff, the end of which was covered in a leather thong. One wore a black shemagh made of what looked like leather wrapped over his shoulders and draped in front of his chest in a loose triangle like an over-sized bandanna.

Joon-baek emerged through the hatch and stuck his hands in the Armatron's controls, ready to execute a plan to lighten the rover by unloading some of the cargo. Tommy tapped him on the shoulder, and Joon-baek turned to see the colonists for the first time. Tommy waved toward the colonists. Joon-baek waved with his arms still in the controls of the Armatron, causing it to imitate the gesture.

Waters, Molly, Beau, and Jazzy donned their environmental suits and gingerly made their way across the bog to solid ground where the groups stood considering each other for a few moments. The missionaries stood at a distance, still wary of the Polus bears.

One of the colonists, relatively young by his looks, rode toward Waters in a few bounds without seeming to give his mount any commands. Waters held his hands up, palms forward, less in a gesture of surrender than of self-preservation; the Polus bear on which the rider sat was a beast every bit as large as the one they had seen the previous day and it was terrifying having it lumber towards them snorting and huffing as it came.

"You do not belong here!" the rider shouted. He gestured at them with his staff. Waters got the impression he meant the staff as a tool of emphasis rather than a threat, but it still felt like he was brandishing it at them.

None of the missionaries spoke, but instinctively they began to slowly back away. The rider swung the Polus bear's massive flanks around and repeated his statement from the left side.

"You should not be here!"

"Jonathan," said the rider with a black shemagh. His tone was scolding, though it carried notes of agreement.

The rider, Jonathan it seemed, paused for a moment while the Polus bear stamped its feet then rode back to the troop, never taking his eyes from them.

The rider with the black shemagh slid off the back of his Polus bear. Without a word, the animal lifted its front leg and caught him in his slide. He rode the leg down as the animal knelt on all fours and lowered its head, gently bringing him to the ground. He patted the side of the bear and gave it a hug. This seemed to make the bear exceedingly glad, and it tossed its head happily. He was taller and broader of shoulders than any of the members of the mission. He was intimidating, but Waters was determined to stand his ground. He waved to the missionaries in greeting, as Tommy sidled up to the rest of the team.

"Hello, Tommy," the colonist said.

"It's good to see you again, sir," Tommy replied, shaking the man's hand. In response to the questioning looks from the missionaries he explained, "We met before, when I came on the first contact trip out here."

Waters and Molly shook the colonist's hand as well. At last, Waters feeling responsible as Mission Director, spoke. "Are you members of the Polus Four colony?"

"I am, and we are," the man said in return. Though he spoke normally, it sounded to the missionaries like his voice boomed across the bog with the piercing clarity of a trumpet's call, unlike any voice they had yet heard. "I am the mayor of the colony. You appear to be stuck," he said.

They shuffled uncomfortably. Their predicament was obvious. This was not the first impression any of them wanted to make upon those they were meant to be helping.

"How did you find us?" Waters asked, redirecting the conversation.

"An arkouda told us," responded a woman, still atop her bear. Her voice carried the same clarity as the man's, but its pitch had a different character. It reminded Waters of high piano keys.

"Arkouda?" Waters asked.

"Yes. Arkouda. One of these good creatures. You met him last night," she replied.

"I see," Waters said. He turned aside to the rest of the team and said in a low voice, "This is more concerning than I think we could have imagined. There is clearly some kind of animism at work even beyond what we expected. We should review additional training on our way to the colony to prepare us better." Beau and Jazzy nodded their heads solemnly. Molly looked perplexed.

Waters looked back over his shoulder, and the woman met his gaze, smiled ironically, and waved her fingers at him. He quickly turned back to the team. She could not possibly have heard him.

"This is not going to help our goals at all, I'm afraid," Waters finished.

"Well," the mayor said, done with waiting. "Do you want out?"

Waters, embarrassed at having been caught by the colonists in a compromising situation, took time to consider the offer. While he was certain that the colonists' beasts possessed enough strength to pull the rover from the bog, he also feared that they might damage it in the process. More importantly, however, he did not want to admit they could use the help.

"No. No thank you," Waters replied. "We'll get the rover out with our technology. It's delicate, you know. And expensive."

"Waters, that rover is about the toughest thing around for miles right about now," Tommy said.

Waters shot Tommy a look that said "shut up!"

The mayor turned back to the arkouda. "What made you think we wouldn't use technology?" he said as he mounted the bear again.

Waters could only imagine what they might consider technology. The Administration could at best estimate how much the colonists' equipment must have degraded after so many decades without upkeep and the benefit of Earth's specialists. He was certain of that fact now that he saw them riding animals. "They must truly be devolving into a primitive civilization," he said to himself. Though, perhaps it was not too late. This would be of great interest to Director Stanisdottir.

"Here," Joon-baek called, holding a winch out from the rover's side with the Armatron.

Together, Beau and Tommy carefully maneuvered the winch to the front of the rover and attached it.

"Be careful to ensure the locking pin is completely in place," Waters said, supervising from the shore.

"Got it," Beau finished as the winch snapped into place. Waters nodded his approval.

Tommy unstrung several meters of cable, and then tossed the bundle to Molly on the shore. She backed up, unstringing more cable as she went. She saw that she was headed straight toward their visitors with their enormous Polus bear mounts, blushed a little, and detoured to the side.

"It will be more likely to pull free if we take it at an angle," she called back.

"That's right," Beau replied, understanding her intentions completely.

She found the nearest tree. It was large enough that it could have been hollowed into a house and still have room left over. She disappeared for a minute as she walked around the tree, then came back around and hooked the cable back on itself.

"All set," she shouted.

Tommy hopped in the rover and powered it up.

"Huh," he remarked.

"What is it?" Joon-baek asked behind him.

"It's already charged more than I would have expected. Must be the morning sun."

He activated the winch, and it began to pull, jerking the nose of the rover to the side. He gave it a little throttle, slowly turning the wheels to take some of the strain, though he knew it was unlikely to matter. The cable was at least ten-ton test, and the torque from the winch's motor was more than capable of pulling it straight up a cliff if necessary.

A few minutes later the rover was on solid ground. Waters and Jazzy were worried that the razor grass might be hard on the tires, and they both spent a few minutes walking around the rover, clicking their tongues, tsk-tsking this and that, and disagreeing while saying the same thing. Eventually, they concluded that with care it was adequate to the terrain and agreed to move on.

Tommy tapped the control screen and noted the batteries were indeed charging nicely. They were not full, but if they kept a relatively slow pace, the sunlight should keep up with their power usage.

"It would be better if we could drop some weight," he suggested.

"I don't support that," Jazzy said. "There is not a thing aboard that isn't mission critical."

"I agree," Waters said. "We'll have to just take it slow."

"Well, some of you may as well walk then. It's going to be that kind of a pace," Tommy said.

None of the missionaries seemed eager to hoof it, especially not with six large Polus bears in the area, and they all climbed back inside the rover.

CHAPTER FIFTEEN

THE NARROW GATE

The troop of colonists rode into the forest, revealing the path as they departed. The missionaries peered after them through the rover's windows.

"The path they took should lead straight to the city," Waters reasoned.

Waters was not wrong, but the path was not straight. Although it was wide as a Polus bear and permitted the rover to pass, it was not designed for a vehicle. Travel was even slower than on the plains, and much, much more rough. The path ambled around trees and up and down hills. Small streams regularly crisscrossed the path. Where there were no streams, there were large rocks. The rover regularly tilted precariously as it negotiated a boulder or massive root. They occasionally drove through vast meadows filled with glorious wildflowers of all kinds. The relatively flat trail through the meadows offered relief, but the meadows did not make travel any faster as they were often sopping wet with dew and hidden springs and had to be traversed with care lest the rover's wheels become trapped again.

Whereas on the plains the missionaries had been able to sit on the floor and lean against the walls, there was no chance of comfort here. The rover rocked and jostled constantly so that even Joon-baek could not rest. They sat on the benches and held onto cargo straps for handholds. They said nothing, needing all their energy to stay upright.

As the day wore on the terrain began to change. The hills became steeper, and the rover leaned more. Instead of driving over hills they drove through them on trails cut into the mountains. The rover climbed higher and higher. A great river roared through the valley below.

When at last they stopped for the night, they were too fatigued to even prepare food. They consigned themselves to munching on rations and sipping from water bottles in dejected silence.

Only Tommy found the energy to speak, "I said this would be the worst trip of your life."

Five pairs of glaring eyes told him if he chose to point it out again it would be the last trip of his life.

Exhausted, and the motion of travel finally having stopped, they fell into the restless sleep of people in a strange place, physically tired but mentally alert.

Dawn warmed the rover, waking the missionaries to a mutual but unspoken commitment to procrastinate driving again. None of them desired to suffer more travel, so they made sure the equipment was double-secure and ran diagnostics on the rover's systems. Tommy took his rifle from its lock and practiced disassembly and reassembly while he waited for the others to make up their minds to depart. He oiled and cleaned it again and again, testing the action with a 'click clack' sound. Beau watched with curiosity.

They stepped outside, careful to stay on the path to avoid injury, and ate a morning meal of rehydrated mush mixed with bits of dehydrated apple out of the aluminum mugs from their mess kits. Joonbaek sweetened his with the juice of a Polus fruit, ubiquitous and easily gathered even in the mountains, and the rest soon followed his example. The mush was not unpleasant, but the texture and presentation left something to be desired. Tommy made cowboy coffee, which they shared eagerly, grateful for the warmth.

As the sun rose, they saw that they had stopped at the base of a vast, wide valley. The river whose roar had been their constant companion the previous day broadened into a wide, shallow tract of clear water coursing gently over pebbles and rocks below a sloping bank. There were places they could wade across and barely wet their ankles. Minnow-like fishes darted through the shallows. Polus's ubiquitous pink freshwater krill played tag in the deep pools where the river turned. Sometimes larger prawns, the only predator they had encountered yet, chased the smaller krill. A field an intense green filled the valley, the stalks of grass waving in the morning breeze. On either side the valley gave way to sloping hills. Ahead the valley turned where the foot of a tree-covered mountain obscured their view. The path was blessedly flat and appeared dry. Having run out of excuses for remaining stationary, the missionaries eventually climbed back inside and Tommy started the rover.

The going was smooth, and they soon realized their hesitation was unfounded. They rounded the foot of the mountain and a vast sloping hill opened before them. At the top of the hill, large, clear, and bright, stood the colonists' city.

The city was surrounded by high walls of golden luminous energy that shone like the dawn and stretched for kilometers across an enormous bowl between mountain peaks. Beyond the walls towered buildings of white stone and glass built on tiers seemingly carved into the mountainside. The stones themselves shone with light that was visible even in the bright morning sun, but none compared to the towering spire that rose from the city center. Its glow lit the city and filled the entire valley.

The river flowed out of the city through the wall to the right side of a tall gate, cascading down the hill through orchards of fruit-bearing trees and fields of tended vines and other crops. The trees appeared ancient, with great gnarly tapered trunks full of thick bark, massive roots, and large branches that came out in twists and bends, ending in pads of smaller leaves and needles. The branches emphasized the shape of their trunks, while their crowns were thick with tight growth. The leafy trees were in blossom and covered in flowers. Here a deep magenta, there a brilliant amber, there pink or peach. Some trees were still covered in bunches of lavender or red berries from the winter season. There were flowers the color of rose wine, and even orange and violet flowers the colors of a sunset. Where blossoms fell, they bathed the floor with color. Their fragrance penetrated the rover's filtration system. The missionaries inhaled deeply, unable to resist. Native insects flew between the trees and wildflowers of the valley, going about their work to and from white hive boxes stacked in periodic intervals throughout the orchards and fields. Birdsong hung in the air, and herds of animals trapsed about the hills. The valley was alive with life. In and through the orchards moved machines as tall as trees. These tended to the orchards, hives, and vineyards autonomously.

"Where are the worker positions?" Joon-baek asked.

"Maybe those machines serve the same purpose," Molly speculated.

"It's tragic when a machine takes a position from a person," Jazzy said. "This will have to be something we discuss with them. A change like that should help their employment rate as well."

Six-winged birds flitted among the trees. Their morning song resonated through the walls of the rover. Above them high in the sky massive creatures the size of whales swam among the clouds on wings like fins, flying upwards and breaching backwards through the low cumulus, scattering water vapor in turbulent whorls.

The rover drew nearer the city and the path turned to pavement. A tall, narrow gate flanked by white pillars inlaid with a kind of amber energy stood next to the river where it flowed from the city. Colonists came and went out of the gate. Polus bears and other creatures milled about in the fields or gamboled amidst the colonists. Some colonists walked, some rode. The animals seemed delighted to have a rider. Other colonists flew by in vehicles that hovered on pillows of air emanating from hoops set parallel to the ground evenly spaced around a cabin in sixes, imitating the wings of Polus's native birds. The hoops rotated to steer and maneuver the vehicle. There were no visible blades, but the hoops seemed to serve as engines, moving air or pure energy to provide superconductive lift. They gave off a bassy but pleasant electric thrum. Duck-like birds made a game of flying through the hoops where they swirled down and sideways, riding and tumbling on the current of air as they shot out the bottom like a slide.

"Why didn't we have those?" Joon-baek asked.

"They're great, aren't they? I want one," Tommy said.

Waters and Jazzy watched, mouths gaping.

As they continued toward the city it became clear why the path was not a developed road: there was no need. It had only been worn by the passing of walkers and riders. When the colonists needed to be somewhere quickly or farther away, they simply flew. They saw one flyer towing a cart back to the city, itself stabilized by several of the hoop-like engines; yet elsewhere they saw a Polus bear towing a cart as well.

"See how they don't make full use of technology," Jazzy said, a tone of desperation in her voice. "They live with a mixture of technology and more pastoral means. This is something we can help them with."

"It doesn't look much like they need help," Joon-baek mumbled.

The colonists gave a variety of reactions as they passed. Some waved, some took no notice, some flew by too quickly to see, others scowled. The rover rolled onto a flat plaza set in white marble pavers with tall, interspersed columns that supported banners and sails of shade cloth. There the rover stopped at last, just a few meters from the narrow gate.

Waters inhaled deeply. "We're here," he began, taking his talking stance as best he could inside the rover, readying a speech he had obviously prepared for the occasion of their arrival. "I know this has been a hard trip, but now, at last, it's time to get to work. Remember your training. Remember that the full force and confidence of Earth, MFASA, and the Administration is behind us. You are the best Earth has to offer. Never forget that. Despite what you see, we know these colonists are in need of much, and we can offer that to them. So let's go. Let's complete our mission and do it well. For the glory of—" Waters was interrupted as the rover rocked back and forth.

"I thought you stopped us?" he said to Tommy, his voice shaking. "Disengage the drive!"

"I did!" Tommy said.

A Polus bear had sidled up to the rover and was indulging itself in a scratching session, rocking the vehicle side to side. It turned its rump toward the rover and began scratching its haunches and tiny tail against the rover's wheels. It squatted down and pressed its rear into the rover and gave it such a lift that it brought the rover's wheels off the ground. The Polus bear stepped away and the rover crashed back to the ground, jostling back and forth on its suspension.

"You were saying?" Tommy said, finding the whole thing very amusing.

"Is everything okay?" Waters asked.

"I think we're alright," Molly said.

"It's fitting that the first thing to greet us should be a gigantic ass," Tommy said, not done amusing himself.

"That's enough," Waters said. "And I'll remind you that word could be considered offensive. Please don't speak that way around the colonists. Let's get out while we can."

They opened the door and climbed down the ladder to the pavement below. The marble reflected not only the light from the sky, but the light of the city itself back at them. It was like being in a snow field on a clear winter day, and more intense in contrast to the rover's dark interior. They blinked and shielded their eyes as they struggled to adjust.

As the missionary group gathered on the ground, a group of colonists was there to meet them. They recognized the mayor and Jonathan from the previous day. A small group of other colonists had come to greet them including the woman they had met. They no longer wore the ponchos, boots, and slitted glasses, nor did they carry staffs. Most of the men dressed in simple button-down shirts with the sleeves rolled up and tucked into slacks or pants. Many wore hats. Most, but not all of the women wore dresses, but all had hair that fell in long tresses. Some wore their hair in thick braids woven with ribbons falling down their backs. Those who did not wear hats wore gossamer thin circlets or crowns, each unique, some tipped with precious jewels. All of them had a bearing of confidence. The men seemed more than men and the women more than women. It intimidated the missionaries. Although there was nothing especially formal about the colonists' appearance, the missionaries felt underdressed in their jumpsuits, mission jackets, pants, and caps.

"They must be dignitaries here to welcome us to the city," Waters said in an aside to Jazzy. "It's good they already recognize our authority." Jazzy squeezed his arm in acknowledgement and stepped forward pulling Waters along with her.

"Are you sure we should approach them?" Joon-baek asked. "Don't they look, I mean, don't they look like we should ask first?"

"Nonsense," Jazzy said. "We represent the Administration and Earth. The colonies have recognized Earth's superiority for generations."

The missionaries climbed down from the rover and immediately shielded their eyes from the intense light of the city and high mountains. A small group gathered around the missionaries, curious, though most continued past on their way to the orchards, fields, and vineyards with tools in hand. Some rode animals. Some stood. All of them offered the same impression as the mayor and his entourage: an air of dignity somehow coupled to humility. Hound-like animals bounded about or sat at the feet of the colonists, eagerly looking up for some acknowledgment or instruction. Like the Polus bears, they had six tiny wings set between their shoulders. One colonist threw a stick; half of them took off after it like so many fur projectiles.

Among the animals were creatures with long necks and comforting faces with puffy snouts and wooly thick piebald coats. A herd of animals with spindly legs and crowns of antlers bounded down the hill a hundred meters away before stopping and turning their heads, preferring the view from a distance. Small chooks milled about, and billed fowl played in pools by the river. All the animals had six wings, whether they appeared vestigial or not. Smaller birds hopped about the plaza, pecking for snacks and bits here and there. Swallow-like fliers snapped up insects.

Jazzy stepped forward with Waters, both holding their hands at their brows to shield against the light, and the rest of the missionaries followed. A woman from the welcoming party stepped forward carrying a bag and began handing out glasses. They were of the same kind the riders had worn the previous day.

"Welcoming gifts?" Waters asked.

"You might say that," she said. "They're for your eyes. It will take some time for you to adjust to the light."

"Why aren't you wearing them?"

"We only wear them when we need them. We're part of this world. You, however, need them now," she replied.

It was true, very few of the colonists were wearing the glasses though some went about with them on their foreheads or tucked into their pocket.

Waters pondered the glasses in his hand. They appeared hand-made, carved from a piece of sun-bleached white wood, and had only a single slit that ran horizontally across the face to admit light. They looked primitive. He put them on and was surprised immediately.

"The slit will both shield your eyes from the light and sharpen your vision," the woman said.

"They're smart glasses!" Joon-baek exclaimed, putting his on and looking around in wonder.

Indeed, they were a piece of technology beyond simple glasses. Aside from blocking the light, the slit brought everything into sharper focus. The interior projected a heads-up display. The amount of information was overwhelming. It seemed to react to thoughts, first showing the names of those in the welcoming party, and then the full names of the missionaries. The glasses described the architecture of the city, the materials composing the walls and buildings, overlaid a map of the terrain, gave the scientific and common names of the animals, birds, and insects in the plaza, identified a failing mount in the rover, and showed that Molly was tachycardic even beyond the excitement of the other missionaries.

"There're different modes," Joon-baek said, swiping his hand across his face. "Huh. Why would you need to detect gravimetric distortions?"

"I don't recommend that you use them all the time. Only when you need them," the woman said, who the glasses told them was Ai, an assistant to the mayor's office. "Otherwise, your eyes will never adjust, and you'll grow lazy and never learn anything for yourself. Having information handed to you all the time does you no good. Only use them when you need them."

Jazzy stepped forward and began to speak: "Colonists of Polus IV. We are pleased to be here on behalf of the Administrations of Earth on a mission from MFASA. We thank you for these gifts and for your welcome. We hope in time to get to know all of you better." She glanced at Waters, who took the cue and stepped forward and continued.

"Yes, thank you, for the gifts and the welcome. We know that it may be hard to accept our presence and purpose here, but we think in time you will come to understand and appreciate what we have to offer."

Jonathan huffed, and turning on his heels walked back to the city, apparently having decided he had better things to do. As he left the small crowd began to disperse, though a few of the colonists stayed out of politeness.

The tone of Waters's voice rose a pitch as he continued, "As you have given us gifts, we would like to bring you gifts as well: gifts of education and science, of technology, of health and medicine, of culture, and knowledge of better governance and society. With time, I'm confident that you will come to see our ways as beneficial and for the best."

Jazzy began clapping and turned to look at the missionaries behind her who broke out into tepid claps. The colonists did not clap, though a few smiled courteously.

"Well, Mayor," Jazzy continued, "shall we meet in your city? Perhaps we could have a tour?"

The mayor glanced at the rest of the entourage with a lift of his eyebrows, and the colonists began to disperse, though Ai remained. Patience, according to the glasses, the woman they had met the previous day, joined the mayor and Ai. She had a glorious head of curly hair that stuck out in all directions like a globe.

The mayor spoke, "I don't think that will be possible. Not at this time," and sent a questioning look Tommy's way.

Jazzy was visually perturbed but maintained a polite smile, "We have just arrived, mayor, and would very much appreciate the opportunity to see where we can stay."

"You may make a camp wherever it pleases you, as long as it does not interfere with any of the people's work," the mayor replied.

Jazzy dropped the appearance of politeness.

The mayor held his hands in a pacifying manner and explained, "Please do not misunderstand me. We would in time be overjoyed to welcome you into our city. I do not think it will be possible, however, though you are welcome to try. Not until you share our faith. Please excuse us, we have work of our own to do."

With that, the mayor, Patience, and Ai turned and walked back toward the city gate. Waters heard Joon-baek chuckle, and thought that he must be seeing her name through the glasses too. It was an odd name and a bit funny. It was also archaic, like a name out of nineteenth century books.

Jazzy stepped forward with a look back at Waters, who himself looked back at the missionaries and motioned for them to follow. They all stepped forward except for Tommy who did not seem interested.

"Aren't you coming?" Waters called back.

"That's alright. You go ahead," Tommy said.

"Don't worry about him," Jazzy said to Waters. "He's not officially part of the mission anyway."

The trio of the mayor, Ai, and Patience passed through the gate and back into the city. The missionaries gathered as a group. A massive wall made of white limestone surrounded the entire city. The same amber energy that coursed through inlays up the pillars on either side of the gate served as its mortar. To call it a gate was something of a misnomer. There were no doors. It consisted instead of the open area between the pillars. Nor was it particularly narrow up close. From a distance the tall pillars and vastness of the wall stretching to either side made it look small.

Jazzy looked up at the height of the construction, and then stepped over the threshold. She looked back with a smile and motioned for the others to follow. However, she soon slowed and struggled as she met greater resistance. She pressed forward, but at last whatever restraint held her reached its limits and she could go no farther. All at once she fell, thrust backward out the gate.

Tommy burst out in laughter. Jazzy looked back at him, her face red with embarrassment, frustration, and anger. Waters helped her up and they both attempted to pass through the gate, slowly this time with their hands held out as if to stave off whatever would hold them back. The farther they progressed, the more the city resisted. The rest of the team, excluding Molly, stepped forward and tested the gate with the same effect: not a one of them could push through. Molly stood back in apprehension, not wanting to test the gate herself, perhaps afraid of what might happen to her or what it might mean.

Joon-baek pounded rhythmically on the invisible membrane that prevented their passage, making it a game.

"Stop that," Jazzy scolded. Joon-baek stepped back with his hands at his sides.

"This is absurd," Waters said as colonists, vehicles, and animals on either side of them continued to come and go through the gate at will. "What kind of trick is this to play on guests?" he complained.

Patience returned to them and motioned them to the side. "Please stand out of the way so that the others may pass freely," she said.

"What's going on here? I demand an explanation," Jazzy said.

"It is as the mayor said: it is simply not possible for you to pass at this time. Not until you share our faith. Tell me, did you have trouble with the grass?"

They nodded their heads.

"Did anyone explain to you the reason for the difficulty you had with something as simple as the grass?" She did not wait for an answer. "I was there among the riders, though you may not have recognized me under the hood behind the glasses." A look passed between the missionaries that suggested her hair would be near impossible to miss, but Patience continued. "You were not made for this world. In the same way, neither was this world made for you. Even the plants, the air, the light could do you harm. And that is why you cannot enter the gate. Though perhaps one of you might," she said, looking at Molly, who for her part avoided eye contact.

"No thank you," Molly replied.

"When you are ready, then."

"Her?!" Jazzy said incredulously. "The exobiologist? She does not even hold a leadership position, she has no doctorate, and she's the one you would permit to enter?"

Molly looked hurt.

"Please understand, miss," Patience continued to explain. Jazzy took offense at the use of the honorific. "It is not a matter of permission. You simply will not be able to enter the city as you are. It is not up to us."

Waters finally spoke up. "This has to be a mistake. You see, we are on a mission from MFASA, and we have the full backing..."

"The full faith and credit..." Jazzy interjected.

"...The full faith and credit of Earth's...the Administration behind us," Waters continued. "It is simply unthinkable that we would not be permitted to enter. This is our mission. It's what we are here to do."

Patience, true to her name, did not seek to explain further, but apologized once more. "I am sorry that you will not be able to join us, I truly am. Please understand. I have told you what you must do."

"Share your faith? What does that even mean? Perhaps you could speak to the mayor for us?" Jazzy asked.

"Yes, you're part of his staff. You can speak to him for us," Waters said.

"Please try to understand. Good day to you all." She turned and walked back into the city.

"Ugh!" Jazzy shouted in frustration, slamming the heel of her hand against the wall. "Now what are we supposed to do?" she said, turning to Waters.

Waters stood there looking between the faces of the missionaries, looking for an answer that was not to be had, not really knowing what they could or should do with this unexpected turn of events.

"We could go set up camp like the mayor said," Joon-baek offered.

Jazzy glared at him.

"Are you all done playing yet?" Tommy called from where he had stayed by the rover. He found the whole thing very amusing. Dejected, the missionaries rejoined him, uncertain what to do.

CHAPTER SIXTEEN

FULL GEAR

Fields and orchards surrounded the valley on all sides, so the missionaries could not encamp anywhere near the walls. They boarded the rover and drove back down the hill, where they chose the spot at which the valley had opened to show their first view of the city. It was beyond the fields, but near water. The forest and mountains provided cover, and the location had plenty of open space between the river and path. Importantly, they felt they could manage the plant life in the area and that it would not interfere with their efforts to make camp or cause more injuries with a little care.

Joon-baek, who had become an expert at the Armatron, unloaded equipment. The others arranged and opened crates. Shelter was the first necessity. MFASA supplied modular tents: strong fabric stretched over lightweight composite tubing to form a domed habitat. They first assembled and anchored a circular floor. Four long tubes crossed in the center and connected to the outer ring. Over this they stretched a white PTFE shell. The result was a durable, well-insulated four-walled shelter with enough room to walk around inside. The shelters had only one zippered entrance and no windows, though the PTFE shell, while opaque, did admit diffused light. They had enough shelters to pair up again.

"You know, we had the same experience during the first expedition to the colony before you arrived," Tommy began as they set up camp. "We walked right up to the gate ready to enter the city, and it was like running with a stretch band tied around your waist. The more you struggled to get in, the harder it resisted. None of us could get in. We couldn't believe it then either. One of the specialists thought it must use a genetic coding system of some sort."

"Right: a genetically mitigated authentication code," Joon-baek said, pondering how that might work.

"That's it," Tommy said. "We must have spent days trying to get in, though we didn't try begging like you did, at least that wasn't the first thing we did. We tried to override the system with a resonance cancelling signal; we tried hacking their networks; we even tried brute force, driving a rover through the gate. About the only thing we didn't try was blowing the thing up, which would not have gone over well. It didn't matter what we tried though; we never could get in. We eventually tried outright ordering them to let us in, but it made no difference. Either they would not let us in, or they could not let us in."

"When did you plan on sharing this information with the rest of us?" Jazzy scolded.

Tommy shrugged off Jazzy's comment, "This way was more fun. Besides, would you really have believed me if I had said you wouldn't be able to get in?"

"He has a point," Waters conceded quietly. Jazzy was not the type to accept anything she did not already know herself. Even after experiencing it first-hand she was still not ready to accept that they could not enter a city.

"There's nothing there. There must be a way in. They have to let us in!" she muttered to herself as she finished unloading a crate and moved to the next, only to have the lid of a crate became stuck. "That mayor!" she cursed as she tried to force the lid. Beau moved to help her.

"Your hands," he said as they popped the lid off.

"What about them?" Jazzy said.

"They're almost healed already. You were just injured a couple days ago," he said.

"I've always been a fast healer. The inoculations MFASA gave us probably helped too," Jazzy said.

Joon-baek climbed onto the rover's tires and looked at his reflection in the glass. "My face is better too. It must be the Polus fruit. It was rumored to have terrific healing qualities."

"That's impossible," Jazzy insisted. "Nothing could be that effective on its own without significant refining and study, including rigorous peer review. As far as I'm aware, no papers have yet even been written on the subject."

"But just look—"

Jazzy cut Joon-baek off, "I won't hear anything else about it."

"But it's my primary directive on this mission!" he protested.

"Nothing else about it," she repeated.

Jazzy lifted some equipment out of the crate and carried it off to her shelter. Joon-baek walked over to help Beau.

"I've already started writing the first paper, actually," he said.

"When did you have time for that?" Beau said.

"You know, while we were traveling," he said.

"This June Bug guy is something else," Tommy said. "It was enough for the rest of us just keeping our lunch down."

"I've decided to submit *Vitis Polae kimensis* to the Administration for consideration as its official scientific classification," Joon-baek said.

"Naming it after yourself, are you?" Beau said, poking fun.

"I don't think 'Kim's Polus fruit' would market very well at the grocery store," Tommy said.

Joon-baek smiled. "That's just for classification purposes. No one knows the Latin names of things anyway. I think we should just call them 'vitis.'"

"Like kiwis?" Beau said.

"Like kiwis," Joon-baek acknowledged.

Later that day they finished unloading and setting up their shelters. They occupied themselves arranging their living quarters and workspaces.

"Look over there," Tommy said as they assembled portable furniture. "June Bug's already set up his workbench."

"How?" Beau asked.

"If he keeps making that workbench appear when none of us are looking, that guy's going to get a reputation as a witch," Molly said.

"There's no such thing as witches," Jazzy said. "At least not magical ones." Jazzy shuffled around in a crate, found the screen she was looking for and trotted off with it under her arm.

"Thank you, Jazzy," Molly said sarcastically after she had left.

Joon-baek overheard them. "These are amazing," he said from his workbench. "These aren't individual plants. The entire vine appears to be connected and span several square kilometers. It may even cover the entire planet."

"You mean moon," Beau said.

"Right, the moon. Are you familiar with aspen trees on Earth? They're a kind of poplar."

They nodded.

"Well, an aspen grove is made up of many individual trees, but they share a common root system. New trees grow when the roots send up suckers, meaning that each tree is a clone of the other trees around it. Entire groves come from just one seed. The individual trees might only live through a few generations, but the root system can be ancient, thousands of years old, and span hectares and hectares, covering entire mountains. The vitis appear to behave the same way. The samples I collected here have the same genetic makeup as those we found near the space elevator. I need to do a larger survey, but if the vitis are really one enormous organism, it could be the largest living thing on the moon, possibly the largest organism ever discovered."

"Gather around, everyone," Waters said, approaching the other missionaries. He was wearing a full MFASA enviro suit, including its heavy boots and gloves. He had a helmet under his arm. "In spite of what Joon-baek may learn, I want everyone dressed in full gear, like this, anytime we're outside to help protect against further injury. That means boots and gloves too. No T-shirts, tennis shoes, or casual pants outside of the shelters."

"You don't mean for us to wear the helmets too," Beau asked with a little despair.

"It wouldn't be a bad idea," Waters said, "but I'm not going to require it."

"I don't understand how the colonists don't need the same protection," Jazzy protested.

"It's like they said: we weren't made for this world, and we haven't adapted yet," Joon-baek said.

"That mayor…" Jazzy said. His name was becoming her favorite curse.

They saw little of the mayor and his associates except by chance in the following days and weeks. The blossoms mostly fell from the trees to be replaced by tight flushes of growth whose colors were as varied as the flowers before them. Strange leaves of red, yellow, orange, blue, lavender, violet, magenta, and even the more traditional green, colors of every shade imaginable grew on the trees. Spring on the fourth moon of Polus threatened to fade into summer.

Their first effort to enter the city proved a fitting start to the mission, which showed signs of the same degree of success. They tried persuading other colonists to let them in. When that failed, they tried other means of reaching the colonists, yet still they made no progress. The people had little interest in hearing what they had to say, and the city itself sheltered them. The colonists could speed away on one of the six-engine flyers or on a Polus bear, or even walk away, leaving the missionaries huffing for air and struggling against the grasses and plants. Just walking through a field was difficult. The moon itself seemed determined to impede them.

Unable to enter the city and unable to keep up with the colonists, Jazzy and Waters planned to set up her medical clinic just outside the city walls. She would provide medical care, and Waters could use the opportunity to speak to the colonists. Jazzy was determined to set up her clinic in the plaza as close to the narrow gate as she could. She recruited Beau, Waters, and Tommy to help with the set up. Together, they moved her clinic from the camp to a spot in the plaza near the city gate. They partitioned off the back as an examination and consultation room, and she opened shop.

Molly's, Joon-baek's, and Beau's purposes were much more straight-forward. They seemed to struggle less to work on their goals. Molly cataloged Polus' fauna. Patience and other colonists sometimes joined her. The animals in the immediate area around the city alone would provide years of study, and Molly had plenty to keep busy. Curiously, none of the animals were domesticated, yet they neither feared the colonists nor posed any threat. To the contrary, the animals seemed to delight in their presence, and the people were happy to keep company with the animals.

Joon-baek could not have been happier studying the plants around them, particularly the vitis, which he found fascinating. He had yet to successfully cultivate one of the fruits on its own, but that did not bother him. Instead, each failure led to a fascinating discovery. He sat with a bowl of fruit at his side as he studied at his workbench. Periodically he trekked off with Tommy to gather more samples. His face, pockmarked since his youth, had begun to clear. He attributed this to a combination of the cleaner environment of Polus and the vitis themselves; Jazzy reminded him not to draw hasty conclusions until his work had been peer-reviewed and published.

At first, Beau was intent on documenting everything, remembering his failure to capture the storm at the space port. As the days turned into weeks and the season began to drift into the moon's version of summer, he found there was simply not that much new to record, exactly as he had on the Arca. Instead, he helped Joon-baek and Tommy collect samples, sat with Jazzy in the clinic, or accompanied Molly on her explorations. Footage of animals was always worthwhile. They were a hit on the Administration's broadcasts. And the animals here were surprisingly easy to capture since they did not flee; in fact they walked right up to Beau and Molly, eagerly seeking pats and scritches, almost anticipating, even awaiting a command. This behavior was helpful, because hiking off the path through the dense and rigid foliage remained a chore. Despite Waters's orders to wear additional protective gear, they still had to move carefully to avoid injuring themselves. For the same reason, the team remained limited largely to the area around the city and the path. Despite the limitation, there was plenty for them to do. Still, they grew frustrated at not being able to see the city or leave the valley.

CHAPTER SEVENTEEN

ANIMALS DON'T SMILE

A commotion in the plaza uncharacteristic of the colonists was enough to get Jazzy and Waters to leave the clinic, which was an extraordinary feat. They had taken to spending the whole day, and some evenings, in the clinic as the weeks and months wore into routine and it became clear that meeting their objectives was going to be difficult. The few colonists who came to visit, including the mayor, never sought treatment, and never listened to what they had to teach. Instead, the few visitors that did come debated and argued. In whatever ways they spent their days, it was certainly not fulfilling their mission.

Molly and Beau passed by on a morning survey of the wildlife and joined Waters and Jazzy in the crowd. They were watching Patience and Jonathan have a serious conversation with several other colonists.

"What is it?" Molly asked.

"This is not your affair," Jonathan said. "Leave it to us."

Patience placed a calming hand on his arm and stepped toward Molly. She motioned toward one of the colonists. "This is Leroy. He believes he sighted an apoch in the area." The man nodded his head. "Tell them," she said.

"Early this morning I was checking the lower vineyard near the MFASA campsite as I do every couple of weeks. I noticed a dead animal on the ground near the trees at the edge of the field."

"A dead animal isn't so unusual in itself," Molly said. "Animals die all the time. It's part of nature."

"This one had clearly been killed, not simply passed away," Leroy said.

"Again, animals get killed all the time," Molly said.

"Not on Polus they don't," Patience said. "The animals care for each other as much as they do for us. They may chase and play, but they never hurt each other unless by accident."

"Could this have been an accident?" Molly asked.

"Not this one. Not in the way I found it," Leroy said.

"What do you mean?" Molly said.

"The apoch doesn't just kill its prey," Patience said. "It flays its prey alive, torturing it as it feeds on its life and light. It doesn't even eat the flesh. The signs that an apoch has made a kill are unmistakable."

Jazzy blanched at the description.

Patience continued, "But even so, tell us why you are sure it was an apoch's kill."

"I have never seen one before, but it matched all the descriptions: the poor skiouros had the skin torn from its chest and stomach. Something had pinned its little arms and legs to the ground with something like needles or spines. And it was grey, almost colorless. But when I spotted the carcass, a distortion in the tree line caught my attention, like the light was bending through a lens. When I looked closer it seemed to disappear, but I could tell something was there because the underbrush kept moving. That's when I came here. There is no doubt this was an apoch."

"Could I see it? Examining the carcass might help me learn more about how it died," Molly asked.

"I'm afraid not," Leroy said. "I buried it hastily where I found it in the field and came straight here."

"You should have waited for us so we could examine it. Study of the wildlife of this planet is part of our mission," Waters scolded.

"The wildlife and what happens to them are a matter for the colonists," Jonathan retorted.

"I know you have trouble accepting our role here," Waters began, but Jonathan simply turned his back and walked away to meet a group of colonists who had begun to assemble on arkouda carrying the colonists' traditional staffs. They wore the same attire as their first encounter with the missionaries near the bog: boots, ponchos and parkas, and slitted glasses. Small drones hovered around their heads.

"It looks like you're getting ready for something," Waters commented.

"I appreciate the parameters of your mission, Director Waters. However, you do not seem to understand the gravity of the situation. An apoch is extremely dangerous and a threat to all life in the area, including human life," Patience said.

"Predators have predictable behavior," Molly said. "If we can study it and understand it, we might be able to arrive at an understanding where you do not need to hunt it."

Patience looked at Molly with compassion, but her reply was firm. "No. I'm sorry, Molly. You must let us deal with the apoch in our own way."

Waters looked as if he were inclined to protest once more, but Patience excused herself and joined the other colonists preparing to depart.

Waters reddened at the rebuff. "I cannot believe these people. They ignore everything we try to do for them. They even refuse our offer to help understand one of the creatures of their own planet a little better."

"Moon," Beau corrected.

Waters was not in the mood for word games and signaled as much with a piercing look.

"Maybe," Molly hesitated, "we could try to find it first. If we could capture it, we could study it even more effectively than we could in the wild. We could protect it from the colonists at the same time."

"I don't think that's a good idea," Jazzy began.

"I think that's a fantastic idea," Water said. They looked at each other sideways for a moment. Jazzy crossed her arms and marched back to the clinic.

"Beau, you go with Molly and find Tommy," Waters said. You three are in charge of capturing the apoch before the colonists find it. Joon-baek and I will set up an enclosure back at camp. We'll have it ready by the time you get there."

"What's Jazzy going to do?"

"It looks like she's going to watch the clinic while we're gone."

Beau, Molly, and Waters trotted down the hill to camp as fast as they could, and were out of breath by the time they arrived. Tommy was at the camp with his feet kicked up on an overturned crate talking to Joon-baek while he worked. Tommy, to their surprise, was skeptical when they explained the situation.

"I don't know," he said. "I feel like you should trust the colonists on this one. They know this place pretty well. They've been here for decades."

"We can't allow something as barbaric as hunting to take place," Beau protested. "It doesn't matter how well they know the moon. This is one area where Earth knows better. It's just one more indication that despite all their technology, the colonists have a lot to learn."

Molly chimed in. "Tommy, normally I would agree with you. But I think capturing the apoch is in the interests of the mission, and in the interests of the creature," she said.

"Thank you, Molly," said Waters.

Tommy relented.

"So, how are we going to find it?" Molly asked.

That question ended discussion. They had been so engrossed in the prospect of capturing the apoch they had not considered how they should do so. At last Joon-baek spoke up.

"You said that the apoch disappeared and 'bent the light' as it left. We might be able to track the distortion."

"That's it!" Waters said.

Joon-baek continued, growing excited. "We would just need to synch with the geotracking data from Polus Station…"

They fell silent again. They had not yet been able to obtain a LiFi signal from anywhere, let alone synchronize with the space station.

"What about the glasses the colonists gave us?" Beau finally suggested.

Joon-baek lit up again at the suggestion. "That would work. They have a wide number of functions. They might even be able to track the kind of distortion the animal would make without any modification."

"The colonists getting ready to hunt were all wearing glasses," Waters said.

No one needed another word. They set out to locate their glasses. Beau, who had his with him, had already put them on. Joon-baek returned and donned his as well.

"These are hard to get used to," Beau said, trying to focus his thoughts to cycle through the various modes.

"I've got it. Try this mode," Joon-baek said as he handed his glasses to Beau. "The one after ultravision and infravision. I was wondering why they had a mode for gravimetric distortion."

"They have a setting specifically for that?" Tommy said, a bit incredulous.

Joon-baek shrugged. "They may have created it specifically for the apoch, now that I think about it."

"How can you tell?" Beau asked, handing the glasses back to Joon-baek. To him it looked normal.

"Well, I can't," Joon-baek admitted. "But the name suggests it."

"It's worth trying," Waters said. "We need to hurry. The colonists have probably already set out. Joon-baek, you work with me to set up the enclosure. You three, do what you can to catch the animal first."

Waters walked behind their shelters to a stack of crates. He threw off the lid and began unpacking poles. Joon-baek looked like he would much rather have gone after the apoch but followed Waters anyway.

As the trio of Molly, Beau and Tommy were about to set out to find the apoch, Beau posed an important question. "Even if we do find an apoch, how are we supposed to catch it, let alone contain one?" he asked.

"I have these," Molly said. She shuffled through her equipment and produced three pipes held together with wire. She pulled the wire taunt and the pipes snapped into a pole with a long loop at the end. "MFASA sent these specifically for capturing larger specimens."

"Animal control uses those for catching strays," Tommy said.

"Exactly right," Molly said. "You slip the loop over the animal's neck, and then lock the rope in place. That keeps it tight around the animal's neck. The long pole keeps it far away so it can't hurt you. It should work, anyway." She handed one to Tommy and Beau, who assembled them into the same long shaft.

"Where do we start?" Beau asked.

"Where the colonist saw the apoch is as good a place as any," she said. "It shouldn't be far from here."

They approached the vineyard wearing their glasses. It was not far from their camp, just along the border of the trees and meadow. They bent over and held their poles in front of them, tense and ready.

"It looks like the colonists have been here already," Tommy said. "See? There are Polus bear footprints everywhere."

"I don't think we're going to beat them," Beau said.

"Guys," Molly said, her tone changing in a way that caused their toes to tingle. She lifted her glasses and pointed to the treeline. Tommy and Beau lifted their glasses, hardly able to believe what they were seeing.

At the edge of the forest, no more than thirty meters away, a creature sat hunched on the ground with its back to them. Its skin, or fur, or hair, was completely black, which made its features difficult to distinguish in the shade of the trees. Something held its interest, and it sat hunched over.

"I don't think it's noticed us yet," Molly said.

They approached slowly, poles ready, loops dangling and twitching loosely. As they drew nearer the animal made no attempt to move. Its chest rose and fell with each breath. At least it appeared to be breathing, although it was difficult to make out. It was black save for a few barely perceptible spots like spilled red wine, but that was not quite right either. It seemed to have no color at all. Neither light nor shadow could touch it. What they saw of its skull bore a long snout resembling that of a wolf, but much longer and completely hairless save for a scraggly mane. Two holes suggested ear canals. Hints of white teeth showed under its lips. Blunt spines protruded from its back and the lower parts of its chest as if the bones themselves had penetrated the skin. It had terrible sharp claws. In shape, it resembled a gangly and extremely emaciated human. It hunkered there over its prey, a formless nothing.

"Damn it's ugly," Tommy said.

"It's starving," Molly whispered.

"How did the colonists miss it?" Beau asked.

"Maybe it doubled back on them," Molly said and motioned the others forward.

Gently and slowly, Molly and Tommy slipped the loop of their poles over the animal's snout and head, then with a nod to each other sinched them tight.

The apoch erupted with furious energy. It lunged, pulling Tommy and Molly to the ground.

"Beau!" Molly shouted.

Beau ran forward to loop the apoch's head, but it thrashed so violently he only managed to beat it about the head and shoulders. This made it angry. The apoch's jaws clamped down, vice-like, on the pole. Beau pulled, but it held fast and unmoving. Tommy and Molly stood up and pulled with all their might. The apoch planted its feet in the ground, then took one step back, then another, dragging them against their will.

"It's too strong!" Molly said.

The apoch gripped the poles tightly and pulled its arms close, then it exploded in a great leap that carried the three of them bodily into the air. They let go and fell to the ground with a thud. The apoch landed near the trees. It spit out Beau's pole with disdain and pulled its lips back over its teeth in a terrible and toothy snarl before its shuddered and disappeared before their eyes except for the poles that still hung around its neck. They watched the poles bounce off into the forest still around its neck, banging off trees and bushes as it carried on at a terrific pace, breaking branches as it went.

"I think we underestimated it," Molly said. Beau and Tommy looked at her incredulously.

"We'll never catch it like this," Tommy said.

"We have to hurry. The colonists are sure to have spotted it by now. If we don't beat them, they'll kill it," she said.

"Guagh!" Beau cried, scrambling backwards.

"What is it?" Molly said, rushing to see if he was okay.

"It's dead," Beau said. He had landed next to the carcass of the apoch's prey.

"I don't think it's dead," Molly said.

They looked again. Indeed, although the animal's skin was pulled back to reveal the muscle tissue beneath, its chest still rose and fell in tortured breaths. Tommy stomped down hard and crushed the animal's head under his boot. There was a sickening crunch, and it was still.

"What'd you do that for?" Beau said, alarmed.

"It was the best thing to do," Tommy said.

Molly too looked disturbed at what Tommy had done but said, "We don't have time to argue. We need more help."

Joon-baek and Waters turned at the sound of six tromping boots approaching. Molly, Beau, and Tommy ran up and stopped with their hands on their knees, gasping at the effort.

"I take it you were unsuccessful?" Joon-baek said.

Their breathing slowed, and they explained their confrontation with the apoch and how they had lost it.

"There's no way we can capture it by hand," Beau said. "That thing lifted all three of us off the ground like we were ragdolls."

"We would need military exosuits at least. And even then, I'm not sure we could handle it," Tommy said.

"How do the colonists deal with these things then?" Waters asked.

"They don't. They just kill it," Beau said.

"We need something much, much stronger and tougher," Tommy said.

"Tough like the rover?" Joon-baek offered.

"Exactly," Tommy said.

"What about the Armatron?" Joon-baek suggested.

That caught them by surprise. "That might just do it," Molly said.

"We don't have much time," Beau said. "If we don't hurry, the colonists will get there first."

"Even with the rover, how are you going to catch it?" Waters said.

"Beau, can you link one of your drones to the glasses?" Joon-baek said.

Beau thought for a moment. "Probably. But the drones just have standard cameras. You could see what the drone sees, but you wouldn't get the information the glasses give."

"I have an idea," Joon-baek said. He walked over to a crate and held up a roll of grey tape.

Minutes later, one of Beau's drones ascended into the sky, a pair of the colonist's glasses duct-taped over the camera lens. Beau watched the feed on his phone from the passenger seat. Molly drove. Tommy and Waters watched anxiously, leaning forward with their hands on the front seats to get a better view. Joon-baek stood in the hatch ready at the Armatron's controls.

"There it is," Beau said.

The feed showed a pulsing dot where the glasses had identified an anomaly. They all leaned over his phone. The rover lurched as Molly bent to see too.

"Sorry," she said, righting its course.

"It doesn't look like it's moving, Tommy said.

"Steer that way, Molly," Beau said, pointing to a break in the trees.

"Why would it have stopped?" Waters asked.

As the rover plowed into a clearing, they saw why. The poles around the apoch's neck had become lodged in the branches of a tree at the far end of the clearing. The apoch dangled three meters above the ground, stuck fast. It had one of the poles in its mouth and appeared to be trying to bite through the metal. It pawed and clawed at the cables that held its neck, even using its hind legs to rake at the restraints. It thrashed against the poles, heedless of injuring itself.

"We have to hurry. It'll suffocate!" Molly said.

"Back the rover up," Joon-baek called down from the hatch.

Molly swung the rover around. When the apoch saw them, it began thrashing even more violently. They could not believe its strength. The enormous trees shuddered. Leaves and twigs, even branches pelted the top of the rover as they fell, dislodged by the apoch's protestations.

"If we don't hurry, the poles will snap," Beau said.

"You'll have a different reason to hurry in about two seconds," Tommy said, pointing through the rover's front windshield.

A dozen arkouda with colonists on their backs burst into the clearing. Three colonists slid off the beasts in a clammer and charged toward the apoch. The others surrounded the clearing, staying mounted on the arkouda.

"I've almost got it," Joon-baek said.

He swung the Armatron around toward the apoch. The animal twisted and kicked violently, knocking the rover itself sideways as it struck the arm. It flailed left, then right. A lance sailed past the Armatron and lodged deep in the tree, just missing the apoch.

"That's what those things really are?" Beau said.

"You didn't think they were going to beat it up with sticks, did you?" Tommy quipped.

Then Joon-baek, reading the apoch's movements, ducked the arm under a kick and deftly grabbed the apoch around the chest as it swung left again. Joon-baek lifted it upward with the arm, freeing it from the branches. The apoch pushed down against the Armatron's grip and writhed, shaking the whole rover.

"It's going to break the arm!" Waters shouted.

"It won't. I can hold it," Joon-baek yelled.

"It's slipping!" Beau said, alarmed.

Joon-baek lowered the apoch onto the roof of the rover behind them, holding it tight in the grip of the Armatron. Another lance sailed past them over the rover. Joon-baek ducked as a third lance flew past and sliced a deep gash across the apoch's face. Something white and viscous like wax flowed from the wound. The creature turned toward the throw and screamed. Everyone covered their ears, its cry filling them with fear and anguish as if for a moment they too felt its pain. Joon-baek had to fight the urge to let go of the Armatron's controls.

"Whoa whoa whoa!" Waters shouted, climbing through the hatch past Joon-baek. He stood on the rover's roof with his arms spread wide between the colonists and Joon-baek. "What the hell do you think you're doing?!"

The apoch scratched and raked at the Armatron; it seemed to be tiring and the Armatron held fast.

Jonathan rode up beside the rover on an arkouda. He brandished a lance, ready to throw. Waters moved between him and the apoch. "Move, Director!" Jonathan shouted, a fire in his eyes. "You endanger us all."

"Lower your spear, colonist," Waters shouted back. "How dare you threaten us! How dare you threaten a MFASA mission!"

The other colonists surrounded the rover, some mounted, some on foot, all shouting. Waters shifted left and right trying to shield the creature, but all too aware that if the colonists chose to attack there was nothing he could do.

"Enough!" came a booming voice that shook the clearing.

Instantly the colonists quieted and backed away. Even Waters lowered his arms at the command. Jonathan too backed away, but kept his eyes on Waters, still seething. The mayor rode up, his lance unsheathed and propped on his foot.

"They've captured the apoch. It's not going anywhere," the mayor said. "Tell us, Director: what is it that you intend to do?"

Waters stood struck dumb for a moment. "We…"

"Study, Mister Mayor. We intend study, nothing more," Molly said climbing up through the hatch.

The mayor seemed surprised at her appearance. The colonists softened and back away farther.

"Think, mayor. Think, my friends, what we could learn and share together through study. How much we could gain and understand. Will you let us take this opportunity? You have been generous to us thus far, through your gifts, allowing us to stay in the valley, and letting us set up our clinic outside your city, though we know you do not consider us friends. Do not let your welcome and generosity end here. Please, allow us this request."

The mayor was astonished. "You wish to study this thing? You know what it is…"

"I know, Mayor," Molly said.

"And you believe there is something to be learned still," he asked.

"I do," Molly said.

He considered Molly carefully. It took only a few moments, but time seemed to wear on endlessly as they stood in opposition.

"Very well. We will allow this. For you, Molly. Because it is you who asked," he said.

Waters and Molly sighed with relief. Molly muttered her thanks and turned to climb back into the rover. Beau stood up to help Molly back inside and the apoch locked eyes with him. It ceased its struggles, seemed to relax, and sat down, still secure in the Armatron. It folded its front arms across the metal arm and let its head come to rest, still staring at Beau.

Waters climbed back into the rover. "Holy hell," he said and wiped his brow.

"Offensive language," Joon-baek called down.

"It's wounded. We need to get back to camp soon," Molly said.

"I wouldn't get too close," Tommy cautioned.

"I don't think you need to worry about that from anyone," Beau said and plopped down on one of the benches.

"I think it likes you," Joon-baek said.

"That's not funny," Beau replied.

The missionaries arrived at camp with an escort of colonists, and within a few minutes of arriving, together they finished securing the enclosure.

"Go ahead, June Bug," Waters said. Then he turned to the others, "As soon as he releases it, lock the door."

Joon-baek maneuvered the apoch through the enclosure door, dropped it, and quickly withdrew the Armatron. The missionaries practically fell over each other trying to get the door closed. Waters swiped his phone over the panel and with a click it locked. Despite their caution, the apoch rested calmly inside the enclosure, and stared at the missionaries.

"Are you sure this can hold it?" Beau asked, testing that the door was really closed.

"It should. The documentation says it's rated for any weather on Earth," Waters answered. "If it can withstand a hurricane, it should withstand an animal."

"This is like nothing from Earth though," Tommy said, who had collected his rifle and held it with the butt pressed into his shoulder, muzzle down; safe, but ready to use at a moment's notice.

"Did it just smile?" Beau asked.

"Don't be silly, Beau," Waters said. "Animals don't smile."

CHAPTER EIGHTEEN

THE CLINIC

The medical clinic sat empty except for its proprietors. It often sat empty. The result was a pair of listless, bored missionaries. A feeling that they were not doing their jobs plagued Jazzy and Waters. Yet they were unwilling to adjust for fear that MFASA would see improvisation as contributing to failure should the situation worsen. Better the mediocrity of familiarity than the unknown.

Today was no different, except that the days were becoming hot. The PTFE shelter was good at keeping the elements out, which was part of the problem. The only air movement came from the zippered flap at the entrance. However, without an outlet, the air inside the shelter tended to stagnate even with the flap open. Behind the privacy screen that separated Waters's office in front from Jazzy's clinic in back there was even less air movement. This tended to bring the pair into close proximity throughout the loathsome days. As soon as the sun hit the shelter, she sought respite closer to the door, in Waters's office space.

Today, she stood in the shelter door, arms crossed, and watched the colonists pass. "When is our next report due?" she asked.

Waters was at his desk reviewing their mission training as he had done every day for weeks. He spun in his chair to face her.

"It's past due. MFASA wanted weekly updates. We have not been able to provide an update since we left the spaceport. The atmospheric interference is too strong here for us to contact Polus Station, let alone obtain a LiFi signal to report directly to MFASA. Why do you ask?"

Jazzy stood in the doorway, not moving, not really looking at anything, and not answering either. She was silent long enough that Waters turned back to his desk.

"How many times are you going to review our training and mission parameters before you start to implement them?" she said.

"What was that?" Waters asked, spinning his chair around again.

"When are you going to stop flicking through our training and actually put everything that we were taught into practice," she said, this time turning to face him, her arms on her hips. "Are you this mission's Director or not?"

Waters stared for a second. "You know very well that I am the Director. And you also know that these colonists have been intractable. How many have come to see us? A half dozen at most? How many have come to your clinic, Doctor Bebe?"

Jazzy shifted on the balls of her feet and stomped back behind the curtain to her clinic, drawing it sharply after. Waters turned back to his desk just in time for the curtain to fly open as Jazzy emerged again. "You realize that when the LiFi window opens I will have no choice but to report to MFASA and the Administration the situation here as I see it."

"What do you think my role is? I will be doing the same. I'll report on the progress of each missionary, including the status of our clinic. What were your target numbers again?"

"Who do you think is going to have credibility when they report?"

"What are you implying? I am the Director of this mission. It is my responsibility to make the report. I expect the missionaries to confine their communication to the areas for which they are responsible. And what about your responsibility? We all have specific tasks; yours is to treat patients. How many have you seen so far?"

"I could get better numbers than you in a second."

"I'd like to see you try for once. You've had months to get someone in the clinic. Anyone. And how has that gone for you?"

"I'll bet my numbers will be better than your numbers."

"You're on."

They both stomped out of the clinic, Jazzy to the gate and Waters down the hill back to camp. He needed to strategize. She may have been out of line, but she was right. He had to show some measure of success before their LiFi window opened, even if it just meant increasing his number of contacts.

Waters was breathing heavily when he arrived and felt dizzy. In his anger he had forgotten that, as the colonists liked to remind them, he was still not accustomed to the moon's atmosphere. He had jogged too quickly down the hill in the heat of the day. He moved into the shadow of one of the shelters and rested his head on a water purifier. Taking a drink, he fanned himself with his hand and wiped the sweat from his brow. After a few minutes he felt comfortable again. The last thing he wanted was to suffer heat stroke and need to have Jazzy treat him. He had to show that he was a strong director. He walked to the shelter he shared with Jazzy and resented it. He thought of the rover, which sat parked in the shade, but resented that too. He remembered it as a place where he and Jazzy had been too close together for too long, a space like what the clinic was now becoming.

Not really knowing where to begin, he began to walk. He passed Joon-baek working outside his shelter. Most days Tommy would be sitting with his feet kicked up on a crate next to Joon-baek, but he was nowhere to be seen for once. Joon-baek had yet to succeed in cultivating a vine, let alone growing one of the fruits, but he still worked happily and diligently. He had collected and propagated several other species. The bandages on his hands and fingers testified to fresh injuries from recent work; the Polus fruit, vitis, which they all ate now, would heal him by the afternoon.

Molly was in camp too working at a bench opposite Joon-baek.

"Hi, Alex," she said as he approached.

"Good morning, Molly," he said. "What're you working on?"

"The apoch is fascinating. June Bug's been helping me with the research."

"She's not kidding," Joon-baek said, leaving his plants behind for once to join them. "I know I think everything is fascinating, but this really is. You know how the colonists have a mode on their glasses? The one we used to track the apoch?" Joon-baek said.

"Of course."

"Well, we think they use it almost exclusively to track apochs," Molly said.

"Wasn't it for gravitational anomalies?" Waters asked.

"Yes, but that's part of what's fascinating. We think the apoch has some measure of control over gravity itself," Molly continued. "That's why it can be so hard to see. It doesn't just camouflage itself or have chromatophores like a chameleon; it absorbs and bends light, even feeds on it. Its physiology is different from anything we know."

"We think it may actually 'jump' using its control of gravity. That's what creates the distortions, and why it's so strong and fast," Joon-baek said.

"It makes its own wormholes?"

"Possibly."

"So, if it's not 'bending the light' or 'jumping,' the glasses wouldn't be able to spot it," Waters said.

"Probably not," Joon-baek said.

"Doesn't that mean it could jump out of the pen?" Waters asked.

Molly and Joon-baek looked at each other uncomfortably, and Molly said, "We're not sure why it hasn't already. The pen might act like a kind of Tesla cage and prevent it from leaving, but truthfully we just don't know enough to say."

"If it hasn't left on its own then either it can't leave or it wants to stay," Waters said.

"That's plausible," Joon-baek said. "I think we should still take precautions, maybe ask Tommy to keep his rifle handy."

"That's not a bad idea, but I think we're probably safe. The chase and capture, and the colonists' hunt, probably agitated it. It's just an animal, remember. If it feels safe and well kept, it doesn't pose a threat. Have you seen Beau?" Waters finished.

"Not today. He must be off shooting video," Molly said.

"Good. I hope his edits are ready to transmit when the LiFi opens up. His last wildlife film was fantastic."

"It really was," Joon-baek said.

"The more success you all have, the better our report to MFASA will be," Waters said.

Walking past the shelters, Waters followed a path through the trees. It led to the clearing with the apoch's pen. It was quiet there. The clearing lacked the valley's characteristic birdsong and buzz of insects. The colonists were extremely hesitant to let them keep the apoch for study. "It is only because the knowledge you gain may yet help us that will we allow this," the mayor had said. That mayor. The colonists had absolutely refused to provide them an animal as food for the poor creature, even a deceased one. It ignored the food they gave it, only playing with the fish and shrimp they netted in the nearby river. It did not bother with its fodder at all. It had recovered from the stress and wounds of its capture but still looked just as emaciated. Despite its refusal to eat, it looked no different or worse for wear. "Its physiology is different from what we know," Molly had said.

Waters noted a couple of small animals, skiouros the colonists called them, who must have wandered too close and been caught. Their skinned carcasses lay on the floor, but the apoch had not eaten the meat. The sight of the dead animals hurt Waters, but he reflected it was simply the way of nature. Humans knew better; animals did not.

The apoch sat on its haunches in the center of the pen, intent on something as Waters approached. Waters turned, following the apoch's line of sight and flinched. Beau sat on a crate just outside the apoch's reach, but close enough to observe the creature. He was sitting so still that Waters had not seen him.

"Oh, you startled me," Waters said. "I thought you would be off filming."

Beau did not answer.

"Mind if I stay a while?"

He dragged an empty crate next to Beau's. He turned and was

surprised to see that the apoch had moved right up against the wall of the pen while his back was turned. It was so close he could hear it breathe. The air from its long snout blew against the walls of the pen as its bony chest rose and fell. It stared at him, black eyes unblinking, limbs folded against its sides. Waters had to fight the urge to stare back.

"On second thought, I think I'll find something else to do. You alright?" he asked Beau.

Beau nodded. It was barely perceptible, but still a nod. "I'm fine, Alex. More than fine. I don't think I've been better this entire mission. You know, I really like this guy. I'm glad we didn't let the colonists kill it. Did you know that in the absence of Higher Authority, the self determines what is moral?" he said, never taking his eyes off the apoch.

"That's what you've been thinking about? That's why we have the Administration," Waters said. "We are certain of what is right."

"That thinking is too narrow, Alex. Like the city gate, it leaves much out," Beau said. "What if there were no Administration? What if the Administration were not there to pass judgement? What if the Administration never knew someone's actions? What if no one ever knew?"

"Isn't that why we have a conscience?"

"The conscience is a construct of Higher Authority's influence and not native to the self. It only makes sense for the self to do what's best for the self."

"This conversation's a bit more philosophical than I'm in the mood for right now," Waters said. "I need to get back to work. I'll see you later. Don't spend all your time here, okay? We have a mission to carry out."

Waters avoided Jazzy's clinic the rest of the day and the next morning, but out of obligation he made his way up the hill late in the afternoon. He was surprised to see a colonist leaving the clinic, and a group of colonists milling around outside in the plaza. There were so many that they had set up shade sails on the columns. Despite the presence of so many people, no one else seemed to be entering the clinic.

"Good afternoon, Director Waters," one of the colonists said from the shade with a tip of his hat as Waters passed. Waters nodded in acknowledgement and entered the shelter to see the screen pulled aside and Jazzy sitting there. She leaned against a table and rubbed her forehead. She looked exhausted.

"It looks like you had a patient," Waters said.

"I've had sixteen patients," Jazzy replied.

"Sixteen!? That's fantastic!" Waters said. "At last, a result that we can show in our report."

"Is it? Is it fantastic?" Jazzy asked with frustration.

"What do you mean? That's more than twice as many patients as we've had in all the months up 'til now."

Jazzy looked up, exasperated. "Not one of them needed any treatment. From old to young, every one of them is the picture of health. They weren't here for treatment."

"Did you examine them?"

"Every one."

"And none of them needed treatment?"

"Not a one."

"Then why on Earth were they here?"

"I have heard about 'Jesus' more today than in my entire life, including the required MFASA course on comparative religions."

"You mean they were here to convert you."

"That's exactly why they were here. Every one of them sat patiently through my exam, babbling all the while, asking if I had read the gospels. Of course, I have not. Everyone knows it's on the DID's cautionary list. I wouldn't touch that book if you bashed me in the head with it," she said, removing a pair of latex exam gloves and tossing them into a waste basket with more force than was necessary. "And where were you? How was I supposed to handle a mob of colonist proselytizers? You were supposed to be here to do your job. We're supposed to be educating them, Alex!"

Waters and Jazzy narrowed their eyes, but they were spared another argument when Tommy burst in.

"The LiFi is working!"

CHAPTER NINETEEN

SEE YOU ALL AGAIN SOMETIME

The camp was quiet that evening. The missionaries waited patiently for their turns to use the LiFi. There were two places they could access the LiFi: the rover's transmitter and a terminal in the shelter that housed their equipment. Waters and Jazzy claimed the rover for making their reports to MFASA and eyed each other as they swapped places. Beau noted the tense looks they exchanged as he waited.

The others stood in line outside the equipment shelter for privacy's sake. Beau and Joon-baek agreed to let Molly go first. Joon-baek waited in front of Beau; Tommy had smartly taken his turn before he announced the LiFi's availability and had no further need of it. He had his arm elbow-deep in the engine compartment of one of the colonists' flyers.

"They just gave that thing to you?" Beau asked to pass the time while he waited his turn.

Tommy pulled hard and almost fell backward as something broke off in the compartment. He grinned at Beau's comment and held up a tarnished and scored bolt, which he unceremoniously tossed over his shoulder.

"It's an older model. It had apparently been sitting for years. No one was using it, so I asked if I could have it," Tommy replied.

"It was that simple?" Beau asked.

Tommy shrugged and volunteered nothing further.

Beau had the feeling it had not been that simple, but Tommy was not saying. No colonists had come looking for it at any rate. He turned his attention back to waiting. Beau had volunteered to go last. He did not really have anyone he needed to talk to. Both of his parents had passed a few years ago, and his best friends were with him on the mission. He mostly hoped to use his bandwidth to catch up on the news and transmit his edited footage to MFASA.

Molly's turn ended, but Beau and Joon-baek hardly noticed her leave because Waters walked up looking like he had taken a beating.

"It didn't go well?" Beau asked as Joon-baek took his turn.

"It did not," Waters said. "MFASA and Interim Director Shepherd are 'disappointed at the lack of progress the mission team has shown toward its goals.'"

"Ouch," Beau said.

"No kidding. I'm held responsible as mission director. If we can't increase our contact ratios, MFASA will move the mission to phase II. That means on-site supplemental education and remediation, possibly relocation for the colonists. It'll be worse for me. That could mean the end of my position with the Administration."

"I'm sorry, Alex."

Waters brushed off Beau's condolences with a wave of his hand. "I should have known better. The metrics MFASA gave me were impossible. No one has ever achieved one hundred percent in any colony anywhere. It was foolish of me to attempt to achieve all the optional objectives as well. You might suspect MFASA designs the missions to fail as an excuse to proceed to the next phase sooner."

"But what about all of us?"

"Are you kidding? You all were the best part of my report. You guys have been great: Joon-baek, you, Molly. Molly's cataloguing Polus's fauna, and has shown no sign of deviation from her denunciation, not to mention our success with the apoch. Without you and especially her work, my entire report would have been a disaster. The Administration was quite pleased about that at least. Thank you for what you did, for keeping an eye on her."

"But what about you?"

Waters did not seem upset, but contemplative. "Don't worry about me, Beau."

Waters walked away and Beau did not have a chance to ask more questions, as Joon-baek emerged from the shelter looking relieved, and it was Beau's turn.

The next day Beau awoke and went about his usual morning routine. His partition of the shelter was looking untidy. He had a pile of dirty clothing on the floor that needed to be washed, and another pile of clean laundry that needed to be folded and put away. He selected a jumpsuit from the clean pile. Molly did not seem to mind his mess so long as the common area was clean. He decided to clean up anyway. She must have gotten an early start because she was not around. "Maybe I'll shoot some B footage today, visit the apoch again," he said to himself as he worked. He finished tidying, grabbed a drone, and headed out.

It was a long day. Beau did not return to camp until evening. He found Waters almost frantic. Joon-baek, Tommy, and even Jazzy were searching the camp.

"Beau, I'm glad you're here. Have you seen Molly?" Waters asked him.

"What? Why? No. I've been filming all day," Beau said.

"No one has seen her. When do you last remember seeing her?" Waters said.

"Yesterday when we were taking turns on the LiFi, I think," Beau responded.

"Was she home last night?" Waters asked.

"Yes—wait. Now that I think about it, I don't remember seeing her last night. Did you check her room?"

"We did," Waters said.

Beau and Waters entered the shelter and peeked behind the partition that separated Molly's room from the common area. "All her stuff is still here. We can't call her phone either," Waters said.

"She hardly uses her phone anyway," Beau said.

Jazzy walked into the shelter. "No one's found her yet."

"I wouldn't worry about it," Beau said. "She's probably off doing her research. You know how the signals are here. She'll probably show up tonight. What's that?" Beau said, spotting a tablet on her bed. It flashed a notification indicating she had a message. "It's unlocked," Beau said, picking it up. Tapping the notification, a message popped up. It was from Molly herself.

"It looks like she recorded a log recently," Beau said.

"But why send it to herself? Hit play," Waters said.

Molly's face filled the screen, and she began to speak. "Beau, I think you're probably the one who will find this. I'm sorry. I've decided to leave the mission. By the time you find this I'll already be with the colonists in the city."

"How the hell could she get in the city?" Jazzy said.

Molly's recording continued, "I made a mistake. I should never have agreed to come on the mission. I should never have done what I did. I should have defended my family and defended my faith." She grew tearful as the message continued. "The only thing for me to do now is ask everyone to forgive me—my parents, my brother, the colonists, the other missionaries, and you. I hope you can forgive me, and I hope that you understand. At least you'll have the shelter to yourself now. Goodbye, Beau. Say goodbye to everyone else for me. I hope I get to see you all again sometime."

The message ended.

"It looks like she recorded it in her room. The time stamp is from last night," Beau said.

"No," Waters said. "She was the best thing this mission had going."

"Speak for yourself. I've been able to report multiple successful contacts," Jazzy said.

Waters ignored her. He pushed the door to the partition aside and walked out with a vacant look on his face.

Jazzy watched him go and gave Beau a look. "Some director," she said.

"He's doing the best he can with a difficult situation," Beau said.

"Psh," she said, and walked out herself.

Beau decided to go find Waters.

Beau wandered aimlessly because he had no notion of where Waters would go. Jazzy may have reported successful contacts to the Administration, but Beau was certain that she had mischaracterized her interactions with the colonists; they all did, to an extent. He knew she had not actually administered any treatment. On the contrary, based on her own accounts, the colonists had attempted to treat her, in their own way. With an unsuccessful report and now Molly gone, the mission appeared to be collapsing around Waters. They would need a breakthrough and a lot of luck to turn things around. Jazzy was sure to take advantage of the situation as well. Her relationship with Waters was collapsing, and he needed to be there for her too. As a friend, of course. Anything else, well, he would see what happened. Waters would need to report that Molly had absconded, and the Administration would be furious. He was the director. He would be held responsible. Fortunately, or unfortunately, the LiFi window had closed, and they did not know when it would open again. Waters had some time; they had some time, but Beau did not know how long.

Beau's feet carried him to the apoch's pen. He took his seat on the crate where Waters had found him last time. He adjusted and turned to find the apoch staring at him from the other side of the wall.

"Still using that trick, are you?" he said. Beau sat, and thoughts began to fill his head, thoughts he had had before, but now they arose spontaneously, almost as if he had not willed them.

You know why she left, don't you? She went to be with them. With them! She is one of them. She believes in Him. *You've known this. Against all she knows, against the mission and what the Administration teaches, she's still a Christian.*

And why shouldn't she still be? What they did to her was terrible. What they did to her family.

This is better for you. Less of a distraction. You don't have to be her keeper any longer. Waters is falling apart. His directorship, his relationship. Now's your opportunity.

I shouldn't take what was his though.

And why not? Jazzy is not property; women are not property. Isn't that what the Administration teaches? She can choose you if she wants. In the same way, the directorship is not his; it is given by the Administration and can be taken by the Administration...and given to whom they choose, for Their Glory.

But he's a friend. It wouldn't be right.

Oh, my friend. Don't you see yet? None of that matters. Nothing at all matters. Your ideas of morality, what are they for? What consequence would you suffer for breaking them?

I would hurt them. I could lose standing with the Administration.

Only if they found out. Don't you see? You don't believe in God, do you?

Of course not.

Then why worry about consequences if your execution is sound and your path clear? If no one will find out, why worry? All that matters is what you can get away with. Jazzy could be yours. A directorship could be yours, maybe even the directorship of MFASA.

Impossible.

Then the presidency.

No.

It's happened before. You know this. Don't you see? Can't you see? Do not let sentimentality bind you. Go. Do. Achieve. All you desire can be yours if only you are willing. This life is all you have so make the most of it, isn't that what they say? Why waste it quivering and quavering over morality? Those are just rules that keep others in power. Stop worrying about how when you could simply do.

"What are you doing here?" Jazzy asked as the mayor, Patience, Ai, and Jonathan galloped up to the camp on arkouda. They dismounted quickly. Waters came out of the shelter. He had to watch and re-watch Molly's message yet again. He could not understand but kept watching it anyway. Joon-baek put down what he was doing. Tommy stepped away from his machine and walked over to the group.

"We came to warn you," the mayor said. "A storm is coming." Tommy, Joon-baek, and Waters tensed up immediately. They remembered the storm at the space port too well and were in no mood to repeat the experience. "A storm is coming," continued the Mayor, "and you must take shelter."

"Then let us in the city," Jazzy said.

"That's not possible," Jonathan said.

"Then we do not need your help," Jazzy replied.

"I think we should take whatever help they're offering," Joon-baek said.

"Hush!" Jazzy said.

"Director Waters?" the mayor asked.

"He's preoccupied, unable to act just now, and you know very well why. I'm the deputy of this mission, and the Administration and MFASA have empowered me to take action and make decisions for the mission."

Waters did not argue but let her proceed.

Patience dismounted her arkouda and walked to the team with her arms extended forward in a conciliatory gesture. "Please, let us help you. You need to come with us. We cannot let you in the city, but we can shelter you elsewhere in the valley where the storm will not harm you."

"The best way to shelter us would be in the safety of the city," Jazzy said.

"We told you that is not possible," Jonathan said sharply. "Don't be fools."

Waters was already upset at Molly's departure. The prospect of another great storm raised an alarm inside of him. Jonathan's tone with Jazzy, a member of his team, spurred him at last. "Don't speak to her like that. You've no right to take a sharp tone with her. She's a doctor. She deserves your respect."

"The only way through a head so dense is with a sharp tool," Jonathan replied.

Waters seethed, but before he could reply, the mayor interjected.

"Enough, Jonathan!" the mayor said. "Doctor Bebe, I understand your trepidation. I even understand that you do not understand. But this is not a time for arguments and rivalries. Eventually you might choose to enter the city, but that time is not now. Now we need to get you all to shelter for your safety. Please."

"Why does everything have to be on your terms, mayor?" Jazzy said. "We brought ourselves here. We survived one storm unharmed; we can survive another. We don't need your help."

"Jazzy," Joon-baek said calmly, attempting to reason with her. "Remember the last time? You lost everything."

"I urge you to come with us. We will not force you, but you need to know this is serious. You are not accustomed to this planet, and you are not prepared to weather a storm. For the last time, will you let us give you shelter?" Patience pled.

"I will not," Jazzy said, ignoring both Joon-baek and the colonists' pleas.

The mayor looked to Waters, who knew deep down that the smarter move was to go with the colonists, but just then he did not feel like giving them the satisfaction. Not after Molly had left, and for them no less. Not after being reprimanded, largely due to their intractability. His apathy and complacence faded, replaced with anger. "I'll stay with my team."

"I need to stay with the mission," Joon-baek said with resignation when the mayor looked to him.

"Tommy?"

"These guys may be out of their minds, but part of my job is to try and keep them safe. I need to stay."

"Then we have done what we ought. It was in our power to help and you refused. We pray that no harm may come to you, but neither are we responsible for anything that may befall you. Though we leave, our prayers stay with you," the mayor said.

"No thank you," Jazzy called as they departed.

Patience was the last to leave. She kept turning to see whether one of them might change their minds until she passed out of sight.

"Now what?" Tommy asked.

The storm ripped the shelter right from its base where stakes anchored it to the ground and cast it into the night where none could see, leaving three missionaries and one marine staring at the elements, pelted by rain and hail alike, both of which fell mercilessly on and about their backs and heads. They stood frantic with panic for a few moments amidst a surreal display. The skeleton of the poles that had once supported the PTFE roof was all that remained, their living quarters exposed and on display, a diorama of vainglory open to Polus's mockery. As one and without a word, they ran for the trees, waving their hands and arms above their heads in a futile attempt to fend off the hail.

"Over here!" Tommy shouted, barely heard above the wind.

Through the sheen Tommy waved his arms, beckoning them to a fallen tree. Its enormous trunk offered protection at least from the watery elements, if not the wind. Tommy pulled a glowstick from one of his pockets and ignited it with a snap. Under its illumination they saw that the tree had fallen in front of a rocky outcrop, and they moved deeper under its shelter. It was dry at least, though they all began to shiver from the wet and cold.

They huddled together for warmth, as Tommy attempted to light a fire. Although the outcrop protected them from the rain and hail, the wind would have none of it and he could keep no flame alight. After a few minutes of fruitless fighting against the wind and his own shivering hands, he gave up and joined the others. They encircled their arms, forming a small pocket of warmth instinctively with their backs to the outside. The glowstick provided a modicum of comfort if not heat.

Then all at once the wind stopped and a musty but pleasant smell filled the air. They could hear the wind blowing still, now as if it were at a distance. Tommy tried again and at last got a fire going, and they took turns casting twigs and dried needles and leaves into the flames. Eventually it grew to a small but warm fire. Without the chill of the wind and a fire at last lit, they began to stop shivering. First Jazzy, then Joon-baek finally lay down on the dirt floor and fell asleep. Waters was determined to stay awake, but as the adrenaline drained from his system, he found that his eyelids weighed on him more and more and he was unable to resist sleep.

The light of day suddenly shone beneath the overhang and Waters awoke. Through blinking eyes, he saw Tommy slap the sides of a Polus bear as it rose from where it had spent the night.

Tommy looked back toward him and answered a question he never asked. "There were three of them. They lay in front of the log and blocked the wind. If it weren't for them, we might have caught hypothermia, even died."

This was the most somber Waters had seen Tommy yet. He seemed to be taking something very seriously for once. The Polus bears moved away as a group, though not too far. Tommy stood watching them with a contemplative look.

Joon-baek and Jazzy soon awoke as well.

"Has anyone seen Beau?" Waters asked.

They all shook their heads.

Tommy, Waters, Jazzy, and Joon-baek made their way back to camp. As they broke through the trees they saw Beau at last, still so soaking wet that his hair and clothing clung to his body, giving him a pitiful thin appearance. He stood alone in what had been their camp, now a complete loss. The wind and storm had carried away everything or scattered its contents across the face of the moon. One of the shelters was bodily gone with no evidence it had been there at all save an imprint of packed dirt and flattened grass.

The rover, despite the sturdy machine that it was, had been blown on its side. Its external equipment, including the Armatron and communication antennae, was misshapen and bent out of order. Blessedly,

Joon-baek and Tommy's shelter was mostly untouched except for some tears in the fabric.

Jazzy went to see that Beau was alright while Tommy, Joon-baek, and Waters moved through the camp, picking up bits of equipment and trying to find what they could salvage. After a few minutes Jazzy turned from Beau and began picking through the wreckage with the others. Waters stopped and stared, seemingly lost in some endless depth from which only he could choose to return. Beau found the drone he had used to record so much of their mission, or what was left of it. Its electronic guts lay strewn out in a line. The storm had smashed it against something, or something had smashed against it, leaving it unusable. He did not even care to think of what had happened to the rest of his footage. He assumed it was a total loss.

Waters emerged from his trance at last. "Gather the scrap PTFE cloth from the base of that shelter. We can use it to repair the holes in Tommy and Joon-baek's shelter. Beau, you and I will move in with them.

"What about Jazzy?" Beau asked.

"After we right it, Jazzy can have the rover to herself as the last remaining woman on the mission."

Jazzy nodded as a silent acknowledgement passed between her and Waters. Beau dropped his broken drone, and his face flushed a little.

"We're continuing the mission?" Joon-baek asked.

"Of course, we're continuing the mission," Waters said.

They righted the rover with the help of the colonists and some arkouda, then spent the next several days scouring the valley and hills trying to recover what they could. It was depressing and difficult. At the same time, Waters thought it was nice to work together for a change. Except for Jazzy. Her clinic had remained mostly intact, except for some holes in the fabric, protected by its proximity to the city wall. She retreated to the interior of the clinic, alone except for Beau who occasionally visited, and did not rejoin the group until night when she went to sleep in the rover by herself. It took nearly two weeks to scour the valley sufficiently for them to be satisfied they had recovered as much as they could, which was not much: just a few empty crates and some miscellaneous equipment. Everything else was simply gone, torn to pieces by the storm or scattered across the moon. The last thing they had which remained intact was the apoch pen. Its walls had withstood the storm.

"Probably because the metal mesh allowed the wind to pass through rather than pushing it over," Joon-baek mused.

The colonists helped, which made the work both easier and more difficult. Most of the colonists were kind enough, but Jonathan enjoyed reminding them that they could have been safe if they had only listened. In the end it did not matter, because the missionaries received the care they needed. As only Tommy and Joon-baek still had their clothing and personal items, the colonist provided clothing for Waters, Beau, and Jazzy, and other items from the city as well. Waters expressed begrudging gratitude for their assistance but refused to accept what material goods they offered and went about instead in an environmental suit from the rover, one of the last pieces of clothing native to the mission that he still possessed. Beau accepted their gifts but following Waters's example, persisted in wearing his mission jumpsuit.

"It would not be fitting for the director of a MFASA mission to subordinate himself to the very people he came to educate," Waters reasoned.

CHAPTER TWENTY

CHUNKING TWIGS

Waters lay in the shelter, perturbed but unmotivated to do anything about it. The breeze had died down with the heat of the day, and the open door of the PTFE shelter he now shared with Tommy, Beau, and Joon-baek listed gently. Weeks had passed since the storm destroyed their camp. Summer on Polus IV was at its height.

Beau emerged from his small partition in the shelter. Despite the summer heat and sun, he was pale. His face had grown lined and dusky. His shoulders slumped. He had not trimmed his hair or shaved. The environmental suit he wore perpetually was now starting to show wear.

"You don't look good," Waters said.

"I know, Alex. I know," Beau said.

"Where are you going?" Waters asked as Beau moved toward the entrance. "There's nothing so important that it needs to be done today. Why don't you take a day off, get some rest? Stay at camp with us."

"I think you're right," Beau said. "Maybe I'll go pay our friend a visit."

"Is that where you've been spending all your time? Sitting with that animal?" Waters asked.

"No, not all my time, but it helps me think. Somehow, it helps me think," Beau said, slipping out the door.

Watching Beau leave, at last Waters resolved to do something. He needed to speak to the mayor. He was bored; they were bored as a mission team. They had made no more progress in the weeks since the storm than they had in the weeks leading up to it. As much as the mission's progress weighed on him, it was clearly a burden to the team as well. He was determined to learn what was so special about the city that none of them could enter. What was so great about their way of life that they had nothing to learn from the missionaries? At least that would be something to do. At least it might help. At worst, nothing would change. Waters pulled on his boots and stomped up the hill toward the city.

For no reason other than desire for something different, he turned aside from the path and followed the river. He wound his way over the grass towards the water, careful not to slip and injure himself or damage his suit. The sound of the cascades babbled pleasantly in his ears and sent a cooling mist into the air that worked wonderfully against the heat of the afternoon. Then he saw someone across the river. No, not just someone: a lady walked down the opposite bank. Her long dark hair hung in great waves upon her shoulders. She wore a flowing light blue dress. Although it was midday, her gown glowed like the light of the city itself, or was it she herself who gave off the light? A Polus bear accompanied her, but she was not riding. It approached, nuzzling her. She rewarded it by taking its cheeks in her hands and blowing across its nose. The Polus bear tossed its head with delight. A pair of hounds walked at her heels. They gamboled about, running away from her into the bushes, rocks and trees, sending skiouros and other small creatures scattering up tree trunks and into rocks and crevices, chittering and scolding as they fled, before the hounds bounded back to the lady for affirmatory head pats and ear scritches, reenergized for the next chase.

Waters stopped to watch the lady. He could not help but do so. As she drew near the opposite bank, she took notice of him and waved. He looked to his side and behind before realizing that she was waving at him. He wondered why such a lady would take notice of him when he looked again and recognized her. The lady was Molly. Or rather, Molly was the lady. She walked a few meters back up the cascade to where the rocks formed a serviceable path and crossed. She stepped lightly over the stone path to the other side, the hounds bounding after her, eagerly following. Their paws and claws struggled to grip the rocks, dipping their hindquarters in the cool water when they slipped, but that only strengthened their enthusiasm. The Polus bear forded the pool above the rock path with ease, dipping its head and taking a large drink before spurting the water through its baleen, filtering out a snack of fresh-water krill.

Molly no longer wore the garb of their mission. She had discarded the cap which bore the MFASA logo. In its place was a delicate crown in the style of the colonists, gossamer thin with a tiny jewel that hung on the ridge of her brow. Her hair had grown since he had seen her last several weeks ago. Only now, he seemed to see her as she truly was or as she was meant to be. He felt both delight at her presence and ashamed that he should look on her. He fought the urge to lower his eyes and felt a strange compunction to bow as she approached. He thought that absurd, and resisted by standing especially and awkwardly upright. He felt even more clumsy when she embraced him and kissed his cheek. He blushed, filled with embarrassment and confusion. Not that she should display affection to him, but that she would deign to do so. He became self-conscious of his dirty enviro suit. Nor had he washed or bathed. He doffed his MFASA cap in what he thought the best gesture of respect he could muster, and immediately regretted doing so. He ran his fingers through his hair in a hopeless attempt to straighten what must have been a disgraceful mop of disarray.

Molly smiled, finding joy in his dis-ease. It was not a smile of condescension or abasement; it reminded him of the way a mother would look at a child, and he calmed at once.

She asked how he was, and he told her everything that had happened: their ongoing frustration at being unable to enter the city, the mission's stagnation, uncertainty at what had become of her after she left and why, their arguments with the colonists, how the storm had destroyed their camp, Jazzy.

Waters did not know how long he talked, but they must have

walked along the banks of the river for many hours, because the day passed through its golden hours, making way for Polus to dominate the sky above, and the luminescent display of night to take the sun's place.

Molly finally spoke, "Alex, may I join you back at the camp tonight?"

Waters hardly felt he could refuse her request, nor did he want to. "Of course," was all he managed.

She motioned in the direction of the camp.

"Right now?" Waters said, feeling foolish.

"I think that now is the best time," she said.

Having earlier been self-conscious about his jumper and hair and how he must smell, oh how he must smell, his thoughts now turned to the shelter. They were not untidy, but it was no place for her to visit.

"Let's have dinner under the sky tonight," she responded as if she knew. "We can set up a table and chairs, and I can ask for the colonists to bring us something to eat."

"That would be fine," he said. She had put him at ease once more.

Joon-baek and Tommy saw them approach the camp, but Beau was nowhere to be seen. The two men were sitting outside the shelter at Joon-baek's workbench, jabbering about whatever it is that causes friends to jabber. As Molly drew near, they stood automatically. Both removed their hats, Tommy his cover and Joon-baek his MFASA cap, as if it were involuntary. Molly hugged them both, Tommy first and then Joon-baek, who actually did return a bow. Jazzy saw from the rover that a colonist had come to camp and climbed down to investigate.

"Molly?" she said.

"Hi Jazzy. I'm so happy to see you again," Molly replied with a hug.

Jazzy was dumbstruck.

Together they cleared a small space of ground and surrounded it with rocks. They gathered some dry wood and built a fire. Tommy showed them how to light it, first putting together a nest with some dried grasses and small wood shavings that he made with his knife. Scraping some ground aluminum flakes into the bowl of the nest, he struck a metal rod against the spine of his knife and ignited them into a small coal with a few sparks. He blew on the coal gently, catching the grass and wood shavings on fire, before placing it in the center of a neat alternating stack of small wooden sticks, which quickly caught the flame. Then they stacked larger branches along the perimeter of the flames, forming a fine campfire. And what a delight it was!

Waters had never seen such a campfire. Sure, they had huddled around a small fire during the storm, but this was different. Regulations forbade open flames on Earth due to the possibility of wildfire. They normally did all their cooking with electric heat, but he could see no reason why they should not have a fire. It was not an especially cool night, but the fire offered comfort and warmth in a way that penetrated his bones, warming him from the inside, even his spirit, if he dared say so.

Joon-baek offered his workbench as a table. A few colonists brought them a small pot, its savory smell made their mouths water when they lifted the lid. The colonists joined them, and they sat and ate and talked. Tommy told stories from the Marines. Joon-baek told stories of his large family. The colonists were eager to hear about Earth and asked many questions. Waters felt he had nothing interesting to contribute and chunked twigs into the fire while he slurped his stew, but that was satisfying in itself. Molly listened and laughed.

The stew itself was a mixture of vegetables grown in and around the city with grilled freshwater prawns, covered in a viti juice reduction and spices. They devoured it. Waters was afraid it would run out too soon with so many around the table, but each time they dipped the ladle into the pot it came out full.

At last, they had eaten their fill and leaned back in their chairs, a satisfying and comforting silence rested over the table. That was when Molly began to speak. Molly inhaled the way a person does when about to reveal something important. The missionaries all sat forward, ready to hear what she had to say. The colonists, seeing that a more intimate moment was about to begin, excused themselves. Molly hesitated, then began.

"I was never supposed to be a member of the mission. The Administration sent my mom and dad upstate for training. Before that happened, my parents had enough foresight to send my brother to stay with friends. In reality, the Administration wanted to reprogram them, or if you want to call it something nicer, re-educate them. For the same reason MFASA relocated those colonists from Alpha Centauri b; the same reason our mission came here to Polus."

Waters shifted uncomfortably at the mention of Alpha Centauri b. He did not like his mission being compared to a disaster.

"You've probably never seen pictures of one of the facilities where they do the training either. With good reason, photography and video are strictly forbidden. They're not facilities: they're gulags. And there's no training going on. It's forced labor.

"My parents were sent away. I didn't go with them because I was at school, but I found out quickly what had happened. A member of the Administration showed up at my apartment escorted by a couple of officer positions. She came on the pretense of an informational visit, but she was really sounding me out.

"That was the start of when I agreed to go on the mission. My parents were members of the Good Samaritans board, and the Administration was especially eager to make an example of them. What better way than to have their own daughter go on a colonial mission? You probably saw them on the news. I'm sure you'd recognize them. In exchange for my denunciation and participation in the mission, my parents were moved out of the gulag and into house arrest and got to bring my brother home. Well, they didn't call it house arrest, but that's what it amounts to. They are only permitted to use Administration phones that track their movements. They also don't get to work anymore, so they're dependent on the Administration. At least they still have a home. Before long, they'll probably end up on the streets like all opposition members.

"You saw me on the news. I had to read several prepared statements denouncing GS and praising the Administration. That's how I got my celebrity status: by denouncing good people like my parents."

"But you said you're not a celebrity," Jazzy interjected.

"That's right. I never wanted to be one. Especially not for that reason.

That was about the time I developed depression. I wasn't just sad in the way anyone would be if their parents were in trouble, but I had a *bona fide* mental illness. Jazzy, Doctor Bebe, I want to thank you for the way you helped me through all that."

Jazzy acknowledged the compliment but looked a little uneasy.

"I last spoke to my parents the night I left to join the colony; the night the LiFi window was open. My parents told me to join the city. Even though they knew they would be sent back to supplemental education, they told me to join the colonists. Though I denounced them publicly, they understood my reasons. But they were only concerned about me. I confessed to them, and they forgave me. So, I left the mission."

The missionaries were not quite sure how they should react to Molly's story. It was late by the time she finished, and they said their goodbyes, leaving their questions for another time. After Molly said goodnight and returned to the city, the four missionaries retired to their bunks. It had been a more satisfying evening than Waters could remember in a long time, yet he could not sleep. Molly's story had left him with many thoughts. While she had spoken, everything she said seemed right; however, now that he was on his own again doubt and skepticism loomed. He got out of bed, went to the open tent flap and breathed in the cool night air. He went to the water purifier, which they still used although the colonists assured them the water was quite safe, and got himself a drink before returning to bed, hoping that the change in posture and activity might calm his mind. Instead, when he lay down, their conversations kept re-treading his conscious. He questioned her new-found association with the colonists, how she had lied publicly about her beliefs to save her parents and join the mission, which also meant she had lied to them. How she could still believe those things despite their training and everything they knew. How could she?

Restless, he found himself sitting at the table again outside the shelter, only the shelter seemed more like a house. A woman came and sat

across from him, though he could not see her face for a light surrounding her. She plucked fruit from vines that grew along the wall of the
house and placed them in a bowl on the table. "Look," she said, pointing to the chair between them. A tree began to sprout there and grow.
Its trunk grew thick and put out branches and shoots and leaves. Birds
came to rest in its branches, and animals sheltered in its shade. Tiny
blossoms emerged and produced olives. He learned forward to touch
a branch, but could not reach it, not yet.

CHAPTER TWENTY-ONE

FIRST RIDE

Waters awoke as the morning light struck the table where he lay his head. So he had fallen asleep at some point after all, though he could not remember when. He got up, washed, and resolved to visit the city to see if he could speak to Molly again. He wanted to confront her about the things that kept him awake.

He panted up the hill, and arrived at the plaza in front of the narrow gate determined and puffing. Colonists came and went around him and paid him little mind though some nodded or waved a polite greeting. They had become accustomed to the missionaries by now. Jazzy's clinic, still standing after the storm but with scars in the fabric from their attempted repairs, stood empty. She was never one to get an early start. As of late, it seemed she had mostly abandoned the clinic, and Waters did not know how she filled her days. That was something he should probably know as director, but he could not bring himself to associate with her too closely, not yet. He was surprised the colonists permitted the structure to remain, semi-neglected, vagrant, and dilapidated as it was. Resolved in his mind, he walked to the gate only to meet the mayor himself.

When Waters found the mayor, he watched the man pause for a moment and consider him, before joining him. A Polus bear ambled up beside him, and the mayor patted the animal absentmindedly, the bear responding with coos of delight as waves of magenta shivered down its coat. The mayor stopped in front of Waters then mounted the Polus bear.

"Come with me, director," he said, extending his hand to pull Waters onto the beast's back. The arkouda knelt with one leg extended. Waters did not feel he could refuse, so he took the mayor's hand and joined him for a morning ride. He sat behind the creature's vestigial wings, which fluttered. He looked down and realized just how tall these animals were and grasped the wings as a handhold. The Polus bear shuddered but did not seem to mind. For non-functional wings they were surprisingly warm and muscular in his hands. Waters imagined one of these great animals flying, tiny wings fluttering madly, and smiled at the image. The mayor sat atop the Polus bear's shoulders, comfortably, confidently. He needed no handhold himself.

"Hold on if you need to," the mayor said, "but it is his responsibility to see that you do not fall, so have faith."

He did not take Waters back down the hill, or through the groves, or to the river, or the vineyards, or to any of the places near and around the city the missionaries had visited many times before and with which they had become quite familiar. Instead, they rode past Jazzy's clinic and around the wall and ascended the bowl that held the city close to the mountains.

The path was wide and rocky. It rose here as it climbed the mountain, descended there as they came into a meadow, broadened in a field of vigorous green plants where a mountain spring broke from the rocks before it gave way to a boulder field as they rose above the treeline. Each rock might have required a few minutes to negotiate on its own on foot, but the Polus bear navigated the field with ease. It huffed and kept pace as if determined to please its riders. Waters's breathing quickened as they gained altitude. He was grateful for their mount as he was certain he could not make the climb himself. The mayor breathed no differently than if he were seated on a couch.

The boulders gave way to tundra filled with tiny flowers and close grasses when at last they came to a stop next to a cairn in the saddle between two peaks. They rode for several hours to get there, though as the distance and altitude increased time began to matter less and less. The mayor was content enough with the morning ride and made no conversation. Waters's resolution to have Molly answer his questions faded the farther the mayor took him from the city.

The mayor dismounted and fished around among the rocks. He dug out a large piece of a mineral like quartz but with an aquamarine streak and added it to the cairn.

"What's that for?" Waters asked.

"For fun," the mayor answered. "And tradition."

Below they could see the city as if drawn on a map. A great cathedral stood at the center with its back to the city wall. It rose on the highest tier above the rest of the city, its spire towering over everything, visible from all around. Tiers of buildings fanned out in all directions. Even in the full sun, visible light emanated from the cathedral. The city filled the valley for several kilometers. Waters was surprised to see that it was a veritable metropolis. He assumed it was a small town or borough at best. Parks, buildings, and homes large and small dotted the landscape from wall to wall, yet it still seemed small and comfortable. The mayor pulled a bag from a pocket inside his poncho and passed Waters a muffin.

"Patience made these," the mayor said.

They were delicious. No doubt they were viti muffins. Waters swore the bits of fruit scattered throughout the baked goods glowed, even after cooking.

He was not sure what he was supposed to do. The mayor did not seem to have much purpose in bringing him here, though the view was nice; he was at ease gazing out on the mountain, the city, the valley, and forest. Beyond, Waters swore they could see the plain, covered in low clouds. Faint in the distance, he squinted at what he thought was the space elevator's cable and scaffolding, though he could not be certain. The thought was reasonable. They were only a few hundred kilometers from the space port. If construction had made good progress since the missionaries' departure, it could be tall enough to be visible over the curvature of the moon.

The mayor finished his first muffin and munched on another. Waters was certain they would do nothing but sit when at last the mayor said, "You must have questions."

Waters was not sure what the mayor meant. He did have questions, many questions, specifically about and for Molly, but was that what he wanted? Waters did not need to ask because the mayor continued.

"Molly told me what happened yesterday. That she told you her story. I'm sure you must wonder how we could welcome someone who abandoned her family and faith."

Waters did not know how the mayor could hit the question so exactly, but Waters needed no more encouraging.

"Yes," he said.

All that kept him awake the previous night poured forth. The mayor sat and listened. He pulled out a third muffin and continued eating and periodically drinking from a thermos as Waters spoke.

"Molly used to be a Christian on Earth, or her parents were. To keep them from undergoing supplemental education, she denounced her parents and their religion publicly—we all saw the news— and agreed to join a mission whose specific purpose was to educate the colonists— you—about the benefits of the Administration's programs, which most would argue are incompatible with any system of belief. She underwent the same training we did, albeit abbreviated, spent weeks on a spaceship with us, months on the moon, came here with a purpose, and then she abandoned the mission to join the very people we were meant to educate."

Waters paused, considering his words before continuing.

"I don't know how she could do that to her parents, though I think any sensible person should reject religion. If she had just done that, maybe the Administration would have gone easier on her family? But then she rejected us too! It turns out she believed all along despite our training and mission. She pushed it all aside to join up with you the first chance she got. Where does she even stand? She's a liar and a traitor to a lot of people right now, and I'm not sure I understand what I think about that let alone what I should do about it as a mission director, or why you seem okay with it." Waters finished and felt a little relief at sharing his thoughts.

"What do you know about forgiveness, Alex?" the mayor asked.

"You mean saying you're sorry?" Waters responded.

"Something like saying sorry, but forgiveness runs deeper," the mayor continued. "It doesn't even require an apology. A person can ask or give forgiveness, and if it is genuine, they free themselves from the burden of their wrongdoing. Did you know that Molly spoke to her parents before leaving your mission?"

"She told us she did," Waters said.

"When your LiFi window was open, she called and asked her parents to forgive her. Not that she harmed them; on the contrary, her denunciation saved them from your Administration, even if it meant house arrest. She told them everything, though they knew all she had done already, and they forgave her. Did she tell you what her parents said?"

Waters nodded. Molly did not give details, but he knew enough.

"Knowing the consequences, knowing the best they could hope for was a return to supplemental education but the more likely was remediation in a gulag, her parents told her to join the city," the mayor said.

"You're telling me her parents remanded themselves to supplemental education so she could live in your city? I don't get it. I don't get it! What's so important about some stupid, archaic beliefs? It's not worth your lives, your possessions, your daughter. How stupid can a person be."

"Molly has a brother as well," the mayor added.

"That's even worse! They put their children through this? Who would be so selfish? To put your children through this, all so you can subscribe to some outdated traditions?

"Wait. I see," continued Waters. "Here we are, up on a mountain, hours away from anyone, and you want to have a *conversation* with me. You've got me in the perfect place, I see. No place to go, no one else to argue with you. Just a misguided missionary with no choice but to sit and listen. Just like you tried to do to Jazzy. Well, I'm no fool. I'm not like *her*. I'd like to go back."

The mayor looked hurt. Waters refused to make eye contact.

"There's no need for me to take you back," the mayor said.

A Polus bear bounded up without a word. Waters looked between the beast and the mayor. He felt it was a fool's choice, but in the end, he took the ride. The Polus bear bowed to the ground and bent its knee. Waters wasted no more time. Waters stepped onto the creature's knee and it lifted him onto its back effortlessly. He sat in front of the tiny wings and gripped the scruff of its neck.

"Let's talk more later, Alex!" the mayor shouted as Waters and the Polus bear hurried back down the mountain.

Beau and Jazzy had been working on the rover's communications system since she awakened later that morning. It had functioned poorly since the storm if it functioned at all.

"I'm afraid our director is losing sight of the mission," Beau said.

"I've had concerns about his effectiveness for many months now," Jazzy said.

"We are overdue on our reports to MFASA," Beau said.

"We are, but they understand. They know about the atmosphere on Polus IV. Besides, once we get this working, we can report the damage from the storm, and that will include the damage to the rover's communications systems," Jazzy said.

"And Molly's apostasy," Beau said.

"That too. Of course, they'll need to know about that," Jazzy said.

"Do you think Waters was planning to tell them?" Beau asked.

"I'm sure it is already part of his next report," Jazzy said.

"You could be the one making the report instead," Beau suggested.

Jazzy shrugged but did not argue.

"You aren't the only two who can benefit from the mission's success. It means a lot to all of us. Sure, you are ahead in line, but who knows? All of us could end up as directors someday. Maybe even of MFASA itself. Maybe even president," Beau said.

"Beau, I'm surprised at you," Jazzy said. "I didn't know you were ambitious."

"I've learned a lot of things on this mission. I feel I have a different perspective than when we first arrived," he said. "You should be director now. MFASA needs to know what's happened."

A piece of cable broke loose. Frustrated, Jazzy tossed it over the rover's side. "Look, I know I've been hard on Alex, but that's only because this is so important to me. To us. We need to give him a fair chance and support him."

She touched Beau's arm gently.

"Still, I'm glad I have your support," she said.

"It's important to me too," he said. "When will it be time?"

"Not yet. I'll tell you when it's time, but not yet."

CHAPTER TWENTY-TWO

A LONG WALK

Waters's anger churned as the Polus bear took him to the city. "Not the city. Let's go back to camp," he said, surprising himself both to be speaking to an animal and that he should do so without a second thought.

The Polus bear did not argue nor did Waters sense that it would, even if it had a different preference. Instead, it practically flew down the hill to the camp. Waters climbed down and paused to say "thanks." He wondered why he bothered as he walked away.

Waters could not tell if he was truly angry, but he was uncomfortable and that was enough. It would be appropriate to appear angry in such circumstances after all. He should probably tell his superiors about the incident. He could probably make it appear to be a sign of progress, which they struggled to achieve. And with the mayor himself! It could be a long time before the next LiFi window opened so there was time to work on the report.

The conversation left him thinking in so many directions that his thoughts were difficult to sort. He decided that he was genuinely a little angry, yes, but not so angry that he should cut off communication. He should not appear too eager to meet again; that would place him at a disadvantage. By waiting, say, a week at least, he could put the mayor back on his heels and gain the upper hand. He had responses for things the mayor had not said, but which the mayor could potentially say. He was grateful he would have time to practice and prepare in advance before he saw the mayor again. He felt grateful for their training too.

Waters ruminated on their conversation the rest of the day. The next day, however, he could not find enough busywork inside the shelter sufficient to excuse himself from stepping outside. He had amended his report already, and there were only so many times that he could check and recheck the regulations and guidelines for conformity.

He decided to take a walk; a long walk. Part of him reasoned that no one could question whether he was working and contributing if he were out of sight. By choosing where he walked, he could also avoid an encounter with the mayor or a colonist. That meant avoiding the city and plaza, and the fields and orchards as well. He wanted to avoid seeing Molly again if he could too. He certainly could not stay at the camp, as that was the first place visitors would stop. So, he decided to hike into the hills and mountains.

As he departed, he stuffed his phone in his pocket and mumbled something to Joon-baek, who was engrossed in his workbench as usual. Joon-baek was lucky. It could take weeks for anything to grow. He could justify lengthy amounts of time between progress.

Water still felt he had to be careful, although begrudgingly, he was now sure the colonists were right that there was little to fear on Polus. They captured the only apoch in the area, so things were safe. He was still not acclimated to the moon, however, as they liked to remind him. That meant he wore his full enviro suit as he walked for protection against the plant life, tattered and dingy as it had become with daily wear. He also wore the colonist's glasses, their gift to the mission. Although he could blaze trail, that was tiring, difficult work, so he kept to game trails. The flora on Polus was universally and remarkably resilient and difficult, and resisted his efforts terrifically. The colonists, even Molly, seemed to have no trouble moving about as they pleased. This puzzled him.

Although it seemed threats surrounded him, Waters was not worried about his safety since he was never completely alone. Within minutes of leaving camp animals and birds followed him, clustering around him, coming and going, looking at him intently as they walked, hoping for some sign of recognition or a request. He was anthropomorphizing he reminded himself. Although animals deserved conservation and care, they did not think; not like people.

He no longer felt in danger around them. The Polus bears, the colonists' 'arkouda,' huge and lumbering beasts that they were, and the other animals were ever gentle and careful. While at first, they seemed frightening and formidable, now they seemed tame as puppies and strong as elephants. As good for riding as a horse, just like he had seen in old movies. More so since they needed no saddle. They were naturally attentive and would not permit a rider to fall. When they felt pleased, which was often, they made a friendly chuffing noise and ruffled their fur with color. Molly called it "prusten." She explained it was like a sound tigers used to make on Earth. She had played a recording for them of one of the last tigers making the noise, and she was right: they were remarkably similar.

The game trails were astonishingly random. Their jibes and zigs across the fields were generally directional without being straight. The animals tended to put one foot in front of the other and walk in single file, which meant the trails were narrow. It was frustrating to see where the trail headed and know the path did not arrive there directly. He reflected, however, that it did not matter much since his goal was to waste time.

After walking in this way for several days, his breathing did improve somewhat, though he still became winded walking on any grade. The composition of the atmosphere was virtually identical to Earth, with fewer emissions, as would be expected since the moon was undeveloped. More interesting was that relative to their altitude atmospheric pressure was not much lower. It should not have been difficult for the missionaries to breathe, yet it was. It was like hiking fourteeners with his dad as a kid all over again. He needed to catch his breath every so often, which was helpful since regular rest periods killed more time. His inability to move about normally and as he would have liked in the environment irritated him, however.

He developed a new routine by the third day. He would set out each morning, taking just a few things and not packing food or water. They kept the water purifier but accepted that the water was pure, without pathogens. Aside from taking a tea bag for flavor, he only needed an empty bottle. The viti were ever-present, and both nutritious and satisfying. One fruit sustained him for several hours.

In this way Waters hiked. He stopped and drank directly from the springs that came from the rocks, identifiable by patches of green plants, and when he was hungry, he plucked a viti.

On the sixth day of this routine, one day earlier than his plan required, Waters decided it had been long enough. He had considered what he would say to the mayor, and it was time to speak to him again. Waters even looked forward to the opportunity. Where the mayor had not spoken much to Jazzy, he specifically made time for Waters. He needed to be careful, however. This was both his and Jazzy's responsibility in their leadership positions, and he did not want to be perceived as redirecting duties away from her. Although, he had not seen her in the previous week—no, longer—and he wondered if she would even notice. He had been making himself scarce to be sure, but he should still have seen her from time to time, even if they had not interacted much. She must be busy.

He had grown accustomed to the walks and was even beginning to like them. That morning he set out thinking he would only walk a little before going to meet the mayor, maybe even Molly. There was no need, however. For the second time, the mayor approached him first.

"Good morning, Alex!" the mayor called from the back of a Polus bear. "Are you going for a walk? Do you mind if I join you?"

Waters got the impression the mayor not only knew he was out for a walk but had known he would be out for a walk and had been out for a walk these past several days. Though irritating, it did not matter. He intended to speak to the mayor anyway. Whether he walked to the city or they met not so coincidentally was unimportant.

"Sure. I was just coming to see you," Waters said.

"Why don't we ride?" the mayor offered.

He was not in the mood to share a ride with the mayor. He had no need though. A pair of the mayor's entourage of Polus bears ambled up and knelt before him, competing for the honor. Waters obliged a beast, who chuffed excitedly. The other tossed its head, not disappointed, but happy that its partner had been chosen. "You're anthropomorphizing again," Waters said to himself as he mounted.

He had become used to a much slower pace walking on his own. The Polus bears had no compunction about sticking to trails or need to rest or delay from tough, obstinate vegetation, and they made terrific progress. Waters took out his phone to take a picture. The mayor took note.

"Do you mind?" Waters asked.

It was more of a courtesy than a genuine request for approval, but the mayor nodded.

Waters did not permit hours to pass in silence this time and began his prepared conversation straight away.

"Mayor, there's something I do not understand. How can you continue to be a religious society in the face of everything we know? Just look at what we can do. We can travel between the stars. We have colonies on distant planets. It was people who accomplished this. We can see into the reaches of space and know the depths and scope of the universe. It is vast, far greater than any god. We can see into the space between atoms and have named the particles and quarks that compose the building blocks of life. Our engines carry us to distant worlds. It is only a matter of time before we have mapped the universe. We can measure the depths of the oceans, the height of mountains, the distance between the planets and stars. All creatures have come under our dominion, though we learned to treat them well; indeed, we could fish out leviathan with a hook, but choose not to. We looked into the depths of the Earth and the vastness of the universe, and what did we see there? We saw the infinite, but not the Infinite. I do not understand, mayor, how you can still have faith when we understand the universe and how it works from the tiniest speck to the greatest expanse."

"And yet, something as simple as a thunderstorm destroyed your camp," the mayor replied.

Waters blanched a little at the comment but continued. "We don't need religious explanations anymore. No one looks for krakens because we understand the wind and tides. We don't need Zeus and Thor tossing thunderbolts because we understand electricity. We don't need God to create the world—let alone in seven days—because we can explain how it was created without God. Even the things we can't explain are vanishing. All we need is time, and we'll know. We don't need God to fill in the gaps."

"Did you think that God would not follow His own rules?" the mayor said. "When something can be explained, that's called consistency, not superstition. Did we ever claim that God was an explanation for the unknown? That oceans must be populated with monsters until we know better? We never claimed that God wouldn't tell us how he did something. Our ability to know things about the universe is a feature of creation, not in any way something that disproves God."

This was not how Waters had planned for this conversation to go. Why didn't the colonists just listen? If they would only listen, he could make them understand that his, that the Administration's, way of thinking was right.

"It's all just rhetoric," he said.

"If you can explain everything with knowledge alone," the mayor continued, "then all things must be within the realm of what can be known, including our own thoughts. How can you trust your own thoughts to be telling you what is true when they themselves must be explained? What you describe assumes that our ability to explain is somehow outside explanation itself, which has never been the case, and never will be. When you will not consider God, you eliminate a possibility before you have even asked the question."

Waters could hardly keep from rolling his eyes.

"But I understand. I understand more than you realize, Alex," the mayor continued. "Were it not for that one great miracle that settles them all, I could be led away. I'm surprised more people have not attempted to unset it. Perhaps once someone concludes that any miracle is impossible, it becomes easy to dismiss The Miracle."

"What on Earth are you talking about?" Waters said.

"You mean 'what on Polus,' don't you?" said the mayor, a twinkle in his eye.

This was no time for word games. The mayor did not seem to be taking this as seriously as Waters would have liked.

"I'm talking about the defeat of death itself, Alex. The one act at the center of time. The Resurrection," the mayor said.

"Now you're just being ridiculous."

"I have never been more serious."

"Look, you can keep your zombie Jesus—" at this the mayor winced. Waters had scored a point. "Something like that is impossible. That you would believe in it makes you ridiculous. Not knowledgeable, not credible, not special. Ridiculous. We know it's impossible. That you continue to believe it says something about your intelligence, I'm sorry to say."

This was a conversation that was going nowhere, and would go nowhere, thought Waters. There was nothing left to say, and they were making their way back to camp anyway. Waters decided to walk the rest of the way back and dismounted.

"Thank you for the ride, mayor," he said mustering what politeness he could. He turned his back on the mayor and walked back to camp. The Polus bear followed him.

CHAPTER TWENTY-THREE

WE SHALL SEE

They had travelled farther than he thought on their ride, and it took more than an hour to get back. He fumed all the way back to camp. What foolishness. What arrogance. Waters knew what it was. There was a term for that kind of psychological issue, but he could not bring it to mind just then. A word for when people were shown to be wrong but persisted anyway. He would ask Jazzy when he saw her next. She was not a psychologist by training, but she might be able to give him the word.

Why should he continue to meet with the mayor if the conversations went nowhere? It was his duty as a member of the mission, of course. It would not really be a failure; it would only mean MFASA would step in and resettle the colonists and submit those who did not comply to supplemental education. That would be better for the colonists anyway. They would get a seat in the Colonial House and have the benefits afforded to people who still lived under the Administration. Best of all they could to live on facts instead of myths.

He approached the camp and passed the enclosure where they kept the apoch. The Polus bear stopped and remained at a distance. Its fur flashed green and orange and it stomped nervously. The apoch had refracted the light to blend into the environment and was hardly visible. Waters knew it was there and knew to look for a distortion in the light to spot it. He saw a slight shimmer like hot air rising and made out an outline.

"Poor creature," he said to himself. "The colonists are so wrong about so many things, they can't be right about this animal either." He approached the cage. As he did the apoch surprised him by becoming visible. "It must be starting to trust us," he said. "Why can't they see, these creatures just need the same care they give to all the other animals, and it will be no different."

Before Molly left, her analysis found that the apoch's skin absorbed more than ninety-nine percent of all light, more than their instruments could detect. It seemed a creature of pure shade. It absorbed so much light that it cast no shadows on itself and so appeared with hardly any form. If not for its bony protuberances and spines, its true shape would have been very difficult to see.

Waters approached the gate and the creature materialized and gazed back at him with unimaginably dark eyes. The Polus bear turned and fled.

He spoke aloud to the apoch, "With Molly gone, there's really no point in continuing to keep you captive. She completed her studies anyway. The only point of holding you would be transport to Earth. It would be cruel to take you out of your natural environment. Cruelty to animals is one of the worst things a person can do. Yes, it's time: time to set you free."

Waters passed his phone over the door panel. With a beep, the latch opened. Waters pushed the door inward and stepped back. The apoch approached and showed its teeth. Whatever its color, or lack of color, its teeth were the purest white. If he had not known for certain that animals were incapable of higher emotion, he would have sworn it grinned at him.

"What are you doing!" came a shout from behind.

He turned to see the mayor riding at full speed. Waters stepped with his arms held out wide between the apoch and charging Polus bear. He regretted his brave moment, cringed, and expected to be trampled, but there was no need. The apoch darted from the enclosure into the trees and disappeared.

"Have you any idea what you've done? And so close to the city!" the mayor shouted, his voice booming. He was angry in a way that Waters had not seen from any colonist, not even Jonathan. The mayor pulled out his phone. A screen projected in front of him with a map. It pulsed and sounded as if it tried to detect something.

"It must have made itself visible again," the mayor said to no one in particular. "What you've done is extremely serious," he said as he turned back to Waters.

"All I did is return an animal to nature where it belongs," Waters replied, defiant.

"What you've done is the height of foolishness, and it must be dealt with immediately. We will need to decide how you should be disciplined for this," the mayor said, extremely serious.

"Disciplined?!" Waters cried, exasperated. "What I've done is right. And you have no authority over me to administer 'discipline' in any case. In fact, it is the other way around: it is you who should be listening to us. We represent Earth and have the full authority of MFASA and the Administration behind us."

"We shall see about that," the mayor said.

"We shall see," Waters repeated.

The mayor rode away from their camp up the hill, the Polus bear carrying him at a terrific pace. They were incredibly fast for their size. Waters admitted to himself he had been scared when the mayor charged. Not frightened, but the apoch stirred something deeper in him. He was proud he stood his ground.

However, there was something else to deal with now. The mayor had threatened him. This was something he would need to discuss with the missionaries. Jazzy would want to be a part of the conversation, but regardless of who participated in the discussion, he was confident he had acted in the right, and that they would support him. Jazzy had developed no great love for the colonists in her time here either, which was in his favor.

He did not find her at the rover. He tried to call Jazzy on her phone, then Beau, but neither answered. Thinking they might be at the clinic, he resigned himself to walking to the plaza and Jazzy's clinic. Joon-baek, however, was at work in a plot of soil nearby.

"Are you headed to the city?" he asked.

Waters told him about his encounter with the mayor and his decision to release the apoch. His acts seemed increasingly impulsive in the telling, but it did not matter.

"I guess I didn't need to release the apoch. I probably should have left it in the enclosure," he said.

"That probably would have been best, but it's too late for that now," Joon-baek agreed.

"Where's Tommy? I could use his help now," Waters asked.

"Probably flying with the colonists. He got his machine working. I really wish we had one of those," Joon-baek said.

Joon-baek followed Waters up the hill, and together they approached the plaza. A cadre of colonists was already there including the mayor, Jonathan, Ai, Patience, and several others all mounted on Polus bears. The dilapidated clinic still stood on the side of the plaza, but neither Jazzy nor Beau seemed to be there.

The colonists surrounded Waters and Joon-baek, not threatening them, but they knew they were not free to leave either. The Polus bears were intimidating, but he had learned they would not hurt him.

The mayor spoke first. "Director Waters, you are accused of having released an apoch near the city, thereby putting all of its people in danger. Do you deny that you have done this?"

Waters did feel guilty, but his hackles raised at the accusation. "I released the apoch, yes, but mayor, none of you are in danger. It's just an animal—"

"That's enough," interrupted the mayor, his voice echoing off the city walls.

Jonathan spoke, "You put all of the people in this city, including your own team and all of the surrounding area, at risk with your stupidity. We tried to warn you, and you ignored us, assuming in your arrogance that you knew better."

"That's enough, Jonathan," the mayor said. "Although what you say is true, it is not your place."

"If you please, mayor," Waters said, not at all plaintive, "as I mentioned earlier, neither you nor anyone here has the authority over me to take any action. I am here on a mission from MFASA and Earth and carry the full weight of the Administration's mandate with me."

"How strong does that mandate feel now?" Jonathan retorted.

Waters admitted he was in a difficult situation.

"I said that's enough, Jonathan," the mayor admonished before turning back to Waters. "I know you do not understand what you have done. We share part of the responsibility as well. We should not have allowed you to keep the apoch as your pet, and should have slain it outright, captive or no. Therefore, we will aid you in correcting the error. We lay before you two options: you shall either undo this grievous fault by hunting and killing the apoch yourself. Not re-capturing mind you, but killing it. You must remove this evil from among us."

"Mayor, really—" Waters protested.

"Failing this," the mayor continued, ignoring him, "you and your team shall disassemble your camp and depart. You will return to the space port and not come near the city again. Do not fail to take us seriously in this, director. We have tolerated your presence here hoping that you might come to see the Truth, and we rejoice that one has done so. Permitting you to stay so long has proven a mistake. We will not compound it should you refuse. It may be that we should not have allowed you to enter the valley at all, as you have brought wickedness among us, but that is done. All we can do now is make it right. What do you say?"

"If I refuse to kill an animal?" Waters said.

"Then we will effectuate your departure immediately," the mayor replied.

Waters looked to the clinic, hoping that Beau or Jazzy would emerge to support him, to shut down the colonists' ridiculous assertion of authority over their mission.

"They will not come to help you. They are lost deep in themselves," the mayor said, following the train of his gaze. "Make your decision."

"You leave me no choice. I cannot allow our mission to fail, even based on threats from those who have no authority to end it."

"This is the beginning of making it right then," the mayor said. "Jonathan, you will go with him."

Jonathan's jaw dropped and the smug look he wore fell from his face, but he made no protest. Instead, he satisfied himself with an angry look at Waters.

"You have not yet killed an apoch yourself, Jonathan. Besides, you need to atone for the hostility you have shown our guests. They may not have been entirely welcome here, but you should have treated them better."

Jonathan reddened but said nothing.

"Can I go too?" Joon-baek asked. Everyone looked at him in surprise. "I'd just like to go is all."

"You may take any of your companions you want, but you must leave immediately. We cannot permit the creature to escape. We will provide you with the supplies and tools you'll need."

Waters looked around, hoping Tommy would appear with his rifle, but he too was nowhere to be seen.

The circle of colonists opened, and a pair of Polus bears sidled up. Ai brought forward a poncho and saddle bag for the missionaries, and Patience passed each of them a lance. A leather thong sheathed and concealed the blade.

"Direct this only at that which you intend to kill. Nothing else, ever," she said.

"They don't even know which end to point," Jonathan taunted, who received as reward another stern look from the mayor.

The three set out immediately. Waters and Jonathan rode side-by-side, or as close as two people could on massive Polus bears. Joon-baek rode behind. All were silent. Waters pretended to be very interested in the map on his phone. Jonathan flew a tiny drone that projected a screen. It searched for anomalies that would signal the apoch had camouflaged. Waters would not look at Jonathan, who for his part could not keep from boring angry holes through Waters with his eyes.

"You could have borrowed one of our drones," Jonathan said, finally breaking the silence with a gesture at Waters's phone.

"It's fine," Waters said.

"What is your problem?" Jonathan said.

Waters had enough and was ready to voice his frustration. "What is my problem? How could you ask that? How could you not know? Since we arrived you stupid, ignorant people have done nothing but ignore and ridicule everything we've been trying to teach you. As if a bunch of colonists could show Earth— Earth!— anything! We try to bring you education, ignored; healthcare, ignored; government, ignored! And now, you threaten to execute an innocent animal, an animal we were trying to study and protect, for having done no more than be taboo in your backwards society. And to make it worse, you force me and Joon-baek to participate in your barbarism! How in the hell could you ask me what my problem is?!"

Joon-baek kept his head down.

"Your problem is you don't listen! To anyone!" Jonathan responded. "Not to the mayor, not to me, not even to Molly. To the people who have lived here for decades and know this planet, helped shape this planet. Your heads are buried so deep in your precious Administration that you can't even see anymore. You know nothing of Polus, nothing of the city, and nothing of what is true," Jonathan said.

"True! What do you hicks know about truth! Truth comes from the Administration. Glory to the Administration!"

"You and your precious Administration. You cling to it as if it were the ending of all arguments. Have you any idea how often your precious Administration has been wrong? Any idea how often your Administration has killed? We are not the one's worshiping a false god. We serve the Living God! Your god tells you to tie your shoes one way today, and tomorrow it will tell you different, and none of you will even question," Jonathan said.

"The Administration is no god. It just is. You're the one who can't see what's right in front of him. You believe your stupid mythology is real like a child!"

"God is real!"

"There is no such thing as god. If there was, we would have found something, anything, the smallest bit of evidence that there was a god. Any god. But no. We can see distant stars. But sorry! No trace of a god! Haven't discovered him yet. We have telescopes that can see distant galaxies. Have any of you seen god yet? Nope. Sorry! No god. We can measure the width of the pieces of the components of a proton. Hey, guys! Did you see god there? What's that? No? No god here! There is no such thing as god. If there really was this benevolent old man floating on a cloud in space around the Earth, we would have found him by now. There. Is. No. God!"

"You're so blinded by what you can pick up, what you can put down, what you can measure, what you can destroy, you've convinced yourself that the only things worthwhile are those you can put on a scale. But it's worse than that! You're so blind you think anything you cannot describe is without value."

"There is nothing we cannot describe."

"You proclaim, 'we have measured a thing; we are its master,' and you actually believe it!" Jonathan continued, ignoring Waters. "Then worse, you are so far gone that you believe something only has value if you can tie a string around it and measure the length of the line. You think you know what a star is because you have named its elements. You name the parts and think you understand the thing. Is that all you are? A pile of dust? Is that all this planet is? The fourth moon of Polus? A thing's value only just starts well past your pitiful measurements. People have value beyond their use to your fallen Administration. When you cannot reconcile your ignorance, when you don't understand, when something doesn't fit your precious Administration's plan, you toss it aside. Or destroy it. Like you did with the colonists on Alpha Centauri b. Like you do on Earth. Like you tried to do with Molly."

Waters's face tightened. He leaned towards Jonathan and gritted his teeth, his face red and his eyes flashing in anger. Jonathan gripped his lance. Joon-baek watched, horrified, certain they would come to blows. Why had the mayor insisted these two go together? Certainly, there were dozens of colonists who had more experience with apochs. Why didn't he send one of them? Then Jonathan's drone chirped, that blessed drone, interrupting their argument. Its screen flashed an alert. Jonathan brought up a map of the area. It showed a spherical ping. Jonathan leaned forward on his lance. Waters unclenched his fists but kept one eye on Jonathan.

"He found something. Let's go." Jonathan's Polus bear broke into a canter without a word or movement from its rider. Its legs rolled underneath it smoothly and gracefully.

"It's not a 'he.' It's a drone," Waters called after him.

He beat his heals against the side of his mount frantically in a vain effort to move faster.

Joon-baek rode up beside him. "You just have to ask it," he said.

"I am not asking an animal's permission to move faster," Waters insisted.

Joon-baek rode to catch up with Jonathan.

CHAPTER TWENTY-FOUR

OVER SOON

Through the trees, in a clearing ahead, they saw the creature. It was not at all as Waters expected. The creature before them was sickly pale, as if it had not been exposed to daylight for years. Its skin both clung and hung from its bones at the same time. Its ribs, spine, and pelvis were visible, giving it the appearance of starvation. The spinous processes were elongated, and protruded through its skin, as did the ends of its free-floating ribs. It squatted in front of something, and concentrated, manipulating whatever it had with hand-like paws and pointed claws.

"It must be starving," Waters whispered.

Yes, starving.

"It needs help."

Yes, help.

"Quiet," Jonathan hissed. "It doesn't know we're here yet. We can surprise it."

Do not kill. Just an animal. Innocent. Do not kill.

"I don't think we should kill it. It's just an animal. We should try to recapture it."

Yes, capture. Let live! Live!

"We need to kill it. That's our only purpose right now," Jonathan said.

"It's not right to kill it. It's just an animal."

Clear thinking. Many choices, many options.

"Alex, we must not allow it to escape. Get your lance." Jonathan stepped into the clearing. He crouched and moved on the balls of his feet as quietly as he could. Joon-baek looked at Waters uncertainly then followed. He stepped slowly and imitated Jonathan's movements. Waters gripped his lance with both hands and considered it.

"I've never killed before," he said to himself.

Have never killed. Should never kill.

He looked up and saw that Jonathan was now fully in the clearing. In a few moments he would be in striking range. Waters's heart was beating so hard he could hear it.

"This is not right," he said aloud. "We're not supposed to kill animals."

Not kill.

Waters looked at the lance again, then at the apoch. He suddenly let out a cry, "Gah!" not sure what he even meant to say.

The apoch turned and looked directly at him. Membranous, large, pupil-less eyes saw through him. Jonathan lunged and missed. Waters swore the creature grinned before it leapt out of the way and into the trees where it disappeared.

"Alex!" Jonathan called out, stifling a curse.

Joon-baek stumbled up behind Jonathan. He held his lance, resolute but clearly glad he had not needed to use it. Waters held his lance like a walking stick and stepped into the clearing. They came closer and could see the object upon which the apoch had been so intent.

The apoch had splayed a small animal, like a squirrel Waters thought, one of the moon's skiouros, against the bark of a tree. A splinter of wood pierced each of its tiny paws and pinned it to the tree. Folds of soft skin hung from its frame where the apoch had carefully pulled it away from the fascia to expose the muscles as it flayed the creature alive. Pulses of red flashed over the animal. It was in pain.

"It's still alive," Jonathan said.

He plunged the point of his lance into the animal's chest. It flashed bright and then slumped, dead.

"I'm sorry, little one," Jonathan said. After a moment he turned to Waters. "Do you see? Do you see now, Alex? The apoch is a creature of pure evil. It knows only cruelty and wants only the worst kind of destruction. It feeds on suffering."

Don't know.

"I don't know," Waters said. "Maybe it was only eating. Maybe this is just how they feed."

"Can't you see what's right in front of you?" Jonathan said.

"I think he's right, Alex," Joon-baek said.

Can't be right.

"No, that can't be right," Waters said, almost mumbling.

Jonathan looked at Waters intently, grabbed his cheeks between his thumb and forefinger, and pointed Waters's eyes at his. Waters stared back blankly.

"It's still here," Jonathan mouthed with dread and raised his lance.

Jonathan had barely moved when the apoch dropped from the trees onto Joon-baek, who collapsed in a heap. It leapt in the air again and came down a second time and crushed him. Joon-baek's clothes tore under the apoch's claws and spurs. The apoch spun around on its heel with a kick and slammed Jonathan into a tree, knocking the wind out of him. The apoch held him there with its hind leg. Jonathan let out terrible gasps as he struggled to get air back into his lungs. The apoch was on him instantly. It grabbed Jonathan under his chin and lifted him high against the tree, leaving his feet dangling. Jonathan flailed and beat against the arm that held him with all his might, but the apoch did not move in the least. The apoch turned a blank, membranous eye to Waters who stood as in a haze. This time there was no mistaking its sneer.

It turned back to Jonathan, grabbed his arm in a claw, and forced it away from his body. Jonathan resisted with all his strength but could do nothing. A strange, uncanny smile crept across the creature's mouth as it watched Jonathan struggle. The apoch let go of Jonathan's neck, and held him against the tree by the wrist. Reaching into its side it snapped off one of its spines, then slammed it through Jonathan's forearm and pinned him to the tree. Jonathan cried out in anguish and kicked at the apoch's face to no avail.

"Alex!" he yelled with desperation.

Waters looked at the scene vacantly and knew he should do something but did not seem to have the will. He felt as if he watched a film play out in front of him, that he was merely an observer. All of this would be over, and the next scene would start soon enough.

Over soon.

Yet, he had to act. How would it look if he did nothing? He looked at the lance in his hands and thought he should at least attempt something. He raised the lance, pointed it at the apoch, and allowed it to make contact with the creature. The lance left a shallow mark in its back hardly worse than a scratch. A white waxy substance immediately coagulated around the area his lance touched. The apoch flinched and released Jonathan, who cried out in pain as he dangled from the tree by the spike in his forearm. The apoch screamed and with a backhanded swipe sent Waters flying across the clearing.

Instantly, Waters's eyes opened and he saw. He saw the tiny animal hanging from the tree, pinned with the apoch's own spines. He saw Joon-baek unconscious and dying in the dirt. He saw the blood streaming down Jonathan's arm where the apoch pierced him. He looked up and saw the creature approaching, no longer smiling, but wearing a look of genuine malice and vengeance. It walked, then trotted, then charged.

Waters did not know what to do. He tried to bring the lance up, but the end was caught in viti vines at the base of the tree. There was no time to struggle. One more bound and the apoch would be on him. He pointed the blade with the shaft still caught in the vines, turned his head, closed his eyes, and braced for the impact.

Jonathan braced his feet against the tree where he hung and with a cry of terrific effort pulled his arm free over the spine that pinned him. He fell to the ground but did not stop. He picked up his lance and stepped forward. He drew his throwing arm so far back the ligaments popped. The lance traced a line across his arm and chest. With a tremendous heave, he arced the lance toward his enemy.

The point of Jonathan's lance transfixed the apoch, and the point stopped mere centimeters from Waters's face. The apoch arched backward in pain. It howled and pulled at the shaft desperately before it collapsed onto its knees and slouched forward into Waters. Its head bowed, and with a sigh let out the last air from its lungs. Something like wax sloughing off a candle oozed from the apoch's body as it passed. Its skin turned inky black as the light of thousands of victims left its body and flowed into the earth below. A pattern emerged in its skin like blood red leopard spots as its hide drained.

Across the clearing, Waters saw Jonathan standing once more. He clenched a mangled and bloody forearm tight with his good hand. Waters pushed off the apoch's body and ran to Jonathan.

"I'll be okay," Jonathan said. He removed his belt and wrapped it on his bicep above the wound. He inserted a stick under the belt and twisted until the blood flow stopped. "Tie the belt around the stick, please," he said to Waters. "I can't with one hand. We need to help Joon-baek."

Joon-baek lay still where the apoch had leapt on him. He was unconscious and had many broken bones but was breathing. Jonathan's drone arrived with a first aid kit from his saddle bag.

"They can do that?" Waters asked.

"They can do that," Jonathan said.

Gently Jonathan used his forearms to secure Joon-baek's neck and rolled the unconscious man onto his back, protecting his spine. He poured a swallow of viti juice into Joon-baek's mouth, then he fished around inside the kit and pulled out a small glass ampule. He broke and waved it under Joon-baek's nose. Joon-baek awoke instantly and gagged. Even Waters recoiled at the pungent smell from a distance.

"All our tech, and still smelling salts are the best way to wake someone up," Jonathan said.

Joon-baek tried to sit up, but they stopped him.

"You are severely hurt," Jonathan said. "I gave you some juice from the fruit of the vine, but even that needs time to work. Lay here. We don't know the extent of your injuries yet. An arkouda will come soon and we can take you back to the city."

Then before their eyes, the fallen apoch began to deflate. As if the decomposition process accelerated, all that had been substance, bones, organs, blood, flesh, were devoured in seconds. The lance fell to the ground as form left the apoch's body leaving nothing but a black pelt. It would have been pitiful had they not known the creature to which it belonged.

Jonathan picked up the pelt and held it at arm's length. He looked from the pelt to Waters. "Here. You can have the pelt. I'll get the next one."

Waters did not really want it, but he did not have a mind to argue any longer. He took it gingerly. The texture surprised him. "I've never felt leather before," he said.

Jonathan bit into a viti, and tossed a piece of fruit to Waters, which he ate as they rode. A few minutes later Jonathan removed the tourniquet, and Waters was surprised to see that the wound in his forearm was already healing. Joon-baek dozed comfortably in a makeshift stretcher on the back of an arkouda.

"He'll be alright?" Waters asked.

"He'll be fine, but he'll need time to recover," Jonathan said. He paused as if hesitating, then continued. "The apochs are not native to Polus as far as we can determine. You can tell just from observation. All the native animals have wings, even if they don't use them. The apoch have two legs and two arms, like a human. But they're not human, and they're hardly animals. Besides that, we've performed genetic assays that show they're not from Polus. This planet is practically paradise. The apoch are wicked. Pure evil. They do not belong here. We don't know where they're from, and as far as we know, no one does."

Waters felt obliged to argue, but he lacked the will just then. He pondered the pelt lashed in a roll on his saddle bags and wondered how they had been so wrong. Animals could not be cruel. They were incapable of higher behavior. Yet this one delighted in suffering. Killing animals was wrong, yet was it wrong to kill this animal?

They rode back in silence, left to their own thoughts.

CHAPTER TWENTY-FIVE

ITS TOOTHY GRIN

Joon-baek sat up in his bed and munched on a viti fruit. Tommy and Waters sat with him. Jazzy tended to him, happy to use her skills at last. Beau was not with them. He took the news of the apoch's death especially hard and had been despondent since their return.

"Careful," Jazzy said. "You must have a natural ability to heal to have come so far in only a few days, but you still have a ways to go."

They left the shelter door unzipped, a breeze moved the door flap gently and allowed in fresh air. The overcast clouds had begun to clear, and light filtered through the white PTFE fabric to illuminate the interior.

"Jonathan's right, you know," Joon-baek said.

"About the apoch, I know," Waters said. "I see that now. I still don't understand it, but he's right. They're right. It makes sense that the people who live and work on a planet would be the most knowledgeable about a planet. But they're colonists. It's such a contradiction."

"I don't mean the apoch. I mean what he said before then," Joon-baek said.

Waters looked up at Joon-baek, who continued, "I love learning about the world, about worlds. I love new discoveries. I love knowledge. I love understanding the way things work. I love technology. I love the process of science; the thought that if we've done everything right, we can know that we've learned something real, added something true to our understanding of the universe."

Joon-baek looked intently at Waters before continuing. "But somewhere along the way we got it wrong. Suddenly the Administration's goals were science, and science was just a formality preceding a foregone conclusion, and we couldn't disagree anymore. We started treating everything there is to know as if it was somehow the Administration that gave us that knowledge regardless of where it came from. As if all you needed to do was ask a question, and the Administration would provide the answer. And if it couldn't, it was a question you shouldn't have asked. That's not what knowledge is; that's not what it was ever supposed to be. Learning is a process. It's ideas you test, then observe the results. Nothing more than that. Yet lifting the Administration and its definition of learning so high hasn't made either of them greater. Just the opposite. By giving these things a status beyond what they deserve, they diminish in significance."

Jazzy's hands stopped mid-examination, Joon-baek's words having caused her to forget what she was doing. Waters sat back, surprised to hear him speak so frankly. Tommy looked at his friend with respectful admiration.

"The Administration didn't build and design Polus Station or the space elevator. Engineers did that. Sure, they had the backing of the Administration, but it didn't build, or envision it. The Administration didn't create these plants or animals, but it will claim them as its own by the time we're done. We name them and the Administration thinks that somehow it has accomplished something. It didn't. These animals existed and had names before someone from Earth came along, as if the first person to write a paper for the Administration were somehow responsible for the animal itself."

Joon-baek took another bite of fruit. Waters felt like he should interrupt this potentially damning speech before Joon-baek damaged himself irreparably and looked to Jazzy for support, but she remained dumbfounded that a member of the mission would speak so about the Administration.

Joon-baek swallowed and continued, "Don't you see that we lift the Administration up so high that we forget that it's not the only thing, that it depends on many other things to function. Math isn't the Administration, but the Administration depends on math. Reason and logic aren't the Administration, but the Administration depends on reason and logic. There are other ways we can learn, other ways we can know things. We learn history not from the Administration, but by studying what people wrote and did. Sure, experts from the Administration can help answer some questions, but they can't tell us what motivated someone, why someone started a war, or painted a painting, or believed.

"We think of what we know as if it has always been, and as if what we know will always be. But what we know changes. You know that by the time we're fifty, half of what we know now will either be shown to be dead wrong or replaced with new knowledge? It's even worse if you're in medicine. How long ago did you graduate from medical school, Jazzy? I hope you've kept up, because within five years of graduation, half of what a doctor learns is no longer current, superseded by new guidelines and treatments and the Administration's own messaging."

Jazzy bristled at her profession being singled, but Joon-baek didn't let that stop him. "Think about what we know. How many times have we been told one thing only for it to be superseded and contradicted the very next year? Sometimes the Administration is spectacularly, horribly wrong. The most modern centuries on Earth saw some of the worst instances of human death and suffering, not from wars, but from plans and models developed by the Administration's predecessors. But people pushed forward anyway rather than admit a mistake. You could say this is not a problem with the Administration but the people in it, but what is the Administration without the people interpreting and enacting its regulations? The Administration isn't some monolithic, all-knowing, omniscient entity with poor, dumb humans just getting it wrong. Without people, the Administration is nothing."

Joon-baek saw the others were uncomfortable and let his eyes fall to the floor, but after a moment he lifted them, resolute, and continued. "Jonathan is right. These people are right. I mean, look at them! They're not primitive, or hicks. They have all the technology we have and more, and freedom to do and say things like I've never seen. They don't worry about losing their status if they don't keep up with the DID's list of offensive words. And here we are, a team whose mission is the precursor to MFASA doing just that: resetting them for doing nothing more than believe something the Administration says they shouldn't, which I guess is just unacceptable.

"Somewhere we became a people who believed so much in ourselves we could see nothing else. At the same time, we became so fragile we could not bear even the thought we might be wrong. We're wrong, Alex. We're so wrong, and because of it we have no business telling them they're wrong." Joon-baek finished and sat back in his bed, staring at the wall, lost in his own thoughts.

Waters and Jazzy said nothing. They had listened because this was not some fanatic speaking; not some zealot invested in ideology. This was Joon-baek, June Bug, their friend, their colleague. The worst part was that Joon-baek could be right. These colonists did not need them to educate them, or teach them about governance, or about health and medicine, not about anything. Since they first arrived, the missionaries were the ones receiving an education. They could barely tread the grass without the colonists' help, let alone teach them.

Then there was Molly. They had never seen her happier since she left the team. No, she was not simply happy. That was too trivial a term. It was like she was home. She belonged here. She was joyful. The colonists let her in the city, but none of the rest of them. Why? She was special, that was why. From the beginning the colonists could see something in her that the rest of them did not have.

Jazzy stepped out of the shelter. What Joon-baek said frightened her. Missionaries were not supposed to speak like that. The Administration was beyond reproach. It was part of their oath: they were never to criticize the Administration. It made sense. You could not open and close a door at the same time. How could someone advocate for the Administration and disapprove of it at the same time? Yet she did not want to report Joon-baek. He was a friend, yes, but what frightened her the most was that what he said might make sense. Waters had changed since they killed the apoch. Joon-baek had changed, too, or developed the courage to say what he thought all along. These were not colonists. These were her colleagues. These were her friends. What did that mean for her? She found that if she were honest with herself, she did not want Waters to report it either.

She looked and saw the rover was gone. "He took it," she said aloud in her surprise. "He's going to make the report now. We're not ready yet. Not now. It's too soon." She had to stop him, to reason with him. He would listen. He loved her, yes, though she did not love him, but she would not need that. Not this time. He would listen to reason first.

Her equipment was in the rover. She could not don her enviro suit or use her phone to track it, but it did not matter. The rover carved deep ruts in the earth wherever it traveled. She could follow its path easily enough.

The rover's treads led up a hill away from the city. She knew the valley well by now but had never been so far away from camp. She was surprised at how difficult the trek was. Although the rover's tracks made it manageable, the effort was tiring. She breathed heavily and needed to stop often. She turned and jumped at the sight of Polus bears following her. "You startled me," she said aloud.

The Polus bears stomped their feet with pleasure at her words, but she turned and kept going. They followed her, and other animals joined them. Birds sang, and insects buzzed. Although physically exhausting, the walk was not unpleasant. It was like a good bout of exercise. It filled her with energy even as she worked. She could see why the others enjoyed hiking in the hills.

The trees broke near the top of the hill, and she saw the rover at last. She stopped to rest and noticed the Polus bears had gone. The birds had too, and the top of the hill was quiet. She could see Beau on top of the rover, fiddling with the communications array.

"Is this why you took the rover? So, you could make a report without me?" Jazzy said as she approached. "This was something we were going to do together."

She climbed into the rover and through the hatch onto the roof.

"Waters has failed to show himself an effective director. It's time MFASA knew about it, and it's time for a change," Beau snapped.

Jazzy was surprised at his tone.

"Stay back, Jazzy," Beau said, holding his palm out towards her. "I can almost get a signal, and I don't need you messing up what I've accomplished here the way you've helped mess up everything else."

"You plan to make a play to take over as director yourself," she said.

"Our report to MFASA is overdue," Beau said. "There are many crucial pieces of information we need to share. The intransigence of the colonists. Their poor reception towards your medical clinic, their unwillingness to let us in the city, how Waters slaughtered the apoch, and perhaps most crucial of all, the loss of a missionary. The Administration's own darling."

"But that's my job. And Waters's job as director. Not yours. You're not even a deputy of the mission," Jazzy said.

"The Administration needs to know about his failures, particularly the loss of a team member to an unorthodox philosophy. You've put off making the report for too long. Someone has to tell them so they can make appropriate changes," Beau said.

"You're wrong. You think they'll put you in charge, but they won't. All it will mean is the premature end of the mission and an excuse for MFASA to step in and resettle the colonists. You'll get nothing from this," Jazzy said.

"That may be, but at least he won't be in charge anymore," Beau said. *She can't stand the thought I might report her failures too*, he thought. "You were only ever interested in yourself anyway. That much is clear now, but it should have always been clear. You may deny it, but you want to report my failures too so that I will be removed as competition for director and you will be named in my place. Is that why you slept with me? To make me easier to manipulate?"

That got Jazzy's ire, and she forgot her reason for going after him. "Beau, that was a mistake. I was vulnerable then. Don't deny you didn't take advantage though. You've wanted to sleep with me all along. Everyone can see the way you look at me, the way you have looked at me. But it had nothing to do with seeing you as competition. Truthfully, you're no competition at all. Driving the rover up here, for example. It would have been easier to take the rover back to the plains for a clear signal than to drive to the top of this stupid mountain."

Beau struggled against a piece of equipment on top of the rover and did not answer. At last, a piece of the rover's transmitter broke off and he fell over backwards. He lashed out at the rover and kicked the equipment. Knowing that a tantrum wouldn't help his situation, Beau composed himself and went back to work.

"Come and put your finger here," he said. *It's as I thought. She wants to be director. This whole time she's been acting as if she were in charge anyway. Barking orders at the missionaries. Telling us what we ought to do.*

Jazzy stepped forward and held a piece of wire in place. Beau pulled out his phone and checked a diagram, though his eyes could not help flitting to Jazzy. *Just look at her. Even now she's using me. I'm nothing more than a prop to her. She's so desperate to make this precious report first that she won't look at me.*

"It's no good," Jazzy said. "There's too much interference. These mountains, these trees, even the atmosphere."

"But we have line-of-sight to the space elevator. Look, you can make it out from here," he said.

Beau was not wrong. From the top of the mountain the great tower and scaffolding of the space elevator under construction was visible above the horizon, hazy grey-blue at this distance but there nonetheless.

"Line of sight isn't helping. The atmosphere is filled with the same kind of wavelength the LiFi transmitter uses. It's causing destructive interference. Between that and the mountains, we can't even raise Polus Station when it passes by in orbit," she said.

"Know-it-all," Beau scoffed. "You've always been insufferable."

"Well, this was your idea. And it hasn't worked at all. Now we don't have a working LiFi transmitter, and our rover is on the top of a mountain where no one could use it anyway even if it did work. I hope you realize I will have to report this insubordination once we finally do make contact," she said.

"That's not to mention your clinic, which you haven't even maintained properly. It's no wonder none of the colonists want to seek care from you," he said.

"The clinic was damaged in the storm! We don't have the supplies to make repairs," Jazzy protested.

"I'm not surprised given how abrasive you are to them. From the moment we made contact you were trying to order them around. As if they'd just let us into their city. Can you imagine!" Beau raised his voice.

"Well, someone had to show some leadership with you all just standing there, mouth agape, ogling all the colonial women. That's probably something I should report as well," Jazzy matched his tone.

"I did no such thing, as if you're really one to talk."

"At least they have some real men among them. You're nothing to be proud of."

That hurt Beau. First his hackles rose at the jab, but then he softened and relaxed his shoulders. "Jazzy, why won't you have me? Am I so despicable to you? Am I that much less than Alex to you?"

Jazzy, however, had not relaxed at all. "I'm sure MFASA would be very interested to know more about our relationship when we do finally contact them. About how you inappropriately took advantage when I was at my worst to coerce me to bed. How you demanded sexual favors in exchange for your silence on the status of the clinic."

"No one will believe that."

"Won't they? Are you willing to lie and say we haven't slept together? I can provide them with proof. I have samples if need be."

"No one would believe you. You have access to who knows what from every missionary as the team physician."

"But not samples taken from within my own body," she retorted. "No one will even think twice about what I have to say then. They'll believe me. But they'll have questions for you, oh yes, they will. You'll be done and shipped back to Earth in disgrace, in shackles even. MFASA never supported the mission having a media specialist anyway."

Beau considered her carefully. "That will mean a messy investigation for you as well. And I'll say whatever I care then. It won't matter if it's true or not. They'll still have to investigate it, and who knows what they'll find during the investigation. Perhaps something on how you treated, or didn't treat, a certain missionary."

"I have no idea what you mean," Jazzy said.

"How long did you think you could hide that you were feeding Molly aspirin instead of her proper medication?" Beau said. "You just had to make sure you were better than her, didn't you? What did you call her? 'Our little celebrity?' An ethics violation like that against such a high-profile patient will mean a board inquiry at least. Whatever they choose to do to me, you won't get out of this clean either."

They stood, neither ceded to the other, but they silently acknowledged the stalemate.

I could throw her down the mountain. Right now. I could get away with it too. Isn't that all that matters? A simple slip is all it would take. Everyone knows none of us are adapted to this world, least of all her. She hasn't shown herself to be the most adroit member of the team either, the way she sliced her hands open almost as soon as we arrived.

"I think we're done here," Jazzy said finally. She left the array, dropped in the hatch, and started the rover. Beyond her, Beau thought he saw a shadow leap into the trees.

You're losing your mind. It's nothing.

Their trip down the mountain was as quiet as the very land around them. The usual cadre of animals and birds, even insects that would normally have accompanied anyone who so much as stepped outside was absent. There was no birdsong, no thumping and grunting and hoofing, only they two and their seething silence. Beau sat in the back behind Jazzy, far enough away that she would not hear if he chose to mutter, but close enough that he could watch her. He was safe for now. She could make no allegation to the Administration; neither could he, however.

But does it need to be that way? Polus is a dangerous place. Despite what the colonists might say, it is still a natural environment. Accidents happen, naturally. Not so natural ones too. She could slip. Perhaps she has an allergy to some insect?

An allergy to your own hand perhaps... Why recoil at the thought? Do we not determine our own morality? Have we not ascended beyond quaint notions of crime and punishment, of heaven and hell? You must do what you need to protect yourself. You must advance your interests. Hers no longer align with yours. Fear not the consequences; there need be none.

They reached the bottom of the hill and parked the rover. Beau walked away and paused outside the enclosure that had once held Molly's apoch. Before Waters had let his friend go. Before Waters had killed his friend. It was empty now.

Beau turned and stopped short. He was face-to-face with the apoch itself. It almost smiled at him, but an animal cannot smile. They were so close he could feel its hot breath on his face. Yet it was calm, and he was calm. This was certainly a dangerous creature. Probably a predator. But he knew that whatever peril it had planned was not for him. Then a thought occurred to him as if from outside himself.

"Jazzy!" he called. "Can you come here? Please?"

The apoch shifted instantly. It backed into the foliage, camouflaging itself. Its toothy grin was the last thing he saw as it blended into the trees.

"Jazzy!" he called once more. Then a third time, "Jazzy!"

At last, she appeared around the side of the rover. "What, Beau? What is it? What do you need?"

"Come here for a moment."

Jazzy walked forward and stood directly across from him, her arms crossed, one hip thrust out to the side. "Did you think of something else you need to say?"

Beau stared at her. "I've decided something important. Something we've known all along, but I feel as if I've only just discovered it for myself."

Jazzy shook her head in annoyance. "What have you discovered?"

Beau pushed Jazzy back into the clutches of the apoch, which materialized from the underbrush as they spoke. It stifled her scream with a gnarly paw. Its long needly claws drew blood where they pricked her face. The apoch gave Beau a knowing grin, that is if animals were capable of grinning, and lifted her body as it carried her into the woods. Jazzy looked back at Beau with open eyes full of terror. He took a few steps back and sat down on the same overturned crate by the pen to which he had become accustomed. His heart pounded, but he felt calm. He breathed deeply and told himself: *Don't worry. There will be no consequences.*

She was gone.

CHAPTER TWENTY-SIX

A TECHNICALITY

A lex, we have a problem," Jonathan said.

He rode up to the camp on an arkouda, joining the group lounging outside the shelter. Molly had come to visit again, so she, Waters, Tommy, and Joon-baek looked up at his arrival.

"What is it?" Waters asked.

"The apoch we killed was not the one you captured. I just received the results of the tests on the pelt. It doesn't match the DNA of the apoch you were holding. Your apoch is still loose," Jonathan said.

"Show me," Joon-baek said.

Jonathan pulled out his phone, and with a flick sent the data to Joon-baek. He hobbled to his workbench and with a gesture projected the data onto the side of the shelter. Molly came to stand behind him.

"He's right," Joon-baek said.

"Here are the data we collected on the apoch we captured, and here's the analysis of the pelt that Jonathan just brought. They're different," Molly said.

"There's still an apoch in the area. We have to go find it now," Jonathan said. He pulled out his phone and began searching.

"Has anyone seen Jazzy?" It was Beau.

"Beau!" Waters said. "Where have you been?"

"Hello, Beau," Molly said. He ignored her.

"I don't think we've seen much of either of you recently," Joon-baek said, answering the question.

"We took the rover to the top of a mountain to try and get a signal on its transmitter. I haven't seen Jazzy since we got back," Beau said.

"There, a distortion not far from here. We have to go now," Jonathan said, interrupting any further questions.

As if summoned by thought alone, several arkouda came to them. They mounted and followed Jonathan's direction. Tommy started his flyer and flew above them. Jonathan phoned the mayor. Within a few minutes the mayor and other colonists joined them on arkouda with supplies.

"It's only a couple of miles away. We should find it soon," Jonathan said.

"How far is that?" Waters asked.

"Just over 3 kilometers," Tommy's voice came piping over their phones. "I don't see anything from up here. It's all tree cover. I'm going to come down."

It only took a few minutes to close in on the signal. The arkouda raced through the woods with a speed and agility Waters still found difficult to comprehend. When they were within 100 meters, Jonathan stopped them. They dismounted but Waters spurred his arkouda on ahead of the rest.

"Alex!" Jonathan called after him, yelling as quietly as he could through closed teeth, but he paid no attention.

Waters rode into a small sandy-bottomed clearing but saw nothing. He put on his glasses. He was right on top of the distortion but saw and felt nothing. The arkouda spun around in place, anxious itself but also spurred by Waters's confusion. The others ran into the clearing behind him. Waters began to speak but the mayor pressed a finger to his lips and grabbed his ankle. He pointed to a tree on the far side of the clearing. It was massive like the others, but Waters saw nothing there. No apoch or sign of the apoch.

"What? It's just a dead tree?" he whispered.

The mayor shook his head and motioned for Waters to dismount.

The arkouda left the clearing as soon as he dismounted, and the very air around them became silent. Together they approached the tree. As they drew near, Waters began to see. The tree was dead indeed. Skeletal branches towered high over them. The whole tree was naked of bark and bleached by exposure to the sun. The sap and resin had settled in the wood and preserved it hard like iron. Wind-blown sand had polished the trunk smooth. They walked around to the other side and found a hollow there, carved by years, decades even of elements. They looked inside. Below the hollow the dirt had worn away and broken through the top of a cavern which was all blackness, and into which they could not see.

"Down there?" Waters whispered.

"Down there," the mayor said. "Glasses."

"We have to go in? We'll be at a complete disadvantage," Tommy said. "Besides needing the glasses to see, we have no idea where it is, or the layout of the cave."

"We have no choice. We can't give it time to flee again. It may already be too late," Jonathan said.

They all put on their glasses and prepared their lances. Tommy walked to the hollow and kicked a stone into the hole. It landed with a plop. "It can't be that deep," he said. He lowered himself over the edge and dropped himself down while the others watched. "It's just a few feet. The bottom is sandy. We should be able to get in without a problem," he said.

"Waters, Jonathan, you must go to complete your responsibility in this," the mayor said.

Neither of them argued.

"As for the rest of you, they will need help, but you know the danger. Only volunteer if you are willing. Joon-baek, you should remain here," the mayor continued.

Joon-baek looked disappointed but did not protest.

"I'll go," Molly said.

Several colonists stepped forward as well.

"I'll go too," the mayor said.

Waters was surprised, but grateful.

Tommy helped them down into the hollow. Everything was complete darkness just a few feet beyond the entrance. They could see with their glasses, but it was a strange sensation. They showed everything in stark chiaroscuro, all outlines and shapes in red and blue. There was no gradient or shadow to show depth or form.

It was not a cavern after all. The walls were dirt, not stone. The tree's petrified roots extended in all directions around and above them and supported the walls and ceiling like arteries, long dead and hardened.

"How do you make something like this?" Waters asked. "There's no water, no wind."

"You carve it," Jonathan answered.

"It would take years to make something like this," Waters said.

"Think on what that means," the mayor said.

They walked deeper, following the only path before them.

Molly placed a hand on the wall as she looked at the data her glasses gave her. "Nothing is alive here," she said. "I mean nothing. There are no worms, no beetles, no ants, no roots or tubers, nothing you would expect to find in soil." She tapped her glasses again. "Not even bacteria. The earth is truly dead here."

"We must be right under the clearing by now," Tommy said.

"Hush," the mayor said. "Something's there."

They heard something like cloth rubbing together. They did not so much see as feel that the apoch was there.

Waters did not hesitate; he took his lance and drawing his arm back he hurled the lance forward into the darkness. He was not experienced, but he caught the apoch by surprise. His throw connected and struck the apoch in the back between the shoulder blades where the lance clanged off its spines. From the wound the lance left, a tiny stream of light flowed forth and dripped to the ground where it left glowing splotches in the dirt, the only light in the darkness around them. The apoch shrieked. They covered their ears at the terrible sound.

"Together! Stay together!" the mayor called. His voice boomed in the cavern and cut through the apoch's scream.

They gathered back to back, their lances pointed outward.

Tommy held his rifle up and ready. "The glasses aren't showing it," he said.

"It will only show on the glasses if it camouflages. It doesn't need to do that down here," Jonathan said.

"Watch for the blood. It will give it away," the mayor said.

"Watch above you. This is a 3D environment," Tommy said.

Several of the colonists pointed their lances up.

In the darkness their fear amplified every sound. Every breath of air, every shuffled foot, every creak and groan, real or imagined became an enemy ready to strike from any direction or no direction. They began to lunge out at perceived shadows with the points of their lances.

"Keep your heads. The apoch is dangerous, but it's mortal," the mayor said.

"Watch the exit. Don't let it get around us," Tommy said.

"Something fell on my head!" shouted one of the colonists. He dropped his lance and frantically brushed dirt from his hair.

"Hold on to your weapon!" the mayor said, thrusting the lance back into his hands.

"There!"

"Over there!"

They began to move frantically. Their formation broke.

"Stay together!" the mayor shouted, his voice reverberating through the cavern.

"Where is it?"

"I can't see it!"

"Dear God, is there more than one?"

The missionaries and colonists grew frantic and were on the verge of panic.

"Be still for a moment," Molly said. Her voice dispelled the fear from among them. "The apoch harms the body, but it feeds on the mind. It's affecting us even now. Be still in your mind and heart. Take my hand," she said to Waters.

Waters took her hand and placed his other hand on Jonathan's shoulder. One-by-one, they reached out to each other. The human contact gave them strength and courage, and they calmed.

"I don't think it's moved at all," Molly said.

"Everyone together. Step toward the glow on the floor," the mayor said.

They took one step forward, then another. They moved as one group toward where the apoch's blood glowed on the ground, lances at the ready. A hiss came out of the darkness, seemingly from everywhere at once, and threatened their composure.

"Stand together," Molly said.

They took another step forward and a shriek pierced their ears through the silence again. Claws scraped against dirt as the apoch charged. Colonists hurled their lances at the sound. Suddenly, the cadence of its steps changed and a thud landed against the wall.

"It's climbing the wall!" Jonathan shouted.

"It's making for the exit," Tommy said and opened fire.

Flashes from his rifle's muzzle lit the apoch's tunnel like a strobe. They hurled their lances at the afterimage as the apoch dodged their missiles. One of Tommy's bullets found its mark and a spray of liquid light covered the walls. The apoch stumbled but continued. A trail of tiny globules of light fell and betrayed its location as it ran back toward the tree.

"Don't let it escape," the mayor shouted.

Waters ran forward to the outline of his lance where it lay in the dirt after his throw. The others fumbled in the dark and searched for their own lances. Tommy stopped firing to reload. Waters grabbed his lance and charged past the group. He followed the tiny drops of light in the dirt back to the entrance where he saw the creature. A shadow just below a shaft of light from the tree hollow to the outside. He drew his arm back and let the lance fly. It hurtled through the air and lodged in the apoch with a sickening sucking sound.

Enraged, the apoch turned and ran toward him. Then as if something inside switched off, it stumbled and collapsed. It turned its hideous head toward Waters and gave a defiant howl before a throw from behind silenced the beast with finality.

Jonathan came up from behind him. "I think that makes this one technically mine," he said.

They all sighed with relief. With a smile, Jonathan slapped Waters on the back.

CHAPTER TWENTY-SEVEN

REGRETS

Molly let out a gasp that caught the group's attention, and they all turned to see what had alarmed her. Jonathan regretted his quip immediately, and his face grew grim.

With the monster dead the situation unfolded before them. The apoch had captured Jazzy and pinned her to a root upside-down through her ankles. Her face was beet red and swollen from blood running to her head. Her jaw was broken and hung askance and loose. Her tongue flapped uselessly in her mouth, bisected down the middle. Streams of blood flowed from the corners of her mouth. She coughed and threatened to aspirate.

"Quickly. Get her down." the mayor said.

Molly ran forward to Jazzy and tried to lift her head but could do no more than tilt her neck forward. Jazzy winced with pain. Waters and Jonathan grabbed at her legs and attempted to pull her down. Jazzy gave a guttural cry of pain so grotesque they could not stand it, and they let go. The clothing around her torso was in tatters. They pulled back the shredded cloth and found that the apoch had rivetted her fast to the tree through her hip and shoulder. They stared helplessly, none of them sure what to do.

"We have to get her down!" Molly said in no small distress, tears flowing down her cheeks.

Jazzy looked back through eyes soaked wet with pain and desperation and pled silently for help. She dared not move. Then her chest heaved, and her eyes suddenly stared out at nothing with an intensity unlike anything they had seen. Her head and neck went limp in Molly's arms. Blood flowed from her mouth followed by an unsettling rattle, and she was still. Her half-open eyes gazed out at nothing, forever.

They did get Jazzy down eventually. They splintered the apoch's spines so they could remove enough of the pieces to take her body down. They had nothing to cover her, so Joon-baek lent his mission jacket. They lay her body on the back of an arkouda and rode to camp. It mourned with them, though it held its head with dignity, honored to carry her. The mayor sung in low tones to himself.

"We will take her into the city and prepare the body for you," the mayor said when they arrived back at camp.

"We appreciate it," Joon-baek said.

"That would be fine," Waters said.

"We'll need to know how you want her body handled," the mayor said.

"That would be a question for director Waters," Molly said.

Waters did not know what to do. No one responded.

"Where's Beau?" Molly asked, suddenly missing him.

"Wasn't he with us?" Joon-baek asked.

"Now that you mention it, I don't remember him, but I thought he was with us the whole time," Tommy said.

"The rover's gone," Joon-baek said.

"He wouldn't have just left with it. He wouldn't have left. Would he?" Waters asked.

"Call him," Molly suggested.

Waters opened his phone, but it was no use. "There's too much interference. I can see you, Joon-baek, Tommy, but not Beau. He must be too far away already."

"Or he turned off his phone," Tommy said.

"I'm sure he had a good reason to go. He probably wanted to report to the Administration," Waters said.

"But he wouldn't have known about this any more than we did until we found her. Why did he leave?" Tommy said.

"Look, we don't even know that it was him who took the rover," Waters said.

"There's no one else who could have," Joon-baek said.

They stood puzzled. "But why?" they asked themselves.

"The guilty flee when none pursue," Tommy said with a note of grave significance.

They looked at him, disbelieving.

"The apoch killed Jazzy. Not Beau," Waters said.

"We all saw it," Joon-baek said.

"All we know is that he came to tell us that he had not seen Jazzy since they got back," Tommy said.

"One may be responsible for killing without doing the act," the mayor said. "But you're also right. We don't know what his part may have been in this, and he may have had legitimate reasons for leaving so quickly."

"Unlikely," Jonathan said, chiming in at last.

The mayor shot a look to quiet Jonathan, but his heart was not in it. "Let's see to what is at hand. There will be plenty of time for answers later. Most likely this is a simple tragedy. We will take care of the doctor; in the meantime, see to yourselves."

The mayor, Molly, and Jonathan parted with Jazzy's body and returned to the city. They left Joon-baek, Tommy, and Waters alone at camp.

Feelings of heaviness weighed on Waters. He both felt the emotional weight of Jazzy's loss, and the physical sensation of her absence in his shoulders and chest at the same time. That night he could not sleep. He was certain none of them slept much. They were quiet, but it was the quiet of people pretending to sleep, not the comfortable wheeze of those in slumber.

Waters arose the next morning before the sun and returned to the place where Jazzy had died. He looked down into the hollow. There lay the apoch's skin in a heap, untouched and forgotten, devoid of life and substance if it ever had any. If there truly was a creature of pure evil, this was surely one of them.

"You should take it," a voice said.

It was Jonathan. Waters did not need to ask what he was doing there; they were there to exorcise the previous day each in his own way.

"An apoch skin is more than just a hunting trophy," Jonathan said. "It is a symbol that you've overcome something truly wicked and made the world safer. It's a sign you are committed to self-sacrifice for the sake of those around you. You should take it. We, we would be honored to make it into a shemagh for you."

"I think I understand its symbolism. I understand what it means to have a shemagh too. I'm grateful for that. I don't think I would have been even a few days ago, but I am now. I don't think I should have it though…" Waters began to choke up, and the words caught in his throat.

Jonathan knelt down next to Waters while he waited respectfully for him to continue.

"You know…I just…" Waters paused for a few moments while he composed himself. "I am responsible for her death. I helped capture the apoch, and it was me who let it go. I was spiteful toward the mayor, toward you, toward the rest of the colonists, and I wanted to show that you're wrong. Not just about the apoch. About everything. I thought if you were wrong about this one thing it would somehow prove you were wrong about the rest too. But it was stupid. I don't even feel like I was myself when I let it go," Waters said after composing himself for a few moments.

"You may not have been yourself," Jonathan replied. "We don't fully understand, but the apoch can affect you. Each person is different, but they somehow influence you just by their presence. They cause thoughts you would normally push out of mind to surface, and you act on impulses you would normally abhor. They search out and amplify the darkest parts of yourself. That's what makes them dangerous. They are strong and can cause great harm, but it's how they torment you with your own thoughts that causes the greatest injury."

Waters nodded, feeling comfort from Jonathan's words.

Jonathan continued. "And you're right: you are responsible for her death."

Waters's heart dropped out of his chest.

"Do not try to delude yourself otherwise that you weren't," Jonathan continued. "That will only form scars of denial, and you would be lying to yourself. It's painful now. The pain will always be there, though it will get easier each day."

Jonathan looked at Waters with great meaning, and Waters understood that what Jonathan said was meant for the sake of offering comfort, but he was also relating something personal but unspoken.

"Admitting your part is the first step in forgiving yourself for what happened," Jonathan said. "That doesn't mean you won't face consequences, but you'll be prepared to accept them. And you can't forgive others until you first forgive yourself."

Waters did not want to believe there might be consequences for his part in Jazzy's death, but Jonathan was right. "I know it was the apoch that killed her, but there's a direct line between when I let it go and her death. I don't want to believe there might be consequences, but you're right. Jazzy already paid the greatest price for my mistakes. I'll accept what happens to me." Speaking these words, Waters felt a wave of relief wash over him. It did not replace his sadness, but he felt he could move forward.

Jonathan placed his hand on Waters's shoulder. "Congratulations, Alex; you have just repented." Jonathan clapped his hand on Waters's back. "Come on. That's enough grief for now. You all should feed me breakfast."

When Waters and Jonathan returned to camp, they found Tommy and Joon-baek in somber moods, but Tommy had his cowboy coffee brewing, and the scent revived them in a way that rivaled the viti fruit's power. Jonathan helped make biscuits of flour, milk, and honey straight from the produce of the valley in a cast-iron pot he seemed to summon from nowhere. Instead of cooking it over a gas stove they set the pot amidst coals. The aroma set their mouths watering. The pot steamed when they opened it a few minutes later, as did the biscuits when they pulled them apart. Pads of homemade butter melted instantly in the steaming biscuits, and they savored their breakfast as each ate his fill. The pot never left them wanting. They drank cool fermented viti juice. It fizzed pleasantly in their mouths and livened their spirits. They cooked up the eggs of some native fowl, which they fried and seasoned with salt.

Just as breakfast was winding down, Molly joined them. They exchanged pleasantries and stood awkwardly. They knew the questions she needed answered. The breakfast had been good. It was a shame to see more serious matters take its place.

"We need to decide what to do with Jazzy," she said.

There was a moment of silence.

"I think by regulation we should contact MFASA for guidance," Waters offered, "but we can't. I suspect that's what Beau and Jazzy… what they were trying to do with the rover before it happened. They don't seem to have been successful, and I can't think of anything we could try that they would not have already attempted."

"Except returning to the space port to make the call ourselves," Joon-baek said.

"We could take my flyer since he took the rover," Tommy suggested.

"We're not supposed to go anywhere near the spaceport," Jonathan said, shaking his head. "Not after the accusations made against the colonists on Alpha Centauri b and what happened to them. We avoid anything looking even remotely like interference with Earth's projects to keep ourselves safe from even the most modest allegation."

"I wish we knew why he took it," Waters said.

"Maybe he was one step ahead of us," Joon-baek said.

"He couldn't have known what would happen," Molly said.

"We could ask for permission though, right? About flying?" Waters said.

"We could ask," Jonathan said.

"I'm not sure we should wait that long," Molly said. "The colonists can keep Jazzy for as long as we need. That's not the problem. It doesn't feel right to not do something sooner."

"Did she have any family?" Joon-baek asked.

"I don't know. Now that I think about it, I didn't know her that well. Not nearly as well as I should have," Waters said with a touch of guilt. "Did she tell you anything?" he looked at Molly.

She looked away. "It's true. She treated me. But we didn't talk about family. At least not about her family. My family came up all the time, but I really don't know anything about her. We could check the records."

"Without the rover, our ability to connect to MFASA's database is very limited. Everything else was lost in the storm. Beau, why did you just leave like that?" Waters said to no one in particular.

No one had a solution. They stood looking at the dirt for a few moments.

Jonathan finally spoke up. "This is really your decision to make. She was part of your group. But if it were up to us, we would bury her."

"Here on Polus?" Joon-baek asked.

"Would you cremate her? We don't usually bury people," Waters said.

"It is our practice to bury people when they pass. We don't cremate the dead. You could pick a place where you would like her buried. Some place you could visit, and others could visit later if they wanted, if there's anyone to visit her," Jonathan suggested.

Waters looked at the other missionaries. "What do you think?"

"I don't think we should wait to contact the Administration. That would take too long," Joon-baek said. "Even if we do find some way to contact them, who knows how long it would take to get a response?"

"If the colonists are offering, I think we should bury her here," Molly said.

"What do you think, Tommy?" Waters asked.

Tommy looked surprised to be asked for his opinion. "I'm not one of the missionaries. I don't think it should be my decision."

"You're one of us though," Molly said.

"Yes. Just because you don't wear the same patch doesn't mean we don't want to hear what you have to say," Waters said.

"I think we should bury her here. It's what the Marines would do if we couldn't bring someone home. It's the best way to show respect for her passing," he said.

They looked at each other and concurred. It was nice to decide together.

"I'll let the city know," Molly said.

The missionaries selected a spot across the river near the base of the valley where the meadow ended and the trees began. None of them had buried anyone before. The funeral was not quick. It was hard work. They had to dig a deep hole, which would have been difficult work in itself, but the moon resisted their efforts, making it harder. Fortunately, the colonists lent their hands, including Jonathan. They could have dug the grave in a few moments with their machinery, but the mayor told them this way would be better. The mayor was right, in a way. It felt better to dig the hole. With each shovel they seemed to be preparing a place for her to rest.

When it came time to finally lay Jazzy in the ground, the team of missionaries and Tommy gathered around the hole. A few of the colonists attended out of respect, including the mayor. They carried Jazzy forward in a fine-looking wooden coffin, hand-made by one of the colonists. It was far simpler than the kind of urn they would have used on Earth, but felt more appropriate. They placed the coffin on the side of the grave atop several ropes. The mayor asked, "Have any of you done this before?"

They shook their heads.

"Would you like me to conduct a service?" he asked.

"I don't think we're sure what that means, Mr. Mayor, but that would be kind of you," Waters said for the group.

The mayor read the funeral ceremony from a book. The words were clearly religious, but none of the missionaries objected. He finished speaking, then motioned toward the coffin. Jonathan and two colonists took the ropes. Jonathan looked over his shoulder at the missionaries. Waters, Tommy, and Joon-baek stepped forward. Together they lowered her coffin into the grave. The mayor took a handful of earth and threw it on top of the coffin, touching his forehead, stomach, and both shoulders as he did so. The missionaries in turn also took handfuls of earth, tossing them on the coffin, though only Joon-baek imitated the sign the mayor had made. Molly added a bouquet of flowers and leaves, then they covered the coffin in the same way they had dug the grave: one shovel full of dirt at a time until at last the ground was level. The colonists set a plain headstone. It read: 'Jazaraiah Bebe, M.D.'

Waters added one last shovel of dirt, then went to stand next to Molly where he planted the shovel in the ground.

CHAPTER TWENTY-EIGHT

MISSIONARY LEE

Going was slow in the rover. The trip back to the spaceport was every bit as rough and rocky as the trip out, only Beau was alone this time. There was no one to take turns driving. No one to help change the batteries. No one to heat water for a bit of MFASA's mush while he drove. No one to keep watch or monitor geomapping or navigate the gullies and washes, hills, rocks, and arroyos. No one to drive while he stopped to relieve himself.

Beau had been energized at first, but the high faded soon enough to something like depression. He was not sad or grieving. In his actions he was resolute, a new man. His path was clear, or at least, his guiding principle was clear. He was sure the details would present themselves in time. No, the lows he felt were the rebound of a fall from the height of a man reborn by his choices.

He could drive for about two hours before he needed to rest: he ached, he was hungry, he was thirsty, he needed to pee, he wanted a nap, he was tired of driving, plain and simple.

The terrain all felt the same on the way back absent the novelty of a new place. Not like the drive out. That trip had been comparatively short, though when every bluff and blade of grass was new it seemed to take more time than it did. Now the plains were just a cloudy expanse, a wide sea interrupted only by the occasional wind rippling through tall stalks of accursed grass like waves. Above, only sky; below, only dirt. And how far must he travel? At night, the glow of vitis dotted the plain with thousands of pointilliste lights that blended into the constellations, making heaven and firmament indistinguishable, but he despised the spectacle. He pulled a blanket over his head. He preferred to drive at night, but the lights mocked him, so he shut out the night and planned.

Like a child with a flashlight in bed too tired to sleep and too awake to dream, he sat under his blanket. His phone showed maps, diagrams, notes, stratagems. Long stratagems. He would need years, but he would gather to himself that which was most important: authority, comfort, his best life now, his eternity. Power. One problem remained: the colonists. Their intransigence ruined his mission. The issue was trivial for the Administration: MFASA would resettle the colonists, and those who would not be resettled would receive supplemental education. He could not have a failure on his record, however. Even the ABS, which had eaten up his footage, ever eager to showcase the popular MFASA in its programming, would not overlook the mission's failure. He needed a solution that evaded him still. He needed the colonists gone, separated from Earth.

The journey to the colony had taken no more than a couple of weeks. His solo traversal back to the spaceport took many times that.

One night he lay restless. He tried to sleep but could not. The lights mocked him. He tore out of the rover and pushed aside the tall rigid grass. He cut his hands but did not care. He snatched up as many vitis as he could carry. In his fury he bit into the fruit deep as he could with one enormous bite, but found the fruit now had the bitter taste of gall. Instead, he tore at it with his teeth. He spilled the vitis as he thrashed. He filled his arms again, and when he could carry no more stomped down hard on those in reach, soiling his pants and boots with the spatter. The juicy pulp glowed still, and that infuriated him even more. He climbed back into the rover and looked at the fruit that had not fallen from his arms with derision. "We'll see how well you survive off the vine," he said aloud, and poured the contents out onto the floor.

At last, the space elevator took the place of the gas giant Polus in its dominance of the sky, and Beau felt that he was arriving back at civilization. Below, the comforting grey concrete and steel spaceport stood with its brown trailers lined up in neat rows. Only a few trailers had not been replaced from the tornado. Above, a dusty cloud of industry and smoke emanated from the factories and scaffolding where worker positions, those engines of society, implemented progress. He rolled into the gravel road between the trailers and main building. He brought the rover to a stop in front of the same doors out of which he had first stepped onto Polus IV proper. That was its real name after all. No more colloquialisms. It was time for the truth, his truth, to dominate.

Alice emerged from behind the sliding doors. A look of surprise flashed across her face only momentarily before she regained her doll-like composure and approached the rover, still dressed all in white. Behind her Beau could see a new group of worker positions being treated to the same stupid, outdated introductory video.

The rover's door opened, and Alice recoiled at the terrific stench that wafted forth. The rover had been home to a single occupant who neither bathed nor cleaned the rover for several weeks. The vitis had rotted on the floor where they lay, seeping their fetid juices into the cracks of the rover's interior where only the most determined refit detail had any hope of finding them.

"Missionary Lee," Alice said, politely waving a white kerchief in front of her face and pretending to stifle a cough as a pretext for covering her nose. "You were not expected. We had no communication from you."

Beau dropped to the gravel on both feet straight from the door and looked around. He breathed and appreciated the smell of civilization. Alice looked him up and down. The environmental suit was faded and dingy. His armpits were stained even through the suit's tough fabric. Viti juice stained his chest and the cuffs of his pants and sleeves blood red.

Alice pursed her lips in ever-so-slight disapproval and repeated herself, "You were not expected, Missionary Lee. We had no communication."

"I know. That is why I'm here," Beau said. "We have not been able to transmit a LiFi signal for several weeks, months. This moon presents too much atmospheric interference, you know."

"I am quite aware. Just as soon as you have cleaned up," Alice emphasized this point with a subtle inflection, "I would be happy to assist you in making use of the space port's LiFi. Or perhaps you would prefer to do so from one of the trailers?"

"A trailer I think," Beau said.

"Then I will need to make arrangements. If you care to follow me," Alice said with a gesture of her palm toward the doors.

Beau followed her back inside. The odor of his accommodations wafted after him, and the worker positions inside took notice as he passed. Alice grabbed and donned a mask from a cart as they passed through the doors. They walked through the amphitheater, and Beau was treated to a second viewing of the safety briefing. Suddenly, two ideas collided in his mind.

"That's it," he said as they emerged from the dark room.

"I'm sorry, Missionary Lee?" Alice said.

"I know what I need to do, Alice. Thank you for your help."

"You are welcome."

CHAPTER TWENTY-NINE

HE WHO HELPED CREATE IT

Life continued for the missionaries as if a shadow had passed from camp. They packed up what remained of Jazzy's belongings to ship back to Earth, should the opportunity present itself. They may have followed regulations in doing so, but they did not know whether they did or not. Regardless, it felt right to do. They packed up the clinic, which sat ragged at the edge of the plaza, and salvaged most of the PTFE cloth and poles. The equipment inside had been neglected, but still functioned.

Several of the colonists joined them in their cleanup, including the mayor, who suggested they move their camp to the square near where the clinic had been. Tommy integrated the clinic and their remaining shelter into a larger habitat so they each had their own room. When they finished, they had a credible house, complete with a common room and bedrooms. Molly had helped with the move but chose to remain in the city.

As the days and weeks wore on, Joon-baek had a fantastic time exploring the moon. He had no more success in cultivating the Polus fruit, but the planet proved a treasure trove for someone with unlimited curiosity. He spent his days working in the fields with the colonists or exploring with Tommy in his flyer. They flew from peak to peak with the excuse of mapping the terrain. They shared stories both fact and fiction with some having a touch of both. Joon-baek held on tight, but still laughed with joy when Tommy threaded the eye of a rock arch with only a few feet to spare.

Tommy found a love for the colonists' machines, even those beyond the flyer he claimed as his own. He was becoming quite the pilot, and a decent mechanic too. The colonists obliged, and he would drag some new machine to camp and take it to pieces in the yard next to their new home while Joon-baek sat at his workbench, dissecting or illustrating some new plant and deciding what to call it.

"The colonists named them first. That should be honored in their scientific name," he said to himself. Tommy grunted his assent, shoulders deep in the chassis of some machine.

Waters missed Beau and worried about where he had gone and what had happened to him. He would want to know what had happened to Jazzy. Waters took to hiking again, though not alone. He often walked with Molly, always chaperoned by a club of bounding but respectful animals. He walked to the top of a peak where he held up his phone in vain, and tried to raise a signal, but it was no use. The response was always the same: static and interference.

Although MFASA required that missionaries keep their hair short and under a cap for the sake of sanitation, Molly's dark hair had grown and now hung well below her shoulders. The uniform cap, which could be flattering in its own way as a symbol of humanity's accomplishments, did not compare to the beauty of Molly's hair. It was like a glory to her, a better covering than any hat no matter what it signified. Waters caught himself looking at her; he felt ashamed and thrilled at the same time when she looked back.

He rode on Polus bears as much as he hiked, often accompanied by Jonathan and other colonists. Their conversations were often filled with less weighty topics than before, with Waters learning from the colonists about subjects the missionaries would never have bothered to learn before. Nearly everything the colonists did was based on interest. Technology took care of their needs. They therefore pursued what activity their talents lent them. Those who worked the fields or tended the trees did so because they enjoyed it. Those who kept the bees did so likewise. There were painters, musicians, poets, writers, sculptors, dancers, and all manner of high art, in addition to athletics. Others studied the planet's ecology, geology, meteorology, and the system's cosmology. Some delved into literature, or studied scripture, or language, or history. Some spent their time with the animals. Some explored, some were engineers and designers, some were architects, and some programmed. Technology freed them to pursue that which they wished, and so the colonists worked each according to their God-given gifts.

Indeed, Waters was amazed that the colonists had achieved a peaceful and prosperous society where people were free to seek their own happiness without the Administration's assistance.

One day, Waters returned from riding. He cast off his poncho, hung his shemagh and glasses on the corner of his bed, and on a whim picked up a mission tablet to kill time before he met Molly for dinner. He ran through their old lessons and training. It was all so strange to him now. He tossed the tablet into a box, which held remnants from Jazzy's clinic, and noticed a second tablet in the box. It was one designated specifically for him as director and labeled sensitive.

He opened the device with his thumbprint. It contained many of the same training topics, but his provided more detail: Administrative Solutions, Free Education, The Administration and Science, Western Religions and other Enduring Myths, Supplemental Education. The last topic reminded him of Molly's story about her parents. It had been incredible if true. Would the Administration really put people into gulags? It would be regressing hundreds of years if so.

As Waters continued to review the training materials, he found most of it standard training, but the deeper he got, the more credence it gave to Molly's tale. He came to a slide deep in the training about supplemental education, and almost dropped the tablet in shock. He grabbed his poncho and rushed out of the shelter. He jogged toward the Narrow Gate and pulled out his phone to make a call. "Jonathan.

I've found something important. Can you put me in touch with the mayor? It's about our mission."

Jonathan, the mayor, Ai, and Patience met him within a few minutes. He still could not pass through the gate, but it had become something he now accepted. One's ability to pass into the city depended on no one's choices but his own. None of the missionaries were ready to make that choice. Molly, by contrast, had come to Polus having made the choice in her childhood.

"Mayor, I just learned something significant for you and the whole city. It will work better if I can show you," Waters said. He led them back to the shelter and invited them in, then regretted doing so: it was the habitation of three single men. While not untidy, it was not what he wished them to see. But no matter. He pushed a spare shirt off a table, it might have been any one of theirs, and set his phone down. Then with a flick and flip of his fingers, his phone projected the slides he had been reviewing above the table.

"I had got so used to being here with you that I nearly forgot why it was we came," Waters began. "Our mission, our purpose, was to convince as many colonists as we could to rejoin Earth's society and government. My mission especially was to persuade you to join the Colonial House. There someone from the colony would represent you and along with members from the other colonies, and cast resolutions concerning colonial government to be considered by the Administration."

"We knew this. You explained this to us many times," Jonathan said.

Molly walked into the shelter looking for Waters. He was late to dinner.

"Did I threaten you with this? Supplemental Education?" Waters said and flipped to the final slides of a presentation. Most of the slides were cheerful enough, showing small groups of people eagerly participating in classes and seminars that could have been for any generic purpose. Deeper into the presentation, the character of the slides changed. The final set was marked "sensitive: not for public distribution."

"These slides describe procedures for what should be done if a team fails," Waters said. "Supplemental Education doesn't just mean you'll have to attend some classes; it means MFASA could join with the military to relocate your entire colony back to Earth. You could be placed in camps. You could remain there until and unless you renounce your way of life." He looked at Molly, who remembered something she had rather not. "That may not be the worst of it though."

Waters advanced the slides and there was an audible gasp. They depicted a gruesome medical procedure. A patient lay restrained on a table as a doctor inserted a metal rod above his eye. With a tap, the rod broke the thin wall of skull above the eye and penetrated the frontal lobe. The doctor twisted the rod and removed a tiny piece of grey matter. As the doctor did so, all emotion left the patient's face. They were not certain what it was, but it looked like medieval torture.

Jonathan grew agitated and ready for a fight.

Ai looked distressed, "Is this true?"

The mayor and Patience were the only ones who did not react, but instead shared a knowing look. "Alex, we're grateful to you for bringing this to our attention, but we knew this already," the mayor said. Then he turned to Jonathan, Ai, and Molly. "I knew this already. I know what supplemental education means. I know what it means because I helped create it."

Those gathered gasped at the mayor's revelation but allowed him to continue.

"I was not part of the first generation to come to Polus. I came around the time the Colonial House was established. It was presented as a compromise to keep the colonies connected to Earth, but most saw it for what it was: a symbolic body that left control in the hands of Earth's government and turned the colonies into nothing more than janissaries. My division was tasked with developing the program, the same division that would send you on your mission years later. As the true intentions of the program finally became clear to me, I made plans to leave myself."

Waters was the first to speak. "Mayor, the Colonial House was established almost a hundred years ago. What you're saying is impossible. You would have to be more than—" Waters did the napkin math in his head, "—one hundred and twenty years old."

"My one hundred and thirty-sixth birthday is later this month," the mayor responded.

Waters was agog. The mayor looked older, but not elderly. Past middle age, but still not old enough to be eligible for the Administration's retirement support. Waters assumed he was in his mid-fifties. "That's not possible," he said. It was not an expression of disbelief.

"It's this planet, Alex. The fruit of the vine not only heals and mends broken bones, it extends our life, though it will never be everlasting. Not in this world. Those born here like Jonathan and Ai will live even longer. Even just the year you've spent here will extend your life. You must have noticed already. The fruit of the vine can do things that are almost miraculous, but it's not just the fruit. This whole planet was made somehow *more*. The air, the water, the plants, the animals, even the weather, they're all more than they were on Earth. I've been away for so long that it's hard to remember things weren't always this way, but it's as if everything here is more itself, more the way it was meant to be all along."

"Beau, where are you? Why won't you answer?" Waters was at the top of a peak once more trying contact his fellow missionary. There had been a brief break in the atmospheric interference. He could see the Beau was receiving a signal, but he would not answer.

"I'm sure he would answer if he could," Molly said.

"You would think he'd answer a call from the missionaries he hadn't seen for weeks—no, months," Waters said.

"It's hard to let go, isn't it?" Molly said.

She was right. Their mission had effectively ended with Jazzy's death. None of them attempted to proselytize the colonists further. Not that their efforts were effective anyway, but the endeavor seemed futile, even counter-productive now that they knew the colonists. Waters kicked a rock with his foot, just hard enough to let it know he was frustrated, if it would listen. "We can try again later, I guess," he said.

They started down the mountain. A brace of arkouda followed at a respectful distance, hoping for riders. A troop of what Molly had

named leercats gamboled and chittered about their feet. They dug
every so often to chomp on a grub. They were small, about the size
of a prairie dog but with a longer face and body and long ringed tail.
Like nearly all animals on Polus they had three pairs of vestigial wings,
though theirs were still somewhat useful. They leapt after insects and
their wings fluttered, contributing to the jump in their own way. Sometimes they caught a bug between racoon-like front paws and sat back
on their tiny haunches and munched gleefully.

Molly took Waters's hand; Waters squeezed hers back. They walked
for a while enjoying each other's company before Molly spoke. "Why
is it that you haven't joined the colonists yet?"

Waters knew this question would come. It was the one thing that
still separated him from Molly. "I'm just not ready yet."

"But why? You know what we believe is true. You can see for yourself," she said.

"It's not an easy choice to make," Waters replied. "You're right; I
know it's true. But it's more than that. I think I do believe, but it's
still hard. Joining the colonists means more than saying some words.
It means leaving behind everything. I could never go back to Earth.
Polus is wonderful. It might even be paradise. But I still feel like Earth
is my home."

"I know what you mean. It wasn't easy for me either," Molly said.
"Even though my parents wanted me to join the colonists, almost
begged me to join them, it still felt like I abandoned them. I hope
they're okay, but they're probably not. Letting go of everything, it's not
easy, not at all. It's almost like dying."

"That's what it feels like," Waters said.

"But my parents were right," Molly continued. "I'm better off than
I ever was, and every day I become more myself. I had to let Earth go
so that I could become who I was supposed to be."

The sun shone bright, but everything around them seemed aglow
of its own accord. The tall grass vibrated with energy, vivid green and
yellow coursed through a layer of soft fuzz. The trees were an earthy
ochre, deep grooves in the bark practically invited them to take hold

and climb as high as they dared. The sky was blue, bluer than the clearest afternoon sky Waters had ever seen in the remotest parts of Earth. And above them the gas giant Polus looked down, so clear they could call by name the jet streams and storms that dotted its surface if they had wanted.

"I just don't think I'm ready," Waters said.

"I know. I'll be there when you are," Molly said.

CHAPTER THIRTY

MY LORD AND MY GOD

Beau's complete plan required him to get off Polus IV and back onto Polus Station. The space port had LiFi thanks to a boost from the station above, the flat plains which minimized atmospheric and geographic interference, and the gigantic antenna that was the budding space elevator to amplify signals. The LiFi was spotty, however. Worse, it was public, which meant unsecure, and neither of those suited his needs. He needed to get back into orbit.

There were no scheduled launches, however. Nor shuttles to launch. And a fuel shortage. The double punch of a tornado and severe thunderstorm damaged the fuel extraction and production facility. Dropships could arrive therefore, but they did not depart except rarely. According to Alice, he needed to, "Get in queue with the worker positions waiting to rotate out. Unless he wanted to contact the Administration for an exception."

No, he did not, thank you very much. MFASA's Interim Director, whom he had not even met and did not even know, would certainly ask for a report that he was not prepared to give. Not until he reached out to Black, the important Black, the Black who was the key. She was the President's wife, which rumor had it was dissatisfied with the nature and limitations of her relationship to the President. Beau felt they were of the same mind. It seemed Black was willing to lie for status; why should she not expose that lie to accumulate more power and status?

"Missionary Lee," Alice said. "Here is a new set of clothes. I do apologize that we do not have any MFASA uniforms available. Please understand that it would require a special authorization from the Administration to manufacture a single order for just you, which is unfortunately not possible due to the inefficiency of such a request."

The clothes being offered matched the white trousers and shirt she had given Waters previously. They were the uniform of civil servant positions on Polus IV.

"Please be careful not to soil them."

"Missionary Lee," Alice said. "I have arranged a trailer for you while you await an available shuttle. Please let me know if I may be of further assistance while you remain at the space port."

"Missionary Lee," Alice said. "I received a request from the Interim Director for a report on your mission status."

"How did the Interim Director find out I was available to provide a report, Alice?"

"I told him of course."

"Please let the Interim Director know—wait, who is the Interim Director?"

"Interim Director Stephen Shepherd."

"Of course. Please let Interim Director Shepherd know that a report would be inappropriate at this time using the space port's unsecure network. My report will need to wait until I am able to access a secure network on Polus Station."

"Of course. Would you like me to advocate for an exception for you in the queue?"

"Yes, Alice. Do that please."

"Of course."

Beau languished in the queue, which was weeks long. Months long. Even after the fuel facility completed its repairs. So, he waited. He celebrated the anniversary of his mission's arrival on Polus IV alone. Then he waited more, and watched the months pass alone. Polus IV's summer would fade into nazomer by the time his turn arrived.

"Missionary Lee, I am pleased to let you know that your turn in the queue has arrived. You are scheduled to depart on the shuttle for Polus Station Monday."

"This Monday? That's excellent news, Alice."

"No, missionary Lee: the first Monday of next month. Shuttles depart only monthly now."

"Thank you for the news, Alice," Beau said, disguising his frustration at the continued delays as best he could. Alice turned to leave when something occurred to him. "Alice? Who is scheduled to pilot the shuttle?"

"Why, Captain Jackson, whom you already have met. Will that be all?"

"Great. Thank you, Alice."

"We're going over the mountains. You should come too," Jonathan said, popping his head into the missionaries' shelter.

Waters, Tommy, and Joon-baek lounged in the shelter. They felt lazy after a day that had been hard and satisfying for each of them in its own way. Joon-baek worked in the fields, Tommy finished repairs on his flyer, and Waters finished a piece of writing he had been working on for weeks. It was a report in its own way. Not for the Administration, but for the pleasure of writing, and in his own style.

"Right now?" Waters asked.

"No, tomorrow morning. Have you seen the ocean?" Jonathan asked.

"Not here. Not on Polus," Waters said.

"You'll love it," Jonathan said.

"Can we swim?" Waters asked.

"Of course. That's half the point of going. Bring swimwear," Jonathan said.

The missionaries looked at each other blankly.

Jonathan read the look that passed between them and said, "Don't worry. We can get you something," before he disappeared, returning an hour later, arms full, and dumped clothes on the floor of the shelter. "Pick one. Make sure you try it on first."

They left the next morning riding on arkouda. A few smaller onos and strong-necked mulari happily trucked baggage. The mulari had comically large ears that stood straight up. As their journey continued, Waters recognized the path he and the mayor took the previous year. A few colonists, including the mayor and Molly, came with them, but it was a small group. The air was cool in the morning, but the warm sunlight boded a hot day befitting Polus' Indian summer.

"This is the best time to go to the beach," Jonathan, said, obviously excited about the trip. He rode his arkouda up and down the group, chatting up people in the train.

"Why don't you just fly?" Tommy asked.

"Sometimes we use technology; sometimes it uses us. This is one of the ways we make sure we're the ones doing the using," the mayor replied.

"Besides, this is more fun," Jonathan added.

"Hmm," Waters grunted. He did not mind riding, but he did not do it nearly as often as the others. He preferred to walk. The colonists always rode bareback, and he knew he would be saddle sore later. It was going to be a hot day, and that meant sweating on top of a hairy arkouda.

They reached the pass and broke for lunch. It was cool, more so for the breeze, but the sky was clear, and the sun warmed their bones to the core even as the breeze raised little goosebumps on their skin. They shared a meal of honey cakes and a fizzy wine brewed from vitis, a tricky prospect given the fruit's habit of rotting quickly. It was cool and refreshing though, and the drink eased their spirits and loosened their tongues.

"I'm surprised," Waters said, "surprised that you drink alcohol."

"Why? Beer and wine are a gift to mankind," the mayor replied.

"It's just that a lot of Christians back on Earth didn't drink. They were kind of notorious for it. I didn't expect you to drink either."

"Well, look at how people use alcohol," Molly jumped into the conversation. "A lot of people don't drink for the joy of it. They drink to get drunk. That's the main reason a lot of Christians abstain from drinking."

"It's the same idea as technology. Be sure you're the one in control, and it's not a problem," the mayor said. "Still, you all should be careful how much you drink. We're at altitude here, and even though you've been here for a while, you're still not completely adapted to the planet. But let's not get too serious. Enjoy yourselves! Look! Come to the top of the hill. You can see the ocean from here."

The mayor was right. They climbed a little farther out of the saddle and up the path. The ocean spread out before them, an endless horizon of the deepest most vivid colors like every shade of wine Waters had seen. He felt anxious to be there all of a sudden.

"We can go there?" he asked with a touch of wonder he had not felt in years.

"That's why we're here. Come on, let's pack up," the mayor said.

They traveled up out of the saddle and over the far peak before they began their descent. This side of the mountain was different from the inland side. Low scrub over sandy soil covered it, and the few trees had broad leaves and bark that peeled off in great stringy sheets to reveal trunks lined with shades of green, blue, orange, and red like they had been painted. The litter from the leaves made the path slippery, though the animals managed it with little difficulty.

At last, they reached the edge of a great bluff that dropped in a sheer cliff to a sandy beach. They dismounted. The onos and mulari knew the way and proceeded down a narrow path on steps set into the cliff.

"You'll have to wait here," the mayor said to the arkouda. "The path is far too narrow for you."

The arkouda looked concerned but did not follow as the group descended. The sun was at its full height in the sky now. Once they reached the beach, Waters took off his shoes. The light sand was uncomfortably hot, and he stepped back onto his shoes and used them as a platform.

"Here, let's get these set up," Jonathan said. He began unloading bundles from the backs of the animals and handed them to Tommy, Joon-baek, and Waters.

"What are they?" the missionaries asked.

"Tents. For privacy so you can change, and in case you want to get out of the sun for a while. Or if you just want to take a nap. Whatever you want! Let's have fun!" Jonathan said.

The tents went up almost automatically once they were unbundled, as if they were eager to unfold and take their given shape. By releasing a spring along the three corners a pin shot into the ground and secured the tent in place.

"That's clever," Tommy said.

"The real trick is keeping the sand out. No one's been able to figure out how to do that yet," Jonathan said.

Waters and Molly emerged from changing in their respective tents at the same time. Around her waist, she wore a blue and white pareo dyed in a pattern after the leaves of the painted trees. Waters thought she looked stunning. He looked down and took hold of the flesh on either side of his belly. Weeks of walking had done their part, but he still felt self-conscious. The other colonists emerged, and even the mayor looked fit and trim by comparison in his shorts and sun shirt.

"How does an old guy stay so fit?" Waters asked Tommy.

"Must be all the Bible thumping," he quipped.

The mayor began. "Before you go swimming, remember that you're still not fully accustomed to the planet—"

"Race you!" Molly shouted as she tossed her pareo aside.

Waters, Molly, Tommy, Jonathan, and Ai took off toward the water. Joon-baek came bursting out of a tent after the others still kicking off a shoe.

"Kids," the mayor said.

"May we ever be the same," Patience said.

Waters hit the water and leapt up sputtering. The cold sapped the breath from his lungs, and he made back for dry sand immediately. Tommy, who had the same experience, followed close on his heels. Joon-baek pulled up short when he saw their reaction to the water, then gave a shrug and plunged in anyway. He too emerged sputtering but forced himself to stay. He grimaced and grunted with the effort.

Jonathan laughed and paddled around on his back. He lounged with his arms behind his head and floated.

"No way I'm missing this," Tommy said from the beach to where he had retreated. He did not plunge this time, instead making his way into the water, inch by inch.

Waters followed, and after a few minutes they relaxed and were able to tolerate the water.

As evening fell, the cool air over the ocean mixed with warmer air pouring down the mountain and clouds began to build. Not storm clouds, but low cumulus. The sun broke through in perfect fingers of light. It touched the ocean only to scatter from the water's surface in a sparkling display that reflected on the underside of the clouds. Jacob's ladders dotted the ocean from the beach to the horizon. The party, missionaries and colonists, took in the scene from a vantage point on the hill; the arkouda glad to have them near again. As they watched, an enormous creature plunged through the clouds and the group pointed with audible oohs.

"A falena!" Molly said.

"I've only ever seen them much higher in the sky," Waters said.

The animal plunged through the clouds and into the ocean below. A jet of vapor from the clouds followed it into the water. Mouth agape, it sent a tower of foam and spray several stories into the air. The group gasped. A couple even clapped. Its tail and wings pumped and the falena rose back into the sky spurting water out through baleen plates.

"It must be feeding time," Molly said.

As she spoke an entire pod plunged through the clouds and into the ocean. They sent up great fountains of water in a spectacular display. This time none could help but clap.

Waters pointed, "Look!" One falena rose back out of the water with a different animal grasping its tail in its mouth. "Is it trying to eat it?"

"It doesn't look like it," Molly said, as they looked on with curiosity.

The creature was stubby, but broad, almost teardrop shaped. Its large head was like a lion. It even had a flowing mane of bright red behind a smooth tawny face. It tugged at the falena's tail playfully before it let go at a terrifying height. With a series of summersaults, it dove back into the ocean. The people laughed. It leapt out again in a great arc, almost in response to the crowed. It plopped in again with only the slightest splash.

"What was that?" Molly asked.

"That was a kytos," Jonathan said.

"There are more!" Joon-baek said.

A great pride of kytos emerged and played in the water below. They leapt and twisted out of the water in synchrony.

"They're showing off," the mayor said.

"They're not done," Ai said. "Here they come!"

The sun set beneath the clouds and giant medusas descended with it. They hovered just beneath the canopy of cloud cover where they caught the setting sun's last light, its rays passed through their translucent bodies and turning red, orange, and gold. The light blanketed the coastal hills in prismatic warmth.

The display of creation and the joy of the day moved Waters, and he thought to himself *my Lord and my God.* "Mayor…" he began, but the words stuck in his throat suddenly. He felt a sense of shame as if something outside himself would stop him from speaking, but he continued. "Mayor, I'm ready to join the colonists."

Molly's hands shot up to her mouth involuntarily. Jonathan looked surprised. Tommy and Joon-baek stopped tossing twigs over the cliff and stared. The mayor's eyebrows raised slightly, and he smiled. "Alright, Alex. Let's go down to the water."

"Why?" Waters said.

"You need to be baptized," the mayor answered.

"Now?" Waters said.

"Why not? Are you ready?" the mayor asked.

"Yes. Yes, I am," Waters affirmed.

"Who would you like to be your sponsor?" the mayor asked.

"What does that mean?" Waters asked. He had heard of this ritual but did not know very much about it.

"Your sponsor is someone who serves as a witness and testifies that your commitment is genuine and true," the mayor answered.

"Jonathan, would you sponsor me?" Waters asked.

Jonathan looked somewhat taken aback, but replied, "Yes. Of course."

They descended to the beach. The mayor stepped into the water until the waves were chest deep. A pod of kytos encircled him. They frolicked and jostled with each other to be the closest, spitting water playfully. The mayor motioned to Waters to join him.

"Are they dangerous?" Waters asked with some hesitation.

"No more than an arkouda," the mayor answered.

Waters began to take off his shirt, but the mayor stopped him, "No, leave it on." He and Jonathan walked into the water together and faced the mayor.

"I present Alex Waters to receive the Sacrament of Baptism," Jonathan said.

"Alex, do you desire to be baptized? If so, answer 'I do,'" the mayor said.

"I do," Waters affirmed.

The mayor turned and addressed Jonathan. "Jonathan, you have presented Alex for Baptism. You should care for him and help him that he may bear witness to the faith, that by living in communion with the Church, he may lead a godly life until the day of Jesus Christ. Do you promise to fulfill this obligation?"

Jonathan placed his hands on Waters's shoulders. "I do."

The mayor addressed everyone present. "I ask you to profess your faith, the faith in which we baptize. Do you renounce all the forces of evil, the devil, and all his empty promises?"

"I do," Jonathan answered, as did Molly and the other colonists. Joon-baek joined in as well. Tommy turned and looked at him with a screwed-up face.

"I do," Waters said.

The mayor asked, "Do you believe in God the Father?" and the colonists proceeded to recite a creed Waters did not know, but he repeated the words. They all finished with, "Amen."

"Here we go," the mayor said, and put one hand on Waters's forehead and another behind his neck and squeezed his chest tightly between his forearms. "Alex, I baptize you in the name of the Father, and of the Son, and of the Holy Spirit," the mayor said, and leaning Waters back, dunked him under the water and pulled him out again. "Amen."

The colonists clapped. Joon-baek joined in, as did Tommy, reluctantly, still not sure what was happening. The kytos responded to the clapping by leaping out of the water. Behind them, the sun set below the horizon and a flash of green lit the sky.

Waters walked and stood where the incoming surf lapped at his feet and ankles and the receding waves buried his toes in the sand. He blew water away from his mouth and wiped the sea foam from his eyes. He opened and wiped them again. The trees, sand, cliffs, bushes, the water, all of it was more vivid. The light passing through the transparent bodies of the medusas was like the flare of a contrail jetting through the sky. The waves came and went over his feet, but the water was no longer cold. It was warm and gave him a sense of comfort. The sea wind that had chilled him earlier was now a caressing breeze carrying away the heat from the sand and relaxing his body. He felt both overwhelmed by the depth of everything he saw and calmed, as if he saw everything for the first time as it really was, as it was always meant to be. He remembered that night spent on the rover's roof in the bog, more than a year ago, only this vision would not leave him. He was glad for the water still streaming from his hair lest the others see his tears.

Molly walked into the soughing waves with him. She took his face in her hands and kissed him for the first time. The others clapped louder. He blushed as she let him go, then looked and wiped his eyes again. A tiny light like a candle flame hovered in front of Molly's forehead. He waved his hand in front of her face to disperse the hovering wisp, but his hand passed through it with no effect. She took his hand.

"You have one too. So do we all," Molly said, motioning to the colonists.

"Has one what?" Joon-baek asked.

Waters looked to each of the colonists. A flame hovered before their foreheads as well. His jaw dropped in astonishment. "Let me see," he said, and rushed out of the surf, splashing sandy mud and water. "Where's my phone?" He grabbed it from the open tent and turned it on himself.

"You won't be able to see with your camera," Molly said. "Here." She took his phone and powered it down, then held it up so he could see his reflection in the black screen. There, floating in front of his head was indeed a tiny flame. He put his hand up and brought it down, looking into his palm.

Molly smiled. "I didn't see the flame until we got to Polus. I thought I was seeing things, that my depression had worsened and I was hallucinating. Until I saw the colonists."

"This is why you can go into the city," Waters said.

"It's the sign of why she can go into the city," Patience said. "The city only admits believers. No matter how hard you, we, or anyone else tried, none but those who believe could enter."

"That means I can see the city now!" Waters said.

"Yes," the mayor said. "You were always welcome but could not enter until now."

"What about us?" Tommy asked.

"You know what you have to do," the mayor replied.

Joon-baek looked hopeful. Tommy was skeptical, and said "I'll take my time, if that's alright with you."

"It is up to you," the mayor said.

They spent the night in tents on the beach. Starlight penetrated the tent fabric like their own private planetariums. Waters thought he would not sleep at all, but the next morning opened his eyes to sunlight peering over the cliffs behind them.

Waters hardly remembered the return trip at all. He rode next to Molly and chatted joyfully while the others made meaningful looks. Tommy made a face periodically, still not sure what he had witnessed. In no time it seemed they arrived back at the Narrow Gate. Waters turned and looked at his two companions. "I'm sorry you don't get to come with me," he said.

"It's alright, I prefer it out here anyway," Tommy said.

Joon-baek said nothing, contemplating everything that had happened.

"Are you ready?" Molly asked, taking Waters's hand.

Waters gave her hand a squeeze and together they stepped forward.

CHAPTER THIRTY-ONE

NOTHING AT ALL AND EVERYTHING

There was only one thing Beau needed as he boarded the shuttle: a memento from his time with the colonists: the lance Waters himself used hunting his first apoch. How unfortunate that had been. To be forced to kill an innocent animal. Though, Beau reflected, seething a little, he had been a willing partner and was therefore guilty. He kept the lance disassembled in three parts in a case, which he carried as he boarded the shuttle, already wearing a full flight suit. It was to his advantage that no one would inspect the case. He was a MFASA missionary after all. Weapons were illegal on Earth; by extension, regulation forbade them on a mission, and no one would expect him to be carrying one.

"Beau? I didn't expect to be bringing you back up until next year," a voice said.

Damn. "Captain Jackson. I'm returning to the station early to provide a report. No signal at the colony, you know." Beau had hoped he would not be recognized in his flight suit.

"Huh," was all the captain said in reply. He busied himself with the other passengers.

The shuttle oriented vertically for launch. Beau climbed to his seat and stowed the case. He fastened the harness and felt his helmet latch magnetically to the headrest. Why a dropship should be called a shuttle simply because it was pointed toward the sky was a trivial matter. Still, as he stared through the cabin at the sky above him, that was the thought that came to mind. Other passengers climbed past him on either side to their seats.

At last, the countdown began. The boosters prefired during the last few seconds.

"Ignition," the radio crackled followed by a deafening roar. Beau heard the radio babble something at Captain Jackson, but it was not discernable above the engines. Beau was pressed back into his seat with a force unlike anything he had ever felt. A bead of sweat trickled under his helmet along his face. It tickled him. He instinctively raised his hand to wipe the droplet away but could not. The force that pressed his body and limbs against the seat prevented it. It was as if the glove alone weighed a hundred kilograms. Even if his hand had not been magnetically linked to his chair, it would have been quite immobile.

A trail of fire a hundred meters long poured from the shuttle as it rose atop an enormous pillar of smoke that billowed out in a column that stretched into the sky. Like a finger arcing into the sky, it pushed the shuttle ever higher. Water vapor accumulated in a cloud on the shuttle's nose and swirled off with a loud crack as it broke the sound barrier.

There was a moment of silence and a loud explosion. "Primary booster jettison," the radio cackled.

"The boosters will land themselves back on the surface where a team will recover them to use again in a later flight," the captain shouted. "Don't start to unbuckle your straps yet."

"Always needing to narrate what he's doing," Beau said to himself.

Sparks like fireworks trailed away from the shuttle as the boosters separated. He had only a few moments to catch his breath before a second roar rocked the cabin and the force of their travel accelerated him into his seat. This time, the shuttle's own engines ignited. A minute later everything went silent. A mechanical thunk signaled the main fuel tank separating from the shuttle. It too fell back to Polus IV.

"A team will collect the booster tank as well after it lands. Everything is reused. It saves a lot of money on each launch," Captain Jackson said, this time over the speakers.

Their momentum carried them out of the upper atmosphere. The shuttle flipped on its back to intercept with Polus Station and Beau saw a vast ocean below on Polus IV which they never visited, the colony being on the inland side of coastal mountains. "It's just a tiny dot after all. Not so important," he said to himself. He tried to see the space elevator but could not. His head was fixed in place and it had passed behind his field of view.

"If you look out the starboard side you might catch a glimpse of Polus Station," Captain Jackson said.

Beau looked left, then right and thought he could just make out the reflection of light and shadow on a distant object. It grew larger and larger like a camera lens zooming in as they approached.

"We'll dock on the inner fixed spire. That way we don't have to expend fuel to match the station's rotation. There's a fuel shortage, you know. Once you disembark, there's only one way you can go. If you get to the other end of the spire, you've gone too far. Or take some time to enjoy weightlessness. As much time as the station personnel will let you have anyway. When you're ready, find a pylon marked with your destination helix."

Their momentum slowed as they approached the station. It was now impossible to see; they were too close. Gases jetted and hissed and sputtered as Captain Jackson made fine adjustments to align them with the station. Then the shuttle jostled with a metallic thud and they were still.

"You may now unbuckle your restraining harness and depart. If you have magnetic boots, please make sure they're activated. If you do not and you're unfamiliar with zero-G, let me know and I'll help guide you to the door. Be sure to collect your luggage before you depart. It'll be a long time before you see it again otherwise. It's been a pleasure serving as your captain."

Beau removed his suit and helmet. The shuttle's hatch opened and a staticky metallic breeze swirled around his face as the air pressure inside the station equalized with the shuttle. There was no gravity in the core. It made carrying his case easier since it floated itself, but it also made walking difficult. Molly's magnetic boots helped, left in the rover a year and more ago, but walking in space was still a learned skill. It was one he had not needed since training, and one on which they had spent little time anyway.

The long corridor stretched the entire length of the station. It was made completely of metal, as much for structural reasons as to facilitate magnetic maneuvering gear. Windows were rare. Light inside came from high-efficiency LEDs, all the same frequency of bright white. After the intensity of the sun on Polus IV, the station lights were both too bright and too dim at the same time. Beau took note of the interspersed airlocks as he moved up the corridor; he would need one later.

Beau found a pylon connecting to the helix he had lived on briefly before taking the dropship to the moon. An elevator sat just inside of the rotating ring. He boarded the elevator and pulled his case inside. A few other worker positions joined him. The doors behind him closed, and lights above the door signaled a countdown that intensified with a beep. When the elevator aligned with the pylon a set of clamps released. Beau experienced gravity immediately as the elevator carried them to the end of the pylon in a few seconds. He was disoriented momentarily as a door opened in front of him where they had entered the elevator from below. No matter. Gravity was once again where it belonged. He stopped a civil servant position. Her uniform looked like Alice's. "Excuse me." *I must be polite to get what I need.* "My name is Beau Lee. I'm with the group of missionaries on Polus IV. I need to find a room where I can stay, and a secure network I can access to make a report to the Director at MFASA."

"Of course," the civil servant replied.

The concierges must all receive the same training. This one spoke with similar mannerisms as Alice. The civil servant pulled up his phone, and in a few moments had located a suitable room. "Please follow me, Missionary Lee. I would be happy to show you to your room."

Once inside, Beau pulled up the network signal. It was full. Finally, a working connection to Earth. He linked his phone, logged into the secure MFASA VPN. He authenticated the connection with his fingerprint and was glad he had not wasted his LiFi allowance. He then made his first call, which was not to Interim Director Shepherd. It was a gamble, but she might pick up. She needed to answer for his plan to move forward.

"Hello?" a voice said. A moment later the video signal synchronized, and Carrie Black's face materialized before him. This was the person with whom he needed to speak.

Waters flinched as they crossed the threshold into the city. His body expected the same resistance he had felt when the missionaries first arrived, but none came. He passed through the gate and was surprised. He expected the first thing that would strike him would be what he saw, but instead he inhaled deeply and a sweet yet spicy scent struck him, like rose blossoms or sandalwood or blooming oleander or vanilla or fresh cut nectarines or plumeria flowers; his senses could not discern the aroma. Then he felt the air itself. Crossing the threshold was like passing through golden honey whose sweetness his very skin could taste. Then he both heard and felt the thrumming of bass-filled low frequencies playing below brass instruments of all kinds, bright and cheerful to the ears. Overtones passed right through his chest while a piano and organ accompanied a great choir in the distance that sang the joy of being. Senses overwhelmed, at last, he looked around. He saw a space that was vast and open with buildings tall and short inlaid and trimmed with precious metal and gemstones. The stone façades glowed. Indeed, cracks in the pavement beneath their feet barely contained a light that fought to escape.

"This is not what it looked like from up on the mountain," Waters said. His pulse quickened, and he breathed deeply. He felt he was about to be overcome by inevitability itself.

"You would not have been able to see inside very well for the same reason you could not step foot inside," Molly said.

He and Molly toured the city, she was excited to show him the things that had been new to her just a few months earlier. She spoke with vivacity and joy as she showed him vast courtyards and parks and gardens filled with trees and flowers of all kinds. They walked along the river that flowed through the city from its center and out under the wall into the valley. They climbed seven sets of steps leading to seven tiers, each level filled with artistry and beauty. There were sculptures, galleries, tapestries, and people making music in the streets or on balconies or in alleyways around them in secret hidden paths. They heard poets speaking verse and storytellers telling tales. They passed an open stadium where athletes competed as a crowd watched and cheered. There were shops where men and women tinkered. Children raced out of a school to a park across the way. They shouted and screeched with delight at being outside. People ran and played, laughing and talking as they shared and created, as they ate and lived.

Late in the afternoon they came to the center of the city on the highest tier where a large square paved in brick from one end to the other ended in an arched doorway a story tall below a tower that grew a hundred yards skyward. Colored glass windows interspaced the tower walls at regular intervals. At the top they saw two tiers above a crenulated parapet. The tallest tier had a clock set into a glass wall. A dome with a spire topped the tower with a rooster weathervane that turned with the wind below a tall cross. Leafy trees strove to match the tower's height throughout the square, its canals full of fish bordered by plants that flowed around the square's boundaries, as birds nestled in the foliage.

"I'm surprised I can see the top so well," Waters said.

Molly just smiled. "That gate leads to the cathedral." She held on to Waters's arm with both hands as they stood in front of the tower in the square. "Are you ready to go in?"

"Let's go," he said.

The tower itself was massive, which belied the size of the gate through which they walked. Two arkouda could have passed through riding piggyback. Looking up from inside Waters saw from the vestibule that the tower was not hollow but had a high ceiling from which hung a wrought iron chandelier. Hundreds of candles cast their light on the ceiling.

"Are those real candles?" Waters asked.

"It looks like it," Molly said.

"I wouldn't want to be the one who has to clean up the wax," Waters said.

"Or change out the candles," Molly said.

To their left as they entered the tower was an open door, through which they could see a staircase.

"I think that leads to the top of the tower," Molly said. "We should climb it sometime."

"Let's do it," Waters said, not really serious but pulling Molly along with him.

"Not now," Molly said, dragging him back playfully. "We're going to see the cathedral."

Through a second set of arched doors opposite the main doors they saw the base of a building.

"You've seen this before?" Waters asked.

Molly nodded. "I don't want to say anything though. It will spoil it for you."

Waters could see the portal at the front of the cathedral through the gate, and said to himself, "It doesn't look so impressive from here," not wanting to disappoint Molly. Then they stepped through the inner gate.

Two towers drew his eyes upwards so that even tilting his head back he could hardly see the top. The stones of the cathedral glowed with light like those in the rest of the city, but to Waters's amazement it flowed forth, thick like sap to the rest of the city as it were a stream. Waters found nothing to say.

"Just wait until you see inside," Molly said.

"Don't get my hopes up; I'll be disappointed," he said, joking a little.

"You won't," she assured him.

They walked through the doors and down the nave. There were ten thousand things to see inside: paintings and sculptures; flowers, plants and trees, both arranged and growing live; carvings of all kinds representing fruiting plants and animals arrayed every surface of the piers and arches inside; every window was itself a masterwork of stained glass that scattered color. The vault of the ceiling was one vast painted canvas. There was not an inch that did not tell a story.

They reached the crossing of the transept and the space above drew them upward even as they stood on solid ground. It was infinite, as if it were the vault of heaven itself and held both nothing at all and everything throughout time without end. The sight took their breath away. They stood for a time whose length they could not tell, nor did they want to, and beheld wonders.

At last, as if he were pulling himself out of a great river whose tides and currents would carry him forever if he let them, Waters spoke. "Tommy and June Bug can't see this, can they?"

Molly sensed immediately where he was going. "No, they can't. Not until they can enter the city."

"We can't get married here," he said.

Molly squeezed his arm and smiled, "No, I guess we can't."

They looked on greatness one last time and walked out together.

They walked on to where a path ran under a trellis covered with thousands upon thousands of magenta and purple and rose-colored flowers. The flowers hung down so low they almost touched the path. Waters and Molly could not help but brush against them as they passed. In the center the path branched at the source of the flowers: a massive tree with a low trunk as thick as any on Polus whose branches spread out over the trellis radially in every direction. The path rejoined itself on the other side of the tree. Waters was not really fascinated by plants, but even he had to stop to admire this tree.

"You live here?" he asked Molly.

"Not here, nearby. Just on the other side of the path," she said as she took Waters's hand.

They approached a small stone cottage that sat inside a yard surrounded by a low fence. It had a stone path leading up to the door. A gable covered the path where it met the fence, which itself was covered with greenery. Light glowed through a window just to the side of the door and illuminated the grassy yard. The stone walls glowed with a light their own.

"This is what I would imagine an old house in Ireland would look like," Waters said.

"It is," Molly said. "It's modeled after a cottage near where my grandparents lived back home. It was always one of my favorite places."

"It's new then? It looks so old," Waters said.

"I guess it is new, though it seems like it's always been there," Molly said.

Waters looked at her with wonder. "Is everything like this?"

"I think it's all part of Polus, once you can see it. Goodnight, Alex," Molly said. She pushed up with her toes and pecked his lips.

"Goodnight, Molly," Waters said, and walked back through the evening light to the shelter he shared with the others outside the city.

CHAPTER THIRTY-TWO

THE LANCE, LONGINUS

Beau was back in the core. Phone in hand, the system map projected in front of him. He pushed off the metal service pipes to give himself a boost and floated down the corridor. The white LEDs flattened everything and gave it all the same texture and appearance, but it would not have mattered much anyway. It was all metal, rubber, plastic, and carbon fiber. His plan was months in the making, pushing a year even. He needed to come out the hero. He needed the colonists to be the enemy. That part would not be hard given the Administration and MFASA's predisposition. He needed his colleagues to be implicated as well. To protect him, they had to lose credibility. That part was more difficult.

"The station orbits Polus IV every ninety minutes," he said to himself. "Any airlock in the lower third of the spire should do. I'll need to secure a guidance system. A phone would work, but that won't do. I can't use Earth technology. It needs to come from the colonists."

Back in his room on the third helix, he sorted the items that looked important: the lance was the main thing. It was the perfect implement, not only a weapon but symbolic too. He felt stronger when he held it. He tossed the glasses from the city onto the bed. Then stopped and put them on. They functioned just as well on the station. Cycling through their functions he found a map. They pinged his location.

"If it has my location, it has a guidance chip."

Sullivan Jakeson was a unique individual among humanity: one born in space who had never lived outside artificial gravity. His parents were civil servant positions. He grew up on the same station where his mother gave birth. He left for the outer planets when he was eighteen, his feet never having touched ground. He was tall and lanky, the weightlessness to which he was accustomed having stretched his spine and limbs and made his muscles stringy. It was difficult to make friends, or even understand why he should have friends. People were around, but Sullivan did not need human contact, not like other people did. That was difficult to understand too. Machines provided him all the interaction he needed.

Beau had to be careful finding him. Sullivan had to be careful helping him. "The job requires discretion. This is a piece of colonist technology, and we're not quite sure what it can do," Beau said.

Sullivan was fascinated. "You want to rig the location chip as a guidance system onto this pole?" He twirled the colonist's glasses in his hands, popped off a cover plate and poked at the circuitry inside.

"That's right. Be careful with that. I only have one," Beau said.

"Circuitry is simpler than people give it credit for. That should be easy enough to do. For the second part, I need a propellant source though. Just a small air tank connected to a four-thruster system should be sufficient," Sullivan said.

"We're testing using the station's trajectory as a launching platform. It won't need its own fuel," Beau said.

"The air is for steering, not for propulsion," Sullivan said, then under his breath he asked himself, "Who wouldn't understand that?"

"I can work on getting that for you," Beau said.

"Don't bother. We have lots of empty canisters that will work. I just need to pressurize them. Fixed aluminum tubing with an actuated waste-gate system attached to a servo should be enough to open and close the tubes for trajectory correction," Sullivan said. "It is so easy to see. Why does everyone always need to be told these things?"

"What do you need me to do?" Beau asked.

"I need to work."

"I'll leave you to it then. When will it be ready for testing?"

"No testing. It will work," Sullivan said. "I know what I'm doing. Why does everyone always question me?"

"It needs to work. We have to test it."

"It will work."

Sullivan and Beau stood in front of the airlock. Sullivan held the modified lance and guidance system like a precious toy. Beau scratched "Longinus" on the shaft. It was uncharacteristically poetic, but he felt inspired. They wore pressure suits.

"Ready for our experiment, Sully?" Beau asked.

"It's Sullivan. It's ready," Sullivan replied.

They stepped into the airlock and hooked their carabiners to the safety rail. The door behind them closed and there was a sucking sound. Their suits pulled away from their skin slightly as the airlock depressurized. Beau opened the outer door and they stared at the moon below. It careened by at thousands of kilometers an hour yet looked serene from hundreds of kilometers above.

"Tell me again how to work it, Sully," Beau said.

"It's so simple. A child could do it. Why does he need me to show him?" Sullivan muttered. "The guidance system accepts the trajectory from the app on your phone here. When we're ready, you release the lance and press this button to activate the thrusters which will keep it on course."

Beau brought up his phone. The lance's path was loaded and set. "We'll be over the launch site in a couple of minutes. Are you sure about this? There's no margin for error in these calculations, you know."

"Of course, I know that. I'm not an idiot," Sullivan muttered. "It works."

"Who else helped you with this project, Sully?" Beau asked.

"My name is Sullivan, and no one, Missionary Lee. I don't need help."

"You did it by yourself? Did you tell anyone else about our project?" Beau asked.

"No Missionary Lee. I don't need help. I did it by myself. I'm not an idiot."

"What did you use to program the trajectory?" Beau asked.

"My phone."

"Do you have your phone with you now?"

"Yes, it's right here." Sullivan held up his wrist. His phone was attached by a piece of velcro.

"You can let the pole go, Sully," Beau said.

Sullivan took a last look at his creation and gently let go. It drifted out of the airlock on its own. "That trajectory will collide with the moon," Sullivan said, glancing at Beau's phone.

"That's right."

"It will collide with the space port—no—with the space elevator."

"That's right as well. How much air did you say these suits have, Sully?"

"They start with one hour of air. More than enough for work in the airlock. The pole is going to collide with the space elevator. That's dangerous, Missionary Lee. People could get hurt."

Beau unhooked Sullivan's carabiner. "I know that, Sully. That's the idea."

"My name is Sullivan."

Beau pushed off the door with his feet and gave Sullivan a shove. He careened out of the airlock. Sullivan screamed. His voice echoed in the speakers in Beau's helmet.

"Missionary Lee!"

Beau shut off the sound with his phone. He watched the screen as the launch point approached. Just a little closer. The lance drifted away slowly, but just barely. It would travel incredibly fast relative to the moon thanks to the station's orbit and impact the space elevator just right. Three, two, one, go. He tapped his phone and little puffs of gas emitted from the lance. It angled down on a course toward Polus IV.

Sullivan saw the lance come to life and stopped screaming. He rotated slowly, trying to crane his neck to see it move and correct its course. He watched until it was out of sight. "I said it would work."

Alice Liddell awoke at precisely six o'clock in the morning and began her routine. Her training specified that the single greatest reason people became upset was unmet expectations. It was therefore important to set realistic expectations, and to ensure she met expectations. Her training specified that the single most effective way to ensure she met expectations was consistency. In her personal life she therefore ensured consistency, as she did also in her professional life. After waking, she used the restroom and weighed herself. Then she showered, dried and arranged her hair, put on her undergarments, brushed her teeth, applied the correct amount of makeup, donned her clothing, which were always white, always clean, always laid out the night before. She stopped in front of the mirror beside the doorway to double-check that everything was in order, adjusted her cap, and stepped outside.

She walked through the spaceport to the orientation room. Part of her routine was to check the equipment to ensure everything worked properly for the day's arrivals and departures. She stepped into the spaceport and felt more than heard a rumble, muffled as in the distance. She heard a speckled and intermittent tapping and looked up to see debris falling on the roof of the space port. Through the glass ceiling she saw coiling and twisting pieces of scaffolding descend from the space elevator as it fell and crashed through the spaceport in a heap.

Hill was not in the mood to go to work today. He was never in the mood to go to work, however. Why did they even permit alcohol in work zones? This would be the day he stopped, not like those other times. The problem was there was little else to do to ease the boredom. Who was he kidding: there was nothing else to do. He silently thanked no one in particular for his golf clubs. He needed to be on site on time or the worker positions would grow lax, perhaps even file a grievance. He was a member in good standing with the Administration himself, but that would not stop complaints. Every worker position was an expert in the regulations unto himself. An expert. They had called them "sea lawyers" when he was in the navy. Enlisted positions who knew the regulations, or thought they knew the regulations, and who complained when they did not think the officers were following the rules. Sea lawyers, though none of them saw ocean the entire tour. There was nothing except the blackness of space. It was an archaic term. "Rock regulators." That fit the setting better, but it would never catch on.

He stepped off the bed into the legs of his jumper where it lay crumpled on the floor after he sloughed it off the night before. He pulled it up over his shoulders and grabbed a nearby beer bottle. He shook it to see whether there was anything left in the bottom. There was. He finished it off and tossed the bottle into the sink. He looked in the mirror by the trailer door and ran his hand over the stubble on his face. He grabbed a hard-hat from its peg and stepped outside.

A low thud that sounded like it was off in the distance vibrated through the ground just before debris began to fall among the trailers. Hill looked up and saw the space elevator's scaffolding twist and collapse like an enormous rope winding out of the sky. Instinctively, he reached for his hip and grabbed his safety mask. He slid it on as he watched coils of the space elevator slam into the space port. It thundered and snaked down in great heaps as it fell, crushing him and his trailer.

CHAPTER THIRTY-THREE

A CLOUD OF FIRE

From their view on top of the peak, Molly and Waters could see the space elevator begin to collapse, hazy blue in the distance.

"Did you see that?"

"What was it?"

"There was a flash. Look!"

"We have to get back. We have to tell the mayor."

They rode back to the city just as Tommy flew in. "The space elevator collapsed," he announced

"We know. We saw it from the top of the mountain," Waters said.

Word had quickly spread to the colonists. Those outside the city gathered in clusters where they stood and talked. Soon the mayor, Jonathan, Patience, and Ai emerged from the city.

"Tommy, were you flying when the space elevator came down? Did you see it?" the mayor asked

"Yes. I was out above the bog when it came down."

"What happened?" the mayor asked. Colonists gathered around.

"It's hard to say. There was a flash in the upper atmosphere, then the top began to bend and flex, then the rest collapsed beneath it. The whole thing came down. The spaceport is probably ruined, not to mention the workers' housing."

"Just like Alpha Centauri b," Patience said with a touch of foreboding.

"We're going to get blamed for this," Jonathan said.

"Yes, we are," the mayor said.

"If the spaceport has been destroyed, nothing is going to be able to land or take off. They're going to be completely on their own," Waters said.

"We have to go help them," Molly said.

"If we do, it will look like criminals returning to the scene of the crime," Jonathan said. "We'll only look worse."

"If we don't go to help, we deserve whatever comes to us," Ai said.

"You're both right," the mayor said. "But we have to help them. We have the ability, and they have the need." The mayor pulled out his phone and broadcast a message to the colonists. The phones of those who stood in the courtyard before the gate began to beep.

"This is your mayor. We have received confirmation from witnesses of what several of you have no doubt heard by now: the space elevator has collapsed, destroying the space port below. We do not yet know how or why, but I'm sure you all understand the implications. Despite the risk, we have a duty to help those in need. We will worry about the consequences later. I'm asking those of you who can to gather supplies and tools and to fly to the space port to render aid. And who knows? Perhaps when they see our acts of mercy, they will rethink placing the blame for this tragedy at our feet."

The mayor put his phone away. Several of the colonists in the courtyard moved to action; others stood and continued talking. Some made their way back into the city. Patience stepped up to the mayor and placed her hand on his forearm.

"We can do more than bring them supplies. You know that," she said.

"We can't risk the city," he said.

"It is not ours to risk," she said.

The mayor stared into Patience's eyes for several seconds. She returned his gaze with earnest.

"I leave it to you then," he said.

Patience turned and returned to the city.

"Will you take me, Tommy?" the mayor asked.

"Tommy, can we go with you too?" Waters asked.

"Of course. What do we need to bring?" Tommy said.

"I don't even know where to begin. Maybe there are some first aid supplies left over from Jazzy's clinic," Waters said.

"I'll grab them," Molly said, and she jogged over to the men's shelter.

She pushed aside the tent flap, left characteristically open, and made her way to the back where they had stacked some of the old supplies. She pushed someone's laundry off some boxes onto the floor and opened the crates. The first one was a box of medications; that would be useful. She pulled out the bottles and looked them over: antibiotics, anti-inflammatories, all useful. Then she stopped. This one had her name on it. 'Molly McDaithi, 1 PO BID.' A bottle of her prescription. She turned the bottle over in her hand. 'Acetylsalicylic Acid.'

"What?" she said to herself. She turned it over again. It was her name on the front of the bottle. She opened the lid. These looked like the pills she had been taking. She crushed a pill in her hand and licked it. It was bitter. "This is just aspirin," she said aloud.

"Molly!" shouted Joon-baek as he came bursting into the shelter. Molly put the bottle into a pocket. "I just heard what happened. They sent me to help you."

"Take these," Molly said, putting the lid back on the crate and handing it Joon-baek. Joon-baek "It's medication. They won't all be useful, but we can sort out what we need when we get there."

"Can't we just use the vitis?" Joon-baek asked.

Molly had not thought of that. She was amazed that even after joining the colonists, so much of her way of thinking had not changed. "Probably, but we don't know what we'll find." She popped open another crate. "Gauze, sterile supplies. We'll take this one too. I'll bring it."

They jogged out of the tent carrying their crates. Tommy was in the cockpit of the flyer. Jonathan and Waters had loaded up a couple of baskets of fruit and vegetables from the fields. The mayor sat next to Tommy.

"What's that for?" Joon-baek said.

"They'll need food too. Wait a minute." Waters ran to a nearby arkouda and grabbed several of the wineskins from its saddlebags. He
filled them up directly from the river. "They'll probably need water too."

"The rover had a purification system. If we can find it and other rovers, we can use them too," Joon-baek said.

"You don't need to purify the water here," Jonathan said.

"We might at the spaceport. You haven't seen it," Tommy said. He
lifted off as they sat down.

Other colonists flew beside them. Below, several colonists loaded
the arkouda.

"It will take them a week to get there if they ride," Waters said.

"It won't take them as long as you think," Jonathan said. "They can
carry more than the flyers too."

The flight to the spaceport took a fraction of the time it took to cross
by land, perhaps no more than an hour, but they all urged Tommy to
fly faster. "I'm going as fast as I can," he said.

Molly rolled the pill bottle around in her pocket and turned to
Waters. "Jazzy was giving me a placebo."

"What?" Waters asked, surprised. Her statement had little to do
with their current situation.

"Aspirin. She was treating my depression with aspirin. I told you she
was treating me for depression on the flight out from Earth. She was.
Well, she wasn't. I found one of the bottles with my prescription on it.
It was full of baby aspirin."

"What were you supposed to be on?" Joon-baek asked.

"I was supposed to be on an SSRI."

"You still use those?" Jonathan asked.

Molly shook her head. "No need for them here, but we didn't have
vitis on Earth. I don't get it. She wasn't treating me; she was giving me
a placebo. Why would she do that?"

Waters's heart sank, but he knew he had to be honest with Molly.
"My dear," he said, "I'm sorry. I knew, but I didn't tell you. I had forgotten. It's an Administration tactic. They use various means to control
people who might pose a threat. Hunger is the most common, but they

use various medical therapies too. In your case, lack of medical therapy. We never should have done it. I know better now, but that didn't make it right. I'm sorry."

Molly turned and looked outside the flyer for several minutes. Waters felt a pit grow in his stomach and wondered if this would mark the end of their relationship, even though they were just at the beginning. Then Molly turned back to him, hooked her arm through his, and said, "I forgive you, my husband."

"You do?"

"Of course I do."

"But why? That was a terrible thing to do to someone."

"It was. Would you rather I stayed angry?"

"No, but…"

"Man, just accept it for what it is," the mayor turned and said.

Waters sat back in his chair. He felt confused, but as he looked over at Molly, he knew it would be alright.

"Mayor," Tommy said. "I have a question I've wanted to ask for a long time now. What's your real name? Everyone just calls you mayor all the time."

"Maior," the mayor said.

"You're Mayor Maior?"

"That's right."

"I guess that answers the question," Tommy said.

"Look!" Joon-baek said. A pillar of smoke rose on the horizon where the spaceport should have been.

"The shuttle fuel must have caught fire," Tommy said.

"Does anyone still have their mask?" Joon-baek asked.

"What mask?" Jonathan asked.

"We were issued masks after we landed to protect us from dust and fumes in case of just this kind of situation. When the space elevator on Alpha Centauri b collapsed, it landed on one of the factories and sent dust from the manufacturing process into the atmosphere. A lot of people who survived the collapse suffered lung problems. Many died," Waters said.

"They didn't have lung disease. The people who died were executed. The Administration killed them because they knew what had really happened, and what really happened was an embarrassment to the Administration," Jonathan said.

"He's right," the mayor said. "Alpha Centauri b was just a simple accident, the result of a careless maintenance crew leaving some garbage behind in space. The debris re-entered the atmosphere and collided with the space elevator and caused it to collapse."

Jonathan continued the story. "The Administration framed a group of religious colonists for the accident. It was a win-win for them: they got to resettle the people they didn't want there to begin with, and they avoided an investigation from families of the people who died."

"How do you know this?" Tommy asked, incredulous.

"Because some of the colonists from Alpha Centauri b escaped and live with us now," the mayor said. "Patience is one of them. It's part of our history. It's one of the reasons we stay away from the space elevator. We don't need to give anyone a reason to resettle us, or worse."

"Supplemental education," Molly said gravely.

The column of smoke over the space port grew larger. The refinery was indeed on fire.

"At least it will only burn until the fuel runs out," Tommy said.

"How long will that be?" Joon-baek asked.

"It could be weeks," Tommy said.

"What can we do about it?" Waters asked.

"Nothing right now," Tommy said. "Get people away from the smoke."

"Pray for a storm," Jonathan said.

"A storm would be disastrous right now," Joon-baek said.

"Everything is crushed," Molly said.

"The cables of the space elevator are lightweight, right? That should help?" Joon-baek said.

"There were miles of them though. That's not trivial," Tommy said.

As they approached the site, they were able to better assess the damage. The lower stories of the space elevator were intact, such as they could be. They stood like the stem of broken mast above the space port, a broken monument to disaster. The upper miles of cable and scaffold coiled around and over what remained of the spaceport, construction site, and trailers like enormous fallen serpents. Some of the trailers were intact between the coils of cable and debris, but the bulk of the cable had come down directly on top of the space port and collapsed the terminal. The coil smashed and crushed the manufacturing facilities, which were a total lost. Mercifully, there was no dust in the air, and the smoke from the fuel refinery billowed straight into the sky. A dropship's bow and stern both pointed skyward, bent in half beneath a section of cable. The cockpit of one shuttle had been sheared completely off; the aft section remained eerily intact as if someone had cut the forward section with a saw.

"There's the rover," Molly said, pointing. It sat parked in front of the spaceport, spared destruction but covered in fine dust and bits of debris.

"That is one tough machine," Tommy remarked.

A few people milled about the site. Some worked futilely at piling debris as they attempted to clean up. Some called out names of coworkers or friends, as they searched the masses of metal, cable, and great splinters of plastic for those who may have survived. The workers looked up at the flyers and shielded their eyes. Some waved hopefully. Most stared, crestfallen.

"What can we even do to help?" Waters asked.

There was no answer to the question.

"Only what we can," Jonathan answered, finally.

"I'll find a place to land," Tommy said.

He circled over the spaceport once more, then landed on the same path the missionaries had taken on their journey out. Others landed next to them. Workers and civil servants slowly approached and stopped several yards from the colonists. None spoke, none moved; all stared.

"Let's start with food and water," Waters said. "Set up a station here. Molly, would you see if we can set up a shelter to treat anyone who needs medical attention? Jonathan, Tommy, will you put teams together to help rescue survivors?"

"Alex, I don't think that will be necessary," said the mayor, looking to the horizon.

"We need to put up shelters. They'll need them," Waters said.

"Shelter is coming to us," the mayor said.

The air hummed and vibrated. They looked back toward the bog and forest and saw a billowing cloud, miles wide and glowing with fire, crest the horizon. Lightning flashed across its surface as it barreled toward them.

"Dear God, what is that?"

"Not another storm. Not now."

People began to flee with panic.

"Stand fast," the mayor's voice boomed. "This is not to be feared."

"Believe him," Molly said, and a calm settled over the grounds.

The cloud bore down on them and stopped a few hundred yards from the space port. It hovered in place. A golden light emanated from its center.

"I've never seen a cloud do that," Tommy said.

The cloud descended to the ground and settled on the plain. A blast of wind whipped past them and the ground shook. Then the cloud and fire dissipated, and they saw stone inlaid with amber energy towering high into the sky, seven tiers behind a great wall that stretched for miles in either direction. At the center of it all, a spire touched the sky. Golden light illuminated the grounds around them.

"The city," Joon-baek said, awestruck at what he was seeing.

"How?" Waters asked.

They stood dumbstruck; even Jonathan could not believe what he saw. Colonists walked out of the city and crossed the plain toward them, help in hand. Patience met the mayor and they embraced.

"Well done," he said to her. Then he turned to the others and smiled.

"Are you certain it was the colonists?" Interim Director Shepherd asked on his call with Beau.

"Yes, Interim Director," Beau replied. He sat in his apartment on board Polus Station in front of the screen in his room. "A preliminary investigation found several items of colonial tech and literature in the room of a station resident, an engineer position named Sullivan Jakeson. He may have been a colonial sympathizer. We are reviewing the station's logs for communication with colonists, either in person or via LiFi. We suspect a colonist may have snuck aboard the station with the rotating worker positions."

"What did he say when you questioned him?" Shepherd asked.

"It appears he was unfortunately killed launching the device that brought the space elevator down, Interim Director."

"Tell me more about the device."

"Understand that everything suffered significant damage in the wreckage, but those on the ground detected several artifacts typical of colonial use, including fragments of a primitive colonial spear."

"A spear? They use spears? Whatever for?"

"That's right. My time with the colonists suggests their weapons are related to a superstition surrounding a particular animal they refer to as an apoch. We captured a specimen, but the colonists killed it before we could complete our studies or transport it to Earth for more in-depth analysis. It seems that engineer Sullivan attached a make-shift guidance system to the spear. It contained colonial circuitry typical of other pieces of technology such as they use in their local GPS and mapping software. The report suggests that circuitry was combined by Sullivan with certain mechanisms from the station to which he had access. We're not sure what it was used for yet, but analysis suggests it may have served as part of a guidance system."

"And you're asking for authority to conduct a planet-side operation?"

"That's correct. A moon-side operation. As the only MFASA official on site, I'm requesting permission to requisition the station's patrol ships and engage in atmospheric flight to conduct a thorough investigation and apprehend the criminals who perpetrated this heinous act of terror."

"Just who do you intend to question, Missionary Lee?"

"The individual known as the mayor, one of my own team who unfortunately went rogue and has been aiding the colonists: Molly McDaithi." *And Director Waters, who was too accommodating after she betrayed us. Who therefore betrayed the mission, and by extension me, and the authority vested in his position. Whose accommodation of the colonists meant he would side with them inevitably. Who aided them in criminally hunting the animals known as the apochs. Who might reveal, if questioned, other things best left unsaid. There can be no consequence. I must proceed.*

"McDaithi? The one who was on the news? The Administration's pick for the mission? You're kidding. That would be devastating."

"I wish I was joking. It appears she may have been a colonial sympathizer from the start of the mission, though she hid it well. I do not yet have enough information to say conclusively at this time."

"This is all very troubling, Lee. I'll need to consult with President Stanisdottir. This is all over the news. Her team will need to formulate messaging and a response."

"President Stanisdottir. Yes, of course. I hope you'll say hello for me when you see her. And the First Lady as well."

"I doubt I'll be seeing the president's wife, but I will if I see her."

"Thank you, Interim Director Shepherd. Is there anything you need from me?"

"Not at this time. Standby, Lee. I am meeting with the president this afternoon and will let you know the results of our meeting as soon as I can. How are the relief and recovery efforts going?"

"Communication with the ground has been restricted to the investigation thus far, Director Shepherd, and I don't have much information about the people below. The space port was completely destroyed when the space elevator collapsed. That is also hampering relief efforts as there is currently no place for a drop ship to land, and no place for a shuttle to take off."

"How many people were down there?"

"Several thousand. Mostly worker positions and civil servant positions at the spaceport."

"And the only vehicles capable of atmospheric flight are the patrol ships?"

"That's correct. The shuttles and dropships require refueling at the spaceport to launch. The patrol ships are the only vehicles capable of entering the atmosphere and achieving escape velocity again without refueling."

"Yes, those are expensive though. Lee, I will need to confer with the President, but I think I can tell you what she'll say: the patrol ships will be needed for rescue and recovery operations first. We need to assist the people on the ground. The colonists aren't going anywhere, and neither are those responsible. We can continue the investigation after the people on the ground are safe."

"Of course, Interim Director."

"I will get back to you as soon as I can, Lee."

CHAPTER THIRTY-FOUR

FROM WHERE
THEY CAME

By the time the sun set that evening, the colonists working together with the remaining missionaries and survivors had a small camp set up for the injured and homeless. A train of arkouda arrived with fresh produce from the valley where the city had been. Jonathan was right: they moved swiftly and could carry a great burden. The colonists brought in machinery to aid the recovery. The cleanup was slow at first, but once they got going, it gained momentum. They worked until the sun went down and then continued working into the night under the light of the city and flyers that shined spotlights on the ground. By then, they had a small tent city arranged neatly on the plain between the spaceport and city complete with an open-air mess. The surviving workers proved resourceful. They gathered what they could and constructed benches and seats.

A medical shelter was set up, although it was mostly a place of comfort. The viti fruit did its miraculous work, but the need was great and the fruit available in the immediate vicinity quickly became scarce. Joon-baek went out with teams to collect more, a tricky task of timing since the fruit would not keep for long. The injured came and ate and were healed. The more serious cases lay down and rested. Some succumbed to their injuries. No one seemed to want to broach the necessity of digging graves, let alone how they would do so on a large scale.

The dead were laid on the other side of the medical shelter as they found them, a larger number than anyone cared to comprehend. A few survivors emerged from the destruction unhurt but thirsty and hungry; most had injuries, some of them grave. Waters walked along the line of bodies, some covered with jackets or spare warming blankets, although most were not. They simply could not produce or procure the materials fast enough. He stopped in front of a woman's body. Alice was unmistakable, dressed head to toe in a white skirt and blouse, her hair still brushed perfectly straight and topped with a cap despite everything.

Work continued at all hours. They rested when they could, sometimes where they sat in their exhaustion. Polus station passed overhead every ninety minutes like a clock, no more than a tiny light in distant sky, but there just the same.

"Why haven't they sent help down?" some asked.

"There's no place to land. And no way to take off again," was always the answer.

"So, we're on our own."

"We're on our own."

"I'm ready for authorization to take the patrol ships to the surface, Interim Director Shepherd. People died and are dying," Beau said.

"The last time we spoke your priority was to arrest the colonists you believed responsible," Interim Director Shepherd said.

"And I still believe that's important. But I've had time to think about what you said after we spoke last, and you were right: the people need help first. The colonists aren't going anywhere."

Beau did have time to think, not about the people he had made to suffer though. The most advantageous persona was the humanitarian one for now. The bringer of justice could come later. The delay while Interim Director Shepherd sought approval from the President had given him more time to prepare, and he was grateful for it.

"In any case, you will have your authorization. It is as we discussed however: your priority is to bring aid to those suffering on the surface. You may further the investigation as opportunity permits, but aid and comfort are your top priorities."

"Understood."

"Do you have pilots available?"

"Station police and security have pilots."

"I see from the manifest that Captain Jackson is currently at the station. He's a navy veteran. That would play well for the Administration."

Beau cringed a little, but Shepherd was right; it would look good for a veteran to be a part of the rescue operation. However, Jackson knew Molly and the other missionaries and would be inclined to sympathize. Furthermore, Beau simply did not like him.

Beau took a chance. "I have reason to believe that Captain Jackson has sympathies toward the colonists, and may not be the greatest aid in the investigation, and…"

"What is it, Missionary Lee?"

This was pushing it but might be effective. "We do not work well together, Interim Director. He was our captain on the flight out, and he was at odds frequently with the missionaries. He also knows the missionaries who need to be arrested, which may hinder the investigation. I feel it would be best to utilize a station pilot who is unaffiliated with the matter."

"Very well, Missionary Lee. Use your judgment."

Success. "Thank you, Interim Director. Will you be sending me official authorization?"

"Of course. You should receive it shortly."

"How is President Stanisdottir? How is the First Lady?"

"The president is as well as a president can be. The First Lady sends her regards."

That is a good sign. "I will proceed immediately. Take care, Interim Director."

They finished the call and Beau pulled a case from under his bunk. He opened it. It was empty, save for three depressions left by the lance.

On his way out, he dropped the case into a garbage chute to be compressed and molecularized beyond recognition.

Beau's phone beeped as the authorization from the Administration came through. He scrolled down through paragraphs of language detailing his role in the relief and rescue efforts. Then he found it:

> "Missionary Beau Lee is also authorized to investigate and apprehend alleged suspects using the force he deems necessary as concerns the collapse of the Polus IV Space Elevator."

There was no mention of lethal force, but it was also not *not* mentioned. It did not matter though. The authorization included activation codes for the patrol ships' railguns. Once the official Administration report of the incident had been published, all potential deaths would be buried as statistics.

Authorization received at last, Beau walked the kilometer or so down the helix to the security station. There sat a civil servant position, dressed in all white. It was Tegan.

"Missionary Lee, it's a pleasure to see you again. How may I assist you tonight?" she said.

Beau flicked the authorization from his phone to hers. "As you can see, the Administration has authorized me to requisition the station's patrol ships along with pilots to apprehend the criminals responsible for the collapse of the space elevator."

"Oh no!" she said. "You know who is responsible already?"

Thank you, Tegan. You will be the perfect vector to spread the idea that colonists have once again brought down a space elevator. Stanisdottir's failure to protect the Administration's deep space projects will not end her presidency, but it will cast the first seeds of doubt and open the door for me to step in. When the time is right, the First Lady will denounce her and join my cause. In a few years, I will be President. It all starts here, dear Tegan, civil servant position on Polus Station.

"I'm afraid it looks like once again colonists have managed to bring down a space elevator."

"It's Alpha Centauri b again," she said.

"Exactly right, Tegan. You're very bright for making that connection."
She looked surprised at the flattery, but also pleased.

"I'll need the patrol ships readied as soon as possible. Are there pilots available?"

"Most of the officer position pilots have gone home for the night. Perhaps you'd consider asking a commercial or veteran pilot?"

"I'm afraid I must stick to the requirements of the authorization, which specifically requires officer position pilots."

"Of course. We must all follow the rules and regulations. They are what hold our society together, after all. I will reach out for you."

An hour later, the pilots' commander, who introduced himself only as "Officer Carmichael," arrived. His private recreation had obviously been interrupted. He smelled of alcohol, and his uniform was wrinkly as if it had been retrieved from a hamper.

No matter. The alcohol will make him more pliable. He only needs to not crash, Beau thought to himself. "Thank you, Officer Carmichael. I apologize for calling you in during off-duty hours, but we have an emergency authorization from the Administration that needs immediate attention. I need your help. We are to pilot the station's patrol ships down to the surface and apprehend those responsible for the space elevator's collapse."

"You will also be aiding those who were injured in the space elevator's collapse," Tegan added.

"We will also bring supplies and aid to those in need below. Your service in the matter will, I'm sure, not go unrecognized."

Officer Carmichael was not amused at having his off-duty hours interrupted. "We get one-and-a-half time for working during off-duty hours."

"I will be sure to submit the requisite forms, Commander," Tegan responded.

"Make sure that you do," Carmichael said. "And you, let's get this straight. We're the pilots. I'm the Commander. You let me know where we need to go, but I'm the one who decides how we get there. I've seen your types before, all bluff and fluff and no buff, standing behind titles and procedures before the action, then hiding behind desks and better men once things get tough. When we're flying, I'll make the decisions. You sit tight. We'll get where we need to go."

"Of course, Commander," Beau said, completely compliant.

They boarded a patrol ship through a hatch in the roof. "Is this it?" Beau asked. He knew its capacity, but it seemed even smaller now that he was inside. It had seating for no more than four. A metal mesh separated the pilot and co-pilot from the cargo area in the back where there were only two seats. Beau could just stand if he hunched his head over.

"You wanted to use the patrol ships, this is what we got," Carmichael said, taking note of Beau's unspoken appraisal of his ship. "Big ships take a lot of energy to move. Small ships are more efficient for getting on and off planet. You want to bring supplies, so we should take out the seats too. Give me a hand. If we take the seats out, you're going to have to sit up front with me. If we leave in a seat or two, we fit less supplies."

Beau looked over the interior of the ship for a moment. Both sides of the ship had sliding door hatches for ease of access on the planet. "Can you open these doors from the back?" Beau asked.

"They're locked out when we're transporting alleged criminals," Carmichael said, "but I can deactivate the locks, seeing as this is a humanitarian mission."

"Leave one of the seats," Beau said. "I'll sit in the back."

"Flying is more comfortable if you can see out the front," Carmichael said.

"I'll sit in the back."

"Alright, missionary. You'll sit in the back. Come out for a second. I'll pass the seat up to you."

"Where are the other patrol ships?" Beau asked.

"On other helixes. Don't worry. My guys will have them ready. We'll rendezvous before penetrating the atmosphere."

Carmichael removed a seat and passed it up through the hatch to Beau just as Tegan arrived with worker positions pushing carts. They passed crates and boxes down through the hatch.

"This is what we were able to gather on short notice," she said. "It's mostly first-line medical supplies for trauma care and rations. Given more time, I should be able to provide more and higher-quality supplies. Missionary Lee? I want to thank you for involving me in this. I feel so proud to have the opportunity to help those suffering down below."

"What? Yes, of course," Beau said, preoccupied with the space the supplies took up in the ship. There would be room only for him and perhaps one other person, but he could say nothing about it. "Your assistance in the matter is greatly appreciated, Tegan. I'll be sure to make note of it when I make my reports."

"Thank you, but that's not what I mean. I'm just glad to be able to help in some small way," she said.

"Right, of course, that's what you meant. Even so, good work deserves its reward," Beau said.

"You going to help with this stuff or what?" Carmichael called from inside the ship.

"I hope to return to the station soon, Tegan. Please have a team of officer positions ready for me when I do," Beau said as he dropped down through the hatch.

"Of course," Tegan replied.

It took nearly an hour to finish loading the supplies and perform the preflight checks. With each passing minute Beau grew more impatient. Just when it seemed that they had run out of space, Carmichael or one of the workers would suggest that they rearrange some things to make more room.

"I can assure you, missionary, that overtime pay is not a factor in our decision-making process," Carmichael replied with a smirk when Beau protested.

At last, they finished loading and readying the patrol ship. They closed the hatch. Carmichael dropped through a forward hatch into the cockpit. "Helmet and buckles," he said. Beau donned a helmet, took his seat, and fastened the harness.

"I hated our drop to the moon," he said. "How rough is it going to be?"

"Smooth as silk and twice as fine," came Carmichael's reply as he released the docking clamp and a hiss signaled that the thrusters were pushing them away from the station.

"Are you having fun with me?" Beau said.

"I would never," Carmichael said.

Thrusters angled the ship toward the moon below, the gas giant Polus itself looming large at their side. Two other patrol ships joined the formation within minutes. Carmichael moved the throttle forward and the ship immediately accelerated and pushed Beau back into his seat. He was uncomfortable for a few moments while they gained speed and then heard the beginnings of a gentle roar. He saw the glow of heat licking the outside of the ship as they entered the atmosphere, but the descent was smooth, like they were surfing, with none of the shaking and vibration of a drop ship.

"Why don't we all use these ships?" Beau asked.

"Too expensive," Carmichael said. "There's a reason the station only has three and everything else moves with shuttles and dropships. Once they clean up and get the space elevator going again, they'll probably move them somewhere else."

"Who?" Beau asked.

"The Administration. They'll put her somewhere they think she'll be of more use. I'll probably go with her. There's no use for pilots on a station with no ships."

"I see," Beau said. "Commander, is it safe for me to unbuckle? Some of the cargo is shifting around a bit back here, and I want to tighten it down."

"Feel how smooth she is? Go right ahead," Carmichael said.

"Commander, do you mind if I tell you exactly what's going on here?" Beau asked.

Tommy made good use of the flyer that night. He ferried colonists and supplies, and transported the injured when someone was recovered from the rubble. He could never carry enough people at a time though; less if someone needed to lie down, and there were always more being uncovered. The sun was setting, and the low light of dusk was taking over. A low cloud bank typical of the plains settled in. He just finished dropping someone off when a glow in the clouds above indicated an object entering the atmosphere.

"It looks like something's coming down. Maybe the station is sending help. I'm going to go check it out," he said to Joon-baek.

"Okay," replied Joon-baek. "Let us know what you find."

"It's probably your mom coming to check on you," Tommy said.

"Don't even joke about that," Joon-baek said.

"When was the last time you called her?" Tommy asked, laughing. Not waiting for Joon-baek's response, Tommy jumped in the flyer and angled it up toward the descending glow, which faded a few moments later.

Carmichael and Beau had reached an understanding.

"Tell me again, Commander Carmichael, just so that I'm sure you understand the seriousness of the situation," Beau said.

"The colonists are responsible for bringing the space elevator down. We need to deal with them before we can safely deliver the supplies and help the worker positions. You, me, and my pilots are acting with the full authority of the Administration," Carmichael said. "Is that about the long and short of it?"

"I think we have an understanding," Beau said. He anchored himself to the patrol ship's frame with a carabiner. "Now, if you will please release the door locks so I can open the side door. Thank you," he said and slid the port side door open. The cabin filled instantly with noise but little wind thanks to the streamlined shape of the ship. They could see nothing, however, as they descended through the cloud. "This truly is a fantastic machine, Commander," he said.

"You could have just told me we were going after terrorists," Carmichael said. "Hell, I might even have volunteered."

"That could be considered an offensive word," Beau said.

"Whatever you say. Let's just get these guys."

Tommy hovered just below the cloud bank. He pulled out his phone and called Joon-baek. "I don't see anything yet!" he said.

Even as he spoke a patrol ship descended through the cloud directly above him.

"Shit!" Tommy said. He dropped his phone, banked the flyer, and slammed the throttle forward. The ship just missed him. A second ship descended beyond the first, and then a third passed through the clouds directly into his path.

On the ground, Joon-baek dropped his phone. There was an explosion and a second later the sound reached them on the ground. Pieces of machinery fell out of the sky onto the plains in the distance, followed by the remains of Tommy's flyer as it slammed into the ground a mile away with a thud.

"Jesus, what is that?" Carmichael said.

As they descended through the clouds, the spires of the city towered into the clouds in front of them high beyond their sight and captured their attention. The light from the city lit the underside of the cloud bank. Beau shook his head, wiped his eyes, and looked again in disbelief. "It's the city, but it can't be." At that moment, he knew the Administration would never be able to resettle these colonists.

"Look out!" Carmichael shouted into the radio as one of the colonists' flyers veered close to them. A third patrol ship descended through the clouds and struck the flyer. A fireball engulfed both ships. The patrol ship rocked as its pilot struggled to regain control. Engines sheared off the flyer and it went tumbling to the ground, though the patrol ship steadied itself soon enough.

"You alright, officer?" Carmichael asked.

"I've got it, sir," came the reply. "I'll need a new paint job, but all systems are good. Are they attacking us?"

"Lee, let's go get these sons of bitches," Carmichael said, angry, and pushed the nose of the patrol ship down.

Waters, Joon-baek, and Molly ran in the direction of the crash. Several of the colonists followed them, but before they had gone a few yards a fountain of rock and dirt shot into the air, blocking their path as a shot from a patrol ship's railgun left a deep crater in the ground. The patrol ships descended hard behind the shot and almost touched the ground where they hovered in front of them. The wash from the engines sent their clothing and hair flapping and kicked dust into their eyes. The tents swayed in the wind. In one of the patrol ship's doors stood a figure. The figure took of his helmet.

They saw Beau, who looked out and saw Waters standing there with Molly clinging to his arm and Joon-baek at his side surrounded by colonists. His fury rose.

"Beau?" Waters shouted. Waters ran forward but stopped short as another shot from a patrol ship sent up a plume of earth in front of him. "Beau, what are you doing!"

"You ask me that?" Beau shouted. "You dare ask me that? You, standing there amid terrorists with *her*, have the audacity to ask me what I'm doing?"

"Beau, I don't understand," Waters said. He gestured plaintively and walked forward. He stopped as the patrol ships angled towards him. "Tommy's flyer got hit. Please, we have to go help him!"

"Here you are, aiding them," Beau shouted, straining to be heard above the sound of the engines. "How could you betray us like this? How could you side with them, help them do something like this?" he said with a gesture to the wreckage of the space elevator. "How could you abandon everything our mission stood for, everything we as missionaries were supposed to bring to these people? It doesn't matter, though. I know what needs to be done. The old mission is finished; now begins a new mission. I'm fortunate, really I am, to be here, to be the one who gets to administer the first shot of justice."

He raised a hand to Carmichael, who angled the ship towards Molly and the others. She stepped back and clutched her hands together.

"No!" Waters shouted and stepped in front of her with his arms wide. "No, Beau! It was my fault. I'm the one responsible for this—for all this. I take responsibility."

"Alex, no!" Molly cried.

Waters turned to her. "I love you," he said. "Thank you for everything."

Jonathan, thank you. Tell the mayor thank you." He turned, and arms outstretched walked toward the patrol ships.

"I'm the one responsible, Beau. I let the apoch go. I'm the one responsible for Jazzy's death. Everyone else is innocent. Let them go. Take me."

"Jazzy's dead?" Beau said. "Are you sure?"

"Yes," Waters said.

"And you're responsible?"

"I am. I let the apoch go, and the apoch killed her. It's my fault. I'm sorry."

Waters stopped a few yards from the patrol ship. He had to strain against the force of the engines. The other ships kept their guns trained on him. Beau's eyes carried a severe look. He considered Waters, considered what his admission could mean for him, for the mission. At last Beau signaled to Carmichael, and the patrol ships relaxed their aim.

"Alright, Alex. You're responsible. Get in."

"No!" Molly shouted.

Waters turned and smiled at her. "It's alright. This is just."

Waters pushed forward to the open door. Beau grabbed him by the collar and pulled him inside. Beau slid the door closed, and the patrol ship ascended into the sky. The other ships soon followed. Molly, Joonbaek, Jonathan and the other colonists stared after them. The sun set below the horizon, and the glow of vitis filled the plains. Their eyes followed the patrol ships into the sky, through the clouds, back into space from where they came.

THE END, PART I

TO BE CONTINUED IN

PLANET MISSION: PART II

Made in the USA
Coppell, TX
18 July 2021